When Darkness Follows

PRAISE FOR ATHENA DANIELS

The Seer's Daughter

"…the perfect culmination of paranormal mystery with steamy and sensual romance and just enough suspense and intrigue to guarantee a chilling, goose bump invoking, story line… *The Seer's Daughter* would be a brilliant option for adaption to screen—there's a television series/movie in here for absolute certain."
—*AusRom Today*

"…as chilling as it is sexy… This is much more than a romance. The paranormal aspects along with the secondary characters really make the story. The descriptions, language, emotions, dialogue… are all cleverly written to keep you engaged and the pages turning, while the suspense will make sure you read this story with all the lights on."—5-star Top Pick, *The Romance Reviews*

"If you are looking for a book to give you goose bumps and keep you watching over your shoulder, then I can recommend this one! … I got dragged away from this book late in the evening by my husband, as I had an exceedingly early start the next day. This didn't stop me from thinking about the book and what I had read for well over an hour after the lights went out, as well as dreaming about it!"
—Archaeolibrarian, 5 stars, Amazon review

"I love paranormal books, especially when there's romance thrown in, and this… will send a chill up your spine, raise the hairs on your neck, and make you tremble with emotions. What a rush! One of my most favorite reads this year! … It's almost like Stephen King meets Christina Dodd… I loved it; can't wait for book two!"—5 stars, Amazon review

"…a perfect blend of paranormal fiction and romantic suspense that had me completely captivated to the very last page… flawlessly delivered."
—Faridah, 5 stars, *Readers Favorite*

"One of the best ghost/demon stories I have read in a while! It had romance, witches, demons, AND ghosts! Absolutely loved it!"—5 stars, Amazon review

The Alchemist's Son

"…go the hell out and buy both of these books now because they are freaking FANTASTIC. I am not exaggerating when I say this is some of the best romantic suspense I have ever read, paranormal or otherwise; I literally couldn't put down *The Alchemist's Son* until I got to the final, thrilling climax."—5 stars, Amazon review

"This book is as good as the first, with twists and turns! You get the good ol' creepy feels! You may be wanting to look behind you, or not go in your attic or basement anytime soon! I wish this author could write as fast as I can read; I would never put her books down!"—5 stars, Amazon review

"Kept me on the edge of my seat. Several scenes I was holding my breath reading what was happening next…."—5 stars, Amazon review

"This book had my hair standing on end and gave me chills from start to finish. Once again I could not put it down, and loved how, no matter how hard I tried, I just couldn't guess ahead what was going to happen next."—5 stars, Amazon review

Girl Unseen

"For paranormal fans, *Girl Unseen* can't be beat! The depth of emotion with which Athena Daniels fills her characters provides such intensity that you feel their pain and heartache… Just make sure to leave the lights on! Fabulous read! I couldn't put this down and can't wait for more!"—5 stars, *Readers Favorite*

"A wonderful, spooky story with lots of action. A murder mystery to solve and a scorching hot romance. It has everything and will keep you guessing all the way through. I loved it."—5 stars, Amazon review

"I loved it so much! For me, this book covers a lot of ground when it comes to romance + something else. You like a little bit of scary? You've got ghosts and spirits. You like a little bit of detective work? You've got a badass PI trying to solve the mystery… You want romance? Well, you have one amazing medium falling for the PI, while trying to help out a lost soul. Oh, and maybe, just maybe, you want all these with nice writing? You've got author Athena Daniels. Congratulations for your future book to read!"—5 stars, *Lilly's Book World*

Desperate

"What can I say other than I absolutely loved this book from the start, and the prologue really set the pace for a fast-paced plot with lots of suspense and the right touch of romance. The plot was strong and progressed well and I loved the flirty banter between Eric and Ivy, which added to the growing relationship between the pair and provided a few good sex scenes illustrating their intense chemistry… the author has done an amazing job of penning this novel and I can't wait to read more of their work in the future."
—*The Romance Studio* (TRS), 4 stars

"Suspense and steamy romance line the pages of this fast-paced thriller, with action and drama from start to finish…. If Athena Daniels keeps it up with writing like this, I have no doubts that she will establish her place amongst the most well-known authors of erotic literature…. If you're a fan of romantic thrillers, I would definitely recommend giving this one a read."
—Official Review, *Online Book Club*, 4 out of 4 stars

ALSO BY ATHENA DANIELS

Novels

The Scream Behind Her Smile

Desperate

Beyond the Grave Series

The Seer's Daughter (Book One)

The Alchemist's Son (Book Two)

Girl Unseen (Book Three)

When Darkness Follows (Book Four)

When Darkness Follows

Beyond the Grave
Book 4

ATHENA DANIELS

Sunset Coast Publishing

Dedicated to:

My readers.
It is you who make this dream possible.

May all your dreams come true.

Here's to love,
the greatest power of all.

For love survives…
Beyond fear
Beyond betrayal
Beyond the grave

ACKNOWLEDGMENTS

Thanks once again to the dynamic duo, Dana Delamar and Kristine Cayne, for their sharp eye for detail and for polishing my words and helping turn them into a finished product I am proud to put my name on. My deepest appreciation, as always, for my phenomenal editor, Dana. It means so much to know that you are only an email away, cheering me on through the good days, picking me up on the rough ones. Your constant support, encouragement, and wise words right when I need them mean so much to me. Thanks for never tiring of endless questions, and for being my friend. Thanks for being so much more than an editor.

My love and appreciation, as always, to Leah, my toughest critic. Who knows me warts and all, and loves me anyway. We share a love of reading and know the standard I am striving for. Thanks for always being there for me, and for never letting me doubt myself. Your belief in me is the greatest gift you could ever give me. I love you sis! *You and me...*

Huge thanks to my first-pass readers, Leah Frost and Laura Dawn, whose eye for detail and constructive criticism made this story better than it would have been without you. Thank you from the bottom of my heart for being so honest.

I would like to also to thank the wonderful people I have met online and who I now consider friends. Every time you click "like" or "love" on a post, every time you share and spread the word about the series, please know how much it means to me. I do notice and appreciate each and every one of you! Without you all, this journey wouldn't be half as much fun! I can't name everyone here, but I can't miss the opportunity to give a special shout of appreciation to: Vicki Rose, Dawn Y., Stracey C., Cyndi F., Erin S., Susan P., Sandra L., Mary W., Dina S., Jennifer D., Paula C. L., Tracey M. P., Lori H., Caitlyn L., Jessica C., Ashley M., Denise V. P., Kay S. Y., Karen T., Kelly E., Riah C., Danielle F., Mary W., Staci B., Susan C., Viki K. P. and all the totally awesome readers who hang out in the *Athena Daniels, VIP Readers Lounge*!

Unconditional love to my family: my husband, Ali, and my boys. Thank you for your love, support, and unwavering belief in me. It means so much to know you are always there for me, cheering me on, and making me feel like I've got this.

And thanks to everyone who has read the series so far and taken the time to leave a review or tell me they loved it. Your words of encouragement are the fuel that keeps me going.

Chapter One

Coral Coast
Western Australia

I'm being watched.

The hair on the back of Rachel Sommers's neck raised, and she dug her feet into the thick white sand, fighting a strong impulse to run.

Across a span of clear turquoise water and against the backdrop of a picturesque Western Australian sky, a shipwrecked fishing trawler named the *Anna-Marie* sat wedged against a coral reef. Listing at an unnatural angle, its long poles reached like cranes far into the sky, and waves crashed white and frothy around its grand rusting frame.

An icy shiver trickled down Rachel's spine, but she pushed down the rush of fear that squeezed her chest, making it hard to breathe.

You don't scare me. Though her mouth was dry, she made herself stand straighter and squared her shoulders. *You won't stop me from doing what must be done.*

A gust of icy wind whipped off the ocean and sent sand stinging against her face. In her mind, she heard wicked laughter, deep and cruel. Rachel would rather be anywhere else right now, but she refused to let fear rule her.

Walking away wasn't an option.

A week ago, someone—or something—had killed her friend Trey Norton and sent her friend Rob Madden into hiding. And she wasn't going to stop until she worked out what had happened. And where Rob was.

Rachel caught a movement out of the corner of her eye, and she peered through the low-lying bushes that dotted the sand dunes. She couldn't shake the terrifying sensation that she had been watched ever since that night.

Was what killed Trey lurking behind the bushes and dunes right now? Watching her? Waiting for its chance to kill her too? Or worse?

Something had happened after they'd started using the Ouija board Rob had found on the *Anna-Marie* that night. Something terrible. But she didn't know what. No matter how hard she wracked her brain, she had no memories of the time between then and when she'd woken up on the cold metal floor of that rusting shipwreck to find Rob missing and Trey's body lying in a pool of blood.

The bushes rustled again, and Rachel shoved a fist against her mouth. Her skin prickled, and her pulse raced erratically past her ears. Narrowing her gaze, she focused on the shadows between the bushes.

The bushes moved again.

Rachel held her breath. One… two… She didn't have a weapon. Why hadn't she thought to bring one?

Because weapons aren't going to help.

Despite her fear, she took a step toward the bushes.

A white seagull took off from behind the dunes, squawking as it soared high into the sky. Stumbling back, Rachel wiped her trembling hands down the sides of her jeans. Heat spread across her cheeks. Thank God no one had witnessed her overreaction to a damn seagull.

You're losing it, Rach. They'll be hauling you to the nuthouse next.

Something touched her shoulder.

She spun around, her heart pounding erratically, and raised her fists in front of her. As though that could possibly help against what she feared this really was.

"Jeez, Rachel, you need to chill out. You look as white as a ghost. No pun intended." Mark Collins, founder of Paranormal Research and Investigations and star of the ghost-hunting show *Debunking Reality,* grinned at her, showcasing perfect white teeth. In real life, he looked every inch the television star he was. His toned chest nicely filled out a tight black T-shirt emblazoned with the PRI logo and tucked into well-fitted denim jeans.

"Don't sneak up on me like that," Rachel snapped, taking a deep breath and willing her racing heart to slow. If she was this jumpy now, what was she going to be like when she was back on the ship?

"I just wanted to tell you the team is almost ready," Mark said, sounding slightly hurt.

"Sorry. I'm just a little on edge."

Rachel glanced up the beach to where the PRI crew were preparing for the evening ahead. She'd called *Debunking Reality* for answers. Answers WAPOL, the Western Australian Police Force, were unable to give her. Despite the footage and evidence

Debunking Reality had aired in recent times, clearly a large number of officers in the Major Crime Squad and the forensics team refused to believe in anything paranormal. Which was understandable. Unless you'd experienced something impossible to explain using logic and science, it was extremely hard to believe. Rachel would have preferred not to believe in any of this either.

Except… this had happened to her.

Another flash of movement caught her eye. She whipped her head around, but nothing was there.

Nothing followed me off that ship. Nothing.

She took a deep breath and rubbed at the goose bumps that had sprung up on her arms.

"I need answers," Rachel said to Mark, relieved her voice sounded strong. Determined. "I need to remember what took place Wednesday night so I can let the police know what really happened to Trey." *And prove that Rob didn't kill him.*

"We'll get you those answers."

Mark was a man confident in his own skin. Years of ridicule from skeptics over his life's work and passion for documenting proof of the paranormal gave him an enviable don't-give-a-fuck-what-you-think, I-know-what-I-know attitude. Despite Mark's confidence, she couldn't shake a low-level, stomach-churning sense of urgency, a persistent niggling that something very bad was about to happen.

That whatever *this* was, it was leading somewhere. That the horror she'd already endured had only been the beginning.

Despite what the police thought, Rachel *knew* that Rob hadn't killed Trey. It wasn't possible. They'd been best friends nearly all their lives, the three of them. But without Rachel—the only eyewitness—being able to give her version of events, the police were holding fast to their theory.

She looked past Mark to where the other guys in the *Debunking Reality* team were loading cameras and recording equipment into the small boat that would take them to the ship. The team's psychic medium, Pia Williams, stood off to the side, her arms crossed, staring at the *Anna-Marie*, her long red hair whipping in the breeze.

More than one officer investigating the case believed Rachel's memory loss was a convenient ploy to cover for Rob. She almost wished that were the case. Because this not-knowing, this dreadful blank in her memory, terrified her.

A dog's barking broke the stillness on the beach, followed by a man's voice trying to silence it. A German shepherd charged into view, its teeth bared, its hackles raised as it crested the dunes. "Max! Heel! What's wrong with you?"

Rachel would recognize that deep, smooth, commanding voice anywhere. It reminded her of melting caramel, expensive malt scotch, and endless nights of hot sex on a sheepskin rug in front of a roaring fire.

Daniel.

With a few powerful strides, he stalked down the sandy slope and grabbed Max by the collar.

"What's *he* doing here?" Rachel ignored the painful ache that flared in the pit of her stomach.

Mark raised his brows in surprise. "You know Daniel?"

"Daniel and his special ops unit used to come in to my parents' restaurant all the time when they were in town." And then after dinner, Daniel would turn up at her place…

Mark grinned. "I've heard the women love him."

She ignored the sharp jab of jealousy. There was a reason she'd kept Daniel Jackson Smith at a distance. Men like Daniel didn't do relationships.

And Rachel's stupid heart didn't listen to reason.

The last time she'd seen him had been when he'd walked out of her bedroom door at five a.m. on an overcast morning last September. Almost a year ago to the day.

Seemingly unable to stop his dog barking, Daniel disappeared back behind the sand dunes, and Rachel used the opportunity to clear her head. Whatever he was doing here was *not* going to interfere with her focus on finding Trey's killer.

Daniel soon reappeared at the top of the sand dunes without Max.

"Why is he here?"

"If you watched my show," Mark said with a pointed look, "you would know that in April this year, Pia became engaged to Daniel's friend and business partner, Nate Ryder. Their special ops unit—Daniel, Nate, Ethan Blade, Sam Wells, and Sean Wynter—left the police force some months before and formed a security company. They're all equal partners of Taipan Security and Investigations, TSI. We often work with them now."

"Yes, I know about TSI," Rachel said distractedly, her eyes on Daniel's commanding presence as he walked toward them. The city of Perth was like a country town to a large degree, in that everyone knew who TSI were. Especially the single women. The married ones too. The men of the former elite special ops unit, with their buff bodies, power, confidence, and deadly weapons, were easy to lust over. Even the most hardened dominatrix would reconsider her preferences just to be under their control, if only for a single night.

Daniel's tall, muscular body moved effortlessly across the soft sand. His shoulders were wide, his stride confident, the way that only men truly sure of their ability to handle, well, anything had. His dark hair was longer than when she'd seen him last, and a lock of it fell across one eye. His neatly trimmed goatee had grown into closely cropped facial hair that added sexy shadows to his strong, chiseled features.

Although Daniel didn't meet her eyes, the crackling tension in the air between them couldn't be diminished by distance. Or time.

Daniel walked to Pia first, and Rachel's stomach clenched as she watched them embrace briefly. Her body all too easily remembered what it had felt like to have those muscular arms wrapped around her, a touch her body continually craved.

Daniel and Pia spoke a few words, then began to make their way over. And finally, Daniel's gaze, his intense blue eyes, eyes that missed nothing, locked onto Rachel's as they approached.

Rachel's breath caught, and her pulse began to race. God, would she ever be able to see him and not be affected?

"Thanks for coming," Mark said, shaking Daniel's hand. "I thought Nate would come because of Pia, but I'm glad to see you. I believe you already know my client, Rachel Sommers."

"I've had the pleasure. Many times," Daniel added with an emphasis that sent a shiver of awareness rolling through her. "Although, she's been deliberately elusive of late." His voice was low and clipped, his eyes still locked on hers.

Rachel's body heated, her skin tingling with unwanted sexual awareness. It didn't help that Daniel's gaze remained on her. When he got that focused, he was sexually aggressive in bed, even more so than usual. Her nipples hardened, and a flush burned her cheeks.

"Nate is working another investigation," Pia said.

"Regardless, Rachel is my concern. Not Ryder's or anyone else's." Daniel's eyes never left Rachel.

Mark subtly drew back, an instinctive reaction to an alpha male staking his claim over his female. Rachel blinked in confusion. Despite the sexual chemistry between them, Daniel had promised her nothing more than casual sex. He'd been very deliberate about making that clear.

How dare he turn up here now and pretend there was something more between them?

"You left Max in the car?" Mark's gaze flicked between the two of them curiously.

"I don't know what's wrong with him." Daniel released a breath as he looked back across the beach. "He wouldn't stop barking as soon as he got to the top of the dunes. He normally loves the beach."

But not this one.

The unspoken words hung in the air and their gazes traveled in unison toward the shipwreck.

"Animals and very young children can sense and see things people can't," Pia said. "People call it instinct, but it's more accurate to say they still have an open mind." Pia's long black nails fingered a large pendant around her neck. "And this isn't Max's first encounter with the paranormal. Or yours."

Rachel glanced curiously at Daniel, waiting for him to discount the paranormal references, but he remained silent, his jaw set, a slight furrow between his brows.

That surprised her. The cops back at the station had given each other amused looks when she'd told them Trey's murder had to have something to do with what they'd summoned through the Ouija board. The sergeant had tapped a pen on his notepad, his lips twitching as he glanced at his partner. "So, your story is a ghost killed Trey Norton," he'd said with an arched brow and an ill-concealed snicker. Rachel had known at that moment she was in trouble.

"Right," Mark said, waving his arm in a circle to encompass the beach a few meters away where his other teammates, cameraman Ryan Donovan and tech-guru Joe Clarke, appeared to have finished loading their equipment into the boat. "We're ready. Ryan, grab your camera, and let's get this show started," Mark called across the beach.

Leaving Joe with the expensive equipment in the small aluminum boat they would use to transport them to the ship, Ryan Donovan made his way over to the group.

Ryan turned on the camera and stared into the glowing viewfinder. "Full battery, two spares in the case."

Mark looked at Rachel. "Ready?"

Despite the flutters in her belly, she nodded.

It was time to get answers.

CHAPTER TWO

Daniel steered the small motorboat toward the rusting hulk of the *Anna-Marie*. The air was eerily still; the breeze from earlier had dropped off completely, and the temperature had turned crisp. The distance they had to travel to reach the ship wasn't far, but the tide must be incredibly strong tonight. The waves were unusual in both their size and intensity, and they were somewhat erratic as they crashed against the boat. The tinny's motor sputtered and strained in the choppy water.

This wasn't the first, or even the second, case he'd worked on with the *Debunking Reality* team, and he knew enough by now to safely bet that whatever was on that ship was aware of them in some unnatural and unprovable way—and was doing its best to keep them away. Each wave that crashed over them seemed intent on sending them careening back to shore.

Each unnatural wave was a warning to *stay away*.

A warning Daniel ignored. He gradually closed the distance with each wave he fought.

Ryan and Joe sat on the starboard side of the tinny huddled over their equipment, glaring at Daniel whenever water splashed over the sides. As though he could control the weather. Mark was sitting in the bow, his eyes fixed with excitement and anticipation on the ship.

Pia sat across from Ryan and Joe on the port side. Her eyes were slightly narrowed, her jaw set. Her lifetime of dealing with the paranormal was not by choice. She'd been born a psychic medium and had the ability to communicate with the dead. An ability Daniel would find impossible to believe had he not seen it himself.

There was no denying Pia's gift was genuine, even if he didn't understand how such a thing was possible.

And sitting next to her, gripping the side of the boat with white-knuckled intensity, was Rachel.

My Rachel.

She *was* his. Despite the fact she'd refused to return his phone calls for the last twelve months.

She was dressed in ripped jeans, with an old flanno shirt carelessly thrown over a fitted white T-shirt, her long brown hair tied back in a messy ponytail.

He found her just as sexy now as he had when she'd been standing over him in lacy white garters or her thigh-high black fuck-me boots and a short red skirt.

An abnormally large wave formed, and Daniel powered through its frothy white crest. The tinny crashed hard on the other side of the wave, sending a jarring jolt through the hull. Ryan's black leather case slipped from his grip, and he tossed a glare at Daniel. *Yeah, mate, causing these waves on purpose.*

Daniel kept his attention firmly on getting them safely to the ship, but his mind was constantly on Rachel. And what he had to do to get her alone. He'd get her the answers she needed tonight. Then after that? There'd be no more avoiding him. He had questions too, and he wasn't leaving until she answered them.

"Any more calls from you guys, and Blade said we'd have to start up our own paranormal crime branch." Daniel raised his voice to be heard over the engine, and despite the abnormally large waves, his voice carried easily in the otherwise eerily still evening air.

Mark considered. "Probably not a bad idea."

Daniel smiled wryly. "Jeez, he wasn't serious." Although TSI had been dealing with paranormal phenomena, it was far from being officially acknowledged as a legitimate field of expertise, especially when it came to the legal system. Which of course made working paranormal cases and gathering recognized evidence while keeping a chain of custody a minefield.

That's why, unofficially, TSI were highly respected and sought after among high-ranking government officials for anything the governing body couldn't handle through ordinary channels. Which was surprisingly more often than one would think. It was one of the reasons why Ethan had had the idea for them to leave the elite special operations team and start up on their own. Fewer rules and regulations and a hell of a lot more freedom.

Of course, taking paranormal cases hadn't been their intention. Like Pia, life had chosen that path for them when Ethan had met his wife Sage on a case last September. Although instances of the paranormal made up only about ten percent of their workload, they were the cases that required the most focus and resources and, surprisingly, were the most dangerous.

Nate had wanted to handle this job tonight, as he wanted to handle everything where Pia was concerned, but the moment Rachel's name had appeared on the screen, Daniel had insisted on taking the job.

The *Anna-Marie* was technically still closed off as a crime scene, but since the forensics team had finished up, it had been easy for Daniel to arrange access for *Debunking Reality* tonight. You didn't become part of an elite special operations unit without making powerful friends along the way. People in high places who owed you a favor or wanted one up their sleeve. Daniel and the members of TSI were powerful friends to have in their own right.

All the evidence so far pointed to the fact that Rob Madden had killed Trey Norton. Police had found a bloodied knife covered in Madden's prints. The two, along with Rachel, had been friends since childhood. Best friends. So why would Rob Madden kill his best friend? What had made him snap? Where was he now?

And the question that Daniel was most focused on: Was Madden a threat to Rachel?

Daniel's hands fisted, a wave of emotion rolling heavily through his body. If Madden so much as laid a single finger on her, Daniel would tear him apart, limb from limb. The rush of possessiveness he felt for Rachel was powerful. It always had been. Sexually or otherwise.

Long strands of silky brown hair had escaped from her ponytail and were whipping around her face. Daniel's fingers itched to tuck them behind her ears. He remembered all too vividly how soft her hair was against his cheek, how it smelled of peach and vanilla. How silky the skin on her inner thighs was. The sound of her cries when he made her come…

He adjusted his jeans and forcefully pushed the images away. One whole goddamned year. She'd told him she loved him! Okay, she'd thought he was asleep and he'd let her think he hadn't heard. But her words had terrified him, so it had been more convenient at the time to feign ignorance. And after that morning, she'd cut him off cold. She'd said she loved him, and then she'd stopped taking his calls! What the fuck was that about? Why wouldn't she talk to him?

He'd tried to move on and forget her. Even hate her. But a year later, his feelings for her hadn't lessened, not one stinking bit. He was still perpetually in a state of half-madness with wanting her.

Seeing her again had proved that the attraction between them, that powerful pull, was still there. As strong as ever. Whatever was between them hadn't faded.

So what had happened? What had he done to make her so determined to push him away, when everything else about her screamed that she wanted him?

He wasn't leaving without answers.

But first, his number-one priority was her safety, and that meant removing the threat of Rob Madden.

And then, he'd get Rachel to talk.

CHAPTER THREE

Rachel stepped up onto the *Anna-Marie*, her eyes immediately drawn to the rusty metal stairs that led down into the stomach of the fishing trawler.

She wasn't ready to go down there yet. To the place where this nightmare had begun.

Daniel, Mark, Ryan, Pia, and Joe began touring the ship, and after a while, she could hear their muffled voices disappear beneath her feet downstairs.

Rachel took a moment for herself. She moved to the edge of the ship, breathed in deeply the salty ocean air, and rubbed her arms with shaky hands. It was tough being back on this ship after everything that had happened.

Gripping the rusty metal, she stared out across the bay and watched the fading sunlight dance across the waves.

Standing in the same place she'd stood with Trey that fateful night, Rachel could almost feel Trey's hand on hers, his body standing next to her. Though she couldn't remember what had happened later that night, she remembered every word of their conversation before it had all happened. Tears welled in her eyes. She'd never pictured her life without him—or Rob—in it.

When Daniel, Mark, Pia, and the team came back up onto the deck, Rachel dabbed at her eyes and took a deep breath.

"We're going to do a quick introduction for the show while there's still some light," Mark said. "I want to start at the bow."

Rachel watched the members of the team take their positions, their practiced ease that came from years of working together clear.

The red light on Ryan's camera indicated he was recording. Mark had his back to the lens, his gaze focused out at sea. Rachel could imagine the striking visual effect this would make when it aired—Mark standing at the bow of the rusting ship against the backdrop of the fading sunset. His broad shoulders were pulled back, and the tattoos on his biceps peeked out from beneath his tight T-shirt. Slowly, he turned, his light blue eyes connecting with the camera, and began speaking directly into the lens.

"On Wednesday the thirteenth of September, a group of three friends boarded the *Anna-Marie,* a haunted fishing trawler that wrecked eighteen months ago against a reef off the Western Australia coast near Sharktooth Cove. Rachel Sommers, Trey Norton, and Rob Madden. The three members of the popular Perth band, Trinity Beat.

"And now, that band has been almost wiped out. Trey Norton is dead, Rob Madden is missing... and the surviving member of the band, Rachel Sommers, can't remember a thing..."

Mark paused while Ryan panned his camera in on the ship for a close-up. "Here, we'll show some band pictures, and some private ones," Mark said to Rachel. "You have some we can use, right, Rach?"

Rachel nodded. She had many, many photos of the three of them, performing and just messing about.

Ryan panned back to Mark, who resumed addressing the camera. "Captain Adam Edwards bought this fishing trawler thirty-three years ago and named it the *Anna-Marie* after his wife, Anna-Marie Felicia Edwards—a stunning beauty fifteen years his junior. The ship had a reputation for being haunted, something Edwards dismissed at the time."

Rachel glanced at Daniel. He was watching her, his expression impassive, but something tumultuous swirled behind his eyes.

"The ship and its crew of six were reported missing in 1991," Mark said, "just seven years after Edwards bought it. The trawler was sometimes spotted sailing off the coast of Australia, adrift without a living crew aboard."

Mark stopped walking and stared out at the sea. No one made a sound. Even the wind seemed to have dropped off. "Some believe the ship had its own agenda. After thirteen years of drifting, it ended up here. Near the home the captain had shared with the love of his life, Anna-Marie Edwards."

Mark spoke as though musing over the details. "What happened to the captain and his crew? Is there any truth to the rumors that the murder/suicide that took their lives was related to the ship's haunted reputation, which the locals now refer to as 'Edwards' Curse'? And if not, what caused the otherwise mild-mannered captain to snap and commit such a heinous act of violence against his crew and himself? And does this gruesome history have any bearing on the murder of Trey Norton?" Mark asked dramatically, and Rachel's head began to spin. The whole situation seemed surreal, as though she were listening to a story about someone else.

"During tonight's investigation," Mark said in a back-to-business tone, "we will focus not only on the paranormal, but on facts and hard evidence. We will start with the police's theory that Rob Madden killed Trey Norton for reasons that have nothing to do with anything paranormal. We will ask the question: What could have happened to make one friend turn on another and commit a brutal murder?"

Rachel's jaw clenched as she inwardly seethed. Rob hadn't killed Trey. She knew it. It took all her willpower, but Rachel remained silent.

"What we will do during tonight's investigation," Mark continued, "is re-create the events of that evening, with the hope that we'll help restore Rachel's memory so she can tell us—and the police—exactly what happened to Trey Norton and Rob Madden."

Mark waved a hand to indicate Pia. "Our talented psychic medium, Pia Williams, will do what she does best, and with her assistance, we'll endeavor to discover if the friends summoned something through the Ouija board that night. We'll also try to answer other pressing questions, including, who or what is the ghostly entity that's been seen wandering the decks of the ship late at night? Is it Captain Edwards, or something else? Something that was already on the ship when Edwards bought it? Something capable of murder?"

A chill raked down Rachel's spine.

"As we film this show," Mark continued, "Rob Madden is the prime suspect wanted for questioning regarding the murder of his best friend. He disappeared off the boat that night into thin air. Where is he now, and why is he hiding? And why do the police think Rachel herself could be at risk?"

Mark flashed a perfect smile. "We hope you enjoy tonight's show as we investigate the *Anna-Marie* and attempt to get Rachel Sommers, and the police, some much-needed answers. Cut."

Rachel's stomach roiled violently. Mark had described that night in such a cold, sensationalized way. Like a news report about some stranger. Like Rob was someone horrible.

"I'm sorry about the introduction," Mark said, coming to stand next to her. "I know Rob is your friend and you don't believe he had anything to do with Trey's murder, but I have to state the facts as they are."

"Madden is a very real threat you can't ignore," Daniel said, standing at her other side.

Rachel could punch them both. "As I've said, over and over, someone else must have been on this ship that night. Whoever that was, was the one who killed Trey. Rob would *never* hurt me, and I am not going to be held responsible for my actions if I hear anyone saying he would. Especially on camera. For God's sake, Mark, his mum could be watching!"

She glared at Ryan, making sure he wasn't still filming.

Nobody needed to speak the words, but they hung in the air regardless, for all to hear. Everybody, including Daniel, thought Rob killed Trey. How could they so easily overlook the history of the ship? Especially after everything Mark had just said in the introduction?

Mark shuffled his feet and looked away.

Daniel cleared his throat. "Well, I'm sure it will all get cleared up once he turns himself in and explains what happened. Avoiding the police is not helping him."

"Don't worry, Rachel," Mark said. "Tonight is about getting to the bottom of what happened. And when we do, we will show the truth to everyone."

The anger left Rachel in a rush. She had to trust that Mark and his team would be able to prove Rob's innocence.

"Thank you." Her throat closed over, but she forced herself to speak, her voice thick and strained. "Truth is, I hate myself for not being able to remember. Somewhere inside my mind are the answers to these questions, but it's all a blank."

The sun sank into the horizon, taking with it the last light of the day. Ryan and Joe handed out powerful flashlights and set up some lanterns on the deck. The sea breeze whipped up, not against her, but seemingly *through* her, making a sound as though voices were whispering, like butterflies swooshing around her head. *Swsh, swsh, swsh, swsh.* Like something talking about her in an ancient language.

Pia's eyes flicked to the sky, then the ocean. She reached for the pendant she wore, unfastened it, and placed it around Rachel's neck. "Don't take this off."

Rachel's fingers immediately went to the pendant, still warm from Pia's body.

"It's black tourmaline, for protection," Pia said. "Until I know what we're dealing with and can get you something more specific."

Heavy clouds sprung up from nowhere, turning the sky an inky black. In the distance, deep thunder rolled around in the atmosphere like an ominous message. The temperature plummeted, and the smell of rotting fish filled the air.

Rachel shivered, a prickle of awareness trickling down her spine. They were not alone out here, just like she, Trey, and Rob hadn't been alone. Something standing just out of sight, something that blended into the shadows, was watching their every move with interest.

With malicious intent.

Her survival instincts screamed at her to run. To get off this ship. But leaving was not an option. Not if she wanted answers.

She hadn't heeded her instincts last time.

What was going to happen when she ignored them again tonight?

Chapter Four

As Rachel descended the rusty metal stairs to go below deck on the *Anna-Marie*, her back began to burn. Sometime during that night with Rob and Trey, she'd received three long, deep scratches down her back. The police had photographed the injury but had not been able to offer an explanation. The pain had lessened over the last week, though the wounds were again burning like fire.

She ignored the sting and pushed through, concentrating on forcing one foot after the other down the steps.

Mark placed a battery-operated camping lantern on the table, next to a kerosene lamp and candles. The room looked mostly the same as it had a week ago, except for the black fingerprint dust that now covered most surfaces.

Mark stared at the Ouija board, still on the center of the table where she'd seen it last. "Where'd you find this?"

"Rob found it," Rachel answered. "At the back of a cupboard in the captain's quarters."

Pia stepped forward to examine the board. She closed her eyes, took a breath. "The board was already on the ship when Captain Edwards bought it. He should never have touched it."

"Why didn't the police take that thing as evidence?" Rachel asked Daniel, her voice thick with emotion. She would never forget the moment she'd first seen the Ouija board. The way it had made her feel. Instinctively, she'd feared it, as she would a snake curled up and ready to strike.

She hadn't liked the way Rob had run his fingers slowly, almost reverently, across the ornate lettering carved into the wooden board. She hadn't liked the strange expression that had come over his face when he'd told her and Trey to sit down.

Daniel raised his brows. "Evidence of what?"

Rachel frowned. "The demon… or whatever came through that board. It's evidence."

Daniel shoved a hand through his hair. "The fact is, the people in this room are the only ones who believe that as a possibility. The police took several items into evidence, including what they believe to be the murder weapon. To the detectives investigating this case, the Ouija board has no more significance than a game of Monopoly. It was dusted for prints like everything else, but they don't consider it evidence. The fatal wounds on Norton's body weren't consistent with a Ouija board, but rather that of the knife found at the scene."

Of course, the police wouldn't think the board responsible. Rachel herself wouldn't have believed it either just over a week ago. The police thought the Ouija board was a toy. Harmless, if you didn't believe in its dangers. Rachel's heart continued to pound.

"You'll take it though, won't you Mark?" Rachel asked, feeling a little breathless. *What happened to the oxygen in here?* "That thing is evil. I don't freaking care what the police believe."

"You can't remove anything from the ship," Daniel said. "It's still considered a crime scene. I had to pull strings to allow us entry tonight, and I promised we'd leave everything as is."

"What if it hurts someone else?" Rachel demanded.

"Trust me," Daniel said. "The police aren't going to hold a séance with it anytime soon."

"But—"

"Rachel, relax."

Sure. That was easy for him to say. He hadn't been there Wednesday night.

Daniel moved to her side and placed his hand on her shoulder. He tugged her close, making her hiss with pain.

"What is it?" Daniel frowned.

"My back," she explained. "It feels like it's on fire."

"Show me," Daniel demanded. He turned Rachel around, his hand pausing at the bottom of her T-shirt. "May I?" he asked, as though he hadn't stripped her naked many times before.

Rachel's throat closed over at his tenderness, so she nodded. Mark was standing on her other side, and Ryan was next to Daniel, filming. She wanted to tell him to turn the camera off. Strangely, something about the scratches felt too private, personal. Her cheeks burned as though she had some reason to be embarrassed or ashamed. But why would she feel that way? They were just scratches.

Cold air hit her skin, and she sucked in a breath.

"What the hell happened to your back?" Daniel asked. "Did you scratch yourself on something on the way down here?"

"No, it happened last time, though I don't remember how. The police checked it over, photographed it and everything, but they don't think it was Rob or Trey who did it, so I must have cut it on something."

"It doesn't look like it's healing very well if you did that a week ago," Daniel said, his face creased in concern.

"Oh my God," Pia said, looking over Daniel's shoulder. "It's marked you."

"Are you getting this?" Mark asked Ryan. "I want a close-up."

Daniel pushed him away. "What the hell is wrong with you? Turn the damn camera off. She's been hurt."

Rachel tugged her shirt down, her fingers tangling in the material. "It's okay. The scratches mostly don't hurt anymore, but for some reason they've started to really burn again."

"We know what we're dealing with now," Mark said, his eyes lighting with excitement. "This is demonic. That's not just a scratch; it's a claw mark. You have three defined scratches on your back. Three is the sign of a demon, a mocking of the holy trinity."

Mark's obvious pleasure as he looked wide-eyed around the room turned her stomach.

"We haven't come across a true demon in nearly a year," Mark said, his smile growing. "We thought we might have encountered one back in March, but it turned out to be something else."

Rachel's mouth was dry, and she couldn't swallow. Something demonic had touched her? If it could scratch her, what else was it capable of? Had it killed Trey?

Now she knew why the scratches had made her feel violated. Less like an injury, and more like a... message.

Daniel was a towering presence at her side, anger rolling off him in almost tangible waves. "Can you do this without her? It's too dangerous. I'm taking her back."

"No, Daniel," Rachel said. "I have to remember what happened. Demon or not, I'm staying."

Daniel growled, and the room turned deathly still. She sensed Daniel's overwhelming urge to drag her out of there, willing or not. Pia looked torn, as though reassessing the danger now that she knew what they were dealing with.

"We stick with the plan," Mark finally said, breaking the silence, the only one in the room who didn't look scared. "Rachel?" he asked, his tone soft and cajoling. "Are you ready to take us back to that night, tell us what you remember?"

Rachel's legs felt watery, but she lowered herself to a chair and pressed her fingers to her temples.

Remembering anything about that night sickened her, but she needed to do it if she wanted to find out what had really happened to Trey. She closed her eyes and went back to that evening...

"Shit. It's damned creepy on here," Rob said, navigating around the *Anna-Marie's* rusty deck by torchlight.

Rachel rubbed her arms against a gust of wind that moved over them on the otherwise deathly still night. "My sister is right," Rachel grumbled. "I'm twenty-four now. I need to stop drinking and hanging out with the two of you so much. You're becoming bad influences."

"Babe," Rob said with a tug on her long brown hair. "We've *always* been bad influences."

That was true. And that was just the way Rachel liked it. She was the lead singer in their band, Trinity Beat. She also played rhythm guitar, while Rob played lead guitar and provided backup vocals, and Trey rocked the drums. Other musicians often played with them, but it was always the three of them at the band's core.

"Well, after tonight, you boys are on your own for a while," Rachel said. "I'm here to spend time with my sister, niece, and nephew. And behave like a mature adult," she added.

Rob snorted. "You'll be back to the dark side with us within the week. Adulting is overrated."

That might be so, but lately Rachel had been feeling unsettled, as if there were something incomplete about her life, like it was a jigsaw puzzle missing crucial pieces. Her sister, Ellie, would say she needed a husband and kids, but was that it? Settling down, raising a family, seemed so… dull. She wanted to go on adventures. That was why she'd talked Trey and Rob onto this haunted shipwreck in the middle of the night.

A flash of movement caught her eye, and she whipped her head to the left. Rob and Trey were clearly to her right; she could see the light from both of their torches fading as they descended a rusty set of stairs.

She shivered, and a strange sense of awareness that they were not alone out here settled uncomfortably over her. As creepy as it was up on the deck alone, going down those stairs seemed like an even worse idea. At least there was fresh air up here.

Rachel steeled herself to remain calm. Despite telling the guys she didn't believe in ghosts, that wasn't entirely true. Secretly, somewhere deep inside, Rachel was very aware of something outside the existence of normal reality. There was a reason she sought out ghost tours and visited haunted houses. Curiosity? Fascination? Something deeper? Whatever it was, her attraction to the paranormal had been deeply ingrained from an early age.

Except… something about this ship was different than all the other haunted locations they'd visited. There was a prickling in the air, a strange static charge that made her body shiver with awareness. Her survival instincts were kicking in, screaming at her to get off this ship.

"Come on, chicken!" Rob said, sticking his head up from the top of the stairs that led below deck.

"I'm coming."

What else could she say to the guys at this point? Whatever it was, it certainly wasn't going to be, "I'm scared, and I've changed my mind."

She'd prided herself on being able to keep up with her two best friends as they'd grown up together. The more they had teased her about being a girl, the more she'd set out to prove she could do anything they could. And more. Riding BMX bikes on dirt trails had turned into risky cross-country motorbike adventures as teenagers. And now, as adults, they were kicking around the countryside, visiting haunted places.

With heavy feet, she made her way to the stairs, keeping her torch trained steadily in front of her so as not to fall over obstacles in the dark.

Below deck, the air felt thicker, heavier. Stagnant. She took a deep breath and regretted it. Her stomach roiled, and she clapped a hand to her mouth, fighting down the urge to vomit. "What is that smell?"

"What smell?" Trey asked.

"You can't smell that?" She coughed. "Must be something dead in here," Rachel murmured, but she could see no evidence of that being the case.

Rob was opening cupboard doors, shining his torch into every nook and cranny.

"What are you doing?" Rachel asked, rubbing her arms. *Must be a draft down here.* Though it was warm above, here it was ice cold, and the hair on her skin was all standing on end. "Looking for something to drink?" Rachel teased Rob, in an attempt to hide her discomfort. "Want me to put a pot roast on for you too?"

"Ha ha," Rob said. "Very funny. I'm looking for the Ouija board."

Rachel's heart shuddered to a halt. It was one thing poking around the haunted shipwreck, but trying to find the Ouija board that local legend claimed had turned the captain insane enough to kill his entire crew was another thing entirely.

She forced herself to breathe. "As if you're going to find it. This ship has been abandoned for years." *Please don't find it.*

"And yet there seems to be plenty of shit still here," Rob said. "There are sheets on the captain's bed; they're yellow and disgusting, but they're there. There's even a journal on the captain's desk. It's almost like stepping back in time right to the day of the murder-suicide." He turned some dials on an old short-wave radio in the captain's room, but it was dead. Though what had he expected?

Rob picking through the ship put her already frazzled nerves more on edge. It felt as though they were trespassing, or had opened up a coffin and were pawing through the contents.

All while the previous occupants stood right there watching.

Rachel's heart pounded, and sweat beaded across her forehead.

"Look at this." Rob traced his fingers across some carvings on the timber desk. At first it looked like graffiti. But it wasn't.

Bitch.

Slut.

Cheating whore.

I'm going to kill you both.

"Legend says the captain's wife was cheating on him," Rob said in awe. "Looks like that was true too. Isn't this exciting?"

"Sure," Trey said, evenly. "But we should probably start thinking about heading back before the cops catch us on here." Concern reflected clearly in Trey's eyes when they connected with Rachel's. Thank God she wasn't the only one who thought this shit had started to feel just plain wrong. "I'm heading back up on deck."

"Poor bastard," Rob said. "Imagine being trapped out at sea while someone is screwing your wife in your own bed back at home."

"Jeez, Rob. Stop being so morbid," Rachel said. "Let's go."

I can't breathe down here.

The air was thick, like milk that had curdled.

Rob put a hand on his hip, his expression mocking. "I wondered when scaredy-girl would make an appearance."

Rachel rolled her eyes. "Stop being a child."

"You're no fun," he teased.

"The things you're going through belonged to real people," she said, taking the tattered captain's log out of Rob's hands and putting it back on the desk. "This is like snooping around someone's house while they're not home. It's not right."

"Well, it's not like they're going to come back and catch us, is it?"

And yet, that was how she felt. Actually, she felt as though the captain and his crew were watching them right now. Rachel's eyes searched the shadows in the corners of the room. Empty. They were alone.

Weren't they?

"Whatever." Rachel shrugged. "You and your drunken ass can stay down here picking through graves. I'll be up on deck with the moon enjoying the starry night." Trey had definitely had the right idea.

The deck turned out to be nowhere near as pleasant as Rachel had hoped. The clear, starry sky was obscured by swirling dark clouds.

"I don't remember there being a storm forecast for tonight," Trey remarked.

"There wasn't." Wind whipped strands of hair into her face.

"It looks clear over there." Trey pointed to the left, and then to the right. "Look, you can see stars along the horizon. It's almost like the storm is just over us."

Trey was right; it was odd. Just like Rob's behavior down below. "Rob's acting strange," Rachel said.

"Don't let him freak you out. He's just trying to scare you. He's disappointed that the haunted houses we've seen so far have turned out to be so ordinary."

"Did he expect a real ghost would step out of a closet and say hi?"

Trey grinned. "That would have been polite. Ghosts these days are so rude."

Rachel smiled. At five-foot-eight, Trey was the same height she was; she didn't have to look up when they were close to each other. She tucked a strand of his reddish-brown hair behind his ears, and his hazel eyes twinkled at her.

"Leave him down there for a little while longer," Trey suggested, clearing his throat. "You saw how he was drinking back at the campfire. Breaking up with Bianca hurt him more than he'll admit. He'll soon get tired and want to go home. Or he'll pass out, and we'll have to carry him off."

"I'm sorry it didn't work out for them. I really thought she'd be the one."

Trey nodded. "You ever think you'll find the right one?" he asked, keeping his gaze on the ocean, not on her.

"Me?" Rachel laughed. "I'm not really looking." *Liar.* Daniel's face filled her mind, but she pushed his image away. Trey had asked about finding the right one. Whatever Daniel Jackson Smith was, he certainly wasn't the *right* one.

"What about you?" she asked. Girls threw themselves at Trey all the time, but he'd been single for a while now. Quite a few months, actually. There had to be a reason.

Trey paused, a moment too long. "I've always loved you, Rachel. You must know that. I've had girlfriends, but no one has ever lived up to you."

Her chest squeezed. *Oh.* She thought he'd gotten over that long ago, that time he'd tried to kiss her when they were sixteen and she'd turned him down.

Sure, Trey was attractive. So was Rob. But they felt like brothers to her. She fumbled around for something to say, some way to let Trey down gently without breaking his heart.

She was saved from answering when a scraping sound came from their left. She jumped away from it, smacking into Trey. "What was that?" She peered in the direction the sound had come from, but all she could see were shadows.

"Just Rob banging around." Trey's laugh was forced.

"Rob's downstairs still. You can hear him moving stuff around." Whatever had made that noise, it wasn't Rob.

Trey frowned. "Who's there?" he called out.

Silence.

He let out a nervous laugh. "Probably just a rat."

"How'd it get out here?" Rachel asked dryly. "Hitch a ride on a shark?"

She tried to smile at the image but couldn't. She'd had enough. She pushed off the side of the boat. "I want to go back." She didn't want to be there a moment longer.

"Rach, wait—" Trey covered her hand with his, sandwiching hers between the cool metal railing and his warm palm. He stepped closer to her. "I've wanted to tell you how I feel for a long time, but I didn't want to ruin our friendship."

"Let's not do this, Trey." Her voice sounded strangled, tight.

"I've started now; I have to finish." Trey took a breath. "Every woman I meet, I compare to you, and they come up lacking. They don't have your sense of humor, your strength, your sense of fun and adventure." He reached up and ran his hand down her hair.

"Don't," Rachel repeated, barely able to manage the word. Her throat had closed over. "Don't do this."

She'd hoped he would just drop it. What if he couldn't accept how she felt? Would he end up walking away from her and the band?

He dropped his hand, his shoulders slumping forward, then he turned away. "It's that guy, isn't it? The special ops guy, Daniel."

"No," Rachel immediately said, ignoring the painful twist of her stomach at the lie. At the mere mention of his name, her heart had fluttered in her chest, and her skin had heated.

Damn Daniel for always having that effect on her.

"He's no good for you." Trey's voice was clipped, his back stiff.

"You're right. He's not." On that they could agree.

There was a drawn-out moment of tension, then Trey released a long breath and rolled his shoulders. He turned to her with sad eyes and his familiar smile.

"Look at us," he said. "Both of us pining for someone we can't have."

"Oh, Trey…" She leaned her head on his shoulder. "We'll both find the right people for us one day."

The staticky sound of a radio cut in and out below deck. "Did you hear that?" Rachel asked.

Trey frowned, and they both went silent as they listened. This time the sound was closer, clearer, as if it were up top with them. A faint, but audible, male voice transmitting across the airwaves. "There it was again. Tell me you heard that," Rachel whispered.

Trey nodded. "I did."

"That sounded like the ship's radio."

"Probably just Rob messing around down below."

"He was playing with the radio in the captain's room earlier, but this… doesn't it sound as though it's coming from the bridge?"

"The electrical equipment was all dead when Rob tested it earlier," Trey said.

A crackling sound followed by distorted voices echoed faintly, but undeniably clearly, in the air around them, and a hum, as if from powerful engines, reached their ears.

Trey's eyes widened. "It almost feels as though the ship is coming back to life."

Rachel swallowed. That was exactly what it felt like. The movements she kept seeing out of the corner of her eye now seemed to be the fleeting images of a captain and his crew walking the deck.

Except that wasn't possible.

But… didn't it feel as though the ship was more upright now? Not quite at the same angle wedged against the reef as it had been when they'd boarded? If she didn't know better, she would almost believe the dead captain and his crew were about to sail the *Anna-Marie* off into the ocean, taking them along for the ride.

Impossible, Rachel reminded herself sternly. *It's my mind playing tricks.* She'd had too many drinks herself back at the campfire.

Rob was coming up the metal stairs, each step clanging. Rachel and Trey abruptly pulled away from each other.

Rob stuck his head up through the hole and eyed them suspiciously. "What are you two doing?" His words held an edge that Rachel didn't like.

"Are you finished snooping around down there?" she asked. "It's time to go."

"I've got something to show you. Both of you." He ducked back down the ladder.

"On our way, mate," Trey said. Then to Rachel he said, "We'll see what he wants to show us, then we'll go home. Okay? Just five more minutes. I promise."

Rachel caught his arm. "It's creepy down there. You go see what he wants. Tell him I drank too much earlier and need the fresh air."

What she actually wanted was to get a bit of distance from both of them. From Trey's declaration and Rob's newfound obsession with the dead captain's things.

It was time to call it a night and go back to her sister's. That was, after all, what she was supposed to be doing. Visiting her sister, not messing around on a shipwreck in the middle of the night.

"Hurry up, you two! What are you doing up there?" Rob demanded. "If I didn't know better, I'd say there was something going on between you." The darkness in his tone sent a shiver down her spine.

"He couldn't hear us, could he?" Rachel whispered.

"I don't think so," Trey said, frowning slightly. "But we'd better go down there."

The feeling wouldn't leave her. That little voice of warning inside her head telling her not to go. To leave. *Now.* So what if Rob got upset? He'd get over it.

Trey grabbed her hand and tugged her forward.

When she reached the bottom of the stairs, Rob was in the middle of the room, watching them with his hands on his hips. He shined the beam of his torch directly on Trey's face.

"Jesus, mate!" Trey said, shielding his eyes.

A strange look had entered Rob's eyes, and he seemed... different somehow, something Rachel found hard to put into words. His face was Rob's face, but it seemed to be shaped differently. He wore an expression Rachel didn't recognize. It was almost as if someone else was wearing Rob's face like a mask.

"What were you two doing?" he asked, his tone harsh. "You're acting very suspicious."

Trey ignored the question and directed the beam of his light around the room. Plates had been set on the table. They were chipped and mismatched, but placed as neatly as though they were fine china.

And they hadn't been set up that way when they'd been down here before.

"You hosting a dinner party?" Trey asked, shining his torch back on Rob, then letting the beam travel down Rob's arm. He was holding something flat and square. A piece of wood.

Rob raised his hand, an unfamiliar, lopsided grin on his face. "Look what I found."

A chill rolled through Rachel's body.

A Ouija board.

Rob turned his back and crossed the room, used the sleeve of his shirt to wipe down a wooden table, and placed the board in the center.

"Where did you find it?" Trey asked.

"Is it the same one?" Rachel asked.

Rob laughed. "Questions, questions. Be patient, old friends. We need to prepare."

Rob reached for a whiskey bottle and proceeded to pour the alcohol into three chipped melamine cups, his movements neat and precise, careful not to spill a drop, as though he were pouring Moët into champagne glasses. Where had Rob found a bottle of whiskey?

Rachel swallowed past the lump in her throat. Sure, Rob had had too much to drink, but he wasn't even acting like his drunk self.

He placed his torch base flat on the table so the light shone upward and acted like a lamp. From his jacket pocket, he withdrew a tear-shaped black object.

"The planchette, my loyal subjects!" Rob announced with a flourish and placed the pointer on the center of the board over what appeared to be a carving of a horned demon's head.

"Where did you find that?" Trey repeated, moving to stand at Rob's side. The board was clearly old, centuries perhaps, and around the ornate letters of the alphabet were carvings of skulls and pentagrams and symbols Rachel didn't understand or like the look of.

"Right at the back of the cupboard in the captain's quarters, behind a false wall. I found this too," Rob said, placing a strange crystal ball next to the board. There was an indentation on the table, so the ball didn't roll off. It was as though whoever had gouged the table had done it specifically for the crystal ball. Which meant that person had likely been standing or sitting right where Rob was now.

Fingers of ice raced down her spine. "What's that?" Rachel struggled to speak past the constriction in her throat.

Rob shrugged and stroked the glass surface of the ball. "Who knows? But it's cool, isn't it? Makes you feel all tingly when you touch it." He ignored the cup of whiskey he'd just poured himself and instead took a swig directly from the bottle in his hand.

"You're drinking the captain's whiskey?" Trey asked.

"You think he's gonna care?" Rob slammed the bottle down on the table. The board jumped, the sound jarring in the otherwise silent space. "What's he going to do? Whatcha gonna do, captain psycho?" Rob called out belligerently to the room.

Rachel's pulse fluttered erratically. Something was wrong with Rob. Seriously wrong. He looked like Rob, but he didn't sound like Rob, and he didn't act like Rob.

The man before her was a stranger.

"How did you know to look behind the wall?" Trey asked, caution in his tone. He was concerned about Rob as well. How were they going to get him off the ship and back to shore with him acting so… irrational?

"Just knew." Rob shrugged and made a sound that should have sounded like a laugh. Except it didn't.

"You just knew," Trey repeated slowly.

Rob glared at him. "I was looking for it, and I found it, all right? What the fuck difference does it make? When you lose your keys and you find them, I don't ask you how you found them. I just accept that you found them. I found the fucking board. You going to make it a capital offense?"

"Don't get your knickers in a twist. Jesus! I was just asking." Trey's tone was light, but Rachel could tell he was nervous. Rob's anger was uncharacteristic. He'd always been the most easygoing of the three. She couldn't remember the last time he'd been riled up like this.

"Wanna have some fun?" Rob asked with a lopsided grin, his mood flipping to playful.

"No." Rachel crossed her arms.

"Why? You scared?" Rob's tone was jeering.

She shrugged. "Of course not." But she was.

She didn't like this Rob. She wanted the Rob she knew and loved back. Not this one with the frightening eyes and the unfamiliar cadence to his speech.

Instinct told her to play along. *Get this over. And get off the ship.*

"Prove it. Prove you're not scared." Rob stared directly into her eyes. His voice belonged to a crazed psychopath in a dark alley, not to her best friend since kindergarten.

"Rob! What the hell?" Trey playfully punched Rob in the arm, but there was a clear warning in his tone. Rachel's heart was beating unreasonably fast in her chest and refused to slow down.

Rob glared at Trey. "She's been prick teasing us for years, and you're the only one allowed to act on it, right?"

Heat flashed across Rachel's face. *What?* She'd never led them on… Why was he saying this? It had to be the alcohol talking.

She took a step forward, preparing to intervene between them if necessary, but Trey pushed Rachel aside and angled his body protectively between her and Rob. Something he'd never had to do before. Ever. "Don't talk about Rach like that. Jesus Christ! What's gotten into you?"

Rob's shoulders relaxed, his leer abruptly replaced by his familiar grin. "Just messing with you. Jeez, you've both got all the courage of frightened little rabbits tonight."

Trey stepped back, some of the tension leaving his stance, but caution was still clear in his gaze. "Cut it out, mate."

"Calling me a prick tease? Not funny," Rachel said, hugging her arms around her stomach.

"I'm sorry," Rob said, crossing the distance and putting an arm around her shoulders. Instead of feeling warm and comforting, his arm felt cold and stiff. And he used the gesture to urge her forward, toward the board, her feet somehow deciding to obey him, shuffling along the metal decking.

"Just five minutes, then we'll go," Rob said, echoing Trey's earlier words.

Five minutes, and then we get off this godforsaken wreck.

CHAPTER FIVE

The room below deck on the *Anna-Marie* slowly came back into focus for Rachel, even as vivid memories of that night clung to her peripheral vision, refusing to be pushed aside. Pia, Ryan, Joe, Mark, and Daniel stared at her with wide eyes and stunned silence, their gazes filled with both horror and sympathy. She blinked back tears.

Mark cleared his throat. "Wow, Rachel. That was a pretty fucked-up night. You get all that?" Mark asked Ryan, who had just lowered the video recorder.

Ryan nodded to indicate he had.

"Why can't I remember what happened to Trey?" Rachel asked, frustration riding her hard.

Pia stirred, began walking slowly around the room, touching objects with her fingertips. "Let's see what we can do to fill in the missing pieces."

Rachel shivered and hugged her gooseflesh arms around her stomach. A shadow moved to her left, and she whipped her head around, but could see nothing.

Oh, Dear Lord, it's happening again…

"The EMF detector has just picked up a sudden change." Ryan angled the camera onto a little black box to read the numbers on the screen. "Three point five… four… back to two… no, up to six."

"Something is here with us," Mark said. "Joe, make sure you keep the wide-angle camera rolling." Joe was across the room, using his camera to capture the room as a whole, while Ryan was using a handheld for close-ups on Mark.

Pain throbbed between Rachel's eyes, and the scratches on her back burned as though someone were holding a lit cigarette to her skin.

Rachel... A deep, raspy, disembodied voice whispered her name and cold breath washed over her neck. She let out a small cry and jumped backward.

"Are you okay?" Daniel asked, concern creasing his brow.

Rachel nodded and shivered against the bitter chill in the air.

The electronic device Ryan had set on the table continued to flash, and another unit started beeping.

"The EMF detector picks up unexplained changes in the electromagnetic field, which indicate the presence of something paranormal," Mark said to the camera. "Especially out here on the ship, where there is no risk of interference from electricity or manmade devices, such as mobile phones, which can ping off nearby towers and make false hits. We already knew there was no reception out here, before we turned ours off. The anomalous phenomena is compelling."

Mark had been circling the room, and he was back at the Ouija board again. Rachel swallowed. Somehow, it seemed more visible in the darkened room than any other object. Even when she turned away, she could somehow still see it in her peripheral vision. It was just so... *loud* in the otherwise silent space. If it were a sound, it would be a drum kit relentlessly pounded in a primal rhythm.

A rush of highly charged energy washed over her, and she had to physically concentrate on fixing her feet to the floor so she didn't run from the room. The events from last Wednesday night were too fresh. Too painful. *Too real.*

Mark ran his fingers over the ancient lettering on the Ouija board, caressing the horns of the demonic goat's head in the center, much like Rob had that night.

"What are you doing?" Rachel's voice was high and tight, the constriction in her throat threatening to strangle her. Every time she looked at that board, her head swam. The floor moved as though the boat were out at sea, and not still wedged against the reef.

Just like it had that night.

Mark continued to stroke the ancient board, his expression one of awe. "It's beautiful."

"It's not beautiful!" Rachel choked out. "It's pure evil."

"Mark?" Pia moved to his side and took his fingers off the board.

He glared at her, and Daniel shifted, focused on the sudden tension between them. Something was not right about that board. It... *changed* you.

"Ouija boards have the power to open a doorway between this realm and another," Pia said. "Although we can never really know what will be waiting on the other side."

"Whatever was on the other side of that board that night, it was most certainly never meant to come through into our world," Rachel said.

But it had. They'd unwittingly invited it through. By messing with what they didn't understand.

What did that mean for them all now? What did it mean for Rachel?

Mark signaled for Ryan to focus the camera on him, the glowing red light showing it was recording. Mark spoke directly into the lens, his tone theatrically dramatic, but not overdone. "Pia, have you picked up on anything yet?"

"Yes." Pia's all-knowing eyes briefly met Rachel's, and Rachel saw concern there. Pia took a deep breath. "I haven't seen what happened to Trey, but I have picked up a fair bit of what happened with the captain and his crew."

Rachel instinctively leaned into Daniel's body, absorbing some of his strength and calm. If he was at all disturbed by anything going on, he wasn't showing it. His face was set in hard, unreadable lines.

Rain lashed against the metal ship, pounding hard on the deck above. Drips landed in loud splashes on the floor.

The temperature in the room turned from icy to arctic, and Rachel could see Mark's breath as he exhaled near the light. Just as she had seen Rob's that night.

The putrid smell of rotten flesh filled the room, and Rachel's heart beat erratically in her chest.

Her throat closed over. "It's here."

"Yes," Pia confirmed.

A circle of seven shadowy figures formed around the board. Rachel wanted to scream but couldn't suck enough oxygen into her lungs, and it came out as a whimper instead.

Her fingers dug into the skin on Daniel's arm, and although he didn't flinch, she knew she must have drawn blood.

The camping lantern flickered, turning off and on. Mark grabbed it and slapped it against his palm, and it went out, plunging them into darkness.

"The camera just died," Ryan said.

"Mine too," Joe said from across the room.

"I'm turning on my phone," Daniel mumbled.

"It will interfere with the EMF readings when it tries to find a tower," Mark said, sending something crashing to the floor while he fumbled about in the dark. A moment later, he struck a match, and the smell of kerosene filled the room as he lit the lamp, bathing the room in an orange glow.

"Not as bright as the battery-operated lantern, but it will have to do," Mark said, lighting the candles as well.

"Fuck the readings," Daniel growled. "Something is goddamn wrong here. I…" He stabbed at the power button on his phone. "Jesus, the battery's dead."

"There's no signal out here anyway," Mark said.

A flash of lightning turned the room into day, and Rachel saw the Ouija board hovering about six inches off the table before the room plunged once again into semidarkness.

Mark and Pia instinctively backed away from the table, their mouths open in shock as the board began to vibrate, making a strange buzzing sound. The air was charged, crackling with the electricity that accompanies a violent storm.

Daniel was the only one who moved forward. "What the fuck?"

There was a terrifying noise, the sound of a hundred tortured animals screaming in pain.

Before Daniel could grab the board, it hurtled at Rachel. There was no time to duck, not that it would matter. The board was aiming for her, like a surface-to-air missile locked onto its target.

The board smashed against her head, sending her careening backward. She cried out and hit the floor, the board hovering above her as it lined up for another attack.

CHAPTER SIX

Daniel scooped Rachel off the floor and sheltered her body with his as the Ouija board rose again. The board crashed against his back in a furious attempt to get to her. A spear of wood pierced his skin like an arrow.

"Fuck you!" Daniel screamed to the unseen presence in the room.

"You can't leave," Mark shouted, watching the attack with wide eyes. "We're in the middle of an investigation. You're getting this, aren't you, Ryan?"

"Fuck the investigation!" Daniel growled. "This ends now." The board smashed into his back again, a searing pain ripping through him, as though it were a knife and not a hunk of wood. Between his body and the wall, Rachel was protected, and he assessed how to make his trip across the room to the stairs without her being exposed.

"Mark! We have to go now," Pia shouted over the howling noise. "I don't know how to protect us. Don't know how to make it stop."

"Show no fear!" Mark shouted. "You know better than that, Pia." Addressing the room, he yelled, "We are *not* scared of you!"

"Mark," Pia said, tugging on his arm. "We really need to leave. Now."

Mark cursed, and the team snatched up their equipment. Something flew across the room, smashing against the wall. A bottle of whiskey?

Daniel bolted across the room in a crouch and hurried up the steps, sheltering Rachel in his arms as more objects began flying around the space. Over the din, Pia called out phrases he didn't understand. Something heavy landed on the floor at the bottom of the stairs, but he didn't look to see what it was.

Daniel didn't stop until Rachel was in the tinny. Rain pelted down; flashes of lightning and thunder roared in the sky. Above them, Pia stood on the deck, her hair plastered against her face, while the team tossed down equipment for Daniel to catch.

"What are you?" Pia shouted in frustration, and Ryan began filming again. "Tell me what you want with Rachel!"

"Hurry up!" Daniel roared. He didn't give a flying fuck what it was. He needed to get Rachel as far away from that ship as possible.

The tinny listed heavily to one side when the team climbed aboard. Daniel tugged Rachel to his chest, even though she struggled to pull free. Fuck that. She mightn't need him, but he sure as fuck needed to know she was safe.

His free hand on the throttle, he revved the motor, eager to set off.

The foul air on the ship seemed to have followed them onto the tinny. He'd almost expected the engine not to start, and he hoped they got to shore before it died.

The little motor screamed each time the tinny crested the waves, then crashed down, sending ocean water flooding into the boat.

"Collins! Grab that bucket and empty the water out."

"I've got it." Rachel pushed out of his grip and began bailing water. He eyed her critically, but she appeared to be holding up okay now that she was off the boat. A trickle of blood ran from the gash on her head, but otherwise she appeared fine. With several inches of water in the bottom of the boat, and more pouring in from each new wave, Daniel feared they would sink before they reached the shore. The ocean tossed the boat around like a dolphin playing with a ball.

The freak storm raged overhead, soaking them all through. But Daniel was chilled to the bone more from what had happened on the ship than the sudden wild weather.

The boat finally hit shore a good two or three kilometers down the coast from where they'd started.

The storm calmed, ending almost as abruptly as it had started. Thunder became a faint rumble in the distance as the clouds left the area above the *Anna-Marie* and headed back out to sea. A few stars peeked through the lingering cloud cover, the moon again visible, providing enough light to navigate the beach.

Daniel eyed Rachel, shivering with cold and fright in his jacket. He didn't want to leave her, but it would be quicker for him to run and get the car than for everyone, shaking and soaked, to walk the distance laden with equipment.

Pia tugged on his arm. "Rachel's still not safe," she whispered urgently.

"From what?" Daniel scanned the beach for an immediate threat.

"I don't mean right now. She'll be okay tonight. But those scratches… He's marked her. I saw… I saw—"

"You saw what?"

Pia, wide-eyed, shook her head, as though the images were too terrifying to even speak of. "He's not finished with her yet."

Daniel's vision reddened around the edges. *He's not hurting her again. Not on my watch.*

"Why would he mark her, then try to kill her with the board?" Daniel asked. He needed to understand this thing if he was going to fight it.

"Fear," Pia said. "He wasn't going to kill her. Demons get their power from fear. Fear is the doorway they use to enter the human soul."

"Is that why Mark shouted to show no fear?"

"Yes," Pia said. "No matter what, you can't show weakness in the presence of a demon."

A howl came from the ocean, like a pack of dingoes out at sea.

"Look after her," Daniel ordered. "I'll be back with the car straight away." He waited until Pia sat next to Rachel on the beach before he took off at a run, powering through the soft, thick sand. He pushed past the burn in his thighs, reminded of his special ops training. He'd been starved, subjected to horrors that had seen him on the brink of death, and he'd made it back. Endured extended torture that would have killed an average person.

That training had been several years ago now, but he still kept in peak physical condition. His muscles were unusually fatigued by whatever had been using their energy on the ship, but that wasn't going to stop him.

He heard Max barking before he saw his vehicle. Max's head was poked out the open window. When he opened the door, Max bounded into his arms and licked his face, and he gave his best friend a fierce hug.

"We need to hurry back to Rachel, buddy."

Daniel whipped out a tire gauge and wasted no time lowering the tire pressure to help keep them from getting bogged. He selected a low-range gear and powered across the soft sand, his 4WD snaking through the dunes. His only thought was getting to Rachel as soon as humanly possible.

A shadow moved in the bushes along the shoreline. It wasn't paranormal. Daniel knew human flesh and blood when he saw it. And although it was impossible to be absolutely sure, Daniel would hedge his bets that the shadow was a five-foot ten male who went by the name Robert Leonard Madden.

And Daniel would also bet Madden hadn't been far from Rachel since the night Trey Norton was killed. Daniel's fear for Rachel escalated.

She'd been marked by a demonic entity and was being stalked by Madden. Rachel was up to her eyeballs in danger.

Madden he could handle.

But even after all his extensive weapons training and years of stoically staring down death, none of that could help him with the demon. All that experience was useless when it came to fighting something you couldn't see with your eyes, couldn't kill with any weapon known to man.

How the hell was he going to protect her?

CHAPTER SEVEN

THREE A.M.

From his position hidden in the shadows across the road from Rachel's sister's house, Rob Madden watched Daniel Smith lower his lips to Rachel's.

Watched the tender way she looked at him.

And he at her.

Daniel's reluctance to leave her.

And hers to let him go.

Daniel kissed her again, roughly. She wrapped her arms around his neck, and he pulled her close. She arched her head back, her body curving backward as he ran a hand through her thick, long hair.

Rob raised his fist and imagined his fingers wrapped around the handle of a blade as it plunged into the handsome detective's flesh. Visualized the bright blood pooling at the wounds, before running in red rivulets down his body. The distinctive meaty, coppery smell of fresh blood, the metallic taste in the back of his throat.

Horror ripped through Rob's body. He made a choking sound, and the detective whipped his head around, eyes scanning the darkness. For a heart-stopping moment, Rob thought Daniel could see him where he hid in the shadows like a coward.

And then Rob wished that Daniel could.

I need help.

Tears streamed from Rob's eyes unchecked. He still had lucid moments, brief periods of time when painful memories flooded back to him in an overwhelming rush. The images were soul-shattering, as terrifying and overwhelming as a horror movie to a six-year-old child.

I killed my best friend.

His one consolation was that Rachel didn't appear to be able to remember. Rob had picked up pieces of conversations as he'd followed behind the cops when they'd taken her to the shore, watched when she'd stared out at the ship. She'd cried that afternoon, huge gut-wrenching sobs, as she'd described what she could remember from that night.

She'd cried for Trey.

She'd cried for him.

It had broken Rob's heart when she'd fallen to her knees in the sand and cried out his name. "Rob Madden, where are you?" The broken words had pierced through the darkness and into what was left of his blackened soul.

It had killed him then not to go to her, to hold her, to comfort her.

The two detectives had just stared at each other over her head, had done nothing other than wait for her to finish. To regain her composure. They hadn't believed her. They'd waited for her to find the strength to stand. And when she had, her face, her voice had been devoid of all emotion, all the joy of life sucked right out of her.

She'd sent prayers to the universe later that day, and Rob's physical body had shaken when the demon's wicked laugh had erupted through Rob's mouth.

Rob barely had any control over his body anymore, his thoughts and emotions rarely his own. The darkness was devouring his soul, slowly but surely, the way a terminal disease ate away at a human body.

An icy wind chilled him from the inside out, and Rob knew the beast was watching Rachel and the detective through his eyes, its evil consciousness alongside Rob's.

Rob studied Daniel long after Rachel had gone inside. The detective waited for a light to turn on, so he would know which room her bedroom was. Rob watched him make a few calls, saw a car with tinted windows pull up at the rear of the house, saw him wave to a patrol car that cruised slowly past. Saw Daniel position his fancy 4WD so he had a perfect view of the side of the house where Rachel slept.

Rob was grateful the detective was watching over her.

When he wasn't imagining killing him. Slowly…

A heavy fog clouded his thoughts again, and something not himself shifted inside him.

Unlike Rachel, Rob remembered exactly what had happened that night.

Remembered the heinous beast as it rose not from the board, but from the scry. Rachel had no reason to fear the board the way she did; that was merely a tool for communication.

The demon they'd invoked resided in the crystal ball. *The scry.*

The archdemon Sohn-Zae. A very powerful and dark entity, who could be summoned through an act motivated by jealousy and revenge.

The beast's face filled his mind, and Rob stood and backed away. As though he could run fast enough or far enough to elude something that was inside him.

Sohn-Zae opened its mouth, and thousands of sharp, needle-like teeth gleamed in the moonlight. *Take me to her.*

Rob shook his head, and did his best to resist the demon's influence. The demon wanted Rachel. Not to kill her. He understood that much. At least he thought he did.

However, Rob felt the demon's desire to kill Daniel powerfully, knew that would happen soon. The detective's time on Earth was limited.

But Rachel…?

The demon wanted her for some other purpose. It had a kind of affinity with her. Something about her bloodline made her special.

Take me to her.

The beast wanted Rob to deliver the scry to Rachel.

I won't!

Rob had no control over what the demon did when it fully took over his consciousness during the blackouts, but so help him, he would fight with everything he had to protect Rachel during his rare lucid moments.

In his mind, the beast raised one clawed hand and brought it down. Rob's back began to bleed and burn with white-hot pain.

Take me to her.

"No!"

Rob doubled over as though he'd been hit in the gut with a sledgehammer. From the inside.

The fight always began like this. Rob's resistance. The mind-numbing pain as the demon abused him. The blackout.

The horror when he awoke, when he remembered what he'd done…

"Take Rachel and run!" Rob screamed at Daniel's car as it slowly cruised past.

The demon's raised claw was the last thing Rob remembered before the pain sent him into oblivion.

CHAPTER EIGHT

Y ou look terrible," Elise said, placing a mug of hot coffee in front of Rachel.

"Thank you," Rachel said dryly. "You always say the sweetest things."

Elise was wearing her light blue nurse's uniform, her chocolate brown hair styled in a sleek bob.

"I mean it," Elise said. "If you don't start sleeping better, people will start thinking I'm the younger sister."

Rachel sat at Elise's large Tasmanian oak dining table in the spacious, open-plan living room. She cupped the mug of strong coffee with both hands and inhaled its rich scent.

"I'll sleep when I find Rob and remember what happened to Trey."

Elise gestured to Rachel's forehead. "You're hurt." A frown narrowed Ellie's beautiful green eyes. The same color as their mother's, a feature Rachel had always envied. Hers were gray, like their grandmother's. Satin gray, an optometrist had told her once. But gray, satiny or not, was still gray.

"Just a scratch." Rachel rubbed a finger across the small bandage covering the angry raised bruise on her forehead left by the Ouija board. Daniel had tended to her various cuts and scrapes with a medical kit in his car before dropping her off.

His darkly sensual scent had lingered on her skin long after he'd left, as had the taste of him in her mouth after he'd bruised her lips with a passionate kiss. While reaching for the spare key, she'd found herself lifted off the ground, then pressed against her sister's front door by a six-foot wall of solid, hot, hard male. She'd been too surprised to stop him. Not that she'd wanted to; the magnetic pull of being anywhere in his vicinity was too powerful to resist. Daniel could seduce her—and often had in the past—with a single glance.

She'd damn near orgasmed from his mouth on hers alone, the way his tongue had hungrily searched hers, the rough way his hand had found her breast. The soft growl that had come from the back of his throat…

It had been far too long since she'd had sex. Not since Daniel. Had it really been a whole year? For heaven's sake, she was twenty-four, not eighty-four. She was free to have casual sex. It was just that… *Daniel.*

That damned man had ruined her for other men.

Unable to sleep, Rachel had stared at her book, the latest Kristine Cayne suspense, until the sun rose at twelve minutes past six. The same time she'd heard her white Lexus being dropped off in the driveway. Daniel just… *handled* things. A woman could lose herself in a man like that if she wasn't careful.

"How did it go last night?" Elise asked, bringing her out of her reverie. Her sister wiped a cloth over the marble island in the kitchen. "Did you remember what happened?"

"No."

Elise crossed the room, gave her a quick squeeze. "This will all work out. You'll see."

Rachel released a breath. "I hope so, Ellie." Her eyes stung as she looked up at her older sister. "I'm sorry this has taken away our time together."

She'd come to spend time with Ellie and to catch up with her sister's kids, who were growing and changing so fast. Sally was a beautiful five-year-old with blonde hair and gray eyes like Rachel's, and Liam, a sweet baby boy who looked the image of Ellie, would be two in December.

"Me too." Ellie closed her eyes and pressed a quick kiss to the top of Rachel's head. This was the first opportunity they'd had to really spend any time together since the death of their mother last Christmas. When Ellie had called, asking her to visit, Rachel had jumped at the chance. The band had had a couple of last-minute cancellations, so the timing had been perfect.

Rachel's stomach twisted painfully. She no longer had a band. With Trey and Rob gone, Trinity Beat was over.

But she couldn't think about that now. Her priority was trying to figure out what had happened. If Rob was alive and out there somewhere, she had to try to reach out and help him, somehow.

"I'm meeting *Debunking Reality* this morning, then I'll be back for dinner with you and the kids," Rachel said.

"Let's hope Mark and Pia give you the answers you need." Elise pushed off from the table and dropped two pieces of bread in the toaster.

"I hope they can."

Rachel eyed her sister now, at home in the kitchen. Ellie was so much like their mum, slim, petite, and stunning, whereas Rachel had always been tall and curvy.

"So," Elise said, her tone brighter. "Who dropped you off last night?"

Rachel's heart skipped, and she flushed, something her sister did not miss.

"He looked familiar," Elise persisted. "I know he wasn't Mark from the show. Although Mark Collins is hot, that man last night took sexy to a new level. And built! Jesus, the muscles on that guy. I thought you two were going to have sex right there on my welcome mat!"

Rachel's already warm face started to blaze. "You saw that?"

Elise grinned. "Security camera at the front door. And why were you wearing his leather jacket? You looked like a drowned rat. Tell me you didn't go swimming!"

Rachel grinned at the rush of questions as Elise buttered a piece of toast, swiped on some vegemite, and passed it to Rachel.

"No swimming. We got caught in the rain."

"It rained?" Elise raised her brow in surprise.

Rachel took a bite of toast. "It did at the ship. Just briefly. The weather patterns last night were bizarre."

Elise's hand that held the knife stilled momentarily, her face creased with worry. A local well aware of the haunted reputation of the shipwreck, Elise had been less than impressed when she'd learned Rachel had gone out there the first time, let alone that she'd intended to go out again last night.

"Well? Where did you find that guy? I've been living out here for five years," Elise said, her light tone slightly forced, "and in one night you manage to find two of the most gorgeous creatures alive and bring them with you out here in the sticks. A TV star, and Mr. Tall, Dark, and Dangerously Sexy."

Rachel grinned at her sister's description of Daniel; however, Sharktooth Cove was hardly the sticks. It was a stunning, picturesque tourist attraction, but at four or so hour's drive north of Perth, it was remote by city standards.

"You were always the one who knew how to have fun in life. Nothing routine for you." Although her sister's tone was jovial, Rachel saw the shadow that flickered across her eyes.

"Nothing wrong with routine," Rachel said, wishing she had some in her life right now. "Kids need it."

Elise shrugged, wiped another dish and put it in a cupboard. "Suppose you're right."

Rachel looked a little closer at her sister. There were dark shadows beneath Ellie's eyes that weren't completely covered by concealer and lines on her face that Rachel hadn't noticed before.

"Looks like I'm not the only one who hasn't been sleeping," Rachel said with a stab of guilt for not noticing sooner.

Had she been so consumed with what had happened to Trey that she'd missed something important going on with her sister? Elise looked a little drawn, like she'd been going through a difficult time recently. But that couldn't be right. She hadn't said anything.

Except for being very persistent about this visit. But that was just because they hadn't seen each other in months. Phone calls and text messages just weren't the same. Everything was going well for her sister, wasn't it?

"Are you okay, Ellie?"

"Me? I'm fine. Just worried about you. Now, stop changing the subject and tell me about that gorgeous guy."

"You remember Daniel Smith? Taipan used to come to Dad's restaurant all the time," Rachel said, still studying her sister.

"Of course! He's the one with the gorgeous German shepherd."

"Max."

"That's right. I'd heard the guys went out on their own late last year. I just didn't recognize Daniel last night in the dark with his tongue down your throat. What's he doing here?" There was a tinge of hurt in her tone. "Did you bring him along as well?"

"What? No." Rachel frowned. Elise had been disappointed when she'd found out that Trey and Rob had come with her. Did this trip mean something more to Ellie than just a chance to catch up? Again, Rachel watched her closely.

"Why is he here then?" Ellie asked. "You used to have a thing with him, didn't you? About a year or so ago? I thought you ended that."

Rachel nodded. "A thing" was one way of putting it. What she'd had with Daniel was way too much—and not nearly enough.

"Mark called Nate, Pia's fiancé, for assistance, and Daniel turned up instead. Mark just wanted to make sure everyone would be safe."

Elise's brow wrinkled. "Why wouldn't you be safe?"

"They still think Rob could be a danger to me, but they're wrong."

"Let's hope so." She didn't sound convinced.

"Oh, come on. You know Rob. He's spent our whole lives protecting me."

"When he wasn't getting you into trouble first."

Rachel grinned. "When he wasn't doing that." She took a deep sip of her coffee. Time to change the subject to something lighter. "How's Don doing on his quest for world domination?"

Was it her imagination, or did her sister's eyes harden at the question? "The same."

Elise's husband, a wealthy mining magnate, worked on a FIFO—fly in, fly out—basis for his company. Rachel had always believed her sister and her family lived the perfect life: expensive, picturesque house, two perfect kids. Had trouble come to paradise? Perhaps they'd had a tiff? Probably over Rachel's visit. Wouldn't be the first time. Rachel sighed.

Don had never approved of her. One night after he'd had too much to drink, he'd described her as "the wayward sister, singing and teasing men in seedy bars like a common whore." Of course, he'd apologized the next day, but she'd never forgotten—or forgiven—the comment. Alcohol loosened the tongue only enough to let the truth out.

"Ellie, is everything okay between you and Don?"

Elise waved her hand and shook her head, as if the question were absurd. "Tell me how you left with the paranormal team and ended up playing tonsil hockey on my front doorstep."

So she didn't want to talk about it, whatever "it" was. Rachel would get to the bottom of it later. She sipped at her coffee, holding it between her palms and blowing steam off the top. "It's complicated."

Elise glanced at her watch. "Well, uncomplicate it. I have to start work soon, and I need the story before I go."

Rachel sighed. "I don't know how to explain it. Things with Daniel…"

"You were the one who ended it, right?"

Rachel frowned. "I'm not sure what there was to end. The only time I saw him was when he had a case in town."

"I hope you don't mind the observation," Elise said carefully. "But from what I could see on the video, I think it meant more to him than you think. His eyes never left you for a moment."

"No," Rachel said. "He made it very clear what it was—what it could be—for him." An arrangement that had suited Rachel as well. At the time. Her heart squeezed, and she struggled to swallow past the lump in her throat.

"I ended it when I started to want more, and I knew he wouldn't be the one to give it to me."

"Good for you," Ellie said, then wrinkled her brow thoughtfully. "Although, how did you know he didn't feel the same as you?"

Rachel blinked. "He would have said something."

"*You* didn't," Elise pointed out.

Rachel pushed up from the table, walked over to the sink. "That's different. Plus, how would I ever trust a man who was interstate most of the time?"

"Ah," Elise said, nodding in understanding.

"Ah, what?"

"This is about Dad."

Rachel's face heated. "This is not about Dad."

"This is *so* about him."

Rachel finished rinsing her cup under the water and tossed her phone into her bag, anger over what her father had done to their mother, to their family, sending adrenaline racing through her veins.

"Daniel isn't the right man for me. Let's leave it at that. Now, I have to go, or I'll be late meeting Mark and Pia."

Rachel slung her bag over her shoulder. Ellie was standing at the table, an expression Rachel couldn't quite read on her face. "You'll be back tonight, promise?"

Rachel exhaled, trying to release the tension in her body. She closed the distance between them and wrapped her arms around Ellie.

"I promise." She kept her tone light, while all the time her stomach was twisting in knots.

Something wasn't right with her sister.

What secret could be so bad Ellie wouldn't share it?

CHAPTER NINE

The beachside bar/café Daniel had chosen in Sharktooth Cove was bustling with tourists and locals. The outdoor table he was sitting at overlooked the clear, turquoise water, soft white sand, and powder-blue sky. But Daniel was oblivious to the scene's beauty or his companions.

He'd deliberately arranged to meet with Pia and the *Debunking Reality* team thirty minutes before he'd told Rachel to meet them. He wanted to ask the team direct questions and understand the precise degree of danger Rachel was in. When Rachel arrived, he'd tell her only what was necessary for her to hear and reassure her that she would be safe. After all, that was why he and the *Debunking Reality* team were there. To deal with this thing she couldn't possibly fight.

He spun his coffee cup restlessly, and while he waited for Ryan to come back with a computer from the team's van, Daniel's thoughts went to Rachel, the way they always did.

The first time he'd seen her was during her first public performance at her father's restaurant on her eighteenth birthday. Daniel had been instantly attracted to her. He was a red-blooded Aussie male, and she was a tall, curvaceous beauty, with flowing locks of lush, gleaming brown hair and the most mesmerizing gray eyes he'd ever seen. Daniel had imagined every man in the room lusting after her.

He'd stayed away at the time, because he'd been twenty-five then and she'd been so young. But right from the start, Daniel had known there was something special about her. She wasn't merely a beautiful woman; the strange, magnetic pull between them told him she was so much more.

His attraction to her was more than just physical. For no rational reason, he could have ripped out the throats of all the salivating men watching her at the restaurant, as though she were his to protect.

As though she were his, period.

Back then, she'd been so young. So sweet, even as she'd sung seductive words in her sultry voice. A voice that made promises he'd known she hadn't yet had the experience to fulfill.

He'd waited three years. Rachel had been twenty-one the first time he'd made love to her, and she'd turned out to be everything he'd fantasized about and, impossibly, so much more. He'd thought the urgency of his desire, his fascination for her, would fade after he'd slept with her.

He'd been wrong.

But what could a man like Daniel promise a beautiful young woman like her except heartbreak?

He'd been just eight years old when he'd seen his cop father gunned down in the driveway of their family home. And his mother hadn't missed a single opportunity to remind Daniel over the years what a mistake she'd made by marrying his father. His death had left her with a child to raise on her own, a burden she'd rather not have had.

Chief Superintendent Liam Smith had been Daniel's hero. Daniel had been watching through the curtains that night, excited that his dad would be home early enough to read him his bedtime story. His father had seen him peeking out the window, smiled and waved. Daniel hadn't immediately understood what had happened next, the sound of the gunfire, the squeal of the car's tires as it had raced away.

Seeing his father's eyes fly open in shock as he'd dropped to the ground was something Daniel would never forget.

Or forgive.

Against his mother's wishes, Daniel had joined the force right out of school. He'd been driven, and he'd made special ops in record time. Throughout his whole career, Daniel had been working toward finding his father's killer.

And now Pia had given him a name. Scotty Fryer. One of Wild Wilson's top henchmen. Pia's psychic ability had given Daniel the first big break in the case in twenty-three years.

Ryan finally returned to the table with the computer. Daniel would get his chance at Fryer soon enough. Right now, it was time to make sure Rachel was safe.

"So, what happened last night on that ship?" Daniel asked, all business, flicking his glance over Ryan, Joe, and Mark, before settling on Pia. He didn't care who answered, as long as whoever it was spoke fast. Before Rachel turned up.

"I'm disappointed we had to call the evening short," Mark said, irritation crossing his features. "But we did get a lot of great evidence." Mark glanced at his laptop open on the table. "Class 'A' EVPs, that's electronic voice phenomena, and a cool full-bodied apparition of what we believe to be Captain Edwards himself. Joe's seeing what he can do to clean up the image so we have something impressive to air."

Good for Mark, but Daniel didn't give a flying fuck about his evidence.

"What did you find that will help Rachel?"

"Not sure yet," Mark said. "But check this out." He turned the laptop so Daniel could see the image. Daniel narrowed his eyes on the grainy pictures, tinged with the green haze of a night-vision video recorder.

The picture had been taken early in the evening. Rachel was standing with Pia at the side of the ship, their backs to the camera. To the left of the frame was the somewhat transparent, but undeniably human, shape of a man, wearing what appeared to be an ankle-length oilskin coat. The man's body was angled toward Rachel, but the face was turned, looking directly at the camera as though aware of its presence.

Beneath the hood, the face was absent, an empty black space, from which eerie white orbs stared right at the lens and, seemingly through space and time, directly at him.

The air was sucked out of Daniel's lungs.

Mark might believe he'd captured the captain's image on film, but the man in the footage no longer had any definable human qualities. The thing in the oilskin coat was something else. Something evil. Something diabolical.

"Do you know what that thing is?" That this creature had been so close to Rachel last night, and he'd had no idea… His hands fisted at his sides.

Was that the thing that had scratched Rachel's back?

Daniel turned to Pia. "You said a demon marked her. Is the demon the thing in the picture? And what precisely does 'marking' her mean?"

If he was to protect her, he needed to understand exactly what the threat was. Even if it wasn't human.

Pia's expression was grim. "I think the demon that scratched Rachel's back was something far darker than what we captured. Something without a human form. Unless it's using the captain's form to appear to us," Pia said thoughtfully.

"Strangely, I don't feel this demon was summoned by Rachel and her friends through the board, despite how it might seem. I sense that the demon was called into our realm many years before that. Maybe a century or more. I've had a vision of a woman, a high priestess I think, who turned to the dark side…." Pia shook her head in frustration. "So much is still unclear."

"What does the demon want with Rachel?" Daniel wanted pared-back facts, and he wanted them before Rachel arrived.

"I don't know," Pia said, nervously twisting a chain around her neck—similar to the one she'd given Rachel last night. "But whatever it is, it won't be good."

No shit. "Is she in immediate danger? Is there something that can be done to keep her safe?"

Pia's brow furrowed. "Simply staying away from the ship won't be enough. Most likely the mark allows him to follow her."

Well, that was just fucked. "Can't you give her a crystal or… herbs or whatever, something to protect her?" It seemed almost ludicrous that a man of his means and training was asking about fucking crystals and herbs.

Pia shook her head. "No."

Daniel thrust both hands through his hair in frustration. "There must be something we can do to protect her. You gave something to Sage last year when that demon was after her, and you yourself wear a pendant on your chain."

"In Sage's case, we were dealing with an ancient prophecy," Pia said, "and there were historical records and a grimoire to work with." Pia fingered a large pendant around her neck. "I gave Rachel my personal tourmaline last night. It's powerful and very effective against low-level negative energy, such as the type I encounter on a daily basis in my line of work, but it's not a match for evil of this magnitude."

A vein throbbed at Daniel's temple. Rachel was in danger, and there was no known course of action he could take to ensure her safety.

"I'm sorry." Pia looked pained. "I'll keep working on it. Once I help your team find that missing girl in time for your takedown this week, I'll be able to focus fully on Rachel."

They'd been asking a lot of Pia these last few months. Although Pia technically still worked for Mark, since she'd become involved with Nate, TSI had started to call upon her psychic ability more and more to help them solve cases when their intel failed.

Pia had been instrumental in helping them get a major break in a case involving Australia's biggest drug lord, Wild Wilson, back in April. She had "seen" the delivery location, and that had given TSI the advantage and ability to intercept a shipment of high-grade cocaine hidden in luxury cars. And now Wilson's gang had crossed their books again.

Taipan Security and Investigation's newest client was a group of parents whose daughters had disappeared. In the last six months, several promising young girls had dropped out of the same university and hadn't been seen again. The police had done what they could, but without much to go on, the case had quickly gone cold.

The girls were all around the ages of eighteen and nineteen, and technically weren't missing. Each family had received some sort of contact, the crux of it being that their daughter wasn't coming home. This behavior was highly out of character for most of the girls, who'd generally been very studious and had bright futures all mapped out. The families had banded together and employed TSI to investigate their disappearances.

TSI's investigation so far had discovered that Wilson's gang had snatched the girls from a succession of university parties, injected them with drugs to abduct them, then continued to give them drugs until they were addicted, at which point Wilson's gang forced them into prostitution. The private-school girl was a popular fantasy, and men would pay an astronomical price for it.

TSI had located five of the missing girls, but the sixth, eighteen-year-old Lilly Randall, despite extensive and exhaustive investigation, still hadn't been located. Their intel had run into a dead end. They hoped Pia would be able to "see" the location of the sixth girl, so that all the girls could be retrieved on the same night. If they didn't take the girls all at once, it was a very real possibility that Wilson would kill Lilly Randall out of spite or revenge.

Pia's ability was Lilly's last hope.

Pia tapped her black nails on her glass of water. "There's something else. I can't shake the feeling that Rachel was destined to be on the ship that night. The band's shows just happened to be cancelled so that she could come here at this time. There's a connection. He needs her for something. He would have already killed her by now otherwise."

What the hell could the demon want with Rachel?

Pia held his gaze. "I saw Captain Edwards with a scry. It's a crystal ball of sorts. And I think somehow, it's the scry that's the connection to Rachel."

"How so?"

Pia scrunched her forehead. "The high priestess I saw is related to the scry and to Rachel somehow. But the priestess wasn't evil. Something bad happened to her, and the conjuring of the demon was deliberate, but with unexpected consequences."

"So, the scry is what… possessed?"

Pia nodded. "Yes. I believe so. I also believe Rob killed Trey. Based on what Rachel described, I think Rob was influenced to do so by the demon."

"Is Madden a threat to Rachel?"

Pia released a breath. "Yes. Although Rachel isn't going to want to believe that…"

"What can you tell me about this scry?"

"The scry is a divination tool, like a crystal ball for seeing the future," Pia explained, her face creased into lines of concentration as though things were finally becoming clear to her.

"At first the captain saw good things in the scry." Pia's eyes closed. "Genuine things that would happen. Like winning that night in a game of cards with his crew. He would be 'shown' the winning hand.

"The captain soon came to believe the scry and trusted it. And then the scry began showing the captain visions of a man visiting his Anna-Marie at night." Pia's eyes sprung open. "*That's* why the captain thought his wife was cheating on him!" She looked around at the others, then closed her eyes again in concentration. "The captain became obsessed, desperately trying to see the man's face in the scry. He drove himself crazy; jealousy and hatred toward his wife's secret lover consumed him. The captain turned the ship toward home, tried to get back to his wife, but storms and freak weather patterns thwarted his every attempt."

Ryan turned a voice recorder on to tape what Pia was saying.

"The more desperate the captain became," Pia continued, "the more he failed, the more he lost his mind. He put the ship, his whole crew, in danger with his unrelenting quest to get back to his cheating wife and take revenge on her lover. The crew rebelled; there was a mutiny on board. But the ship, under the influence of the demonic entity the captain had invited on board, would never reach land.

"Eventually the captain started imagining the face of his wife's lover on the faces of his very own crew, and one by one, he killed them all. The captain, defeated and unable to get to his wife, finally took his own life. A single gunshot to the head. The *Anna-Marie* became a ghost ship, sailing the sea for thirteen long years, unable to return the captain to his wife."

"Jesus." Daniel sank back in his chair and rubbed at his eyes. "Why did it choose to wash up here now?"

"That's something we need to find out. It might help us understand what it wants with Rachel."

Daniel fired off a message to Zach, TSI's tech wizard, asking for a complete background file on Captain Edwards and his crew, and anything that might be relevant in the history of Sharktooth Cove.

Daniel wanted to leave this very second and hunt down Rob Madden, but he held himself in check. TSI were making their own inquiries, but the state police were already all over the case. They'd issued an APB and had Madden's house, car, and known locations under surveillance. So far, he seemed to have just vanished, hadn't touched his bank account, gone back to his house or car. But people didn't just vanish; they hid. Until they slipped up. Through Zach, Daniel would know the moment the cops found anything.

Daniel paused, then asked the question that had been worrying him the most. "Could the same dark entity that attached itself to Madden, attach to Rachel? Is that what the mark means?" Fear churned in his gut as he waited for Pia's reply.

Pia looked pained. "I can't say for certain, but if Rob is still alive, perhaps Rachel is safe."

"So if Madden dies, Rachel could be in even more danger."

"Yes."

Whatever happened, Madden had to be brought in alive.

"I think you're making a mistake not telling Rachel everything," Pia said firmly.

Daniel shrugged. Rachel had already been through enough. She'd dealt with the police and their questions, the loss of her memory, the psych appointments. Daniel was in a position to take some of the burden, and that was what he was going to do.

Pia said, "She's here. Rachel just pulled into the carpark." Daniel didn't need to look to know she couldn't see the carpark from their table. "Don't hide anything from her. She has a right to know."

Daniel shoved a hand through his hair. Was Pia right?

No. This was his domain; protection was what he did. Rachel couldn't fight this herself anyway. She was in danger, and Daniel wanted to be the one to help her. Did he want to be her knight in shining fucking armor? Hell yes. He sure wasn't letting anyone else do it.

Pia leaned back in her seat, looked at him, through him, and a smile played at the corners of her lips.

Daniel ground his teeth. "What?" he grumbled.

"Look at you all twisted up inside." Pia grinned. "It appears we've found your kryptonite."

CHAPTER TEN

The smell of coffee and fresh, savory pastries washed over Rachel as she pushed open the door to the café. She immediately spotted Daniel through the glass window. He was sitting with the *Debunking Reality* team at an outside table overlooking the beach. He had his back to her, leaning forward in his chair, spinning what appeared to be an empty mug of coffee. His jacket was casually placed across the chair next to him, and a tight white T-shirt was stretched across his muscular torso. A tattoo of something—a coiled snake?—that he hadn't had last time they'd been intimate was visible beneath the sleeve of his left bicep.

Rachel walked a direct line to him, watching the way the ocean breeze tousled his hair and how he thrust his hand through it in that way he did when he was tense.

She knew the moment he sensed her approach. His broad shoulders squared slightly, and he straightened and leaned back in his chair. He finished whatever he was saying to Pia, then turned in Rachel's direction.

His gaze met hers, their eyes connecting, and her heart slammed in her chest. But then, it always did. No matter how prepared she was for the jolt, the current that crackled between them always took her breath away. Immediately she was conscious of every step her sandaled feet took as she made her way to him.

No, not to him. *To the table.*

Trey, remember? Rob. The ship. The freaking demon.

Rachel looked away from Daniel and locked her vision on Pia, who was watching her intently. They had seemed to be engaged in a tense conversation earlier, and for a moment, Rachel worried she was late. A quick check of her watch confirmed she was exactly on time. But Mark's coffee cup was empty and pushed to one side. So was Daniel's.

Had they really intended to talk about this without her? She breathed through a fast rush of annoyance. Then hurt.

What were they talking about that couldn't be discussed in front of her? Wasn't she entitled to know exactly what was going on?

She moved to sit next to Pia, but Daniel stood, took his jacket off the spare seat next to him, and indicated the chair, holding it for her as she sat down. She forcefully tempered her body's instinctive response to being in such close proximity to him.

Despite her being left out of the beginning of the meeting, everyone seemed genuinely pleased to see her, and they quickly fell into easy conversation as they ordered what was clearly a second round of drinks along with toasted sandwiches.

"So, what can you tell me about last night?" Rachel asked, bringing the small talk to an end and getting to the topic she needed to discuss most. "Did you find out what really happened to Trey? Rob didn't do it, did he?"

Was it her imagination, or did the team exchange glances? There was a slight pause, as though no one was sure quite what to say.

"What aren't you telling me?" Her stomach twisted, and she shifted in her chair. She couldn't fathom what was so terrible they wouldn't tell her about it. She'd been there when the board had lifted off the table of its own accord and slammed into her head and Daniel's back. What could possibly be worse than that?

Mark ended the silence, his face breaking into an easy smile. He reached across the table and touched her hand. "Nothing sweetheart. It's hard to know where to start, that's all. We went on the ship again this morning." Mark paused while the waitress topped up their water jug and delivered their drinks and toasted sandwiches. "To get the Ouija board and keep it safe until Pia is back in a couple of days from the case she's working on with Nate for TSI."

"Okay." Rachel was relieved that the board couldn't hurt anyone else.

"But the board was gone."

Daniel blinked, the news clearly surprising him. So this wasn't the topic they'd been discussing right before she'd arrived. Had Mark just *lied* to her? What weren't they telling her?

Ryan spoke up. "Sometime between when we left last night and when Mark and I went back, someone must have taken it."

"Media?" Joe asked. "I saw some journos hanging out in front of our hotel this morning. The case is getting even more attention now they know it involves Trinity Beat."

Mark shrugged. "Maybe. But usually they'd come up to us, shoving microphones in our faces and demanding answers to their questions. I can't understand why they'd sneak onto the ship in the darkness and take the Ouija board—and only the board—from what we can tell. Nothing else appeared to be missing, although that would be impossible to know for sure. The place was in chaos when we left it. We really need to locate the board ASAP."

Rachel swallowed. "Why would you need to find the board? Seems to me it's good that it's gone."

"It's a direct link to this specific entity," Mark said. "His point of entry. You can bet your granny knickers that Pia will need it when it comes time to get rid of this thing for you."

Pia nodded. "We do need that board."

Rachel's hand shook slightly as she took a sip of her coffee. She'd been hoping that her night on the ship with *Debunking Reality* would be the end of it. That it would all be over.

"So, you didn't find out what happened to Trey." Rachel's heart was heavy.

Pia reached over, placed her hand on Rachel's arm. Rachel held her breath. Nothing good came from a conversation started that way. "I'm sorry, Rach. Nothing I can say for sure," she said, with a pointed glance at Daniel.

"Was someone else on that ship with us that night?" Rachel asked.

"No," Pia said. "Nothing human anyway."

Rachel's heart sank. "But you still think it was Rob who killed Trey."

"Yes," Pia said.

"That's not possible. You all saw the board flying at me. How do you explain that?"

"You're going to need an open mind to deal with this," Mark hedged, making Rachel feel as though they were preparing her for an answer she wasn't going to like.

"Skeptics will look at all the evidence we provide in the cold light of day and imagine causes for changes in temperature, or say it's faulty equipment, or say the image we caught is lens flare—you name it, we've heard it. It doesn't fit with their worldview, and as they try to reconcile the evidence with their beliefs, they discount it. But when you're there, like you were that night, and you put everything together, there really is nothing to deny. You have to accept the truth. A new truth about the world we live in. What I do by documenting it is let people like yourself know there is someone to turn to when something like this happens."

Rachel finished her coffee. She recognized now that she'd been hoping for an answer along the lines of Pia "seeing" an intruder on the boat who'd killed Trey, and that Rob had fled the scene.

"The paranormal is as real as you and me sitting here, without the flesh and blood," Mark said. "There's a spirit in you, your soul or whatever your individual belief system calls it. The major religions all agree something is inside the flesh we see with our eyes. So when you die, your soul is no longer trapped in your flesh and blood body. Does it simply cease to exist? Where does it go?" He shrugged, throwing up his hands to show he didn't have the answers—yet.

"The laws of physics state that energy can't be destroyed. We have real evidence to prove that the energy that was once in human bodies still exists. There *is* life after death, just not in the same form. The very foundation of our civilization is based on that concept. It's just that some religions want to believe that that energy goes up to a castle in the sky somewhere far away from here. But what if it doesn't? Or at least, what happens if that energy gets trapped here or left behind for some reason? Maybe a soul has unfinished business and can't move on."

Rachel's mouth was dry, but she was determined to do what Mark said and keep her mind open. She'd called *Debunking Reality*; she had to trust that they knew what they were doing.

"Rachel, what Mark is trying to say, is that Rob killed Trey," Joe said, looking bored and impatient with the conversation.

And just like that, Rachel's newfound resolution to be open-minded collapsed. She glanced around the table to find everyone glaring at Joe, but no one contradicting him.

"Was that necessary?" Daniel growled.

Joe raised his eyebrow in challenge. The tension between the two was thick.

"Is that what you all believe?" Rachel asked, looking at each one of them in turn. "After all this talk you just gave me about the paranormal," she said, shaking her head in disbelief. "Something paranormal flung that board at me; it deliberately hurt me. *That* is the thing that must have killed Trey."

There was an uncomfortable silence, as though no one wanted to answer her.

"What aren't you telling me?" Rachel demanded, turning to Daniel. She could at least trust him to be honest with her. Couldn't she?

Daniel held her eyes. "All evidence points to the fact that Madden killed Trey."

"If I wanted that line of bullshit, I would head back down to the police station."

"Rachel," Pia said. "It wasn't the Rob you knew. He was under the influence of the entity."

"What does that even mean?" Rachel hated the way her voice broke, hated that she had to keep asking that question, but she kept her shoulders squared as she glanced around the table. Mark looked like he wanted to answer, but Daniel's expression silenced him. This topic must have had something to do with the conversation they'd been having right before she'd arrived. Something they felt she couldn't handle.

"Under the influence of the entity?" Rachel said, unable to keep the bite from her tone. "Is that a new charge? Driving under the influence of alcohol, killing under the influence of a dark entity? What a load of crap. Rob didn't do it, the… the thing that attacked me did it."

They didn't know Rob. They didn't know how close the three of them had been. They'd been more than old school friends, more than a band. They'd been family.

Rachel shook her head, searching for something to liken it to. "Your mates at TSI are all close," Rachel said to Daniel. "You'd die for each other, right? You've often said that. Would you believe it if someone told you Nate killed Ethan?"

"Yes," Daniel said, a shadow crossing his face. "If the circumstances were right. Look, there was a time I wouldn't have believed things like this were possible either, but now I can't deny the possibility."

"Demonic possession, you mean?" Rachel asked to clarify. An image of a horror movie rose to mind, someone speaking in tongues and frothing at the mouth. Rachel shook her head. "You're all mad. That is not what happened."

"It happened to Mark," Pia said, her voice almost a whisper.

Rachel glanced at Mark in surprise. For the first time since she'd known him, he appeared discomfited. He looked tired all of a sudden, as though weighed down by the memory. He played with his teaspoon, his hand shaking. "I wouldn't wish that on my worst enemy," Mark murmured, not looking up.

"It happened to Jake as well, remember?" Joe said, as though deliberately shifting the focus from what had happened with Mark. Clearly it was still a raw wound.

"We're not discussing Jake," Daniel growled.

"I'll discuss whatever I want," Joe said.

Daniel stood, leaning forward over the table. "I told you not to fucking talk about Jake."

Joe's eyes widened, then narrowed. "Whatever." He shrugged in an attempt to be nonchalant, but it was clear he was unnerved by Daniel's towering presence. Daniel was clearly at the edge of his patience as well. Silence descended on the table.

Rachel opened her mouth, then closed it and shook her head in disbelief. She'd miscalculated in bringing the *Debunking Reality* team here. They were supposed to make things clearer, not turn her life into a horror movie.

"I made a mistake," Rachel said, standing up and taking a step backward. "I thought you were going to help me." *I needed you to help me.*

Rachel glared first at Mark, then at Pia, Ryan, and Joe, and then finally, heartbreakingly, at Daniel.

A lump lodged in her throat.

Her phone buzzed with a text message, and she glanced down. It was from Woody, the surfer who'd hosted the party they'd been at that Wednesday night. They'd all been having beers around a campfire when Woody had told them about the cursed shipwreck.

Saw Rob last night

Hope surged through her for the first time in a week. She hadn't realized until now just how many of her hopes had been pinned on the *Debunking Reality* team to prove Rob's innocence.

Daniel reached for her, and she brushed him off. She hurriedly typed back a message:

See you in 5

She took a deep breath and addressed Pia. "Thanks for attempting to get me answers. I wish you the best of luck with the success of your show."

Pia rose. "I'll keep trying. And please, Rachel, be careful. Keep wearing the tourmaline until I know more."

Rachel nodded and touched the necklace. Whatever. It couldn't hurt.

She grabbed her bag and walked out of the café without looking back.

CHAPTER ELEVEN

The heavy smell of marijuana greeted Rachel as she walked the cracked concrete path to Woody's place. Surfboards lined the front of the timber porch like wooden soldiers, and wetsuits lay open and drying on the plastic outdoor table and chairs. The door was open, so she called out, announcing her arrival as she walked inside, stepping over a thick line of white powder that had been poured along the threshold. When her eyes adjusted to the dim light, she saw Woody and three other guys from the campfire night on mismatched lounges, watching a surfing movie.

Woody turned and held up a joint, offering it to her. Rachel shook her head, wiped chip crumbs off a spare chair, and sat down.

She ran through various pleasantries, how have you been, how's the surf, but the tension from the coffee shop won out and she got straight to the point. "You saw Rob?"

Woody nodded. "I said I'd let you know if I saw him, so I did."

Rachel waited a heartbeat, and when he didn't continue, she asked, "Where did you see him?"

"Here," Woody said. "Rocked up in the middle of the night wanting somewhere to stay."

Rachel sat up straight, glanced around. "Rob's here?"

Woody shook his head. "No way." Woody butted out his joint in the overflowing ashtray and slowly rose from the couch. He indicated for her to follow him, and they walked out to the front porch. Rachel sucked in the fresh air to clear her head from the secondhand dope smoke.

"The cops still think Rob killed Trey," Rachel said.

"I did what I promised, I told you if I saw him. But I can't help you out any more than that."

Woody was watching her curiously, and after she met his gaze for a long moment, he nodded, seemingly satisfied with what he saw. Or didn't see.

"Look, when Rob turned up last night, his eyes looked strange," Woody said. "He was acting strange too. Gave me a chill. I didn't like it."

Rachel looked at Woody's glistening, bloodshot eyes and held back the first comment that came to mind. "What do you mean he looked strange?" Rachel pressed. "Was he hurt? Injured? Did he say where he'd been?"

"He was mumbling something about you being in danger. That I needed to make sure you got far away from here. Or some shit like that."

"He spoke about me?" Rachel said. "Why didn't he come to me?" Her head spun. None of this made sense. Considering how high Woody was, who knew if she could rely on anything he "remembered" about Rob's visit.

"Look, I like you guys," Woody said. "For city slickers, you are all pretty cool, and I like your band, the music you play. But I told you not to go on that ship. I told you it was cursed, that bad shit happened to people when they went out there."

"You lent us your boat," Rachel reminded him.

Woody shrugged. "I was hammered, had way too much to drink. I didn't force you."

There was no point arguing the finer details of what had happened that night. At the end of the day, Rachel, Trey, and Rob had gone out there willingly.

"So, Rob came to you for help—"

"To give you a message," Woody interrupted. "A warning."

"But you also said he wanted a place to stay, and you turned him away."

Woody had the decency to look somewhat remorseful. "Sorry, but I had to. He didn't look like himself. His eyes were black, and his shirt was ripped. And he stank."

"He probably needed a decent shower," Rachel said. "Chances are he wouldn't have had one in over a week. Did he say where he was going?"

Woody shook his head. "Something didn't feel right about him. You should be careful. If you see him, stay away," Woody said. "Call the fuzz and let them deal with him."

Great plan. The police wanted to arrest him. Rachel released a breath and rubbed her eyes. "You're just imagining there was something wrong with him because you believe the ship is cursed. He was probably tired and hungry, and he came to you because he didn't know where else to turn."

Woody moved to the table and began untangling the string on a crayfish pot. "I told you bad shit happens to people who go on that ship. I don't want any of that evil curse brought here." Woody's glassy gaze flicked to the entrance and the thick line of white powder.

Rachel knelt, picked up some of it between her fingers. It was gritty, coarse. "Is this salt?"

"Hell yes."

"You've been watching too much *Supernatural*," Rachel grumbled.

"You didn't believe," Woody said unapologetically, "and look what happened."

Rachel's heart hammered in her chest, and she couldn't help glancing around her. What for, she didn't know.

"This shit is real," Woody said. "The captain's ghost is real, and I'm sorry I ever told you guys about it. Trey is dead, and there's something seriously fucking wrong with Rob. I wouldn't be surprised to discover something is wrong with you too. I'm sorry, mate, but you should go now."

This had been a waste of time. Rob was out there, all alone, and he wouldn't come to her for help. Her throat tightened up, and she turned and left without saying anything.

"Put some salt on your doorways and windows too," Woody called out as Rachel reached her car.

Jesus, what had she really expected from a guy who spent his life in a daze?

"Yeah right," Rachel said. "I'm sure salt is the answer."

———— ♦ ————

From his vantage point a short distance from Simon Morgan Woods's surfboard-cluttered porch, Daniel watched Rachel get into her Lexus. She leaned her head on the steering wheel for a long moment before she reversed out of the driveway.

He gripped the steering wheel and fought the urge to go to her. He'd been curious as to who she'd received the message from and suspected it had something to do with Madden, given the way she'd torn out of the café. Either way, she'd left distressed, and he needed to be sure she was safe. Both from her state of mind, and from Madden. Earlier today, he'd received a report from Zach that someone matching Madden's description had been seen sleeping in the public toilets in the local park. When the police had arrived, he was gone.

Daniel's gut twisted. Rachel wouldn't be safe until Madden was behind bars.

He waited while she backed out of Woods's driveway. Back on the main road, another car would shadow her, make sure she wasn't being followed by Madden. Daniel expected her to be making her way back to her sister's, where he'd already posted another security guard. As the sound of her engine faded, he got out of his vehicle.

Time to have a chat with Woods, and see what light he could shed on this situation.

Chapter Twelve

Rachel pulled over on the side of the road, left her car, and walked across the sand dunes to the beach. She'd been intending to go back to Ellie's but needed time to herself first.

The sky was low and gray, and she sank down into the powdery sand, allowing the tears she'd been holding back to fall. Disappointment was a lead jacket on her shoulders.

At least Rob was alive. She should be grateful for that.

But it was all wrong that he was avoiding her.

Why would he go to Woody and not her? Pain ripped through her, and she hugged her arms around her stomach. What had happened that night on the boat? Was *she* responsible somehow for Trey's death? Rob was angry with her; it was the only conceivable reason he stayed away.

Remember, damn you. Remember! She let out a scream of frustration. How dare her mind do this to her? How dare it be so cruel?

She looked out across the turquoise water, unable to see its beauty. The sound of the waves gently lapping at the shore felt a million miles away.

She had never felt so *alone*. Her grief was the ocean, and she was a tiny island lost in the middle of it. An anguished cry left her heart, and she sobbed until there was nothing left inside.

She picked up a broken shell and squeezed it in her hand. She didn't feel the sharp edges as they sliced into her skin. She held up her hand and watched the blood drops pool and splatter, leaving angry red circles on a bed of white sand.

It was mesmerizing, the way the blood pooled at the wound before trickling down her palm in jagged rivers.

Her wrist was caught in a strong hand, and she gasped. She hadn't heard anyone approach through the roaring of blood in her ears.

Holding her arm gently in his grip, Daniel lowered himself next to her. He tugged a handkerchief out of his pocket and wrapped it around her palm.

Max bounded up, sitting at her other side. She didn't turn to Daniel, instead reaching out to Max, running her fingers through his soft fur with her free hand. He licked her palm, a soft whine coming from his muzzle.

"Why are you here?" She determinedly held fast to her anger with Daniel—and the *Debunking Reality* team—over their conversation at the coffee shop. "I came here to be alone."

"I know," he said. "I wanted you to know that you *weren't* alone."

His words pierced the numbness, causing her to bleed on the inside as well. How did he always read her so well? *Damn you, Daniel Jackson Smith!* She didn't have the strength to resist him right now.

Max whimpered and rested his head on her leg. Rachel ran her hand through his caramel and black thick coat and tried to order her thoughts.

"I'm okay, little buddy," Rachel said soothingly, using Daniel's endearment for the dog. "You don't have to worry about me." Max gave her a look, one that said he didn't believe her. Smart dog. She didn't believe herself either.

Rachel had grown to love Max and had missed him fiercely this last year. Always with Daniel, Max had slept on a special sheepskin rug at Rachel's house on the weekends that Daniel had stayed over. Even though her tenancy agreement for her city unit stated no dogs. Max wasn't really a dog anyway, Rachel reasoned. He was a fur-human. And he never barked out of turn, caused any trouble, or ruined any furniture, so where was the harm?

The numbness inside gave way to the sting from the cut on her palm. She welcomed the pain; it meant that beneath the chaos of her life, there was still a woman inside. A woman who bled.

"How did you know where I was?" It was no use arguing with Daniel to leave. He'd do what he wanted anyway.

"I made it my business to know."

"Are you following me?"

Daniel shrugged. "Does it matter?"

"Would it matter if I said yes?"

A smile tugged at the corners of his mouth. "No."

Rachel sighed, and some weight lifted off her shoulders, something she attributed directly to Daniel's presence. Why was it impossible to stay angry with him?

Her pulse was already starting to kick about erratically as her body became physically attuned to his presence beside her. Every breath she took dragged his scent into her lungs, black leather, vanilla bean, and something dark and spicy. A scent she associated with long hot nights of sex.

She resisted leaning into him. He was wearing denim jeans, a white T-shirt, and sunglasses. A brisk sea breeze tousled his dark hair around his face. Last September, it had been cut short at the back; now she marveled at how the length around the muscled column of his neck softened his chiseled features.

He'd changed this last year, something that might have to do with leaving his position with special ops and going out with his team privately. Or perhaps it was related to the case she'd heard him discussing with the *Debunking Reality* team? The paranormal one he'd been heading to in South Australia when he'd left her last September, the case where Ethan had met his wife Sage. What had happened to them all back then?

Rachel sighed. She'd changed too this last year. Done a lot of soul-searching and questioning what she was doing in life. At twenty-four, she decided she deserved more than settling for casual sex with an absent partner. Despite how amazing the sex—and the man—was.

She looked down at her injured hand. "It's going to get stained," Rachel said, watching the blood seep through the handkerchief.

Daniel made a low noise in the back of his throat and shoved his sunglasses up into his hair. "As if I care."

He lowered his head, pressing his lips to her wrapped hand. The tenderness in the gesture took her by surprise. The kiss was almost reverent, and totally unexpected.

"Don't," she whispered, pulling her hand away.

"Babe." His voice was rough. When she lifted her head, the intensity of his gaze sent a tremor rolling through her.

"You didn't return my calls." Hurt and, yes, anger were reflected in his eyes.

She looked away and concentrated on her toes as she buried them in the sand, contemplated just how much she wanted to admit. "It was time," she finally said, her voice a whisper through her constricted throat.

"Why?" She heard his breath catch and hold as he waited for her answer.

Rachel's chest squeezed. She wasn't ready for this conversation; that's why she hadn't returned his calls. She didn't understand her feelings clearly enough herself. How could she tell him that despite everything that was going on in her life, even right now, her true vulnerability was him?

Trey's death, Rob's disappearance, and still, Daniel was the one who had the power to hurt her most of all.

"I was seeing someone," she lied. *I fell in love with you…*

She glanced up to see Daniel's face harden, his eyes narrow and his jaw clench. "I see."

Her stomach churned with guilt. *Coward! Tell him the truth.*

"Is it over with him?" he asked, a muscle tensing along his jawline.

"Yes." Ugh! Her fictional romance now had a fictional breakup as well. If only she could suck the words back. But it was too late; the lie was hanging in the air like a bad smell.

"You don't get to be upset," Rachel said, feeling her temper rise. "It's not as though you don't see other women." She'd spoken the truth but regretted it anyway. Her anger and frustration were not about Daniel, not really.

Daniel stood, brushed the sand off his jeans, and paced down to the water's edge. She felt the loss of his presence at her side powerfully, like someone had put out a fire, the only source of heat on a blustery winter night. A chill seeped into her veins.

Oh no you don't. You don't get to start this conversation then simply walk away.

Leaving her strappy sandals behind, she walked to him. He had his back to her, his arms folded across his chest, and her body ached for him.

Rachel stood at his side, stared out at the ocean, breathed in a deep lungful of salty air. "You have no right to be angry."

He whipped his head around, his eyes burning brightly. "Don't I?"

Rachel's face heated. "No," she snapped. "It's not as though we were in a relationship or anything." He'd promised her casual; his reaction now screamed anything but.

His eyes continued to blaze. The intensity of his gaze made her feel naked, scorched her skin. Emotions she couldn't read rolled off him in tumultuous waves. He reached out and she involuntarily flinched. His hand froze, then continued forward, taking a strand of her hair and tucking it behind her ear.

"You don't trust me." His eyes searched her face, a muscle along his jaw twitching. "What have I done to cause that?"

Rachel's throat tightened painfully.

I don't know how to be near you and not let you into my heart.

Even now, after seeing him again for such a short time, he had her questioning her resolve.

"Don't do that," he growled.

"Don't do what?" Rachel asked, hugging her arms around her stomach.

"That!" Daniel untucked her arms, ran his hands down to her wrists. His grip was tight, his touch searing her skin. "You stopped returning my calls, refused to see me. You shut me down in the coffee shop earlier, left without an explanation, and you're shutting me out again now."

Rachel pulled out of his grip and began walking along the beach. Daniel watched her for a moment, his long stride making it easy for him to catch up. He kept pace beside her as Max ran off ahead, splashing in the waves.

They were silent for a long time before he spoke. "Tell me what you're thinking."

"I can't do this anymore."

"By this, you mean us."

"Yes." She couldn't meet his eyes.

"I haven't been a detective for all these years without spotting bullshit when I see it. Your words tell me you don't want me, but everything else about you tells me that's a lie."

Daniel stopped walking and gripped her shoulders, turning her to face him. He stared at her long and hard, then pulled her flush against him, his erection pressing into her stomach.

"Do you feel what you do to me? I want you, Rachel, like I've never wanted another woman. And I know you want me too." His voice was deep, rough. It sent a tremor rippling through her. Wanting him wasn't the problem.

He traced the back of his finger down the heated skin on her cheek as she looked up at him. "Your skin is so beautiful when it's flushed, so pink."

His finger trailed across her jaw, down her neck. He lowered his mouth and his teeth grazed the tender skin on the side of her neck. She cried out, desire pooling hot and demanding between her thighs.

It was cruel how much she wanted him. How much her body craved his touch. Her head fell back as his tongue worked its way up her neck, flicking at her skin. He stopped to suck on a particularly sensitive spot. A moan escaped her mouth, and he crushed his lips against hers. *Ah hell.*

She was going to regret this later, wasn't she?

Chapter Thirteen

Rachel wrapped her arms around Daniel's neck and kissed him back with a ferocity that surprised her. All the emotion, the turmoil, of the last two weeks, the last year, moved through her. She couldn't remember why keeping away from him was so important. Something about self-respect and needing to be more than just an occasional fuck to someone.

Daniel crushed her to his body, his tongue delving inside her mouth, tracing across her teeth. He took control of the kiss, like the man controlled everything else in his life. The heat of his mouth set her blood on fire, and her body submitted to his natural dominance.

He groaned, holding her to him so tightly she couldn't breathe. But she didn't need her own oxygen when she could breathe his.

Daniel walked her away from the water to where the sand was dry and still warm from the sun. He fell to the sand, pulling her down on top of him. She laughed in surprise.

His sunglasses fell off his head as he looked up at her. He cupped the back of her neck, guided her head down and kissed her hard. She couldn't think, couldn't feel anything but him.

Her soft, white denim skirt slid up her thighs as she spread her legs and sat on his hips. His erection, firmly encased in his jeans, pressed against her lacy white panties. She rubbed against him, needed to, and his eyes flickered closed. He groaned, the sound sending fire racing through her veins.

"I want you so bad." Daniel's grip tightened on her hips, the roughness in his tone thrilling her.

This was what was familiar between them. This rawness and this uncontrollable desire.

"Tell me you still want this."

Rachel nodded.

"*I said tell me.*"

The bite of authority in the command made her blood race. Her mouth dried, and she swallowed twice before she could speak.

"I want this."

Daniel squeezed his eyes shut, and when he opened them, emotion swirled heavily in his gaze.

"Tell me you still want *me*." His body went rigid as he waited for her answer, and her heart stuttered to a stop.

"I want you," she said, the truth and a lie all at once. God she wanted him! Right now, in this moment, she wanted him more than her next breath.

Daniel sat up, cradling her in his lap, her legs wrapped around his hips as he kissed her again, long and deep. She thrust her hands in his thick hair, holding him hard as his hands ran up her thighs, his thumbs tracing along the seams of her panties and making her core clench with anticipation.

He lifted the hem of her top, his palm scorching the soft skin on her stomach as he moved to cup her breast. His expression looked pained, his chest rising and falling as his breathing grew labored.

As much pleasure as he gave her, she loved watching how much simply touching her aroused him.

"A year," Daniel growled. "A whole fucking year."

She cried out as his fingers found a hardened nipple and squeezed. Pleasure, white-hot and overwhelming, filled her, stole her breath.

His other hand slid the thin fabric of her panties aside, his thumb gently tracing along her slick entrance. Her heart skittered in her chest, her pulse roaring past her ears.

"You need this too," he said, his voice a low rasp. "Don't tell me you don't."

Tears burned her eyes, and she squeezed her lids closed to hide her reaction to his words. She needed him? Dear God! She fucking *craved* him.

And then he'd leave…

And she'd be left empty, wanting him. Frustration caused her to cry out at the same time his thumb slipped inside her, and the sound was disguised as pleasure.

Frustration and pleasure: those two extremes described what she had with Daniel perfectly.

Max barked, and they both looked up to see him bounding through the thick sand toward them. He barked again, and Rachel followed his gaze and noticed two people at the top of the sand dunes, making their way to the water.

"Fuck," Daniel growled.

How like Daniel to always make her feel as though they were the only two people in the world. She pressed her forehead against his, his ragged breath warm across her skin. Before the couple could see them clearly, she rolled off Daniel and tugged her skirt back into place, her body still tingling with the feel of his touch.

Daniel placed his head between his knees, thrust his hands through his hair. They were both silent as the couple walked past them a few feet away. Rachel tried not to notice the easy, natural way they held hands as they strolled with each other. Her chest squeezed painfully at their carefree love.

She and Daniel sat there, shoulders touching, watching the sun make its slow descent toward the horizon. A gentle ocean breeze caressed their heated skin, and Rachel reached out to smooth back a lock of hair that was dancing in front of one of his eyes. His profile was strong, his features chiseled, and in her eyes, perfect in every small imperfection. She loved him so much it hurt. The simple truth was painful to admit.

She turned away, glancing at the couple who were now specks in the distance. Something caught her eye. A glimpse of purple in the desert dunes that lined the beach. Rachel brushed the sand from her legs and walked through the dry and prickly coastal plants covering the small sandy hills to the flowering plant.

Daniel followed beside her and looked over her shoulder when she stopped. "What is it?"

"It's beach morning glory," Rachel said. "I love these flowers. Aren't they pretty? In all these rugged tough plants, you have these delicate flowers. Look how thin the petals are; they're almost transparent." She bent down to get a better look. "They're so pretty, so impossibly fragile. It makes you wonder how they can possibly survive in these harsh windy and salty conditions."

Daniel plucked a flower off the bush and handed it to her.

"Daniel!" Rachel's mouth dropped open. "Little did I know it was in more danger from you than any harsh Western Australian conditions."

Daniel grinned unrepentantly. "It grew especially for you."

He took the purple flower from her fingers and tucked it behind her ear. It was not a frangipani, and it was far too small and delicate to hold its place there, but the way Daniel stood back and admired it made her want to keep it behind her ear forever. The golden glow of the sun softened his features, and his smile was playful, almost boyish. He looked happy and carefree. Rachel's heart leapt, lodging firmly in her throat at the rare glimpse of this side of him.

He cupped his hand behind her head, leaned down and touched his lips to hers. His tongue slipped inside her mouth, and his hair tickled her cheek. Tears sprang to her eyes. How easily he shattered her.

He took her hand, led her back to the soft warm sand where they'd been before. He continued to hold her hand in his much larger one as she sat next to him.

"How are you holding up?" he asked softly.

Rachel shrugged. "I'm coping okay. But it's not about me. It's about Rob. It's about finding out what happened to Trey."

Daniel searched her face. "It's always about you," he said. "It always has been."

Rachel blinked up at him. There was something different in the way he spoke to her now, something else in his tone that hadn't been there before.

"Woody saw Rob last night," Rachel said, changing topics, relieved her voice sounded normal, without the thickness of desire that swirled, unsatisfied, inside her.

"I know."

Rachel blinked up at him in surprise. "You do?"

"You need to be careful of Madden," Daniel said, possessiveness clear in his tone.

"No, I don't." Rachel sighed, already tired of this subject. Not just with Daniel, but with everyone, it seemed.

"Yes, you do." His voice was clipped, his eyes narrowed and serious.

Rachel shook her head sadly. "You're wrong. You're *all* wrong. Mark, Pia, Woody, the police, all of you. Rob is my friend. He's in trouble and doesn't know where to turn. He'd never hurt me."

Daniel spread his legs, lifted her and set her between them with her back against his chest, and she let him. She thought about resisting, squirming out of his grip, for around… half a second. But what was the point? It felt so nice as he rested his chin on her shoulder and they both looked out across the ocean, watched a series of waves crash to shore.

"I want to share something with you," Daniel murmured. "Something that might upset you. I know you don't want to believe that Madden is capable of having anything to do with Trey's death, but I need you to listen to what I'm about to tell you with an open mind."

Rachel tensed, but stayed silent. Talking like this, opening up to each other, was new territory. She was curious to see where it would lead.

Daniel hesitated a heartbeat, as though he struggled to find the words. "I don't know how to explain this, not like Pia could. All I know is that a lot has changed for me this last year. Like you, I didn't choose to get involved with the paranormal. When I left you last September, it was for a case in Cryton, South Australia. That's where Ethan met Sage. That was also the case we were working on when we lost Jake."

His hand went to his bicep, where the new tattoo was. Rachel glanced down to her left at his arm, to the black ink that peeked out from beneath his shirt. Twisting between his legs, she lifted the fabric and ran her fingers across the intricate tattoo. It was a snake, a taipan threaded through Jake's name, against a backdrop of Chinese characters. It was a stunning piece of artwork.

"What do the characters mean?"

"Courage. Loyalty. Brotherhood." Daniel shivered at her touch, and he grabbed her hand, shifting so that he was once again holding her tight in his lap. "I need to tell you this."

She said nothing, waiting for him to continue. When he didn't, she squeezed his hand. "Take your time."

Daniel exhaled a long breath. "Toward the end of the case, Jake came under the influence of a dark entity, the powerful demon that had been stalking Sage. To get to Sage, it attached itself to Jake." Rachel felt him swallow, his throat working behind her head. "It took him over, possessed him. Jake turned on the team, tried to kill Sage. Nearly killed Max."

"Oh God." If anyone other than Daniel had told her that, she wouldn't have believed it. The unit were tighter than family. Brothers. "I had no idea."

"When the demon's influence lessened, and Jake realized what he'd done, he gave his life to get Ethan to Sage so they could destroy the entity. Jake took an enormous risk, knowing how it could end. And he did it anyway."

Daniel swiped his eyes with the back of his hand. "Blade said it was atonement, and I think he's right. Jake couldn't live with himself after what he'd done. Taipan wasn't just a special ops unit; it was a brotherhood. And our team, now TSI, isn't just something we do. We live it. Breathe it. It's our life."

How horrible to have one of them die under such circumstances. "I'm so sorry."

"Jake's actions were out of his control," Daniel said. "But regardless of the reason why, at the end of the day, Jake betrayed us. Our lives depend on having each other's backs. Jake couldn't live, knowing we wouldn't be able to trust him. To have even the slightest doubt is not how we work."

Daniel's voice was filled with pain, still raw. "I lost a brother that night. We all did."

"I had no idea." Rachel ran her palms soothingly along Daniel's thighs. There weren't words to describe how much her heart ached for what they must have gone through.

"I regret that I wasn't there for you." She felt sick now about not returning his phone calls. Would he have told her? Confided in her? Although she would never know for sure, she doubted it. Likely, he would have shown up, determined as always to leave it all behind and share whatever time they had together without the shadow of his work. That was how it was between them. If at any time she asked him about something work-related, he told her he couldn't talk about it. But she knew it was because he didn't want to. Something she'd always respected.

But now...? Talking like this proved something had shifted between them. But what exactly?

"So, you think Rob was influenced by something like Jake was?" Rachel asked.

"It's something we can't discount. We have the evidence it was Madden, but like you pointed out, it was out of character. The fact you had been messing around with the dark side by using the board, and then something like that happened—well, it's the conclusion, however unbelievable, that makes the most sense in your case."

"When we find Rob, will Pia be able to help him?" Rachel asked, hope filling her. At least now they had a plan, and things were finally making sense. Rob wasn't himself. It wasn't Rob who'd killed Trey; it was the demon. All they had to do was find Rob and get rid of the thing that was influencing him. He'd be just as shocked about what had happened as anyone else.

"If anyone can help him, it's Pia." Daniel picked up a handful of sand, let it sift through his fingers thoughtfully, his gaze seemingly stuck on the movement of the grains. His eyes finally rose to hers.

"Rach, I need you to remember that Madden might not be the same person you once knew."

Rachel set her jaw. "I don't care. I just want him back."

"Promise me you won't approach him," Daniel said. "You'll call me if you see him. I need you to promise me that, Rachel."

Rachel nodded. "I'll call you. If you promise me something too," she said, twisting around so she could look into his eyes. "You have to promise me that you'll help him. Not just hand him over to the police."

"I'll do everything within my power to keep him alive."

"I just need to get him to safety. We'll worry about everything else after that."

Daniel nodded. "If he approaches you, or you see him or hear where he is, you tell me. You took off earlier, went straight to see Woods. How did you know Rob wasn't still there? That kind of risky shit can't happen again."

The possessiveness in Daniel's tone, his words, sparked a longing inside her, and for a moment she wished things could be different between them. Last September, she'd watched him get out from her bed, slide into his jeans, his shirt, strap on his weapons belt, then cover it with his leather jacket. He'd walked back to the bed, taken her face between both hands, kissed her once, twice. Hard. Like he'd meant it. Like it had hurt him just as much to leave as it had for her to let him go. He'd closed the door behind him. She'd had no idea when or if she'd see him again.

And that was when she'd made the decision to end it.

"It was good," Daniel said softly, his voice gruff. He placed a finger beneath her chin and turned her head so that she was looking at him. "Between us. It was good, wasn't it?"

"Yes." *It was too good.* It still was. The chemistry between them wasn't the problem.

He leaned in, and their lips touched in the sweetest of kisses. In every way, Daniel was a strong, powerful man, perfectly capable of killing, yet he could be so very tender with her. The contrast made his tenderness all the sweeter. Like the way a heavy metal rock band could perform a heartfelt ballad like no other.

She inhaled his scent, felt the thrill as her body responded to the taste of him.

For a long moment, they stayed like that. He breathed in her breath and she breathed in his. He rested his forehead against hers. "I don't understand what happened between us. The second I knew you were in trouble, I came."

"Thank you, Daniel," she said. "I appreciate your being here."

And she did. But gratitude was all she'd allow herself to feel.

She'd be an idiot to let herself fall in love with a man who honestly admitted he could offer her nothing. She deserved better.

And yet it didn't change a damn thing. She could no more turn her feelings for him off than she could stop taking her next breath.

I don't know how to not want you.

Which was precisely the reason she'd ended it.

Rachel pulled away and turned to look out across the ocean. Daniel sighed, and Rachel didn't miss the tinge of frustration in the sound.

"Your father sold the restaurant," Daniel said. "I was surprised to learn that. That place was such a fixture in the city. I somehow thought your father would be there forever."

Rachel stiffened, the way she now did whenever someone mentioned her father.

"Is he all right?" Daniel said with concern, mistaking her reaction.

"Dad decided it was time he moved on to other things." Other things that didn't involve screwing waitresses.

Last September, a week after Daniel had left, Rachel had walked into the storeroom of their family's restaurant to find her father and a waitress taking up the rear corner space. Her own father! Screwing a girl his daughter's age!

How could he do that to Mum? How could he do that to their family?

I was the one who told Mum what I saw.

And now her mother was dead...

Mum's solution had been to remove temptation. They'd sold the restaurant, and Dad had gone into involuntary retirement and voluntary drinking. Mum went on with life as normal initially, hiding behind her façade, pretending to her friends and family that the affair had never happened. Rachel had suspected she wasn't coping well, the denial not healthy, but was at a loss as to what to do.

Then a week after the restaurant had finally sold, three months after her father's indiscretion, her mother had taken her life. A fatal dose of painkillers.

Rachel couldn't forgive herself for her part in it. For being the one who'd told her. For not doing more after she had. For not reading the signs that surely were there. It meant she hadn't looked hard enough, right?

Rachel suffered greatly for her part in her mother's death, the way she hoped her father suffered for his.

"I haven't seen him since the funeral." Rachel could barely speak past the constriction in her throat. Daniel rubbed his palms up and down her arms.

"I have to go." She stood and brushed sand from her skirt and legs.

He rose, and when he reached for her, she took a step back.

"Rachel, wait—"

"I'm sorry, Daniel. I can't do this." Rachel turned away, but not before she saw the look of hurt flash across his face.

He called out her name, but she kept her head down, walking a direct line to her car.

She'd learned a thing or two, after watching what her mum had gone through. Making yourself totally vulnerable to someone else was a mistake. The price of giving a man absolute power over you, over your life, was too high.

Allowing Daniel to get close again would only cause her more pain. It would be just another loss she'd have to survive when he left. When would that be anyway? Tomorrow? Next week? She had no idea how long he would stay, and only one thing was certain. He would leave.

He always did.

CHAPTER FOURTEEN

In a bar that overlooked the ocean, with Max at his feet, Daniel chugged back the last of his schooner of beer. He needed to stop thinking about Rachel and focus on dragging Madden's sorry ass in.

Sitting on a barstool next to him eating hot chips was Sam "Spiderman" Wells. Sam thrust a hand through his blond hair and smiled at a group of pretty girls walking past, wearing bikinis and short shorts. The girls waved back flirtatiously. Slim and athletic, Sam was never short of female admiration.

Daniel had just hung up from talking with Pia, who was on her way to the bar to meet Sam, who would then take her back to Nate. Pia had insisted she could drive herself, but that wasn't how it worked, something she was still struggling to come to terms with. What Pia had yet to fully understand was that she was now an extension of Nate, which meant she was part of TSI. And TSI looked after their own.

Pia believed the sixth girl they were looking for in the Wild Wilson case, Lilly Randall, was in a small town only thirty minutes away from here.

"How about I swap places with you," Sam said, eyeing yet another attractive girl walking past. "I stay here and keep an eye on the scenery, and you can help the guys nail Wilson's ass to the wall."

Daniel glared at his partner without heat. "I'm not here for the scenery, and you can bet your ass I'll be there when we nail Wilson."

Sam was the youngest member of TSI, which was sometimes more obvious than others. Not that Daniel didn't appreciate a nice-looking woman as much as the next man, and Western Australia had some of the sexiest tanned bodies around, it was just that compared to Rachel, no other women held his interest.

Daniel wasn't a monk, far from it. But having a woman in your bed didn't mean you weren't lonely, and it sure as hell didn't stop you thinking about someone else.

Sam grinned. "The scenery you're pining for isn't blonde, that's all. It's a brunette with killer curves and a voice you'd sell your mother for."

"Drop it." Daniel grabbed one of Sam's chips and lowered it to Max.

The grin stayed on Sam's face, but his eyes turned serious. "What's the issue, mate? Rachel's hot."

Daniel glared at his empty glass.

"You really need to pull your finger out of your ass and do something about it, or you're going to lose her."

"Are you sick of living?" Daniel growled. "I told you to drop it."

Sam put up his hands in mock surrender, and Daniel leaned back as a waitress took away their empties and brought them two more beers.

By a strange twist of fate, the very day before Rachel's name had appeared on Daniel's screen, Pia had "seen" the man who'd killed Daniel's father. She'd been able to give Zach just enough direction and information that they'd confirmed she was talking about Scotty Fryer, Wilson's right-hand man. Between the three of them, they'd tracked his movements outside Australia and back, going through years of old documents with new technology, and they'd finally had a breakthrough.

Despite a massive investigation at the time, the murder of Daniel's father had never been solved. The police had their suspicions, but nothing that would hold up in court. Eventually, the official reports listed the cause as a drive-by shooting. Assailant unknown.

But it had been an assassination.

It had been dark that night, but from the streetlight, Daniel could still remember the shape of the car and the cold eyes of the gunman, the only thing visible through his black mask.

Eyes Daniel would never forget.

Eyes he now knew belonged to Scotty Fryer. And now, twenty-three years later, Daniel would finally get the opportunity to avenge his father's death.

It would happen on the night of the takedown. When they were rescuing the girls, Daniel would seek out Fryer and end him. Killing two birds with one stone, so to speak.

"The cops think Rachel is faking her memory loss," Sam commented, nodding to a girl with a dark tan and a white bikini who smiled at him. "What's your take?"

Sam was tanned, his buff body lean and incredibly fit, but only a fool wouldn't see the tumultuous energy swirling beneath the polished exterior. Like all the members of TSI, Sam had skeletons in his past. Daniel often wondered what Sam's were, what made him take the risks he did, but they didn't sit around talking about their childhoods like a bunch of sissies.

"She's genuine," Daniel replied.

Max stood, his wagging tail brushing against Daniel's leg.

Pia walked into the bar, and Daniel nodded in her direction. Sam saw her, drained his beer, and stood. "No time to stop and chat. Ryder wants his woman back. Good luck finding Madden. I'm only sixty minutes away, thirty if I can get on one of Ryder's bikes."

"Get Ryder to drop a bike off at my place. Going to need it around here."

"Consider it done."

"Thanks, mate."

"Look after Rachel for us."

"Count on it."

Sam rapped twice on the table with his knuckles, then escorted Pia outside to where his vehicle waited.

Daniel scanned the sea of faces, wondering where Madden was hiding out tonight. The best place to hide was in plain sight, as the saying went, and it was something Daniel knew to be true. He kept his head down and studied the crowd. You didn't have to watch long to know which ones were the locals and which the tourists.

At one point, a group of people started talking about the ghost ship, about the guy who'd died onboard, and Daniel listened in closely. When the conversation steered to drunken ghost stories, he drained his beer and pulled out his wallet to settle his tab. He hadn't really expected Madden himself to waltz right in, especially if he was in as bad condition as Woods had described. But locals often told each other what they wouldn't tell the cops. Daniel had had more than one break in a case from listening to conversations in a bar.

He smelled her cloying perfume before he saw her.

"Hi, stranger." The voluptuous blonde pulled her chair closer to his before sitting, so their shoulders would be touching. Daniel angled his body so he was facing her instead.

"Cynthia." He kept his tone reserved, yet polite. "What are you doing here?"

Upset and frustrated by Rachel's refusal to take his calls last time he'd had a case near Perth, Daniel had ended up in a bar numbing his pain, and after way too many tumblers of scotch on the rocks, the night had ended in Cynthia's bed.

Without waiting for an invitation to join him, Cynthia signaled for a waitress to come take her order. Cynthia's long blonde hair hung in a straight curtain down to her waist, and she was wearing a tight red dress and black heels. "I saw a news report about *Debunking Reality* doing a show on the ghost ship, and your name was mentioned."

She put her hand on his arm as she spoke, leaned forward to place her cleavage on show. "You came all the way to Western Australia. I can travel a few teeny little hours from Perth to come and see you," she purred. "I know you'll make it worth my while."

CHAPTER FIFTEEN

Her ears straining to hear the noise that had woken her, Rachel sat up in bed as the digital clock clicked over to three a.m. She replayed the sound in her mind.

What was that?

After all the heavy emotion of the day, it had been a joy to have a fun evening meal with her sister and her kids, to kick back with Ellie and a bottle of wine after Sally and Liam were in bed.

For the first time since Trey's death, Rachel hadn't had any trouble getting to sleep. But something had woken her. Some noise she couldn't identify.

There it was again. The weird noise.

Rachel craned her neck up in bed, held her breath, listened hard.

Thud… scraaape… thud.

Silence, against a low background noise of chirping cicadas.

The breath left her lungs in a rush, and she fell back against her pillow. She was exhausted, she'd drunk too much wine, and she needed a good night's sleep. Her back began to burn, and she shifted from her back to her side.

Pia said the demon had marked Rachel. What did that mean? The scratches burned like fire, the wound stinging and hot, like it was getting infected. Her stomach clenched. The burning seemed to come just before something happened, something relating to the demon and that night.

But surely, she was safe here in Elise's house?

She rolled over to her right side.

Daniel was keeping secrets from her, things he'd discussed with the *Debunking*

Reality team. Despite sharing a rare closeness this afternoon, an intimacy that went above and beyond their physical attraction, he was a long way from an open book.

Why would he hide details about the case from her? Why would Mark and Pia? It was a shitty thing to do in a situation where she already felt confused enough.

She rolled back over to her left side, and something gripped her ankle. She let out a yelp, and lunged for the bedside light, flicking it on. Her heart jumped and beat erratically. Her legs wouldn't move. She struggled a bit, then realized the sheets were wrapped around her ankles.

She barked out a laugh and fixed the sheets. *Get a hold of yourself!*

She turned out the light and tried to slow her breathing. Through the darkness, she peered at the objects in the room. Every shape looked sinister, and the wardrobe doors, the curtains, the dressing gown on the back of the door all appeared to have faces, to be swaying in a nonexistent breeze. She slid down and pulled the covers over her head.

The pain in her back intensified, the scratches burning like someone was raking hot coals over them.

Nothing is there. Nothing is there.

She squeezed her eyes shut.

She heard the noise again.

Thud… scraaape… thud.

Rachel stayed under the covers. She wasn't really hearing that. Just like someone hadn't really grabbed her ankle, and the objects in the room were just that, objects.

Nothing is there. Please don't let there be anything there…

After many long moments of listening, she didn't hear the noise again. The pain in her back faded away, and her breathing finally returned to normal.

She could almost hear Rob's voice in her mind: *Scaredy-girl, frightened of the dark again?*

The old Rachel would have laughed and made fun of herself right along with him.

The new Rachel couldn't.

She took in a deep breath and blew it out slowly. *Get a grip, Rach. It's only the dark, nothing more.*

———— ◆ ————

Rachel woke with a feeling of relief. She'd slept a long time. And it felt good. She'd turned a corner. She swung her legs over the side of the bed… and her heart stopped dead.

Her hand shook as she untangled herself from the sheets and peered closer at the floor. There was a set of wet, sandy footprints leading from the window to the corner of the room. She opened her eyes wide, blinking hard. Because she must still be half asleep.

She crouched next to one of the marks on the floor. Slowly, she reached out a finger and touched it. It was wet, and a whimper escaped her lips as she rubbed the sand between her thumb and forefinger. She wasn't imagining it. The prints were angled away from the window, which was shut. And locked. How could someone get through a locked window?

Rachel shivered and rubbed arms that had turned to gooseflesh. The temperature in the room seemed to have dropped several degrees in a single second. It was probably her fear. She was scared. Who wouldn't be?

Heart racing, Rachel followed the footprints across the room.

No. No. No.

Rachel clutched her chest as she blinked and blinked again. There must be a mistake.

The Ouija board was *not* on her dresser!

It was impossible.

Rachel stumbled, slipping on a wet footprint. She picked herself off the floor, scrambled across the room, flung the door open.

And ran.

CHAPTER SIXTEEN

Rachel bolted down the hallway and through the kitchen, ignoring the stunned expression on Ellie's face, then raced out the front door.

On the porch, she bent over at the waist and dragged in huge lungfuls of air. She lowered herself to the cold timbers, hugged her legs to her chest, took some more deep breaths, and ordered herself to calm the fuck down.

There had to be a logical explanation, because… that *thing* was not in her bedroom.

It was simply not possible.

"Rach?" Her sister's concerned face filled her vision. "What happened? Are you okay?"

"I… uh…" Rachel peered past Elise to where Sally was watching her wide-eyed. Immediately, Rachel pulled herself together and stood. "I'm fine. I had a nightmare."

She smiled at Sally. "I'm silly. And when I woke, I thought I saw a… *spider* on my bed. You know how much I hate spiders, and I just ran. I'm silly, aren't I?"

"There wasn't a spider on your bed," Sally said.

Rachel swallowed the tug of guilt at being caught out in a lie by a five-year-old. Besides, how could Sally say that with such confidence?

"You're not silly, Aunt Rachel," Sally said solemnly. "I have bad dreams too. I see things."

"Sally, run inside and finish your breakfast," Elise said. Sally turned and left before Rachel could question her more.

"I'm sorry I scared her." Rachel hugged her arms around her stomach and tucked her still-trembling hands under her arms. The scratches on her back were burning, and her mouth tasted like she'd been sucking on metal nails.

"Oh, hon." Elise hugged her. "It's to be expected you would have nightmares with everything going on. The talk with the paranormal team, the way they scared you about Rob. Not to mention all the wine we had."

"Ellie," Rachel said, moving her sister away from the door so Sally couldn't overhear. "I'm going to stay elsewhere tonight. I don't feel right being here with Rob still out there."

"But you said he wouldn't hurt you."

Rachel frowned. "I don't think he will. But… look, I was thinking after our conversation last night, what if he *is* a threat? I never would have thought he'd hurt Trey, so who knows what he's capable of? I just think it's best I move out until Rob is caught, then I'll come back, and we'll spend time together, and I won't have to worry about this affecting you."

To Rachel's surprise, tears rolled down Elise's cheeks, and her cheeks flushed with anger. "No. You're not going anywhere. You stay here. Whatever this is, whatever you're going through to cause you nightmares, you need me."

Rachel's heart beat loudly in her chest. "Ellie, it's for the best."

"How is you going off on your own for the best?" she demanded. "Rachel Lisa Sommers, you are staying here with me where I can keep an eye on you. Plus," Elise said, more softly. "I need you. There's something I need to tell you."

"What is it?" Rachel asked, keeping her voice low. "I knew something was wrong. Are you and Don okay?"

"I can't tell you now," Elise said, her eyes flicking to where the kids were inside eating breakfast. "But you're not leaving, to be off somewhere on your own, and that is that."

Rachel thought of the footprints in the bedroom. "Someone was in my room last night," she whispered.

Elise frowned. "No one was in your room, sis. The alarm would have gone off if someone had tried to open the windows or enter through the front door. Since Don is gone a lot, he made sure the security system is top of the range. That's why it's safe for you to stay."

"It's not," Rachel argued, her heart pounding. "I woke up to find the Ouija board in my room."

"There has to be a logical explanation," Elise said, but her brow furrowed with concern.

"Hi, Rach. Hi, Elise." Rachel jumped and turned to find Daniel walking up the path. What was he doing here? Had he found Rob?

His eyes traveled slowly down her body, then back up again, and her face heated. Oh dear God! She was wearing his black Taipan T-shirt. He'd left it behind after their last night together. It was large and soft and comfy, and the fact she was wearing it had absolutely nothing to do with the fact it was Daniel's.

"Uh… I'll be back." Rachel dashed back to the bedroom. She closed the door and leaned against it, closing her eyes for a second.

Then she remembered why she'd left the room in a panic.

Her heart started to pound right out of her chest, and chills skittered across her skin. Her sister was convinced no one could enter the house, which meant no one had been in her room.

Rachel would look over to the dresser and that thing would be gone. She'd realize it was all in her imagination, a bad dream, and life would resume.

She breathed in. And out. Opened one eye and turned her head.

A cry wrenched out of her, and she put her fist to her mouth to smother it.

The Ouija board was still there.

She dug her heels into the floor, refusing to run out of the room again. Cowards ran. She sucked in a lungful of courage.

She checked the window. Still locked, screen clearly in place and untampered with. She checked the floor. Footprints still wet. Why were they still wet? They didn't appear to be drying at all. They were as fresh as when she'd first seen them.

Think, Rachel. Think. There had to be a logical explanation as to how that board got into her room.

Had *she* brought it to the house?

Mark had said the board was not on the ship when he and Ryan went back yesterday morning.

And now it was in her room.

Had she left the house the night before last and gotten the board somehow? Why would she have done that? Had she been sleepwalking? Or had she been possessed, like they suspected Rob was? Like Jake had been? But… she couldn't have left through the window; the alarm would have gone off.

Plus, she was dry and there was no sand on her. She still felt clean and moisturized from the lotion she'd applied after last night's shower.

Someone must have broken in. It was the only explanation for the board being there.

Unless… had someone already been in the house before Elise had set the alarm? A chill rolled through her. Could it have been Rob? But if he'd already been in the house hiding, why would he sneak into her bedroom and leave the board? Why wouldn't he wake her?

It didn't make sense. None of this made sense.

Hot tears stung her eyes and she blinked them back. Now was not the time to fall apart.

Rachel dialed Pia's number, and it went to voice mail. She left a brief message outlining what had happened. With any luck, Pia would be able to explain how this was possible. Next, Rachel phoned Mark, gave him her sister's address, asked him to bring the nastiest steel vault he could find. He laughed, but she wasn't joking.

Rachel chose her favorite denims, took Daniel's T-shirt off, tucked it under her pillow, and chose a simple sleeveless blouse with shoestring straps. She knew it flattered her, but she chose it because it was comfortable. Again, nothing to do with Daniel. It was going to be a warm day, but no matter how hot the day got, the sun wouldn't be able to take the chill off her insides.

Using her smartphone, she snapped a couple shots of the footprints. She swiped her finger across the images to be sure she'd captured them. They were real and not her imagination. Which meant…

Rachel swallowed, forced herself to walk to the Ouija board. It was very old, ancient even, but somehow it was in perfect condition. During the attack on her, she remembered the board splintering and getting damaged.

Perhaps this wasn't the same board?

But what were the chances there were two boards like it? Rachel forced herself to look closer. The ornate carvings and symbols were exactly as she remembered them, right down to the horned demon face in the center of the board.

She shivered. The markings on the board had been carved by hand, and it definitely did not appear factory made.

Sitting to one side of the board was a crystal ball—it appeared to be the same one Rob had placed beside the Ouija board the night Trey had been killed. She picked it up, why she couldn't say. She wouldn't have touched the board for all the money in the world.

The glass was cool… almost familiar. Though she couldn't say why she thought that either. It was heavy, smooth and round, and fit in the palm of her hand perfectly. What was it? She peered closer, finding herself strangely mesmerized by the swirling clouds she saw inside it. She followed the smoky images with her eyes. She started to feel lightheaded, her consciousness altering slightly, as though she were slipping into a light trance.

Far from being frightening, the experience was calming, captivating, like watching the flickering flames of a fire late at night. She saw something in the glass. Something important. Something she should know. But couldn't quite make out.

Without understanding why, she slipped the strange-looking crystal into the top drawer of the dresser and tucked it right in the back. She closed the drawer and left the room in search of her sister and Daniel.

———— ◆ ————

Daniel accepted the hot mug of coffee Elise brought out to the porch for him, noting she didn't invite him inside.

"Thanks." Daniel took a sip of the coffee. Elise looked exhausted. She was thinner, and shadows ringed her eyes. But then, she worked as a nurse at the local hospital and had two young kids with a husband who spent a lot of time away. No wonder she had been looking forward to her sister's visit so much, and the break from routine.

"I'll get to the bottom of this for Rachel," Daniel promised.

Elise smiled tightly. "Thank you. I don't like seeing her have nightmares. Rachel needs to be able to put this behind her, get her life back on track, and find a good man, one who treats her the way she deserves."

Could I be that man for her?

"How long are you staying?" Elise asked, looking directly at him.

"Until we've located Rob Madden." Until after they'd been back on the ship and gotten rid of whatever had left its mark on Rachel's back. Until he could be one hundred percent sure Rachel was safe.

"And then you'll leave?"

Daniel shrugged, his stomach inexplicably in knots. "That's how it works." There was always another case. What other choice was there? His job was more than what he did; it was who he was.

Elise snipped a couple of dead leaves from a potted plant with her gardening scissors.

"How close are you to finding Rob?"

"We're following up some solid leads."

"You're not good for her," Elise said, and Daniel blinked in surprise.

"That so?" Daniel didn't disagree with Elise's assessment of him; he wasn't good for Rachel. He knew that. It just grated to hear it from someone else.

"You'll only end up hurting her, and she's been through enough."

Daniel sipped his coffee, kept his expression neutral despite his surprise at the direction the conversation had taken.

"Rachel knows what she's doing." He refused to be told by anyone what to do. Elise was only looking out for her sister, but still. What couldn't be between them hurt *both* of them, not just Rachel. It was something they needed to work out. Together.

"No she doesn't," Elise said in a loud, angry whisper. "She's having nightmares. She's dropped two glasses in twenty-four hours because she's shaken up so much." Elise looked over her shoulder to make sure Rachel hadn't returned yet. "And then *you* show up, the man who turns up to screw her whenever he feels like it, then walks away without another thought."

"Now wait a minute." Fire simmered in his veins. "Don't presume to tell me what I'm thinking, and don't presume to know what's between Rachel and me."

Elise's lips twisted. "A man like you is not what Rachel needs."

"What do you mean, 'a man like me'?" Daniel's voice was lethally quiet.

Elise's eyes widened, and she adjusted her tone. "All you'll do is break her heart, and I won't stand by and watch that happen again. She's been through enough."

Daniel wanted to challenge her, call her out on observations she didn't have the perspective to make. But the thread of truth woven through her words silenced him.

"If you have any feelings for her at all," Elise said, pointing her scissors at him, "you'll tell her you're not interested. Tell her you've taken a job on the moon. I don't give a rat's ass what story you make up. But don't keep coming back and screwing her and then taking off onto your next conquest without another thought. You treat her like a whore."

Daniel's body turned rigid, and he narrowed his eyes. Having Rachel referred to as a whore made his blood boil.

Although it might have been true at one point that he enjoyed a variety of women, in a variety of ways, it hadn't been the case for a while now.

It had taken a fully ninety minutes and almost a whole bottle of wine at the bar last night to convince Cynthia he wouldn't be sharing her bed. She'd pouted, gotten angry, spilled her drink all over herself, and in the end even put on the tears. But finally, she'd gotten the message.

And why? There was only one reason a man would refuse a willing sex kitten like Cynthia. And that was if his heart was with another woman.

"Rachel's a nice girl with a good heart," Elise said. "Don't ruin her from finding the man who's right for her. She's lost her mother, isn't speaking to her father, Trey is dead, Rob could be out there somewhere trying to kill her, she has no career anymore without the band. Besides me and the kids, what does she have left? She needs a decent man and some stability in her life, now more than ever."

Daniel narrowed his eyes. "What Rachel needs is help and protection. And whether you like it or not, I am the person best placed to give those things to her."

"That's where you're wrong." Elise's lips thinned. "Your protection and help are not the only things Rachel needs. What she needs the most is the one thing you're unwilling or unable to give her. And that," Elise said, "makes you the most dangerous thing of all to her."

————◆————

Rachel felt the weight of Daniel's stare when she came back outside, but she didn't meet his eyes. She waved at Ellie and the kids as they pulled out of the driveway. The kids were spending the day with their grandmother while Ellie did a shift at work.

When she could avoid it no longer, Rachel turned and met Daniel's gaze. His eyes were dark and intense, but his face was impassive, that annoying mask he slipped behind whenever she wanted to know what he truly thought. What she wouldn't do to get into his head for five minutes, know what he was thinking.

"Scary spider, huh?"

Rachel swallowed. "I'll show you."

"Do I need a shoe, or a blowtorch?" Daniel teased with a twitch of his lips.

Did he really think a spider could scare her this much? Rachel paused at the door to her bedroom for two heartbeats, then pushed it open. Daniel followed her inside. She sat on the edge of her bed and pointed at the dresser on the corner. She knew the moment he saw it.

"Jesus Christ! What the fuck is that thing doing in here?"

CHAPTER SEVENTEEN

D id you notice anything else last night?" Mark asked. "Any sudden changes in temperature, any unusual sounds?" The *Debunking Reality* team were all over Rachel's bedroom, and Ellie's house. Ryan was filming, and Rachel swallowed her impatience, wanting them to just take the creepy board and stop asking her questions about how it got there. Was it not enough for it to simply *be* there?

"No." Rachel closed her eyes, remembering. "There were some strange noises, but nothing as definite as actually seeing someone or hearing someone break in."

Through the window, Rachel saw Daniel and Max searching the grounds for signs of entry.

Her head was pounding, a migraine setting in. "I don't understand how the footsteps are still wet. They were wet this morning when I woke up as well."

She turned at the sound of fingernails tapping on the bedroom door. "Pia! You came."

Pia crossed the room and embraced her, keeping her hands well below the scratches on her back. They'd been burning again all morning.

"I can't stay long," Pia said. "Nate and I were only an hour away, well, it might have been closer to two, but the way Nate drives that bike…" A brief smile played around her lips, and her eyes glazed over. She cleared her throat and continued. "Anyway, I came as soon as I heard." Pia scanned the room, a frown creasing her brow.

She was wearing long black boots with a black leather skirt and a red shirt open just enough to hint at enviable cleavage. Her magnificent mane of red hair flowed down her back in luxurious waves.

"Thank you for coming, Pia. I appreciate your help so much. Why do you think the board turned up here?" Not to mention *how*.

"Hmm… To keep you fearful would be my best guess. Demons feed off lower emotions, like fear, sadness, jealousy, anger, hatred," Pia said. "Emotions give off vibrations, and demons and spirits respond to this vibrational frequency. Keeping you scared and powerless makes you vulnerable—and accessible to the demon."

"Show no fear," Mark said, an echo of the words he'd shouted at Pia when it had all turned south on the ship. "No matter what happens, do not show fear. It gives them power."

Rachel swallowed. How the hell was that going to be possible? Knowing something had been in your room while you were sleeping was downright terrifying.

Joe entered the room carrying a large suitcase, which he set on Rachel's bed. He keyed in a combination, and the lid sprang open. The case was lined with metal, a large crucifix attached to the center of the lid.

Pia washed her hands in a bowl of water that someone had placed on the dresser near the board.

"Holy water," Pia said, answering Rachel's unasked question. "Just as demons feed off lower energies, higher energies repel them."

"Higher energies?"

"Because demons are Satanic in origin, they lose their power when confronted by higher energies, emotions like love and compassion. Holy water has been sanctified by a priest to repel evil."

Pia dried her fingers on a white cloth, and after saying a Bible verse Rachel presumed was for protection, Pia picked up the Ouija board and placed it in the suitcase. Joe snapped the locks shut.

Rachel shivered, and even Mark released a breath. "I'm more careful with demons these days," he said. "I know firsthand the devastation they can cause."

Rachel remembered how he'd fingered the board almost reverently on the ship, much the same way Rob had. She hadn't missed Pia's worried glance in his direction at the time either. And after hearing that he'd been possessed before, Rachel understood why Pia had wanted to be here today, to ensure the safe removal of the board. She was very protective of Mark, clearly understanding that his desire and need to be close to and research the paranormal made him a target.

If only Rachel had understood the possible consequences of what they'd done that night, Trey would still be alive. She'd had no idea of the risk they had been taking. Dealing with the paranormal should be taught at school, drummed into kids like all the other gazillion lessons they were taught. Eat your veggies, get your exercise. Don't play with knives. Don't play with fire. Don't drink poison. Don't play with Ouija boards…

Joe took the suitcase out of the room to lock it in the van.

"Listen to Max barking out front," Mark said. "He's a highly trained police dog, disciplined to obey his handler in every way, yet his instincts in this situation are overriding years of training. Max refused to obey Daniel's command to stop barking when he first arrived here today, and now he's barking at the suitcase. He knows there's something inside it that is evil, therefore he's trying to warn Daniel. It's like he's saying, 'What are you doing? Can't you see that menacing thing?'"

"But the house is safe now," Rachel said. "Right? Removing that board removed the demon's energy from the house?" Were Ellie and the kids at risk?

"Your sister and the children should be safe," Pia said, again answering an unasked question. She extinguished the bunch of burning sage she'd been walking around the house with, and selected three crystals from a black bag. "Crystals also radiate a high frequency. I'm cleansing the house thoroughly. With the board gone, and the cleanse to rid the house of any residual negative energy, everything should be back to normal."

Pia flicked a small vial of what Rachel also presumed to be holy water into the corners of the room and recited words from a small Bible she was holding. "Saint Michael the Archangel, defend us in battle, be our protection against the malice and snares of the devil…" Pia moved off, cleansing the rest of the house.

"Max has stopped barking now," Mark said, moving to the hallway, pointing to where Daniel and Max were standing just outside the front door. "See, his hackles are down. But he's still wary; look at him. People are more accepting of dogs' ability to use their sixth sense without realizing that we all have it too. We're just conditioned to pretend it doesn't exist. For some reason, vision is the most valued of all the senses, even though it's the most easily fooled. You just need to watch a magician or illusionist to see proof of that."

Mark looked across the hallway to the pink sign on the door that read "Sally's Room."

"Kids see things too, babies especially. But during the formative years, we tell our kids there's no such thing as ghosts. We tell them they're imagining things. It's confusing for children, especially as more and more are being born sensitive these days."

Rachel immediately thought of Sally. Had she sensed something last night? She'd mentioned having nightmares and seeing things. Even though Sally was Elise's daughter, Rachel had always felt a certain connection—a special bond—with the little girl. Like they were attuned to each other in a way Rachel didn't feel with the rest of her family.

Mark walked back into Rachel's bedroom, and she followed. He paused by the dresser where the Ouija board had been, next to the drawer, the one with the strange crystal in it, and she swallowed a stab of guilt. She should tell him about it, while they were alone. Perhaps he would understand and not judge her unusual decision to hide it. They could work out what it was together.

She opened her mouth, but somehow couldn't form the words.

"Listen, Rach," Mark said, his expression serious. "I know you got upset with us when we suggested that Rob might be responsible, but I just want you to keep an open mind. Don't discount the possibility, that's all. And be careful. Remember, if you do see Rob, he might not be the Rob you once knew."

Rachel's chest tightened. She was no longer able to keep blindly defending Rob. The Ouija board turning up in her room proved that anything was possible. Logic and reality played no part in this situation.

"I wouldn't be telling you this, if I didn't know it to be true," Mark said. "It happened to me with all my experience with the paranormal, so I know it can happen to anyone."

He sank into the chair in the corner, lowered his head and rubbed at his eyes with both palms. "There's a reason Pia dropped everything and came here to remove the board," he said, confirming what Rachel suspected. "Why she used the holy water and said the prayer of protection. Why she didn't leave the job to me." Mark's expression was pained, his voice uncharacteristically flat. "She can't trust me. Hell, I can't trust myself. Maybe I never will."

Surprised, Rachel lowered herself onto her bed and remained silent, stunned and grateful for this private insight into the world's most popular and loved paranormal investigator.

"If it wasn't for Pia, I wouldn't even be alive right now. Neither would Sage, and who knows who else."

"Was this the case you and TSI were working on last September?"

"Yes." Mark stood, walked to the window, and peered out. "In an attempt to work out what we were dealing with back in Cryton, I called out to the demon, invited him to use my energy to communicate. I hadn't realized it at the time, but in my quest to document firsthand evidence, I'd inadvertently given him permission to use my body. I started to become oppressed, the first stage of possession. At first, I sensed the entity as a separate being, a consciousness alongside mine. I remember being me, thinking my own thoughts, and other times, I was horrified as I remembered what I'd said, what I'd done…"

Mark turned his back to the window and shoved his hands through his hair. For a man as unfailingly confident as Mark, failure was probably not something he admitted often.

"You're telling me this because it's what you believe happened to Rob?"

Mark sat down on the edge of the bed next to her.

"It would explain how he behaved in such an extreme and out-of-character way. Rachel…" Mark swallowed hard, his eyes red and welling with tears. "I would have killed Sage, if Ethan hadn't arrived with Pia in time to stop me." His voice broke. "I love that woman. I'd give my life, my everything, to protect Sage, and yet, there I was, under the influence of something dark, powerless to do anything else but watch as I contemplated horrors that I shouldn't have been capable of committing. To this day, I fear the demon left something behind in my blood. When a water supply has been contaminated, can it ever truly be pure again?"

Rachel put her hand over her heart. "Oh, Mark. That's awful. I'm so sorry. I had no idea." How traumatic that must be to live with.

"I still have nightmares about it. But I force myself to remember, frequently. It keeps me sharp. I'm a lot more careful these days. I don't provoke spirits anymore, and I most certainly don't invite them to use my energy."

Which is exactly what Rob had done.

"I'm sorry," Rachel said. "Thanks for being here, helping me with this."

Mark reached out and gave her hand a brief squeeze. "Just be careful for the next few days. Be alert to anything strange that happens, no matter how small or innocent it might appear."

Ryan appeared at the doorway, and Mark stood.

"Ready to go? Pia wants to talk to you about something. I think she had another vision." Ryan glanced at Rachel, and her stomach fisted.

"Right, then." Mark paused at the door, and Rachel glanced at the drawer that contained the crystal ball. That ball was most certainly strange. Wasn't it?

She should go to the drawer now, get it out and take it to the guys and pretend she'd only just seen it. It wasn't too late.

Rachel hesitated.

It was what she *should* do.

Then why couldn't she do it?

CHAPTER EIGHTEEN

Daniel's boot pressed hard against the accelerator as he opened up the throttle along the highway, even though he doubted speed would be able to soothe his nerves this time. He glared out through the windscreen, letting the scenery blur around him, feeling the engine's strain in the vibration of the steering wheel.

Max stared out his window, his mouth open in a toothy grin. The dog was as crazy as he was, loving speed and fast cars. Daniel loved anything that got his adrenaline pumping, made him feel alive and in control. Because sure as hell nothing about Rachel's situation made him feel in control.

He'd left Rachel with Pia, Mark, and the team at Elise's house and checked in with the local police station, where he reported—off the record—what had happened with Rachel to the sergeant. The details, including photos of the board and the wet footprints, wouldn't hit the official files, but the sergeant needed to be fully informed. The report of the break-in at Elise's house had been modified but documented, the suspect wanted for questioning: Rob Madden.

It frustrated the hell out of him that Rachel hadn't jumped at the chance to stay with him when he'd offered, *insisted.* Goddamn it, he'd barely stopped short of forcing her. But what was he to do? Throw her over his shoulder caveman style?

His frustration, his lack of control, was one of the reasons he'd left her with the *Debunking Reality* team. She'd at least agreed to stay in a TSI safe house. She would be safe with Mark and his team during the day, and he'd hired additional security to be positioned at Elise's house as well. He also made sure another car was free to shadow Rachel when she was on the move.

Despite her partial concession to his demands, Daniel had needed to leave to cool off. He'd never *needed* to be with someone before for anything other than the exchange of mutually beneficial sexual pleasure, something he now painfully knew wasn't the same thing at all.

That's how he found himself watching the odometer climb on his 4WD, wishing he was in one of Ryder's Porsches, or better yet, on one of his Ducati 1098s, letting speed soothe his warring emotions.

He hit speed dial on the screen on his dash, and Ethan's voice came through the speakers. "Blade."

Although the former members of the elite Special Ops Group Taipan were all equal partners, TSI had been Blade's brainchild, and he'd naturally assumed the role of coordinator, with his partner Nate Ryder as client liaison. Daniel and his partner Sam preferred the field, getting their hands dirty with the high-risk jobs. And Sean…? Wynter was like sending in a Sherman tank to dig a backyard swimming pool. The death of his partner, Jake Brown, last year hadn't improved his far-from-sunny disposition.

"What are we dealing with here?" Ethan asked, straight to business. "I read your report saying there was an intruder in Rachel's bedroom last night. But no signs of a B&E."

"No sign of forced entry," Daniel confirmed. "Wet footprints that Rachel had the foresight to take pictures of with her phone. Size ten boot maybe."

"What size shoe does Madden wear?" Blade asked.

"My thoughts exactly," Daniel said as anger swelled, hot and painful in his chest. "But if it was him, how the fuck did he get in?"

It pissed him off to no end that Madden was still at large. He was hardly a career criminal, and he had no resources. Locating him should have been a piece of piss. Not being able to catch Madden was a personal insult. The fact he was flaunting his ability to elude capture by scaring Rachel made Daniel want to kill him with his bare hands. But if Pia was correct, Madden's death would endanger Rachel.

Daniel flexed his jaw, slowed down enough to perform a U-turn, letting the skidding of the tires on the road ease his tension slightly. The long drive had helped clear his mind, but it was time he headed back to town.

"What's the security like on Elise's house?"

"Top-notch," Daniel replied. "The alarm would have sounded had someone removed the window screens or opened the windows. The doors were locked, and the security log showed that the system had been engaged all night until Elise turned it off at seven thirty-six this morning."

"What are your thoughts?"

Daniel released a long, frustrated breath. "The facts don't line up. The footprints didn't go all the way to the door, and the footprints didn't dry the way water should. But, running with the theory that it was Madden, I can't discount the possibility he was already in the house. Perhaps he got in during the day and hid." Daniel's grip turned white-knuckled on the steering wheel. "Which means he would have been in the house with the girls all night. But why go to all that trouble, just to leave her the Ouija board?" If it wasn't Rachel, he would be suspecting that the scene was staged. But Rachel wouldn't lie.

"Bastard. Did you check the roof cavity?"

"Of course," Daniel growled. "We didn't see any obvious signs of him being there, or using that space, but that doesn't mean much." Frustration churned like knives in Daniel's stomach.

"I read in your report that Madden turned up at Woods's place asking for a place to stay and Woods turned him away."

Again, frustration was a painful twist in his gut. According to Woods, Madden was on foot. He was close. "Yeah, apparently Madden didn't look like himself. I don't know how much weight to give Woods's stoned observations though."

"It will only be a matter of time before we catch the son of a bitch."

Daniel wished he shared Ethan's confidence. Since last night, Daniel had upped the security on Rachel, on Elise's house, and on the *Debunking Reality* team, stopping just short of overkill. If Madden approached any of them, he'd know about it within seconds.

"Pia believes Madden has been affected by the entity," Blade said. "Tread carefully with this one, Dan." His mate's tone was grim.

If someone as staunchly capable and loyal to a fault as Jake could be possessed by a demon, it could happen to any of them.

No one was safe. Daniel couldn't afford to let his guard down, not for a second.

Blade was updating him on a prior case they'd been working on as Daniel pulled up to the house where he was staying. He keyed the car off, the call transferring to his mobile. He showed his face and fingerprint for access to the house, then entered a series of codes. Inside, he used the remote to open the shutters and let in some fresh air.

"Tell me what you need." Blade's voice was all business. Daniel spent the next few minutes talking through the details and what Blade would need to clear through outside channels, including the police.

"Consider it done," Blade said, then paused. "She's the one, isn't she?"

First Sam, and now Blade. Daniel didn't realize his feelings for Rachel were tattooed across his forehead. "It's that obvious?" he grumbled.

"Is to me. Seeing all the same signs I just saw in Ryder." Blade chuckled, and Daniel's grip on his phone tightened. "But you're going to have to watch how you play this. She's not going to be like your other women."

"Sage and Pia are not your typical women either," Daniel pointed out.

"Why do you think I know what I'm talking about?" Blade said evenly. "Look, none of us ever wanted vanilla; that's why we chose this life. But women like ours create a different type of complication. Our lives are already thirty shades of fucked up, and the women we chose certainly don't make that any easier."

Daniel kicked a towel across the floor until it made its way to the bathroom. See? He could do domestic.

"Where are you at with Wilson?" Daniel asked, deflecting the conversation away from him and Rachel. He could feel Blade's smug grin right through the phone.

"Pia gave us a new lead that we're following up. We're keeping the other five girls under surveillance. Sorry we've taken Pia away from your case, but her ability means she can help keep track of the girls without our guys getting too close. We'll have this wrapped up in twenty-four, forty-eight hours, tops. Then Pia is all yours."

One or two more days. Then hopefully Pia could focus on Rachel and sort out how to get rid of this demon, and then he and Rachel could move on with their lives and figure out what they meant to each other.

After he disconnected with Ethan, Daniel poured himself a whiskey and took it onto the balcony. He drained the glass as he stared across the ocean. Rachel might have chosen not to stay with him tonight, but that didn't mean he couldn't be close to her.

Her insistence on keeping him at a distance was eating away at him. He didn't know how it would work between them, just that it had to.

The thing that cut him the most was that he *wanted* her to want him to save her. He wanted Rachel to need him, to come to him for help. That's what men like Daniel did. They protected the ones they loved.

He wanted all the rights he would have if he was her man. The right to make decisions about her safety, to be close to her without needing an excuse, to share her bed and sleep soundly knowing she was safe in his arms.

But how did he convince her to want that too?

Chapter Nineteen

Rachel had begun to think Daniel would never leave. She needed her privacy. She couldn't risk him knowing what she was hiding from him. Or what she planned to do.

She kicked off her shoes and padded to the bathroom in the TSI safe house. Despite the rustic appearance of the beach cottage from the outside, the inside was luxuriously modern. She stepped out of her clothes and into the large double shower. When the temperature was perfect, she closed the glass door and stood under the water.

Daniel, of course, had tried to insist that he stay with her. He was both angry and disappointed in her refusal, but she needed time alone.

It had been even harder telling Ellie she was staying somewhere else, but it was for the best, Rachel had reminded herself sternly when she'd felt her resolve waver at seeing tears form in her sister's eyes. It was for everyone's safety. If something happened to Sally or Liam or Ellie…

Rachel towel-dried her hair and walked into the bedroom, appreciating the spacious room dominated by a large king-sized bed. Naked, she was about to slip Daniel's shirt over her head, but at the last minute changed her mind, reaching for her sleep shorts and singlet instead.

It didn't feel right wearing Daniel's shirt knowing what she was about to do.

She sat on the edge of the bed and eyed her handbag, staring at the heavy bulge inside.

Why had she brought it?

She'd tried to walk out the bedroom door without it, but every time she'd reached the doorway, she'd stopped, as though walking into an invisible barrier. On the third attempt, she'd turned and crossed the room before she'd even realized she'd taken a step. The crystal was in her hands seconds later, and once she'd held it, it had been impossible for her to leave it behind.

It didn't make sense. Her compulsion to hide and then take the thing troubled her.

Her back began to burn, and she rolled her shoulders in an attempt to alleviate the sting. Rachel opened her bag and reached inside. A profound relief filled her once she held it in her hands, felt the cool weight of the stone in her palms.

What is it?

Rachel peered into the glass. It was solid, and she could see the overhead light reflected in it. Again, she had the sense it was familiar somehow, as if she'd seen it many times before, not only on the night Trey was killed. She stared at it for several long moments, but couldn't see anything in it. No swirling, smoky images like last time.

She turned it over, traced her fingers across the curved edge, the smoothness of the glass, and felt strangely compelled to continue to stare into its bottomless depths. Her eyes felt strained; perhaps she was trying too hard. She relaxed her gaze, allowing her vision to fall slightly out of focus. For some reason, she had the sense she was looking through a window, a doorway to another dimension. Another time and space.

The glass began to vibrate, humming gently, soothingly, and images began to form. At first, all she saw were swirling patterns of smoke, but then scenes stared to appear. As memories entered her mind, the images responded, changing into the people and events she was recalling. She saw the people she knew, past and present, and various places she'd been, all flashes of her own life.

The glass wasn't a doorway; it was interactive. Something you controlled with your mind. How cool!

Rachel played with her gaze, adjusting her focus for long moments, until she "learned" how to see things in the strange object in a more deliberate way.

"What can you show me?" Rachel murmured softly. "I saw pieces of my life; can you show me more?"

Rachel saw herself as a baby, her older sister as a toddler, then a young girl, and recognized herself on her first day of school: scared, excited, clinging to her mother's leg. She saw her primary school teacher and friends in her class, before the image cleared and was replaced by the boy she first kissed on the day he broke up with her, then she saw herself in tears at thirteen years old, on her childhood bed wishing the world would come to an end. She saw many Christmases, a big and joyous event in her family.

She saw her dad laughing, welcoming customers into their family restaurant, and she saw herself singing there in public for the first time. She was standing on the platform beside the grand piano. Her hands were shaking, and she gripped the microphone tighter. Her dad introduced her, and she giggled nervously. Giggled! She could have died of embarrassment. Her dad was proud, his chest puffing out as he told the audience how honored they were to be about to hear his daughter sing. Tears sprang to her eyes, and she wished she could bring back that time.

A time when she'd looked at her dad and seen a hero.

She blinked away the tears and focused on the images in the glass. The piano played the introduction, and she threw the first note. She scanned the tables, her audience, to see if anyone was laughing. No one was, but several shifted in their seats uncomfortably, and a few smiled with sympathy. That was worse.

And then her eyes landed on Daniel. Whoa! *Daniel was there that night?* He was younger then, around twenty-five, his eyes still intense, but less jaded than they were today, six years on. He was handsome then too, his features beautiful, softer, not the raw and edgy masculinity he exuded today.

Rachel was wearing a figure-hugging ankle-length red dress with a plunging neckline and killer heels that her father had paid a ridiculous amount for. Daniel's eyes were hotly focused on her, but he was smiling gently, giving her that smile that crinkled the corners of his eyes and made her stomach flutter. "You've got this," he wordlessly said from across the room.

A warmth spread through her body and dissolved her nerves. She relaxed, and her following notes were flawless. Once she let go and began to sing, the music, the words, took over. She moved her body like she'd been singing in front of people for years, and there was a standing ovation when she finished.

When she stepped down from the stage, Rachel scanned the room. Rob and Trey were at a table, smiling in encouragement and drinking beer. "We should start a band," Rob said. "How cool would it be for the three of us to be together forever?"

"Where are you, Rob?" Rachel asked instinctively, the question so prominently on her mind.

The image cleared, and she was shown an image of Rob as he looked now. Slim, just a little taller than her at five-foot ten, his brown hair cropped short.

The image widened to include his location. He was outdoors, standing on a lawn somewhere. Close to the ocean. She could hear the waves and see his hair blowing in the ocean breeze. Her heart squeezed, and she wanted to reach out and touch him. He stood in the shadow of a tree, dappled moonlight on his face.

Wait!

Rachel's heart began to pound. *I recognize that tree!*

Her pulse racing, she fumbled then dropped the crystal ball. It hit the carpet with a loud thud that startled her, and she jumped back.

She recognized that tree. It was the one in the front yard of where she was right now.

She sat down on the bed and stared at the curtained window. If she went to the window and peered out, would Rob be there? And if so, how had he known where she was? How had he gotten past the guards?

And why after all the images she'd been shown of her past, all of them so pleasant, had she been shown Rob today?

Because she'd asked!

She had specifically asked, "Where are you, Rob?" Just like she'd asked the crystal what else of her life it could show her. Pieces of a puzzle began clicking into place, and Rachel had the strange sense she was relearning something she had already known. Instinctively. She bent forward and picked the crystal ball up.

It was a scry.

She didn't know how she knew that. It wasn't something she remembered learning, but she knew it all the same. The scry was used for telling the future. A divination tool. Was it accurate? Did it work?

There was only one way to find out.

Setting the scry on the mattress, Rachel stood up from the bed, swallowed hard, and turned off the overhead light. Slowly, she stepped to the window and parted the curtains. She peered through the darkness at the tree.

And there was Rob.

He was looking directly at her, as though he knew he'd see her there. She gasped and jumped back. Stumbling, she slung her arm out to the side and knocked over her bedside lamp, sending it crashing to the floor.

Why was she scared? Rob was her best friend. She ought to be happy to see him there. But she wasn't. Something wasn't right.

Something was terribly wrong.

It was in the way he stood. The look she knew she'd see in his eyes if she could see them clearly.

It was the feeling, the chill she got when she saw him.

The Rob standing out there wasn't the Rob she knew.

On her hands and knees, she moved back to the window and peered out.

He was closer.

Still staring directly at her.

Her heart skipped a beat. She let out a small cry, dropped the curtain, and scuttled across the floor back to her bed. She jumped on it and pulled the covers up to her chin.

And waited. Her heart pounded in her chest, so loud she was sure it was audible in the otherwise silent room. Her mind raced. Rob was outside her window. Why? Where were the security guards? Surely, they would have been on him in an instant. Yet he'd still been there the second time she'd looked.

She should call Daniel. Yes. That's what she'd do. She grabbed her phone with trembling fingers. It was dead.

What the…? How?

It had been fully charged when she'd arrived. She'd checked. She ran out to the kitchen, picked up the land line. No dial tone.

There was a knock at the front door, and she gasped.

Was it Rob?

Should she answer it?

Rob was one of her best friends; the fact she would even consider not responding sickened her.

She forced her feet to move and made her way cautiously to the front door.

Knock, knock, knock. Three distinct raps, but this time, it sounded like they were coming from the wall right next to her. Not from the wall's surface, but from *inside* it.

Her head spun, and she rubbed her arms against a rush of icy air that seemed to move not past her, but right through her.

Rachel didn't move.

Didn't breathe.

Time slowed, heartbeats marking its passage. Twenty… twenty-one… twenty-two… Had she imagined the knocking?

She replayed the sound in her mind. *Knock, knock, knock.* Three definite knocks.

Her blood ran cold. Three knocks. Three scratches on her back. Three was the sign of a demon, a mocking of the holy trinity, Mark had said.

Was the demon from the ship here?

What should she do?

She couldn't call for help since the phones were down. She couldn't run outside. Rob was out there. Or something in the image of Rob… Because while the figure she'd seen might have looked like her friend, it didn't *feel* like him.

Rachel pressed her fist into her mouth and bit down. What had Mark said when it had all turned sour on the shipwreck?

Show no fear.

But how did you show no fear when terror sliced your insides like razor blades?

She couldn't just stand in the hallway. She needed a plan. She'd go back into her bedroom, and if nothing was in there, she'd walk to the window, look outside.

Rachel released a shaky breath. *I can do this.*

Show no fear.

Useless though it was, she grabbed the largest butcher's knife from the kitchen and silently walked to the bedroom, keeping her back to the wall.

Her bare feet left the cold timber floor of the hallway and reached the plush carpet in the bedroom. She flicked on the light, scanned the room. Nothing appeared out of place, no sign of an intruder.

She dropped to her knees by the bed, steeled her spine, then looked underneath it. All clear. No Rob hiding there. No intruder in sight. She let out a nervous laugh, her pulse skittering erratically.

Good, Rachel. You're doing good. Show no fear. Now, walk to the window. In six steps, she was there. Rachel took a breath, closed her eyes, then hesitated with her fingers on the curtain.

Would she see Rob standing directly on the other side of the window this time? Would he somehow be able to reach right through the window and grab her? Rachel thought of the wet footprints. How they'd managed to get inside her bedroom at Elise's despite the locked windows.

Heart pounding wildly, she edged aside the curtain and peeked out.

No one was there.

Rob was not in the middle of the lawn, and he wasn't under the tree. She stared for a long time. Continued to stare, as though expecting him to just appear before her, like in a horror movie, complete with sound effects.

But there was nothing except a calm, still night, not even a breeze strong enough to stir the leaves in the tree.

She let the curtain drop. The house was silent, the only sound the slowing of her pulse rushing past her ears.

The scry was in the middle of the floor. Keeping her gaze averted, she put the crystal ball in her bag. She'd had enough experimenting for one night. Feeling a little calmer, Rachel slid into bed, pulling the covers right up to her chin.

She lay on her side, facing the window, almost expecting to see Rob's face staring in at her. She hated that the image of her best friend terrified her. After all, she'd been desperately searching for him all this time. He hadn't answered his phone, and his friends, his family, no one had heard from him, except for Woody. And Woody had turned him away.

Hadn't she just done the same? Had Rob sensed her fear as she'd looked at him through the window? Did he think she'd turned him away too? But how had he even known where she was? Had he been following her? And again… why hadn't Daniel's security team seen him? He'd been standing there plain as day when she'd looked.

Her stomach twisted. She'd been so worried about Rob. It was a relief at least to see with her own eyes that he was alive.

Except… the Rob she'd seen through the window was not the same Rob she'd grown up with.

And what was the connection between his arrival and the strange knocking she'd heard from inside the walls? Or the strange chill that had rolled through her, as though she'd been run through by a train of death?

Slivers of ice slid down her spine.

Why had Rob appeared to her? And what did he want?

CHAPTER TWENTY

Daniel was sitting with Max on the sand outside his beachfront safe house when Rachel's number flashed on his screen. He'd just gotten back in after spending the day at the local station chasing down a new flurry of Madden sightings.

He picked up the call.

"Where are you?" Rachel's voice was lowered, slightly breathless.

"At the beach."

There was a pause. "Are you alone?"

"No."

"Oh."

He smiled, taking satisfaction from the touch of jealousy he'd heard in her voice. "You're welcome to join us."

"Uh… no thanks."

"That's a shame. Max and I would love your company."

"Max." A rush of breath blasted into the phone. "Of course, you're with Max. Well, if you're sure Max won't mind sharing you, I'd love to join you both."

"Want me to come and get you? Where I'm staying is only fifteen minutes north of you."

"No, I'll come to you."

He gave her the address and disconnected the call. Brushing off his jeans, he walked across the front lawn, checking his laptop and comms one last time. With Pia's information, he was closing in on Fryer's location; finally, all the pieces were falling into place. But there was nothing that required his immediate attention.

Daniel grabbed a beer and walked into the bathroom. Leaving his gun on the vanity within easy reach, as was his habit, he stripped off his clothes, kicking them into the corner, and took a quick shower.

He'd just finished sliding on a clean pair of jeans when he heard her Lexus pull into the driveway. He answered the door with his towel-dried hair still damp, but combed back.

His chest warmed. He was ridiculously pleased to see her at his place. All their previous meetings prior to this trip had been at her unit in the city.

Although this house wasn't his personally, it belonged to the company, which, since the entire team were equal partners, meant that technically it *was* his. But it wasn't a house of his choosing.

Daniel had bought a property about ninety minutes south of here, a beachfront property north of Perth, in between the city and Elise's home.

For a reason he couldn't explain, he had a fierce need to take Rachel there. He wanted to see her in his house, a space he'd never taken another woman to. He wanted to know what she thought of it. Would she love it too? Would she love listening to the roar of the ocean crashing onto the shore at night? Would she stay up into the early hours of the morning to watch a storm roll in over the water?

Daniel invited her in and closed the screen door, which still provided high-end security while letting in the cool sea breeze.

Rachel was wearing a tropical-print V-neck dress that hugged her full breasts in a way that tightened his pants. The dress made him think of an island paradise. It was tight at the waist, with loose-flowing, semi-sheer material that cascaded down to her knees and breezed around her long, tanned legs as she moved. She wore her dark silky hair loose, one side held back with a clip behind one ear, leaving the slender column of her neck exposed. His body temperature shot up, and his blood was pumping fast and hot through his veins. She was breathtaking.

"You okay, babe?" Daniel asked, when he noticed her cheeks were red and flushed.

Rachel didn't meet his gaze. "You had a shower."

Daniel gave her a slow grin, leaning back against the wall. "I did. Should I have waited for you?"

Her eyes widened as they traveled over his bare chest down to his bare feet, then back again. She licked a pink tongue over glossy red lips, and it almost did him in.

Max began to growl, low and menacing at the door. "What is it, buddy?" When he pawed at the screen door, Daniel let him out. Max ran straight to Rachel's car.

"Stay here," Daniel ordered. He grabbed his weapon from the table and followed the dog. Max had stopped at Rachel's car, hackles raised and barking. Likewise, the tiny hairs on the back of Daniel's neck were standing on end, but he couldn't see the threat.

"Max!"

"Why is he barking at my car?" Rachel asked at his side.

"Thought I told you to stay inside."

"You did."

Daniel growled, not used to having his orders disobeyed. Whether it be cops or civilians, when he gave an instruction, it was followed without question.

He surveyed the area, peering into the shadows of the surrounding trees, but couldn't see any signs of movement.

"Max." Daniel chastised his dog gently, running a hand over his fur. "That's Rachel's car, you dopey dog."

Max stopped barking but continued whimpering, clearly still distressed.

"Where are your keys?"

Rachel rushed inside and came back with them. Daniel searched the car inside and out. Nothing.

He scoped the yard again. He couldn't see any sign of an intruder.

Max was still growling at Rachel's car. Why? What did Max see that Daniel didn't? The hairs on the back of his neck were still prickling. *Something* was out there.

Something Daniel couldn't counter with a gun. *Damn it.*

But Rachel was here, she'd come to him, and that meant he had another chance to persuade her to stay so he could keep watch over her.

"Max! Come!" he said softly.

With a last warning growl at the car, Max obeyed Daniel and followed them inside.

Daniel walked to the kitchen and poured her a glass of Margaret River Cloudburst Chardonnay. He didn't have much in his fridge, just some beers, a carton of milk… and Rachel's favorite wine.

———◆———

Rachel took the chardonnay from Daniel, her fingers touching his as he passed her the chilled glass. She absorbed the charge at the contact. He looked maddeningly delicious this afternoon, wearing jeans that rode low on his hips and no shirt. He was driving her to distraction, her fingers itching to trace along his nicely defined abs, then follow the thin trail of hair that ran down his stomach to disappear into the top of his jeans.

She cleared her throat. "Nice house." It was deceptively spacious inside, the run-of-the-mill exterior hiding the opulence that was revealed once you opened the front door. Since it was a safe house, she had to assume that choice was deliberate.

Her strappy sandals clicked across the marble tiles as she wandered through the spacious kitchen and dining room. Just that area alone was larger than her whole city apartment. The house was tastefully decorated in blacks and zen neutrals, but it was the traces of Daniel she saw in the space that were ridiculously pleasing. His keys and laptop on the kitchen table, an empty coffee cup overturned in the kitchen sink, a towel on the floor just outside the bathroom door, his worn leather jacket tossed over the back of a chair. She moved to his jacket, tracing her fingers over the soft leather. So well-worn, so masculine. *So Daniel.*

He crossed the room with long strides and opened the large French doors that faced the ocean. "I'd like to believe this visit was purely for pleasure, but there was something in your tone when you called that suggested it's not."

Rachel walked out onto the balcony that overlooked the ocean, and he followed her. Daniel picked up a pair of board shorts that had been left in a heap on the floor from a recent swim, and she took the opportunity to drink in the sexy rear view. His wide shoulders, tapered waist, and well-fitted jeans accentuated the high firm roundness of his ass.

Rachel's nipples hardened painfully, and heat pooled between her thighs. It was cruel how sexy he was, how powerfully her body reacted to him.

She wanted him. Naked and on top of her, satisfying her every need.

Rachel dragged her eyes away from him. Daniel was right; she was here for a reason. Rachel gripped the railing, and he joined her, mirroring her posture and looking out at the ocean. The breeze picked up strands of his still-damp hair and moved it around his face, and she breathed in his clean masculine scent of leather and citrus.

Rachel gulped her wine, and Daniel looked at her with one brow raised inquiringly. She stared up into his intense eyes, framed by long lashes, and forgot what she was about to say. His lips were full, and perfectly kissable, and softened the hard lines of his chiseled cheekbones.

She loved the taste of cold beer on his tongue whenever she kissed him after he'd taken a mouthful, and she loved the freshness of mint after he brushed his teeth in the morning. And she loved the taste of Daniel, when he was just Daniel.

"Rach?"

"What?" *Oh, that's right...* "I saw Rob," she said "At least, I saw what I thought was Rob."

Daniel's body stiffened. "You saw Madden," he repeated slowly, his eyes narrowing in a way that made her shift uncomfortably on her feet. "When and where?"

"Last night, outside my bedroom window."

He slipped behind that impassive expression she recognized as his detective mask, but something dark and fierce swirled in his eyes.

"You sure it was him?"

Rachel swallowed and nodded. "Last night, I could have sworn it was him. At least, it looked like him, but there was something strange about him. But it could have just been me. I was alone, and—"

"Time?" Daniel asked, cutting her off.

Rachel considered. "Around midnight?"

"And you didn't call me?" His voice was soft, his tone anything but.

"The phones weren't working." Heat rose to her cheeks, and her chest tightened.

She didn't like the tone he was taking with her. "I thought I heard a knock at the door, and when I looked out the window again, he was gone. For a while I thought I'd imagined it, but I looked out on two separate occasions and saw him…"

Daniel's jaw was clenched, his expression set in hard lines. He was staring out across the ocean, as though he couldn't bring himself to look at her anymore, his knuckles white as his hands gripped the railing.

"Why are you so angry?"

Daniel turned his head, contemplated her for a heartbeat. She glimpsed his eyes, saw the smoldering embers of pain, anger, and yes, hurt in them.

"You saw Rob Madden outside your bedroom window midnight last night, and you don't tell me about it until…" He looked at his watch. "Two-fifteen the following afternoon."

Daniel pushed off the railing and went to the kitchen, taking long strides to his laptop, which sat open on the table. Rachel watched him, heart pounding, as he typed something on the keyboard. He was only a few meters away, but the distance between them was vast. She hugged her arms around her to ward off a sudden chill, despite the warmth of the afternoon.

She watched impatiently while he finished doing whatever he was doing.

He slammed the screen closed when he'd finished, then straightened, his mouth grim.

"What did you just do?" Rachel's stomach had clenched into a knot. She'd expected him to be upset, but his fury shrunk the room to the size of a closet.

"Fired the security detail I had watching you."

"Daniel!" Her mouth dropped open. The time they'd spent together in the past had been his downtime. Daniel was clearly a man you didn't fuck with, an idiot could see that, but watching the way he worked, how he dealt with men's lives with such cold efficiency, was a shock, and more than a little overwhelming.

"You can't do that!" Rachel was sick to the stomach that she'd inadvertently been the cause of two men and a woman losing their jobs.

"I believe I just did."

"What if I was wrong?" Oh God, what if she had imagined it, and that's why the security guards hadn't seen him? The whole thing, seeing Rob in the scry, then looking out the window to see him there in the yard. When she thought about it like that, the situation was ludicrous.

"Take it back," Rachel said urgently. "Tell them I made a mistake. Send an email and tell them—" Rachel started shoving him in the direction of his laptop, but he refused to budge.

Daniel's hands, large and hot, gripped her shoulders. "Don't tell me how to do my job. You saw Madden in the front yard, you heard a knock at the front door, and neither event was reported to me. I trusted people with your life, *your life*, Rachel." Daniel's voice was deep and raw. "When I trust people with you, there can be no mistakes."

Daniel released her, and she sucked in a ragged breath. He crossed to the window frame, rested his head on his arm, and looked through the opening.

"Anything else you need to tell me, now would be the time."

Rachel swallowed. No way in hell she was telling him about the scry in the backpack in her car. What if she was wrong about that? What if she was wrong about all of it? Nothing about her life made sense, but she'd better have her ducks in a row before she told Daniel anything else. What would he have done if Rob had actually approached her, or worse?

"No," Rachel said. "No," she repeated again, louder and more forcefully. "There's nothing else. And so you know, I very well might have been wrong about Rob, and now at least three people have lost their jobs." She couldn't stop the churning in the pit of her stomach. Even if she'd been wrong about Rob, there was no doubt she'd heard the knocks, felt the chill…

"That's my problem, not yours."

"Don't tell me this is not my problem," Rachel snapped. She crossed the room, yanked his arm down, forced him to look at her. "I'm sorry I didn't tell you sooner. I couldn't last night at the time because of the… technical issues with my phone, and then when I looked again the third time, he was gone. I spent the morning with my sister and the kids, all without incident, I might add, and this is the first opportunity I had to tell you."

Daniel's eyes darkened. "Keep telling yourself that. But the truth is you've had plenty of opportunity. You've had fifty-one thousand opportunities, because that's how many seconds there have been between midnight last night and now."

Rachel stepped back, a subconscious reaction to the intense force of emotion that radiated from him. She'd put distance between them, but not out of fear that he'd hurt her. Daniel didn't frighten her; it was just that being near a six-foot towering angry male was more than a little discomforting.

Daniel was angry, yes, but in absolute control. She ignored the fierce rush of arousal that stirred inside her despite the situation. She loved it when he was all commanding and dominant like that in bed. When he got out his cuffs and told her she'd been a naughty girl…

"I was out on that rusting fucking shipwreck investigating a sighting of him at the time you saw him outside your window," Daniel said in a low voice, tension rolling off him in waves. Her attention snapped back to the room.

"The fact that he got so close to you and I didn't know about it makes me furious. Perhaps if you'd called me last night, he'd be behind bars right now, and we'd be one step closer to putting an end to all this."

Daniel closed the distance between them. "It is bad enough to have to admit that I am powerless when it comes to protecting you from the something *not human* that is stalking you," Daniel said, his expression thunderous. "But protecting you from people is something I *can* do! *Need* to be able to do." Daniel traced the back of a finger down the side of her face, the tender gesture at odds with the fury in his tone.

"The one fucking thing I do have the power to help you with, and I'm unable to do even that effectively." Intense eyes stared down at her, and Rachel trembled as he picked up a strand of her hair and wrapped it around his finger.

His words sliced through her annoyance with him. "I'm sorry," she whispered.

It thrilled her that Daniel was taking this so personally. His reaction proved there was something deeper between them. She'd been steeling her heart against him, telling herself they were nothing more than casual, but with the way Daniel was looking at her right now, the way he was talking… their relationship was anything but casual.

"Nothing can happen to you. Not on my watch. And Rachel? You'll always be on my watch."

Oh God! Her knees felt weak.

Daniel's eyes flickered across her face.

"For me to keep you safe, I have to know everything."

He cupped her face with both hands and kissed her hard, the softness of his lips a powerful contrast to the hunger in his mouth. The sharp tug of guilt over not telling him about the scry disappeared.

Despite her resolve to keep him at a distance, it didn't change the fact she craved Daniel more than she craved her very next breath. The way one single touch numbed her pain more effectively than Novocain ever could.

She shoved her hands through his damp hair and kissed him back, matching the intensity of his lips on hers. He groaned, low and deep in the back of his throat, and an urgent heat burned between her thighs.

Fire raced through her veins as Daniel placed one hand on the small of her back, his heat searing her skin. He pulled her flush against him, the evidence of his desire steely against the softness of her stomach. She rubbed against him, thrilling at the pained, low moan her touch elicited from him. He lifted her, and she instinctively wrapped her legs around his waist. Holding her tight, he moved across the room, kicking a chair out of the way and sending it crashing to the floor.

He backed her all the way to the wall. "I lose my mind when I'm with you," he said, staring deeply into her eyes.

She ran her palms across his chest and down biceps like sculpted stone. He sucked in a breath, his eyes darkening in a way that dried her mouth and made her heart skip. No man could ever compare to Daniel; he was all power, muscle, and take-charge control. She remembered all too clearly how sexually in command he was.

Rachel didn't like being told what to do. Except by him. And only in the bedroom. When she was with Daniel, her mind took a leave of absence, and her body knew only how to obey.

He raised her hands above her head, and her breath caught.

"Ah, Rachel." His breath puffed across her heated cheeks, and he placed his mouth on hers. He kissed her hard, and she kissed him back, matching his intensity and ferocity.

She gave herself over to him, her mind blanking to everything but the feeling of being consumed by him. His size, his strength, his power. The thrill of being under his control. Of being possessed by him.

Here, now, in this moment, Daniel was *hers*.

He released his grip on her wrists and slowly slid his hands down the insides of her arms. She shivered as he caressed the soft sides of her breasts. "You are so damn beautiful." His voice was rough, his gaze hungry. She couldn't help but be hyperaware of him. Her nipples tingled as though he were touching them. Kissing them.

Need filled her, a hot, demanding throb between her legs. He slid his hand beneath her dress and tugged her lacy panties down her thighs. She wriggled, and they slid all the way to the floor. Leaning into her, he pressed her against the wall, lifted her so that she was level with him. She wrapped her legs around him and his fingers moved between her legs. He groaned and closed his eyes. "You are always so ready for me." His voice was low, gravelly, and so fucking sexy.

"I need you, Daniel," she whispered breathlessly against his lips. "That never changes."

"I want you to need me the way I need you." The seriousness of his tone made her heart skip, sent a warmth radiating through her chest.

"I do." Didn't he know that? *Can't he feel what he does to me?*

She gripped the back of his neck, tangled his dark locks around her fingers. He was sexy in that way an outdoorsy male was. His tanned body was carved granite. A scar on his temple ran into his hairline, a knife wound he'd told her was from an arrest when he'd been twenty-seven. His hair was slightly too long, and he needed a shave, but the roughness accentuated his blue eyes and the softness of his lips. And when that intense gaze was focused on her, it was a heady experience. The world shrank away, the effect like one of those fancy camera settings that blurred the background while bringing the subject sharply into focus.

Never had a man made her feel so exquisitely good. Never had a man more thoroughly destroyed her.

Self-preservation made her keep a distance.

Recklessness kept her coming back.

She brought her hands between them, and his eyes darkened further as she undid the button on his jeans, tugged them down on his hips. She gripped his erection, and he sucked in a breath. Slowly, she slid her hands along his length, enjoying the silk over steel feel of him in her palms, thrilling at the tremor that rolled through his body.

"Nobody has ever touched me the way you do," Daniel said, his voice gruff. "Like you really enjoy the way my cock feels."

"I do," Rachel said. "I enjoy the way it tastes even more."

She slid down the wall and sank to her knees. Once again, she took the length of him in both hands, loving the pulsing hardness. She wrapped her mouth around him, sucking as she took his cock in as far as she could from this position. He was large, so she kept one hand fisted at the base as she released him, then took him deep, over and over.

He groaned low and rough, his head resting against his forearm as he leaned on the wall. The other hand was tangled in her hair, and he hissed in a breath.

"Rach, babe. Stop," he panted. "I'm going to come; it's been far too long without you."

Rachel sucked harder, using her tongue to flick along his length. "Ah, God…"

His stomach muscles tightened, his chest gleamed with a thin layer of sweat. He was close to climax, and her core clenched with need. Abruptly he pulled away. His palms on her waist, he lifted her easily, pressing her back against the wall. She wrapped her legs around his hips, and he bent his forehead to hers.

"What you do to me—"

The fire of desire in his eyes scorched her skin, and she arched her body into his. She couldn't wait. Didn't want to wait. She wanted the satisfaction only he could give. His chest rose and fell with his ragged breathing, and she knew he was giving himself a moment to cool off. To hell with that.

Rachel wrapped her arms around his neck, pressed her breasts against his chest.

"Are you trying to kill me?" he asked, his voice husky.

"Can you think of a better way to go?"

The grin he gave her caused her heart to skip. Daniel looked at her in that way he had, the one that made her feel as though nothing existed in the world but them. The heavy-lidded gaze that had kept her warm on those dark, lonely nights without him. She was consumed by him, entwined in the circle of his energy as it wrapped around and through them. His hair fell forward across one eye, and when he swiped his tongue across his full bottom lip, she thought she'd die from wanting him.

Holding her with one arm, he reached into his pocket and withdrew a condom. She wasn't surprised, given their history. He'd always had one within easy reach whenever he'd come to see her. She wasn't upset by his presumption of sex when he knew he'd be seeing her today. It would be a lie to pretend she didn't want him just as much.

Keeping his eyes on hers, he ripped the packet open with his teeth. He raised a brow questioningly, and she reached for the condom. She took her time putting it on him, savoring the feel of sliding it snugly down his considerable length.

Dear God. *Daniel.* That firm jaw and those heavy-lidded, darkly intense eyes. There was nothing like that fierce look that he gave her just before he slid his cock inside her. The one that promised absolute pleasure, complete possession.

But he already possessed her, owned her, body and soul. Had since she was eighteen years old. She just couldn't tell him that.

He paused at her entrance, leaned in, hovering his mouth just above hers, then touched his lips to hers as he drove slowly and deeply inside her. She cried out, and he swallowed her cry. The tenderness beneath his strength and power caused a lump to form in her throat. He filled her so completely, her mind blanked, until she was consumed by him, by only him and how he made her feel. The pleasure he gave. Her whole body was alive; every nerve, every cell, was highly attuned and aware of him.

As he moved inside her, he pulled back so that he could watch her. Resting his forearm on the wall above her, he drove deep inside her, stealing her breath with every thrust until she was writhing and panting. Her body completely boneless as he gave her pleasure like nobody else ever had.

"Open your eyes," he said. "I want you to look at me when you come."

Rachel opened her lids, unaware she'd closed them. He was staring into her, his expression alone sending her directly to the edge. "Oh God!"

He smiled, and her heart skipped. "Right there with you, babe." He increased his pace, harder, faster. She was wild with need for him, desperate and begging, but he kept her on the edge as he drove into her. And then finally, *finally,* he altered his angle slightly, giving them both what they needed, sending them spiraling over into ecstasy at the same time.

"Daniel!" She screamed his name as she came, and he called out hers in a guttural cry. He kept moving inside her until the very last shudders of their orgasms subsided.

He withdrew, and her knees gave way, but he caught her in his arms. He carried her into the bedroom, stripped off her dress, then tossed her on the bed. He disappeared into the bathroom for a moment, before joining her. He leaned over her, brushed his lips against hers.

I love you. The truth was, she had for years. No other man consumed her the way Daniel did. But the words didn't reach her tongue. They never did. She closed her eyes in case he saw the depth of her feelings for him.

He lay on his back, wrapping an arm around her, and she rested her head on his bare chest. Listening to the beat of his heart, she traced her fingertips along the soft sparse hair down the center of his chest to his stomach.

She trailed her fingers down his arm, across the tattoo on his left bicep, and her heart squeezed.

I don't want just a part of him.

I need all of him.

And I want him to need all of me.

Rachel shifted in his arms so that she was staring at the ceiling. He turned his head to look at her. "Everything okay?" She didn't look at him. His eyes always held a rare softness after they'd made love. It would hurt to look at them. She'd always run her hands through his mussed hair, and he'd lean in to kiss her lips tenderly. He'd never say he loved her, but she'd pretend she heard it anyway.

"I'm good," she said. "That was nice."

Daniel rolled onto his side, leaning on his elbow. His hair fell in front of his eyes and his lips twitched at the corners with amusement. "Nice?" He raised a brow.

She grinned. "It wasn't bad." She tried to shrug. His fingers found the dip of her waist, and she screamed as he tickled her.

"All right, all right," she cried, fighting for breath. "Stop! Okay! You're the best lover I've ever had."

Daniel stopped, looked deeply into her eyes, then lowered his head and kissed her. Tears sprang to her eyes, and she squeezed them tight, praying he didn't notice.

She shoved him away, and he rolled onto his back. He grabbed her, slid her close and wrapped his arms around her shoulders. She rested her cheek on his chest so he couldn't see her face.

So he'd never know her heart was fracturing.

Chapter Twenty-One

His freshly showered body sated and languid, Daniel lounged with Rachel on the large white couch, the windows open wide, a gentle ocean breeze brushing over their naked skin. Stars twinkled brightly, a lover's full moon high in the night sky.

She lay against his chest, and he ran his hand across her skin as smooth as satin. They'd eaten take-away Chinese with chopsticks, naked on his balcony, made love in the Jacuzzi, then taken a long stroll along the beach, all the way to the private jetty owned by the retired corporate lawyer, and back.

He couldn't remember when he'd ever felt so… content. Being with Rachel felt so right, so natural. His chest squeezed. She did that. Gave him the painful pleasure of being with her.

Had his father loved his mother like this? His mother rarely spoke of Dad anymore.

"I'm sorry about your mother," Daniel said. Even though Rachel had stopped taking his calls, he'd still kept tabs on her and her family. He'd known about her mother's suicide and the sale of the restaurant. He just didn't know why. He wanted to press her, but given how she'd shut down at the beach, he didn't want to ruin the mood.

Rachel tensed, then she released a long, slow, deliberate breath. "Thanks. It was even tougher on Elise than me, I think. She was closer to Mum than I was. They were alike in so many ways."

Rachel's soft hair tickled his chin, and he ran his fingers through the silky mass.

"What about your mum," she asked. "You never talk about her. Do you see her much?"

"No."

She twisted in his lap and peered up at him. "Why?"

Daniel's eyes traveled across her face, his finger tracing the softness of her cheek. Talking about his childhood—or anything personal for that matter—didn't come easily to him, but judging by the expectant expression on her face, it was important to her.

"My father died when I was eight."

"I'm sorry."

Daniel struggled for words. His mother had resented being left with a child. Donna Angeline Smith, Angel to those who knew her, was young, too young to be left with baggage. Daniel heard her tell someone that once, and it had stuck with him. If he ever gave it much thought—which was rare—it would perfectly describe how he had felt throughout his childhood. Inconvenient baggage.

"You know," Rachel said, "I don't even know what she looks like."

She sat up, and Daniel crossed the room, grabbed his phone, spent a moment scrolling through his pictures. He crossed the room to her, put his palms on the back of the couch, bent down and kissed her lips, then sat next to her again.

"This is her, a year ago on my thirtieth birthday."

Rachel took the phone. "She's younger than I thought."

"Mum was very young when they fell in love."

"She's beautiful," Rachel said. "She's blonde and petite, but you have her eyes. Same unique blue-green."

"My eyes change to green?"

Rachel smiled. "Yes. Depending on the light."

Daniel took back the phone, tossed it onto the coffee table. "Mum fell pregnant with me when she was nineteen. Not intentionally. My father married her, and when he died eight years later, she was still young and not happy about wiping noses and packing school lunches. She always said the best years of her life had been wasted."

"She told you that?" Rachel looked stunned.

"Many times," Daniel said, matter-of-factly. "Marrying my father was her greatest mistake, and her youth had been wasted for nothing."

"You aren't *nothing*!"

Daniel smiled at her outrage on his behalf. He'd long since accepted that his mother couldn't look at him without seeing his father.

"Where is she now?"

"She remarried into the money she always wanted." Daniel smiled wryly. "My stepfather owns and runs an airline, so like my father, I'm sure he's not around as much as she would like, but unlike my father, Bryan has the bank account to compensate for his absence."

"Did she have any other kids?" Rachel asked. "Do you have any brothers and sisters?"

"No. Well, she doesn't anyway. Bryan has two children from a previous marriage. But I don't really know them." Taipan was Daniel's true family.

He leaned back on the lounge, tugging Rachel between his legs. He'd had enough of talking about his family and hoped she'd be satisfied with that. It was more than he'd ever shared with anyone.

Rachel snuggled into him, her fingers tracing the indentations of his stomach muscles, and his chest squeezed.

Speaking about his childhood with Rachel had triggered an unfamiliar sensation inside him. A sense of… longing? His memories of his father were the last memories Daniel had of being part of a family. Would he ever have that again?

Maybe, somehow, he and Rachel could make it work?

"Daniel," Rachel said. "Were you at Dad's restaurant the night of my eighteenth birthday?"

Her question surprised him.

"You were wearing an ankle-length red dress, with a split up the side." As if he'd ever forget. For some reason she tensed up at his reply. "What makes you ask?"

"I don't remember seeing you there."

That gave him pause. "Then what made you think I was?"

Rachel shrugged and didn't meet his gaze. "I was just curious."

Something about both her question and answer bothered him, but he couldn't pinpoint why. He'd let it drop. For now.

He traced a finger languidly along the satiny curve of her back. When this case was over, how the hell was he going to leave?

Would she fight for him to stay?

Rachel had pierced his skin like a splinter the very first moment he'd laid eyes on her, and he didn't know how to get her out. He ran his fingers through her soft hair. She was actually nothing like a splinter. Good thing he didn't want to be a writer; his analogies sucked.

"I love being with you." *I love you. I've loved you since you were eighteen.*

Why couldn't he say the words he'd never uttered to another living soul?

The truth? He was scared. Scared she'd pull away like she continually had this last year.

Her hand on his thigh squeezed, the heat nearly burning a hole right through his skin as he warred with telling her how he felt.

"I love being with you too." Her voice was tender, but her tone was tinged with… pain? Goddamn, he didn't understand what to do about the two of them. All he knew was how he felt. Right here, right now. He didn't know what to do about tomorrow, what was fair to ask of her. Did he have any place in her future? He sensed her resistance, her caution, the way she pulled back when he got too close.

Something she was smart to do.

Her hand remained on his thigh, and it was suddenly all he could focus on. His body was on fire again, and she had to feel his urgent need for her pressing against her back.

Leaving her hand on his leg, she angled her body to look at him. He watched her gaze travel down his chest to his cock. And God help him, the look of hunger in her eyes when she brought them back to his…

His mouth was dry, and hers must be too, because she sucked in a breath, and he glimpsed her pink tongue as it swiped across her lower lip.

She pulled herself up so that she was kneeling in front of him. "You are an insatiable beast," she whispered, kissing a trail down his chest. "Good thing that's just the way I like you."

Her phone rang, and she froze. "That's my sister's ringtone. I need to get that."

She answered the phone and listened for a few seconds. "Oh my God. Yes, I'm coming now. See you soon." Rachel disconnected the phone, swung her long legs off the lounge as she threw her dress over her head.

"What is it?" Daniel slid into his jeans, tucking his pistol into the back.

"Do you know where you tossed my panties?" She brushed her dress down. "Never mind. Where are my shoes?" Rachel rushed around. He heard the jangle of keys.

Finding her shoes, he picked them up and handed them to her.

"What is it?" Daniel demanded, his heart slamming in his chest.

"I should have been there. Staying away was not the right thing to do. Damn it!"

"Rachel!" He gripped her by the shoulders. "What is it?"

"Sally." Tears rolled out of her eyes and down her cheeks. "Someone was in her room."

Daniel grabbed his keys and took hers out of her hand.

"Hey!" she protested.

"I'm driving."

Daniel was already on the phone to the security guards he had posted on Elise's house. There had been no breaches according to the system logs.

Max was already at his side, having heard the jangle of his keys. He guided them both out of the house and assisted her into the passenger side of his 4WD and shut the door. He opened the rear door for Max and glanced over at the Lexus.

He'd already begun reversing when Rachel screamed, "Wait!" She snatched her keys from his console. "My backpack!" She jumped out of the door before he was fully stopped. She dashed over to her car, retrieved her backpack, and rushed back inside his car.

Max growled, and Daniel looked at him in the rearview mirror. "What is it, little buddy?"

Max growled again.

"Hurry!" Rachel said, and he hit reverse and sent the vehicle roaring down the driveway.

Max had reacted strangely when Rachel had first arrived at his house, and he was growling again now. Something was not right about her car, and Daniel was going to get his team to work it over before she got it back.

Why had Rachel looked so panicked when she remembered her backpack?

It could be just that she didn't want to leave it behind. But Daniel had a strong gut feeling that something was not quite right. He couldn't shake the feeling that Rachel was hiding something. Or at least, not being completely forthright about it.

There was something she wasn't telling him.

But what?

Chapter Twenty-Two

The car had barely come to a stop before Rachel threw the door open and raced inside, leaving Daniel out in front talking to the security guards. She found Ellie holding a sobbing Sally in her bedroom.

Sally's blonde curls were tousled, her clear gray eyes wide with fright, her little body shaking as she sat up in her bed with the covers pulled up to her chin.

Ellie's reddened eyes were filled with tears. "I called you straightaway when Sally said she saw someone in her room." She shook her head. "I should have called the police, called emergency, but I knew Daniel and you weren't far away. And like the time with the Ouija board, there was no sign of an intruder."

Rachel lowered herself onto Sally's bed. "Of course I'd want you to call me. I'd be mad if you didn't. Sally," Rachel said softly, "what happened?"

"Someone was in my room," Sally said, pointing to the corner. Rachel's heart hammered. She crossed the room, checked the window. Locked.

Memories rushed back, fluttering on the edge of her consciousness like small black birds she couldn't quite catch. Rachel had seen things in her room too when she was little. Things that had stolen her sleep and threatened her sanity. Things she'd discovered early on couldn't be discussed with her family without serious consequences.

"The alarm didn't sound," Elise said, wringing her hands.

"Someone was in my room!" Sally repeated.

"What did you see?" Dread thickened in Rachel's veins. "Maybe it was just a bad dream?"

Sally shook her head, blonde curls bouncing around her tear-streaked face. "I was awake. I was sitting up in my bed, and I saw him."

Rachel met Ellie's distressed gaze.

"What's your dolly doing all the way over here?" Ellie asked, crossing the room and picking up a doll with blonde hair just like Sally's. She dusted her off and tucked her back into Sally's bed.

Sally tossed the doll across the room. "I don't like Mandy anymore."

"Don't treat your toys like that," Ellie admonished her gently.

"Why don't you like her?" Rachel asked.

"She was talking to the man in my room."

Rachel's mouth dried, her pulse racing.

"Dolls can't talk," Elise said firmly. "Except in your imagination."

"Yes, they can," Sally said, crossing her arms across her chest.

Elise stood up. "There's no one in your room, under your bed, or in your closet. And dolls most definitely can't talk. It's late. Aunt Rachel needs to go home, and you need your sleep."

"I don't want Aunt Rachel to go home." Sally began to cry, and Rachel's heart squeezed.

"Then I won't," Rachel said. "I'll stay here until morning."

"Mummy?" Sally's voice was small, her eyes scared. "Can she?"

"Of course," Elise said. Liam began to cry in the next room. "All this noise has woken your brother." Elise released a breath; she looked exhausted.

"I'll stay with Sally," Rachel said.

"Not for too long," Elise said. "Meet me in the loungeroom when you're ready?"

Rachel crawled into bed with Sally and made up a story about fairies with pet dust bunnies. She had no idea if it made sense, but Sally's giggles assured her it didn't matter.

Moonlight filtered in through the curtains, and Sally began to get heavy in Rachel's arms.

"Do you believe me?" Sally asked sleepily. "Mummy doesn't believe me, but do you?"

Rachel hesitated, unsure how to answer. She didn't want to contradict Sally's mother, but the little girl's question was so earnest it tugged at Rachel's heart.

Did Rachel believe Sally had seen something? Yes. Rachel had seen and experienced things she couldn't explain. Pia had said kids and animals could see things adults couldn't. Dread settled in the pit of Rachel's stomach. But what was it she could see?

"Aunt Rach?" Sally persisted.

"I believe that you believe that you saw it," Rachel hedged.

Sally seemed a little confused by that, but didn't press for more. "I asked him his name."

Rachel froze, her pulse quickening as she asked the next question. "Did he answer you?"

"Yes," Sally whispered. "He said his name was Captain."

———— ♦ ————

Rachel entered the loungeroom to find Elise talking to Daniel. He crossed the room when he saw her.

"I'm going to take care of a few things," Daniel said, kissing Rachel on the lips. She felt an unwanted rush of anxiety at him leaving, but it didn't seem right to ask him to stay, especially as Ellie clearly hadn't invited him.

"I'll call you in the morning," Daniel said, glancing at his watch. Daylight was only a few hours away anyway. "The security team is still in place. If you need me, just call. I won't be far."

When Daniel left, Rachel walked over to her sister, and Elise hugged her tight. "Thanks for coming, sis."

"Of course," Rachel said. "I'm sorry for all of this. I feel it's all my fault."

"It is." But Ellie smiled as she said it.

A heaviness settled on Rachel's heart. "I really am sorry."

"You've already apologized. And it's not like you meant for any of this to happen." Elise sat down on the sofa and invited Rachel to sit next to her.

"Do you believe Sally?"

Rachel sat on the couch next to her sister and tucked her legs up beneath her. "Yes."

Ellie made a choking sound. "I knew you'd say that. She didn't have a bad dream, did she? She really thinks she saw someone like you used to when you were little. Mum would get really angry with you when you woke up saying things like that."

Rachel cast her mind back. "How old was I?"

"You were Sally's age, maybe even younger. I think you were about three when it started, and it went on until you were about seven, maybe eight? Until Mum threatened to take away every toy you had if you spoke of it again."

"Why do you think she got so angry?" Rachel asked. There was so much she hadn't understood. The night terrors she'd had had seemed so very real.

"You know Mum. That subject was off-limits."

"Don't you find that strange?"

Ellie frowned. "Yes. Now, as an adult anyway. As a child, you don't question."

"You didn't have nightmares?" Rachel asked. "You didn't think someone was in your room?"

"No."

Rachel leaned heavily back in the chair, the leather cool against her skin. "Sally said she saw the captain. "What if something did follow me from the ship? That's the real reason I stayed away."

"Clearly, that didn't work." Ellie fidgeted with her fingers, then looked up. "Rach?" Her eyes were teary. "I don't think this started when you went out onto the ship."

"What do you mean?"

Ellie's brow furrowed. "First you as a child, now Sally. Mum's overreaction, her adamant refusal to talk about ghosts in any shape or form. The way it was taboo in the house. And she rarely let us see her mother, and I always wondered why. You know they put Grandma in a mental institution as a child, and then again when she turned twenty-four? The same age you are now."

Ellie chewed her lip. "I heard Mum and Dad arguing about it one day. It didn't make sense to me at the time, but it had to do with your nightmares, Grandma, and something Mum insisted should stay buried in the past. She screamed at Dad, telling him if they weren't careful, they'd lock you away too."

Rachel didn't know what to think. What did all this mean?

"I didn't want them to take my sister away," Ellie continued, "so I went along with Mum, told you it was all in your imagination. Even though I knew by your reaction, your terror, it was something far more real. But what could it be?"

Their mother was no longer alive to ask, and their grandmother had passed away in the institute several years ago.

Tears pooled in Ellie's eyes. "I followed in Mum's footsteps, telling Sally it was her imagination. It seemed to work for you, since the night terrors lessened as you got older. So I keep telling Sally over and over there are no such thing as monsters or ghosts or whatever. And she argues with me every single time."

Ellie choked back a sob. "But what else can I do? My child comes to me for answers. Answers I don't have. I have to say ghosts don't exist, because believing anything else means I'm powerless to protect her."

Ellie walked across the room, grabbed a box of tissues, and set them on the table in front of her.

"I don't want to make the same mistakes Mum and Dad did. I saw what their reaction did to you. How isolated and insecure it made you feel. It stole the beautiful smile my kid sister used to wear so frequently."

Rachel's chest was heavy with sadness. "You think Grandma saw things too?"

Elise started to cry. "Yes. And that's why they thought she was crazy. I think that's why Mum got so mad at you, refused to let you talk about it. She was scared the same thing would happen to you. But it drove a wedge between you two that never healed." Ellie shook her head in determination. "I don't want to do that to Sally. But what choice do I have? I don't want people to think she's crazy. What if they try to take her away from me like they did Grandma?"

"You think Mum believed me?" Rachel asked, shattered she hadn't known that back then. Would their relationship have been closer?

"After one of your nightmares, I saw the way her eyes flicked around the room. She was scared, Rach. As much as she got angry with you, yelled at you that there were no such things as ghosts, I saw real fear in her eyes."

"So, all this time you said you didn't believe in ghosts, but…?"

"It was bullshit. All the times you, Rob, and Trey sought out haunted houses, I knew that stemmed from what you'd gone through as a child. And now it's happening to Sally," Ellie said. "What are we going to do?" Her voice cracked, her hands shaking as she blew her nose.

"I don't know. I don't understand this myself, much less know how to help Sally. I wish Grandma was still around to ask."

"I think whatever this is, it's stronger in Sally than it was in you."

Rachel released a long, worried breath. "I think so too. I don't remember ever seeing things when I was awake. With your permission, I'll ask Pia about it."

Elise nodded. "Yes, please do. Anything you can do to help. I don't know how to handle this, but I'm Sally's mum. She's counting on me to get it right."

"We can still hope it fades with age, like it did in me," Rachel said, struggling to find something to ease the burden on her sister.

Ellie stood, her shoulders slumped forward. "Or she'll turn out like Pia, and her ability will just get stronger."

"Would that be such a bad thing?" Pia seemed to be dealing with her ability quite well now. With knowledge came power.

"I don't know. I'm sorry. I'm so exhausted. I need whatever sleep I'm going to get before Liam wakes up at five. See you in the morning?"

Rachel embraced her sister, squeezing her tight. "Wait. We always end up talking about me. There's something you want to tell me. What is it? You know I'm always here for you too, right?"

Elise looked away, fresh tears springing to her eyes. "Not tonight, sis, I'm too tired. We'll talk tomorrow."

———◆———

Rachael sat by herself in her darkened bedroom long after Ellie went back to bed, thinking about what her sister had told her. What a tragedy she never got the opportunity to speak with her grandmother about this. They might have been able to heal each other, and work out how to help Sally.

A strange feeling tightened her chest, seeped through her flesh, and vibrated her bones. A strange sensation that was not altogether foreign. Something from her past maybe? A distant past?

She sat for a long time in the darkness listening to the scry, humming in her bag. Wait… humming?

She picked up her bag, feeling strangely comforted by the weight. Sitting on the bed, she took out the scry.

Rachel didn't understand exactly what the scry was, and why it had fallen into her hands. But maybe it was here for a purpose. The scry had shown her so much about her past. Could it tell her more about her family, shed light on this situation?

Would it hurt if she took one more little look?

After all, just how much worse could this get?

Chapter Twenty-Three

Rachel cradled the scry in the palms of her hands, peering deep into it, seeing the smoke swirl sooner than last time. Satisfaction filled her, as though she'd learned a new skill.

She stared into the crystal, her anger over something scaring Sally surging in her body. For a moment, she thought it was becoming impatient with her, or was it responding to her inner turmoil?

There was so much she didn't understand. But first, she had something she needed to know.

"Who was in Sally's room tonight?" she demanded.

The clouds dissipated, and the image of an old salt-weathered man filled the glass. *Captain Edwards.*

Rachel's blood ran cold. The name pressed into her mind. The glass didn't speak out loud, but Rachel heard the words just as clearly as if it had.

Sally had said she'd seen the captain.

"You keep away, do you hear? Don't go anywhere near Sally," Rachel said, anger pouring out of her. "She's a child and has nothing to do with this." The image of the captain faded and was replaced by black, swirling smoke.

"Where did you go?" Rachel demanded. "Can you come back? I'm not finished talking to you yet."

The captain's image reappeared.

"You only respond to questions," Rachel said, slowly understanding. That's why it didn't show her anything when she'd ordered the captain to stay away from Sally.

"Okay, then, scry. I get it. You are a tool for asking questions."

The crystal whirled with smoke, and Rachel considered how to make the best use of the mysteriously compelling object.

"Did Captain Edwards have this scry before me?"

The captain's image filled the glass and she saw his weathered hands as he peered into the scry, the same one she was holding right now. A chill skittered across her skin, and she shivered with the sensation she was doing something she shouldn't. Something bad.

But she wasn't ready to let it go just yet.

"How did a burly old fisherman come to have a scry?"

The smoke ebbed, and images began to scroll past, vivid and real. They pulled at her somehow, spiraling her inside the scenes so that she half-watched, half-felt what she was being shown.

It was a starry night, and cold. Bitter cold. The captain turned up the collar on his weatherproof coat and jumped into his dinghy. The ship was anchored offshore at a remote stretch of beach in the Northern Territory.

Rachel didn't just see what was happening, like she was reading a book or watching a movie. She was there with the captain, as though she'd been sucked through a window and was watching what was happening in real life, but one step removed.

The wind whipped through Rachel's own hair as she saw the captain brush a strand out of his eyes. She followed the captain along a path into the bush, farther, farther, deeper into the forest, until he came to a cave. He entered the dark cavern, and Rachel waited by the entrance, too scared to follow. There were strange carvings on the outside of the cave. Many symbols she didn't recognize, alongside stars, and pentagrams in circles. Rachel didn't understand what they meant, but she had the sense they made up some kind of spell. Was it to keep something out of the cave?

Or to keep something in…?

A woman appeared in the glass, wearing clothes from a time gone by; she looked vaguely familiar. The woman was older, her hands wrinkled and marked by time. She stood at the head of a circle, a perfect nine feet around, Rachel somehow knew. The woman was holding the scry, and she was performing some kind of ceremony. She was summoning something dark, an instrument of revenge. The woman's emotions flowed through Rachel, their strength overwhelming, as though they were her own. She wanted someone dead. Her husband. And his mistress!

Her jealousy was fierce; it had turned into a fiery rage at their betrayal.

The woman was summoning a demon to exact her revenge upon them.

But something went wrong.

The demon she summoned couldn't be tamed to her purposes—instead, it used *her*. She did terrible things, unspeakable things. Then finally, the demon killed her and her entire coven.

With her dying breath, the woman looked up through the glass and directly at Rachel.

Rachel gasped. Almost dropped the scry. It was as though the old woman could look directly through time, through the scry, and see Rachel as she was today.

Who was she? Who was this woman who had eyes the same as Rachel's, the same as Sally's?

Rachel's heart hammered and skipped, then the image faded, and the captain returned from inside the cave with the scry. The same one she was staring into right now.

Eyes focused ahead, the captain walked directly back to the ship. Rachel followed, somehow floating from somewhere just above him as he rowed back to the fishing trawler.

"Why was the scry in the cave?"

A woman appeared in the glass, someone familiar. Her grandmother! Rachel hadn't seen her grandmother all that much, but she'd studied the pictures her mother had kept in the shoebox at the back of her wardrobe and often wondered why those pictures weren't in the family album with the others.

What was her grandmother doing with the scry? Rachel watched as she disappeared inside the cave and returned several minutes later without it. Reading from a book, she spoke some words, and carved the symbols into the cave's entrance with an ornate knife.

She then made the sign of the cross over her chest and left.

Rachel was stunned. She didn't understand why, but it had been her grandmother who'd put the scry in the cave!

What did the captain want with the scry?

Rachel saw the captain in a room with six other men in a circle around a Ouija board, the same board that had attacked Rachel on the ship. Next to the board sat the scry.

Captain Edwards leaned back in his chair, his lips curled around his pipe, sending smoke spiraling into the air, mingling with whiskey fumes and the faint scent of fish guts. Rachel had the sense that this tough fisherman, with his wild, scraggly beard, was once trustworthy and kind. But something new had entered his eyes, an edge brought on by dark forces.

His thick, burly fingers struck a match, lit a circle of black candles. He glanced nervously over his shoulder, as though aware he was being watched. Rachel shivered, aware too of the unseen eyes that watched his every move from the shadows. The captain began his summoning verses, a routine now superfluous, as the entity—the demon—was already there. He never left the captain's side, his soulless eyes ever watchful in the darkness.

The air warped and twisted, and something fractured the energy in the room. The men all shifted in their seats, aware of something their eyes told them wasn't there.

A rat ran through the open door, stopped beside the table leg, flipped over onto its back and sucked in its final breath. The captain grunted, then kicked the carcass across the floor with his boot.

"It's time." The captain placed his fingers on the planchette and his crew followed his lead. Candlelight flickered all around, casting long shadows up the walls.

"I did what you asked. I have the scry. Now, you must show me what I need to know." The captain had his fingers on the board, but also stared hard into the scry.

Sweat beaded Rachel's forehead, and her heart pulsed frantically. For a brief moment, she was sucked back into her bedroom, into her time-space reality. She wanted to drop the scry, fearing what it would show her. But it remained glued to her hands, her eyes transfixed by the swirling, smoky images that unfolded within.

"Show me who it is," the captain demanded, thrusting Rachel back onto the ship. The smell of the ocean filled her lungs, and the ship lurched beneath her feet. "I order the scry to show me his face! I did what you asked! Show me who the bastard is!" The captain's voice boomed, the vibrations rolling straight through her.

The scry didn't answer, and the captain's silver hair trembled as his body shook with rage. He slammed his fist onto the board, sending the planchette careening to the floor. One of his crew, a balding man with a tattoo of an anchor on his arm— just like Popeye's, Rachel mused—retrieved it.

"You aren't asking a question," Rachel told the captain, as though he could hear her. "You have to rephrase it, turn it into a question."

As the days passed, the captain's frustration continued to mount.

"Where are you, Captain?" Rachel asked the scry out loud.

The image in the scry panned out, and Rachel could see the ship, battling large waves. The captain was in a rage, barking orders at his crew. A vicious storm raged overhead. "I must get to her!" the captain bellowed.

The crew were casting concerned looks at each other, huddling in groups, speaking in hushed whispers. Rachel knew they were talking about the captain; he knew it too. It infuriated him, but he couldn't stop himself. The desperation to get back to his Anna-Marie was all-consuming, his need to kill her lover just as great.

Rachel felt the captain's frustration, his anger, in her body, as though his emotions were her own. *She* was desperate to get to shore. But the storm was hampering the ship's progress. The captain had the engines cranked to full power; he was going to make it back home, and nothing, not even God's greatest wrath, would stand in his way.

His wife, his beloved Anna-Marie, was cheating on him.

His heart was shattered.

His life was over.

The scry had showed him the betrayal.

Rachel hated her. She stood in the cabin with the captain as the waves crashed over their heads. She laughed maniacally when the captain did. She understood how the captain felt, how her own mother must have felt to know her husband of all those years had been cheating on her with a younger woman.

Humiliated. Betrayed.

The captain's pain, his anguish, tore through Rachel. The pure joy of loving his wife more than his next breath, and the unadulterated torture of needing to be away to support them. Commercial fishing was all he knew, like his father and his father before him. His livelihood meant being away; it didn't mean he didn't love his wife enough to stay.

But his love, his devotion, wasn't enough to stop his wife from cheating on him with another man. Someone who was there when he couldn't be.

If Rachel progressed her relationship with Daniel, would he cheat on her?

The smoke rearranged itself, and the image of Daniel and another woman filled the glass. The woman had long blonde hair and was wearing a tight little black dress. It was her favorite, though Rachel had no idea how she knew that.

A flash of red, her nails, as the woman wrapped her arms around Daniel's shoulders. He lifted her up, carried her across the room, much like he'd done with Rachel earlier tonight. Except instead of fucking her against the wall, he fucked her on the kitchen table.

Cynthia. Her name was Cynthia.

Rachel's fingers trembled, and she dropped the scry. It landed on the floor with a loud, dull thud. She kicked the offensive object under the bed and placed her fist to her mouth, holding back a wave of nausea.

Daniel was seeing someone else.

Cynthia.

Rachel felt as though her heart had fallen from her chest and shattered on the floor. Thoughts, dark thoughts, filtered through her mind. Thoughts, phrases, words she would never use. Her hands fisted as she rode a strong impulse to hurt something. Her insides fired with an intense urge to act. Her building fury frightened her.

Anger over her father's betrayal of her mother, Anna-Marie's betrayal of the captain, and Daniel's own betrayal of her.

Wait…

Rachel fought to clear her mind. She pounded the sides of her head, the sharp stabs in her temples temporarily silencing the wayward thoughts, her roiling emotions.

Daniel *couldn't* cheat on her. They had made no commitment to each other. Daniel was technically free to see whoever he wanted.

As was she.

But… something had changed between them. She knew that. She remembered earlier in the evening, when she'd been wrapped in his arms. He cared about her, truly he did. He'd have to be the world's biggest con man if he could fake their connection. She knew what they had was real. So what had she seen in the scry?

Rachel crawled under the bed and retrieved the scry. Maybe she needed to put it away and not ask it anything else. Its power was intriguing, but frightening.

Wait. She had another question. The most important one. She couldn't believe she'd almost forgotten to ask.

Rachel sat back down, closed her eyes, and took a deep breath, steeling herself for the answer.

"What happened to Trey?"

The smoke swirled again, before images began to form. She saw herself on the ship, laughing with Trey and Rob. A lump formed in her throat, and she blinked away tears as she watched the three of them together. The depth of their love for each other, their friendship evident in the way they acted, the way they spoke to each other. Rachel's heart squeezed painfully. Those times were over. Trey was dead, their friendship no longer possible.

What happened to you, Trey?

Rachel saw herself and Trey at the top of the metal stairs. The two of them had been on the deck, and they were heading down to Rob, who'd been calling for them. He wanted to show them something he'd found. Moments before, Trey had told her he loved her, and Rachel was still reeling inside.

The images in the scry were scattered, a little vague, and she tried to piece them together from what she remembered. Rachel imagined she was going to be shown what happened after she entered the room, the part she couldn't remember after Rob started acting strangely and insisting they play with the Ouija board.

But then she saw her hands reach out, shove Trey hard on the back. He tumbled down the stairs to the steel floor below, his head landing with a sickening thud. Blood pooled beneath him, and Rachel screamed. Rob was at the bottom of the stairs.

"What did you do?" Rob asked, his mouth dropping open in horror.

A violent chill shook her, and with trembling hands, Rachel placed the scry on the bed. She couldn't see any more.

She had killed Trey.

Rachel was the one who'd murdered her friend. Not Rob.

What had happened after that? Had Rob staged it to look like he'd killed Trey to protect her? Was that why he was on the run? To protect her?

Oh God. She was a murderer.

She ran to the bathroom and was sick. Her head throbbed, and her vision blurred, the room was spinning, knives of pain lancing her stomach.

How was she going to live with herself, knowing this?

For a very long time, Rachel stood at the sink and ran cool water over her face. She couldn't handle this new reality. Her brain refused to work, a stick lodged in the cogs of her mind.

Numb, she walked back to the bed and picked up the scry. She'd had enough. There was nothing else she needed to know.

She carried the scry across the room, planning to shove it into her bag. She wasn't going to look at it again, under no circumstances would she do so, but a strange hum emanated from it, and her gaze returned to the scry of its own accord.

The scry filled with thick plumes of dark smoke. An angular face appeared, a beastly one, with black, soulless eyes and curled horns. Rachel recoiled from it, wanting to drop the scry but unable to open her fingers.

A bitter chill bolted out of the scry, racing up her arms and through her body. An electric shock of the purest evil. As well as the face staring at her from the scry, its shadow stared at her from this very room. Icy claws raked her neck, and it whispered in her ear, using an ancient language she couldn't understand. Its breath was foul, and her stomach revolted.

The face became more vivid, and a scream lodged in her throat.

Her heart was racing, her chest painfully tight. She was frozen in place, the beast's eyes staring directly into hers with nefarious, malicious intent.

She was looking into the eyes of the demon. The one the woman had summoned in her fit of jealous rage.

The demon raised a clawed hand and raked Rachel's skin. *From the inside out.*

It grinned, a sickening smile, its needle-like fangs dripping with slimy drool.

Blood thrashed past her ears.

Dear God, help me.

The demon had a plan.

There was a reason the demon had sought her out…

It needed her.

The scratches on her back burned, and the room spun. Black tinged the edges of her vision and her legs started to give way.

A dog started barking at her front window.

Max!

The demon inside the scry vanished.

Like nothing had happened.

Like it had all been in her mind.

CHAPTER TWENTY-FOUR

Max!" Daniel growled. "Come here."

Daniel had parked his vehicle a short distance away, planning on spending the next couple of hours keeping an eye on Elise's house. From his position on the beach, he had a perfect view of the front of the house and Rachel's bedroom window. He had just relieved one of the new security guards he'd hired when Max took off running, barking viciously at Rachel's bedroom window.

Daniel chased after Max. "What is it, buddy?" Max had calmed now that Daniel was at his side, but his hackles were raised, and he was growling.

They had just finished doing a perimeter check of the front yard and surrounding trees. Nothing was amiss. Max would have let him know if there was anyone around. Then why was he barking at Rachel's window? Daniel moved to the window, listening, but all seemed quiet inside.

"Something got you spooked, little buddy?"

Daniel held Max's collar as he growled low and warningly. Daniel's gut clenched. "Is Rachel all right?"

Max growled in answer.

Holding Max firmly, Daniel edged closer to Rachel's window. The curtains moved, and Rachel peeked through them.

Thank God she was okay.

Max lunged at the window, barking viciously. *What the hell?*

"Max!" Daniel whipped out his leash. He rarely needed it, since Max responded obediently to voice command. Well, he used to.

The leash secured to Max's collar, Daniel stepped into the open, so Rachel could see him. Her face was reddened, her eyes glistening as though she'd been crying.

"Daniel?" she said in a loud whisper through the open window, as though she couldn't quite believe it was him. "What are you doing here?"

"Sorry to wake you."

"You didn't. I couldn't sleep. It's morning now anyway."

"Sorry about Max. You'd never believe he'd once been a highly trained and decorated service dog working special ops."

"Yes, I can. I love him. He's the best puppy in the whole wide world."

She put her hand on the screen, and Max whimpered, putting his paws on the sill, trying to lick her palm through the mesh.

"And he loves you too, clearly." Watching the two together, Daniel's heart squeezed. Max and Rachel were the most important things in his life, and outside TSI, the closest things he had to a real family. He couldn't imagine anything happening to either one of them.

"I just relieved the security guard and was going to sit out here and wait for you to wake up." One thought had driven him that morning: *What if she needs me, and I'm not there?*

He had to be close to her. He would take no more chances with her life. If he couldn't be in her bedroom, he'd be just outside the window.

The sun was starting to rise, painting the sky in yellows, oranges, and reds. It had been a long night. Rachel's hand on the curtain was trembling.

"Babe, what's wrong?" he asked, attempting to look past her into her bedroom, but she stepped in his way.

"Wait here." The curtains dropped. Damn it! His hands fisted. She almost looked guilty, as though there was something she didn't want him to see. She'd probably just left her underwear on the floor or something. He'd found hers back at his place beneath a chair. He didn't intend to give them back.

When Rachel next appeared at the window, she was wearing denim jeans and a fitted black sweater.

"I had to disable the alarm; it sounds when the screens are tampered with."

She unhooked the screen and tossed him a small denim backpack. Max growled at it and snapped his jaws.

"Max!" Daniel said. "For Christ's sake. It's just a bag." Jesus, first her car, then her bedroom, now her backpack. What the hell was wrong with Max?

"You got a dead body in that bag?" Daniel joked, and the color drained from her face.

Despite Daniel's warning to keep quiet, Max lowered himself to the ground and continued to growl at the bag, his hackles raised.

Rachel shoved the curtains aside and stuck her leg out. "What are you doing?" Daniel asked, helping her to the ground.

"We can't talk here," Rachel said, closing the window behind her. "We'll wake up Ellie and the kids. Come on." She took his hand, and with Max following, still snarling at the bag she carried, she walked directly to the beach.

At the top of the sand dunes, Rachel dropped Daniel's hand and looked up and down the beach.

"Wait here, I'll be back," she said, hurrying off.

"Hey, Rach, wait up! We'll come with you." She was moving fast, but his strides were twice the length of hers, and it only took a few to catch up to her.

She stopped, placed a firm hand on his chest.

"I…" She wouldn't meet his eyes. "I have to do something. I'll be back. Please stay here."

Daniel frowned. "I'll come with you."

She shuffled her feet. "I have to do a quick wee," she said, looking up at him through her lashes. "I forgot to go before I left the house, and I don't want to go back in."

Daniel grinned. She could still be shy at times. "I'll meet you back here, then." He moved back to the top of the sand dunes.

———◆———

Rachel felt Daniel's eyes on her as she wound her way through the bushes that anchored the sand dunes and kept the strong winds coming directly off the Indian Ocean from blowing them away.

She lowered herself into a squat and pretended to do her business long enough to see Daniel turn away.

How easy it had become for her to lie now. She'd lied about the scry to everyone: Daniel, Mark, Pia, and the team. She hadn't even told Ellie.

She'd picked through the bushes until she'd found a spot she was satisfied with, taking careful note of where she was. Not that she could ever imagine wanting to see the scry again. Ever.

Rachel took the crystal ball out of her denim bag and held it in her hands a moment. Tears blurred her vision, and she blinked them back. She'd been horrified watching what she'd done to Trey. How could she have done that?

She loved Trey!

The image of the demon flashed in her mind. Its eyes, so viciously cold, radiated a foul, ungodly hatred. She felt as though she'd looked into the eyes of Satan himself.

She'd locked eyes with it for only a second or two, but the connection was enough to blacken a part of her very soul. There was a poison in her blood now, from that… that *thing*. She never wanted to see it again.

She looked over to where Daniel was kneeling, patting Max. A cold breeze washed over her, and she shivered. She should never have kept the scry in the first place. What had she been thinking? She should have given it to Mark and Pia with the Ouija board. Why the hell she'd kept it was a mystery. And it was so not like her to be so dishonest.

Nothing made sense anymore.

Terror raced through her veins. *What have I started by keeping it, and how do I stop it?* She prayed it wasn't too late.

She dug a hole, as deep as her fingers would go, put the scry inside, and covered it over. Hearing a noise, she glanced sharply to her left. A dark mist in the shape of a man stood there, staring at her. Her heart leapt into her throat.

Rachel glanced to her right, saw Daniel at the top of the sand dunes, and when she looked back, the man was gone.

A horrible, sick feeling came over her.

Get up, go back to Daniel. Fast.

But she couldn't move. She patted the soil covering the scry, then her fingers began digging. Once again, she held the scry in her palms. It immediately calmed her racing pulse. She choked out a sob. She couldn't leave it.

The clouds over her head began to churn, like the clouds in the glass.

She was torn. The scry terrified her. She hated it.

Then why was it so damn hard to put it in the hole and walk away?

The scry began to vibrate in her hands. She heard the captain calling out to her. Begging her to help him reach his wife. She felt his pain; it connected with her own.

"I'll help you," she said. She put the scry into her bag and stood. "I'll hurt her, like she hurt you."

Daniel was looking at her, hands on his hips. He had to be wondering what she was doing. She gave a little wave, crouched back down again.

What the hell *was* she doing? She dropped her bag and closed her eyes. Forced herself to remember the face of the demon that had stared out at her from the scry's depths.

She never wanted to see that face again. That evil grin, the needle-like fangs, those cold eyes of death.

Rachel retrieved the scry from her bag. It hummed in her hands, the vibration soothing her. *I can't leave it!*

She forced her hands to release the scry.

It plopped back into the hole.

Rachel squeezed her eyes shut, kept Daniel's face firmly in her mind, and covered the scry with sand. A growl, something that sounded like an angry, wounded dog, came from behind her. The hairs on the back of her neck stood on end.

Don't look. Do not look at it.

Rachel stood, opened her eyes, focused on Daniel and Max. On *only* Daniel and Max, to the exclusion of all else.

Show no fear.

The marks on her back burned so intensely she almost cried out. She wanted to turn around, but knew she could not, should not.

Show no fear.

Rachel kept her back to the strange howling behind her. She didn't know what she'd do if she looked and saw the demon's face.

I'm not scared of you.

Rachel brushed the sand off her hands and took note of where she was. The largest round bush of its type. It was covered in flowers, its foliage a lush green. It was two meters in front of the sixth fence post from her sister's gate.

Bearings committed to memory, Rachel walked directly back to Daniel, her heart galloping in her chest. She wiped away the layer of sweat that prickled on her forehead despite the coolness of the morning breeze.

She felt marginally better. At the very least, she had done something significant. Sent a clear message to whatever it was that was watching her.

By getting rid of the scry, Rachel had made sure there was now nothing in her sister's house from that ship. The Ouija board was safe with Mark, the scry buried at the beach.

She released a long, slow breath. She just had to work out how to deal with knowing what she'd done to Trey. How to live with that knowledge without it destroying her.

Should she confess to Daniel?

Would he hate her?

Of course he would. She hated herself.

It was even more important now that she find Rob. He would be able to confirm that what the scry had shown her was true. Because even though she had seen it with her own eyes, a part of her still believed she wasn't capable of doing something so heinous. And if she was…?

Well, that wasn't something she could accept.

Rachel dragged her thoughts back to her sister and Sally. With the scry safely buried, she hoped that the demon would depart and this would be over.

And that the demon—and the captain—would leave Sally alone.

Chapter Twenty-Five

Daniel watched Rachel walk back to him, and his chest warmed. It didn't matter whether she was wearing a skin-tight red dress, jeans and a jumper, or a hessian sack: it was the woman herself, her essence, the being inside her skin, that caused such a powerful reaction inside him.

Reaching him, she raised her brows in surprise and gave him a small smile. "You brought a blanket?" Her voice was uneven, and her hand trembled as he assisted her down to sit with him. Was it just what had happened with Sally that had her so shaken up, or was it something else?

"The team carry blankets as standard equipment for victims and people suffering from shock." He shrugged. "Things like that."

"Oh." After a pause, she said, "You must see some awful things in your job."
You have no idea.

"It's also handy for sitting with pretty girls on the beach," Daniel said lightly. She was still pale and shaking, but some of her color was returning. He handed her a small bottled water.

Max sniffed around, going straight to Rachel's denim bag. Daniel expected him to react again, but he walked away, taking a seat just past their feet.

"Good boy, Max," Daniel said. At least Max had calmed down.

A brisk morning breeze blew as the sun made its slow ascent into the sky. Daniel took off his jacket and wrapped it around Rachel's shoulders. When he put his arm around her, she leaned into him, released a long breath, and shuddered.

"Babe, what's going on? You're trembling."

She tucked her hands beneath her legs and took a moment too long to answer.

"Ellie is upset, which of course is understandable. She wants to tell Sally what parents are supposed to say to their children. Ghosts don't exist; now go to sleep." Rachel chewed her bottom lip. "But we both know she can't. Someone really was in her room with her."

"What makes you say that?" Daniel asked, his muscles tensing. What had he missed?

"Because she said his name was Captain."

Daniel's heart stopped. "Captain. You mean the dead captain from the ship?"

"Too much of a coincidence not to be, don't you think?"

Daniel's jaw clenched. Somehow, he would have preferred that Madden had broken in.

"I need to talk to Pia, but I'll try her at a respectable hour."

Daniel frowned. To TSI, including Pia, there were no such things as respectable hours.

"Want me to get through to Ryder for you?"

"Thanks, but no. I've taken care of it now," Rachel said.

"What do you mean, you've taken care of it?" Daniel asked slowly, not liking the way she'd said that.

Rachel shrugged, and Daniel narrowed his eyes. "What did you do?"

"It doesn't matter," she said dismissively, and his gut tightened further.

"Everything that concerns you matters."

"Listen," she said, her eyes meeting his. "It's sexy when you go all detective on me, but not now. I'm exhausted. There's so much I need to get straight in my head, but I can't right now."

Daniel ground his teeth. He wanted to say no, to press her. But she looked emotionally shattered, so close to tears, he let it go for now. What could she possibly have done anyway while she'd been in her sister's house?

"I won't let anything hurt you." Daniel placed a finger beneath her chin, and she twisted her body so that she was facing him.

"Not everything is in your control," Rachel said, her eyes sad. She wasn't deliberately trying to be cruel, but her words sliced him in the worst possible way. When it mattered most, would he be able to keep her safe?

"I'll go to my grave trying." His voice was low and gruff. He placed his palms on both sides of her face and stared into her eyes.

Then he moved in and kissed her. Hard. She placed her hands on his shoulders and kissed him back.

"It feels different now, doesn't it? Between us, I mean."

"Yes." He held his breath.

She was waiting for him to say more, but he didn't know how to tell her. Did she want a man who was away all the time and could be killed on the next case he worked on? A man who killed people? Even now, he was planning to get revenge for his father's murder. How did that reconcile with marriage? Children?

Yet… somehow his mates Blade and Ryder had found women and made it work. But those were exceptional circumstances, exceptional women. Daniel looked at Rachel, and his heart squeezed. Rachel was every bit as exceptional as Sage and Pia, and in his eyes, even more so.

Rachel was different from every other woman he'd ever met.

He was different when he was with her.

"We'll figure out how to make this work," Daniel said. Because they had to. There was no alternative.

Rachel's eyes glistened in the dawn light, and a tear rolled down her cheek.

"What did I say?"

"Nothing." Rachel turned her head so he couldn't see her tears.

"Don't push me away." *Don't you dare. Not when I know I can't live without you.*

Rachel shook her head sadly. "You wouldn't want me if you knew."

"Knew what?" Daniel tensed.

Rachel shook her head. "I'm not a very good person, Daniel."

"Bullshit." What the hell was she talking about?

Another tear rolled down her cheek. She angrily wiped it away.

He placed his hand beneath her chin, turned her face toward his. "You're the one of the best people I know."

"Don't say that." Rachel squeezed her eyes shut, and when she opened them, he saw a reserve, a distance, he didn't like there.

"I need to be around when my sister wakes up. I need to be there for Sally," Rachel said, standing.

"Want me to come inside with you?" Daniel asked, rising too, refusing to allow the space she was trying to put between them. He wanted them back to where they'd been when she was on his couch and in his arms.

Back to when she'd wanted him to hold her.

Rachel shook her head. "No."

The pain that constricted his chest made his eyes sting.

Her fingers tangled in his hair, and the look she gave him spiked his adrenaline. He was going to lose her, wasn't he?

"Tell me what I need to do." *Tell me what you want me to be, and I'll move heaven and earth to make it happen. Just don't push me away.*

Fight for me.

"I like your hair long," she said, twisting the strands in her fingers.

"Then I'll never cut it."

"Don't be silly," she said, brushing off his comment.

He frowned. He meant it. Not about the long hair part, but about doing whatever she asked of him.

"Daniel, there is something you can do for me."

A small measure of relief washed over him. "Name it."

He traced his fingers over her lips. Her breath hitched, and desire burned behind her beautiful blue eyes. Before she looked away.

What was this about? He didn't believe for one fucking second she didn't want him. She wanted him as much as ever, as much as he wanted her.

If she wasn't going to fight for him, he'd fight for her. For *them*.

She had her hand on his chest, but she was keeping more than just a physical distance between them. Fuck that. He shoved her hand away and yanked her close to him. The beating of her heart against his chest reassured him. She was still here with him. All he had to do was work out how to keep her there.

"What is it you need?" Daniel searched her face.

"You can find people, right?"

"Yes." Daniel was relieved she'd asked something he was confident on delivering. "Who are you looking for?"

"The captain's wife."

Chapter Twenty-Six

The beast wanted him to kill Anna-Marie Edwards. Despite the harsh Australian sun streaming down on him, an icy chill caused Rob to shiver.

The demon was enraged. He was unable to enter Anna-Marie's house. It was just like a church with all the fucking holy light and protection all around it. It was sickening.

There were lots of places a demon could go, but Anna-Marie's house was not one of them. Rob's mouth began to foam, and a low growl like a feral animal's came out of him when he went anywhere near it.

Above Anna-Marie's door was a crucifix. It burned Rob's eyes to look at it, causing him to hiss in pain. He spat on the ground.

He moved to the rear of the property.

Rachel should not have buried the scry.

She was failing to succumb, and the demon was not happy.

Rachel was supposed to be easy prey for the demon; he had only to stir what was already inside her. The girl was pretty on the outside, but so deliciously tormented on the inside. Her psyche was ripped to shreds over dear daddy's infidelity. So much grief, so much anger over her mother's suicide. The demon had messed with Rachel during her early childhood, appearing in the darkness night after night, until she'd been too frightened to sleep.

Until her dear old granny had thwarted his fun. Without Rachel's mother knowing, she'd hidden crystals in the corners of Rachel's room, drawn symbols of protection under Rachel's mattress, and once replaced the water in her fish tank with holy water. Stupid old bag.

The demon had known the time would come when Rachel was older and more useful, and now he had an abundance of riches to work with. How easily he'd gained her sympathy when she'd thought the sweet captain had been betrayed.

Rob heard these thoughts, and more, in his mind, alongside his own. There were long stretches of time now where he didn't remember anything at all. Just woke up, having no idea where he was or how he'd gotten there.

But right now was a rare lucid moment. And he clung to the tiny piece of himself that remained for as long as that might be.

Was he lucid because of the strong religious energy that radiated outward from the house like a furnace? It formed a protective shield of sorts around the building. The demon found the high vibrations repulsive.

Rob knew Rachel would come here; he'd heard her ask the detective for the address. The demon needed Rachel to kill Anna-Marie. Rachel could still enter the house. Rob, with the demon so fully inside of him, no longer could.

And if she failed…?

The demon would kill her.

Anna-Marie was dangerous, the only thing the demon feared.

Rob had done what he could to protect Rachel, but there was little he could do for her now. He was weak. When he lost consciousness this time, he would probably be lost to total possession. The demon would use him, chew up his body, then spit it out.

Then move on to Rachel.

Rob had never been significant, just a tool to help the demon get what he really wanted.

A new high priestess.

Maia had turned her back on generations of lightwork and healing when she'd summoned the archdemon of Hell, Sohn-Zae, in a fit of rage over her husband's betrayal.

Maia had been a powerful white witch, but in that one ill-fated decision, that one weak moment when jealousy had clouded her judgment and overridden a lifetime of spiritual practice, she'd made a mistake. A terrible, irreversible mistake. She had invited into her soul an evil she couldn't control. No one could control true evil; it didn't play by rules.

Maia's followers, her whole circle, had paid the price for her mistake. But not until their entire village was dead. Hundreds of men, women, and children were influenced by the new cult of Sohn-Zae. Sacrifices, both human and animal, had become commonplace, and depravity of the grossest kind had spread throughout the district.

The lives of many now depended on Rachel's ability to resist the demon and cleanse the possessed object, banishing Sohn-Zae back to Hell.

If Rachel failed to live up to the demon's expectations, the scry would continue on to Sally, and then to her children, until Sohn-Zae found a new high priestess.

That was how the scry's legacy worked, following the bloodline of Maia, down through the generations. Only, Maia had summoned a demon, and the scry had become a cursed object.

A demon had no real power to do his evil work on the earthly plane except through a human it had possessed. Through the scry, the demon could reach people.

Through the scry, the demon could possess Rachel. And then Sally.

An influential person, such as Maia, could draw unlimited followers through the power of a cult, brainwashing and manipulating weaker souls. The demon's dark energy was so great, he could influence a mother to sacrifice her very own child. The ultimate. The sweetest taste...

Rachel would make a wonderful high priestess. People gravitated toward her; the rise in popularity of her band was testament to that. Rachel's human body would be an advantageous suit for a demon to wear.

Sohn-Zae was hungry for his new cult.

He was hungry for new souls.

But there was a slight complication this time around.

Anna-Marie.

Anna-Marie held the demon's death in her hands.

Rob finished tying a rope around his wrists, the rest of the rope looped around a tree. He'd tied the knots, so of course, he could untie them. But they were substantial enough to give someone enough time to get away from him if he were overcome again. Though he'd always been strong, this last week had taken its toll on him, emotionally and physically. His grip on sanity was fading fast.

He didn't know how much longer he'd have any recollection of who he was. Certainly not longer than today.

Moving to the end of his rope, Rob kept watch on the driveway. He glimpsed a statue of Jesus in the garden.

The demon bared his teeth, and Rob doubled over in pain. Bile rose from his throat, spilling out of his mouth, running down his neck. It burned, like hydrochloric acid being poured onto flesh.

Rob stilled. Listened intently as a motorbike sped toward them.

The demon inside him hissed and growled.

The detective, on a fancy black Suzuki Hayabusa, came flying down the road, slowing to do a drive-by of the house. Of course, he would want to check out Anna-Marie's house himself; he would be curious as to why Rachel had asked him for the address.

The demon inside him snarled.

Rob smiled.

He'd found his way out.

Chapter Twenty-Seven

Daniel cruised past Anna-Marie Edwards's place: an average-size house, neat as a pin, with a white picket fence and a stunning rose garden. The home was something you'd see on the cover of a magazine. Except for the religious items dotted around the front like garden gnomes.

The property was a bush block, an acre lot with a dirt road at the back. Daniel circled around, riding by the rear entrance.

His eyes caught on a movement. He backed off on the throttle, every sense he possessed on high alert. Standing among the shadows of a tall gum tree was a man. Instinct from years of training told him what his eyes were too far away to confirm.

The man was Rob Madden.

Daniel slammed on the brakes, the tires sliding on the gravel driveway.

The fuck?

He pulled off his helmet and stepped off the bike, grabbing his pistol from its holster.

"Madden!" Daniel called out, holding his weapon in front of him with both hands. "Stay where you are. Keep your hands where I can see them. Put your hands behind your head, and kneel down on the ground." Madden did not comply, and Daniel approached carefully, repeating the order until he was only a few feet away.

The branches of the gum tree twisted like grisly arms above Madden's head, and a five-foot-long western brown snake slithered through the dry grass just behind Madden. Daniel remained perfectly still a short moment, and the snake passed by.

Daniel had the uncomfortable feeling he was being watched. The morning was unnaturally still, not a single birdcall, not a breath of wind. Not taking his aim off Madden, he scanned the area around them.

No one else was there.

But his every muscle was tense, adrenaline keeping his pulse racing, far more so than the situation warranted. Madden was no match for someone of Daniel's size, skill, and training. And he didn't appear to be armed.

And yet, Daniel's instincts warned him to approach with the caution he'd take apprehending a diseased psychopath wielding a blood-filled syringe.

Madden yawned, as though amused by Daniel's brief moment of apprehension. Although barely seconds had passed, Daniel had the sensation that Madden could peer right inside Daniel's head, hear every thought.

Fuck. You. Daniel wordlessly told him.

Madden smiled, and Daniel tamped down his emotions, slid into that cool, detached space that kept him clear-headed and neutral in his assessment and response.

Madden barely resembled the man he'd once been. Aside from the beard and the stench that emanated from him, his face was contorted, his expression twisted into a slack smile, a trickle of drool running down his chin. But his eyes… His eyes were black pools of evil, direct portals straight down into the darkest depths of Hell.

Daniel was no expert like Pia, but he was pretty damn sure Madden had been possessed by the demon.

Madden was tangled in a rope, wrapped around the thick trunk of the tree, knots around both wrists.

If Rachel saw him now, she'd be horrified.

"Madden," Daniel said, this time with less edge. "Don't do this the hard way."

Madden remained still as Daniel read him his rights. There was something slightly crazed in Madden's stare, like he didn't care if he lived or died. And that was the most dangerous kind of man. The one with nothing to live for.

"Sorry to disappoint you, detective. I'm a little tied up at the moment." Madden held out his bound wrists. "Seems this old gum tree has arrested me first."

Remembering how unpredictable Jake had been, Daniel proceeded with caution. Keeping his gun trained on Madden, Daniel reached into his pocket with his left hand for his knife.

"I'm going to cut the rope. Are you going to give me any trouble?"

"You're going to have to ask Constable Gumtree here." Madden's mouth formed something that might have been intended as a smile, but instead just showed teeth in serious need of brushing and let loose breath that could strip paint.

Daniel slid the gun into the back of his jeans and moved closer. In one swift move, Daniel freed Madden's wrists, yanked them behind his back, and had him down on the ground with his knee on Madden's spine before Madden could blink those cold soulless eyes again.

"Aww, detective. I never knew you cared."

Daniel cut the rope that attached Madden to the tree and used the excess to bind his wrists together behind his back.

But before he could tie off the knot, Madden bucked beneath him, throwing Daniel onto his back, momentarily winding him. Daniel scrambled up into a crouch. *What the...?*

He'd had his whole body weight on Madden, his knee firmly pressed down onto his back, Madden's arms tied behind him and useless. Madden's move shouldn't have been possible, the force with which Daniel had been thrown unnatural. Thank God Daniel still felt the reassuring presence of his gun firmly wedged in the back of his pants.

The force of Daniel's fall had caused his knife to fly out of his hands, and it was now in Madden's, who had managed to slice the rope off one wrist. Rope coiled like a snake from the other.

"Detective," Madden said in a rush, surprising Daniel with the abrupt change of tone. "Hurry! I don't want to be brought in. Kill me. I *need* you to kill me." Then he hissed, grunting as though he'd been hit by an unseen assailant.

Daniel pulled his gun and rose cautiously, studying Madden's unusual movements, and put himself face to face with Madden. "I would love nothing more than to grant that wish, but as it so happens, Rachel wants you alive." *And she'll be in more danger if you're dead.*

Madden began to cry. "Tell her I love her." Madden dropped to his knees, burying his face in one palm while he clutched the knife with the other.

Something moved behind Daniel, and he whipped his head around. No one was there. Daniel's heart pounded, and his pulse raced as though an attack was imminent.

And perhaps it was.

"Put the knife down, and come with me." Daniel's voice was calm and clear in the oddly still air.

Madden shook his head and said urgently, "No time. You have to kill me. If you don't, more will die."

"You won't be able to hurt anyone locked behind bars."

"You're an idiot if you believe that. Hurry, I don't have much time. I can't hold him back much longer."

"Drop the knife, Madden."

Madden lunged at Daniel. Daniel jumped back so that the knife only nicked his skin.

"Put the knife down."

"Please," Madden begged. "Kill me. It won't let me kill myself. Do it for Rachel, if you won't do it for me."

"Dammit, Madden! I can't kill you. I'm taking you in." Frustration tightened his stomach painfully, and his finger twitched on the trigger.

Madden lunged for him again, this time landing on top of him. He held the knife high above his head.

Madden looked Daniel directly in the eyes. Daniel watched his eyes change, his pupils dilating until his eyes were pure black. Ice washed over Daniel. He was staring into a face marked by pure malice and hatred. The putrid odor of a decaying corpse poured over him, turning his stomach.

Madden smiled, and Daniel knew he was looking into the eyes of the demon. Whatever was left of Madden was now gone.

Madden brought the knife down—

Daniel swung the pistol sideways, deflecting the blade. Madden dropped the knife and grabbed for the gun. He fought like a wildcat, and they rolled back and forth on top of each other, struggling for the dominant position. With incredible strength, a strength he couldn't possibly possess, Madden peeled the pistol from Daniel's grip.

A single gunshot rang out through the still morning air.

Chapter Twenty-Eight

It was a picturesque morning, the type Western Australia was famous for. The ocean was calm, clear and turquoise, the sun reflecting off the water like tiny shining crystals. There was not a breath of wind, and Rachel inhaled deeply, filling her lungs with warm salty air and the scent of freshly brewed coffee. Was there anything better?

"Come, sit with me." Elise was leaning back on her sun lounger, a hat covering eyes that were watching her children play. Rachel sat next to her and took in the view.

"How is Sally this morning?" Rachel asked.

Elise smiled. "She's fine. Woke up like nothing happened."

Rachel sipped her coffee, Sally's laughter reaching her ears as she splashed in the waves with Liam.

Daniel had left just after sunrise, and Rachel had slept for a couple of hours, waking up surprisingly fresh. She was relieved to have disposed of the scry. With any luck, that would be the last she saw of the demon.

"This is special, isn't it?" Elise said, waving her hand in front of her to indicate where they were, Sally swimming in the ocean, Liam on his little chair in the sand under the shade of a weeping peppermint tree.

"You are so lucky," Rachel said. "We don't do this often enough." She paused. "I'm sorry it's all been such a mess. I'll make it up to you, I promise."

Ellie reached over, held her hand. "A sister is not only there for the good times."

Tears pricked Rachel's eyes. "True."

"Although I hate what happened with the ship, I'm glad this happened close to me. I'd be worried sick about you otherwise."

Ellie stretched out in her sunchair, and at first Rachel thought her sister was relaxed, enjoying the morning, but on closer inspection, she appeared deep in thought. Although she was very still, her eyes pointed straight ahead beneath her hat, her fingers tapped the arms of the chair.

Rachel took off her soft white denim jacket and lay back in her shoestring singlet top to soak up some rays.

Elise tossed her a tube of sunscreen. "Put this on," she said. "And you should be wearing a hat. The temperature is going to heat up again soon. It's going to be the hottest summer on record they predict."

Rachel smiled. She hated being told what to do, but somehow didn't mind—as much—when it came to Elise. "You're such a natural mother," Rachel said, trying to make it sound like a grumble.

She unscrewed the top of the total block-out sunscreen and sighed. "This stuff will reflect enough sun to blind an alien on Mars."

Rachel laughed, but strangely, Elise didn't. She kept her eyes on Sally bouncing through the water, wearing a full-body swimsuit.

Finally, Elise spoke. "Nothing you have means anything at all, if you don't take the time to appreciate it."

Rachel's stomach knotted at her sister's melancholy tone. "Are you talking about you or me?" she asked, unable to shake off a sense of unease.

"I've got a confession to make," Elise said. "Don't be mad."

"What?"

"I told Daniel to stay away from you. That he was nothing but heartbreak you don't need."

"Oh my God!" Rachel said, hitting her sister with her jacket. "You didn't!"

Elise laughed and swatted away the jacket. "Relax, baby girl, it's not as though he listened, is it? When I called you about Sally, you arrived at the house with Daniel and that just-fucked look."

Rachel flushed and hid behind her oversized sunglasses. "I did not!" She knew the look her sister was talking about; she'd seen it on herself in the mirror every time Daniel had visited. "You shouldn't have said anything to him. I feel like my mum has told the neighborhood bad boy to stay away."

"Yeah, well, the neighborhood bad boy didn't listen. Clearly." She smiled. "I've seen the way he looks at you now. I was wrong about him. I can tell a casual fling when I see one, and I can assure you, the way Daniel looks at you? Casual is not it."

Rachel's pulse picked up the way it always did when she thought about Daniel, but she didn't respond.

"The look in his eyes last night was the look of a man in love," Ellie said.

Rachel sat up in surprise. "You don't know what you're talking about. Daniel doesn't do love." She ignored the flutter of her stomach at her sister's words. Rachel knew she was in love with Daniel, had been for years. But was he in love with her?

"You haven't told him how you feel, have you?"

Rachel sighed. "No."

"Why?"

"It's complicated."

"You wouldn't want something to happen and never get the chance to tell him how you feel. Life is short. Sometimes even shorter than we think."

Rachel turned to her sister, her stomach clenching uncomfortably. More than the words, it was the strange melancholic tone in her sister's voice that concerned her.

"Are you talking about Daniel, or something else?"

"I—" Ellie shook her head as though changing her mind about what she was going to say. "You need to tell him. I have a feeling if you do, he'll open up to you too."

"Or else he'll run a mile."

Ellie twisted in her chair. "I bet Daniel is as out of his depth with this—with you—as you are with him. You're probably the only woman he's felt like this about, and he hasn't a damn clue what to do."

"You think so?"

"I do."

Sally rushed up to them, her blonde curls dripping.

"Have you finished swimming already, sweetheart?"

"No," Sally said. "I just came back for a drink."

"Here you are," Rachel said, handing Sally her drink bottle.

"Can I go build a sandcastle with Liam?"

"Of course, honey."

They watched Sally run back to the sand.

"She's so sweet," Rachel said.

"Lay back," Elise said in a strange voice. "Feel the cool breeze on your skin. Go on, it's nice. I've got something I need to say. It can't wait any longer."

A little confused again, by the abrupt turn in conversation and Elise's odd tone, Rachel did as her sister asked, taking a lungful of warm sea air as she did so. The sun hit her cheeks, and its golden warmth felt nice. Even if the sun wouldn't get through the layer of reflective slime on her arms and chest.

"You love them, don't you?" Elise asked. "The kids, I mean."

Rachel turned her head, eyed her sister's profile. "You know I do."

"I mean really, really love them. Like they were your own."

"Absolutely." If someone were to threaten their safety right now? Rachel shuddered. "I'd kill for them," she said, without a moment's hesitation or doubt.

Elise nodded. "That's what I'm counting on."

"Ellie, you're scaring me. What's going on?"

Elise was silent a long time, watching her daughter play with her little brother. Every moment that ticked by increased Rachel's unease.

"I had a scare recently," Elise said, and Rachel's chest tightened. Ellie shook her head. "Ah, hell. It wasn't a scare. Rach, I have cancer. Melanoma. I had it removed, a wide local excision, to reduce the reoccurrence of melanoma around that area. For a while... waiting to find out if it had spread... I was just so scared. That's when I first called you to come. I just... I just needed you. I wanted you with me while I went through it."

The world shuddered to a halt along with Rachel's heart.

"You didn't tell me." Such an inane—and obvious—thing to say, but they were the only words she could form.

"I tried," Elise said. "But you were so excited about that record label that was interested in your band... It was just hard to have that conversation over the phone. So I thought if you were here, we could spend some quality time together, you know like we used to when we were kids. I could tell you what was going on with me, and you..." Elise's eyes glistened. "And you would tell me it's all going to be all right."

Rachel's eyes stung, her heart lodged firmly in her throat. She reached out, took Ellie's hand. Her skin was thinner somehow, more translucent, the bones too near the surface.

"It *is* going to be all right," Rachel said, blood roaring in her ears. "You *are* going to be all right, aren't you?"

Any other possibility was unthinkable.

Elise turned her eyes to Rachel. They were calm. There was a resignation in them that made Rachel's world spin around her. "There's a chance it's spread, but right now, I have no option but to remain positive and hope that's not the case."

Rachel ignored the adrenaline that flooded her veins and made her want to get up and run. Run away from her sister and this new reality. She wanted to scream, pound her head to remove the words that were now the only things she could hear going around and around in her mind. *Cancer. Melanoma.* She kept her body riveted to the chair and pretended to be calm, at least on the outside.

"So what—" Rachel cleared her throat. "So what does that mean? What have the doctors said?"

Elise wiped away a tear that had rolled down her cheek. "Depending on my test results, I might have to go in for more rigorous treatment. My whole life is up in the air at the moment. Of course, the only thing on my mind through all of this has been the kids. Who would look after them if...?"

"But Don... of course he'd take care of them?"

Elise twisted her earring. "He'll do what he can, yes. But it's a lot for him to cope with. He loves his job; he's so high up now that he has to be away a lot. And if he gives up work, what will they all do for money?" She sighed. "It's important that things continue as normally as possible for Sally and Liam if the worst happens. And at the end of the day..." Elise looked at Rachel. "You are the closest thing to *me* those kids have."

Rachel choked out a sob. *No!* Nothing could happen to her sister. That wasn't how life was supposed to turn out. Elise was just twenty-nine. They were supposed to end up little old grandmas on their rocking chairs, watching their grandchildren play.

"I just can't believe this." Rachel barely got the words past her thick tongue. The whole thing felt so surreal.

Elise reached out and took her hand, and the action made her cruel words real. Rachel wanted to take away the last few minutes, go back to bickering with her sister.

Tears streamed unchecked down Rachel's cheeks, burning through lids that were squeezed shut.

"Too much sunbaking when we were teenagers," Elise mused sadly. "Getting the perfect tan wasn't worth the price I'm paying now."

Now she knew why Elise had insisted on the sunscreen. And of course Rachel had had to be flip about it.

"I have to go to Perth to have more tests," Ellie said.

It was on the tip of Rachel's tongue to invite them to stay at her place, but she had a one-bedroom apartment in the middle of the city. Not the ideal setup for a family, especially a baby.

"I don't want to take the kids, unsettle them," Elise said. "But I can if I need to."

"Ellie, tell me what you need." Rachel twisted her fingers in frustration. She felt powerless, frightened, angry at the whole situation. But she wanted to do something. Sitting in this chair while her sister was going through this hell was torture.

"I wanted to ask if you wouldn't mind staying here if needed. Look after the kids if I need further treatment. It all depends on how the tests come back."

"Of course. You don't need to ask. You can count on me." The pieces of the puzzle started falling together. Why Ellie had been so adamant about Rachel helping the kids at mealtimes, making sure she knew how to dry them properly after a bath, the particular way Liam liked his Weet-Bix in the morning, how much Vegemite Sally liked on her toast.

A sheen of sweat broke out over Rachel's forehead, and she shivered with the aching anguish tearing her apart inside.

"What about your singing?" Elise asked.

"With Trey dead and Rob gone, I don't even have a band anymore." She was officially unemployed. But nothing mattered except being there for her sister, for her niece and nephew. "I'm sorry all this happened, and we didn't have the fun this trip was supposed to be. I've been a lousy sister."

"Nonsense," Elise said. "I didn't let this diagnosis take over my life when I got it, and I'm not going to do it now. I just need to know—" Tears rolled unchecked down her cheeks. "I just need to know you'll be here… for the kids. I can't deal with any of this emotionally until I know they'll be taken care of. Nothing else matters to me."

Ah God… "Of course. Of course, I will. But nothing is going to happen to you. It can't be otherwise. I'd never do as good a job as you. The kids need you more than they need their irresponsible aunt, who can't seem to keep her life on track for more than fifteen minutes at a time." Rachel tried to laugh, but it caught in her throat and came out as a choked sob.

Elise pulled a tissue from her pocket and delicately blew her nose with shaky hands. "You are the most capable person I know," she said softly. "All the shit that happens to you, and you always land on your feet. You are gutsy, courageous, and have the biggest heart of anyone I know. Push comes to shove, there's no one I'd rather have on my team. Knowing I have you, now, and after I'm gone is my only light in any of this."

"But you're not going anywhere," Rachel said fiercely. "Right?"

"Right."

Elise pulled her sunglasses down over her eyes. "I'm not planning on giving up easily. I have to take a leaf out of my sister's book and grow some serious balls to fight this thing. I have two kids I want to see grow up and get married." She handed Rachel a tissue.

Rachel blew her nose. "Right. Plus, you need to be here to interfere in Sally's relationships like you have in mine."

"If you aren't married to your sexy hunk of a man by the time Sally is at marriage age," Elise said, "I'll post an ad in the local paper and sell you to the first man who replies."

Rachel grinned. "What if he's bald and has no teeth?"

"Especially if he's bald and has no teeth."

"Well, damn, I'd better snag Daniel then," Rachel said, the fantasy of marrying him setting off a flurry of butterflies in her stomach.

Elise looked at her. "And I want to be here to see you marry him too."

Rachel choked up again. "You and me against this," she said, a slightly modified version of their childhood mantra, *You and me against the world.*

Whenever life got rough—problems at school, cheating boyfriends, getting fired—no matter the issue, the sisters had always turned to each other.

Elise had always been Rachel's rock. Now it was Rachel's turn to be Ellie's. And Lord help her, she wasn't going to let her down.

They fell silent for a time.

"One thing I've learned through all this," Elise said, "is to take time out, appreciate the little things. Because those are the things that matter most in the end."

Rachel's chest squeezed painfully. "This is not the end, damn it."

"No. Bad choice of words. I just meant I know that when the end comes, *many years from now*," she emphasized, "I know that's what will be important. In a way, I'm kind of glad this happened. I was always busy running around, juggling my career with cleaning the house, going to the shops, preparing dinners, making sure the house was tidy. I never took the time to sit and watch the kids play. Just sit, knowing there's nothing else more important to do. Watch Sally's smile when she splashes Liam. Her laugh when he clumsily runs after her with his chubby little legs, the way she always stops and lets him catch her a moment before he gets upset. I remember doing that with you too."

Rachel looked at her sister. "You did?"

Elise smiled. "There are lots of things I remember while watching the kids. Things I wouldn't have, had I not taken the time to do it. This cancer, as horrible as it is, has also been the best thing that happened to me. I'm present now. Like I've finally shown up for life. Like the saying, live each day as if it were your last, because one day you'll be right."

"And that there is the reason I've always looked up to you," Rachel said. "I don't know how you got so wise, but you'd better stick around, because I haven't a hope in hell of living up to you."

"Don't underestimate yourself, kiddo."

Rachel watched her sister watching her children, the sun on her face—the same sun that was stealing her sister's very life—and hated the whole situation.

But peace and acceptance were in Ellie's serene smile, and Rachel remained silent, not wanting to steal a single second of contentment from her.

Elise's smile widened as she turned to Rachel. "At least I can take heart in knowing we exist in some capacity beyond this life."

Rachel felt fresh tears fall.

If no other good came from Rachel's harrowing experience with the ship, at least she'd proved to herself and Ellie that there was life after death. Rachel might have experienced the dark side of that process, but it made sense there were two sides to it, considering there were good and evil people on Earth.

Rachel *had* to believe that good people didn't get to suffer like the tormented souls she'd seen, the captain, the woman who'd summoned the demon…

There had to be a different place for people like her sister. A place of peace and untarnished love, a place where the beautiful souls went.

It was a small comfort, but one Rachel grasped onto with both hands.

Chapter Twenty-Nine

Rachel rinsed the bubbles off Liam's sippy cup and placed it upside down in the dish drainer. When Elise had dashed into town to run some errands, Rachel had insisted on looking after the kids. To reassure her sister—and herself—that she was indeed capable and dependable. She had given the kids lunch and put them down for their afternoon nap. So far, so good.

Ellie has cancer.

That awareness was a heaviness over Rachel now, a lead vise that compressed her chest. Her terrible fear for Elise wouldn't be lifted until the test results came back clear.

Elise just *had* to be okay. Life wouldn't be so cruel. Would it? And yet, bad things happened to good people all the time. Shouldn't Rachel be the one with cancer? She'd spent just as much time in the sun, maybe more so. And she didn't have two beautiful kids who depended on her. She didn't even have a job.

But until she was told otherwise, she'd remain positive for Elise.

At least Rachel could prove the welfare of her kids was one thing her sister didn't need to worry about. So, she'd given the kids a nice bath to wash off the sand from the beach, then made some fancy toasted sandwiches. Okay, they were plain toasted-cheese sandwiches, but she'd used the fancy sandwich press. Then she'd put them down for their afternoon nap, and exhausted, they'd gone straight to sleep.

Rachel glanced at the clock. Two-fifteen. Elise would be back any moment. She dried the last dish and looked around the kitchen in satisfaction. Ellie was going to come home to a clean kitchen and two happy kids, fed and fast asleep.

Rachel made herself a coffee, sat down at the kitchen table, and picked up a magazine.

Sally's scream broke the silence.

Knocking her cup off the table and sending coffee across the floor, Rachel ran into Sally's room.

"What is it, honey?"

Sally was huddled in her bed, blankets pulled around her chin. She spoke slowly, her little girl's voice soft and trembling. "There's a man in my room."

Rachel's heart stopped dead in her chest. *No!* She'd removed the scry from the house!

This has to stop! Elise has been through enough! Leave us alone!

Outwardly, Rachel kept her voice even, kept her rising panic from showing on her face.

"There's nothing in your room," Rachel said gently, in echo of Elise's words last time. "Mummy had this talk with you already." *Liar!* Rachel could feel the weight of unseen eyes on her. A chill down her spine, a breath on her neck.

"Yes, there is, Auntie Rachel."

Sally was visibly trembling, and Rachel moved to her. She tried to wrap her arms around the terrified girl, but Sally hugged her knees to her chest and resisted.

"Shh, honey. Remember what Mummy said? No monsters, just you in your beautiful fluffy pink bed."

"Why doesn't anyone believe me?" Sally started to cry.

Oh God, this was not good. Not good at all. Rachel looked around the room. The room was empty. Visually. But the space felt crowded.

"Where's the man, sweetheart?" Rachel asked, hoping she sounded calm. "Is he still here?"

"Yes. There." Sally pointed at an area not two meters from Rachel.

"Just right there by the wall?" Rachel could barely speak past the constriction in her throat.

"Uh-huh," Sally said. "It's the captain. Can't you see him?" She lowered her arm, tucking it under the quilt.

Rachel tried for what she hoped was a smile, swallowed hard and almost choked on the fear that had tightened her throat. "No, honey." Rachel couldn't see what Sally could, but Rachel had seen the captain in the scry. She scooped Sally up in her arms.

"Come with me. I have some cookies in the kitchen."

As she approached the door, she heard Liam giggling and babbling in the room next door. Instead of giving her comfort, the sound sent a chill skittering down her spine. Liam laughed again, as though he was reacting to someone—or *something*.

Rachel's blood ran cold. What if there was something in Liam's room as well? "Let's get your brother too," she said, but before they could leave Sally's room, the door slammed shut, trapping them inside.

Liam's babble was muffled now, but he was still talking to someone.

"The captain is upset," Sally said, her eyes wide with fear. "You've made him mad."

"Too bad," Rachel said, shifting Sally's weight in her arms. "Tell him I'll show him what mad is if he doesn't go away and leave you alone."

Rachel tried to turn the doorknob, but the metal seared her skin, and she jumped back.

She wanted to scream; it almost killed her to stifle the sound. But she didn't want to distress Sally any more than she already was. Rachel sucked in a shaky breath. *Show no fear.*

"The door handle isn't working."

Liam started to cry loudly in the next room, and Rachel's stomach twisted. *I have to get Sally out of this room. I have to get to Liam.*

She tried the door handle again, but it was still too hot to touch. A car pulled into the driveway. Was Elise back, or was it Daniel? She couldn't get out of the room to answer the door.

Rachel eyed Sally's lamp. She'd throw it through the window to attract attention if she needed to. The broken screen would also alert the security monitoring company.

The front door opened, and someone tossed keys onto the kitchen table. *Elise!*

"Ellie!" Rachel called out in her loudest, and hopefully calmest, voice. "The doorknob is broken! Sally and I are stuck. Can you open it for us?"

"She can't hear us," Sally said in a flat voice.

Liam continued to cry, but Rachel heard Elise next door with the baby. It gave her a small measure of relief that at least Liam was being cared for.

The temperature started to drop in Sally's room, and Rachel's teeth began to chatter. "Can you still see him?" she whispered, even as she knew the answer. The room was crackling with energy, and the scratches on Rachel's back had started to burn.

"Yes," Sally said. "Why can't you see him? He's right there."

Rachel swallowed. "Sally, I can't see him." *Except in the scry.* "So you need to tell me what he's doing, okay?"

"He's angry with you," Sally repeated.

"Why? What does he want?"

"He said he wants to show you something. He said you aren't listening."

The scry. Rachel had buried the scry, and now he couldn't communicate with her. Was that why he was making himself known to Sally? To force Rachel to listen? To retrieve the scry? Sally could see him with her eyes, whereas Rachel needed the scry.

"You want me to find your wife," Rachel said to the room. "If I find her, what do you want me to tell her?"

Suddenly, the air in the room turned opaque, a thick, roiling fog with a pungent smell. Rachel gagged.

"Did he answer?" Rachel asked.

Sally shook her head.

"I'll get the scry, so you can talk to me again. But you have to promise to leave Sally alone. Sally?" Rachel said. "Did he answer me?"

"The captain is gone now," Sally said. "*He* doesn't like you talking to the captain."

Rachel didn't need to ask who "he" was. Pure evil was in the room with them now; she felt its menacing presence chilling her bones, sending her heart racing erratically. She winced as the pained cries of tortured souls, their screams of agony, the horror of their violent deaths, filled her ears.

Can Sally hear that too?

It sickened Rachel to think so.

I have to get her out of here.

What damage would this do to a little girl? The emotional scars would last a lifetime. Rachel was no less terrified than if a flesh and blood serial killer were standing over them. Even more so. The demon's evil ran so much deeper than anything human ever could.

Blood thrashed past Rachel's ears, and she couldn't breathe. Her whole body trembled uncontrollably, and she struggled against an almost unbearable fear to remain calm and in control for Sally.

"I'm scared," Sally said, burying her head in Rachel's chest.

"Don't look, sweetheart." Rachel held her tight. She couldn't let Sally see the demon; the horror of his horned image had been burned forever in Rachel's mind.

She tried the doorknob again, ignoring the pain, knowing her skin would blister. The door still wouldn't open. She banged on it with her fist and screamed for Elise.

She eyed the window. Should she break it?

Rachel grabbed a T-shirt off the chair, wrapped it around her hand to protect it from the heat and tried the handle again. The handle still wouldn't turn, and the heat scorched the fabric.

The window.

Rachel crossed the room to Sally's lamp.

Sally peeked over Rachel's arm. Whatever she saw caused her to shriek. "Don't look at him," Rachel repeated, running her blistered hand over the back of Sally's head soothingly.

Anger tore through Rachel's body.

"Get out!" she shouted at the room, the lamp in her hand.

"He's in the corner." Sally pointed. "He's coming toward you."

Rachel instinctively threw the lamp in the direction Sally pointed. She knew the action would be futile against this threat, but it provided an outlet for her anger. The lamp smashed against the wall, the crash jarring in the small space.

Sally let out a little scream, and Rachel turned her back to the wall, sheltering Sally in her arms.

"Stay away from her!"

Something hissed in Rachel's ear. She felt a burning on her neck and knew without looking that the demon's claws had raked her skin.

There was a loud knock on the door. "Sally?" Elise called out. "Rachel? Are you in there? Open this door!"

And then, in a single moment, the room felt different. The temperature normalized, and it was instantly easier to breathe.

"He's gone," Sally said.

Rachel felt dizzy; the room spun. She stumbled as Sally wriggled out of her arms. Rachel blinked, struggling to adjust to the startling contrast of one moment experiencing blinding terror, the next being in the calm serenity of a little girl's room.

Sally ran to the door, turned the handle, and the door opened easily. "Mummy!"

Elise walked into the room and tugged on Rachel's arm. "You've got to come with me," she whispered urgently, her eyes bright with fear. "Sally, you stay here."

"What?" Sally screamed. "I'm not staying here. There's a—"

"You'll do as you're told, young lady," Elise snapped, and Rachel glanced at her with surprise. That was not like her.

"Ellie?" Rachel asked. "Is everything okay?"

"No," Elise said. "It's not okay. Stay here, Sally."

Rachel didn't want to contradict Elise in front of her daughter, but she also couldn't leave Sally in her bedroom either. What if the demon returned and Rachel was on the other side of the door and couldn't get in?

Rachel hugged Sally to her hip. "I've got her," Rachel said.

Elise shook her head. "She can't come."

Okay, this must be bad. She let go of Sally. "Go into the kitchen, sweetheart, and grab yourself a cookie. They're on the plate on the table. You can reach them."

Sally ran off.

Dread moved sluggishly through Rachel's veins as she followed Elise. In the hallway, Rachel saw Liam's little bed. It had been dragged out of the room and was now jammed across the hallway.

Ellie stopped and shook her head. "No, I can't do it."

"Do what?" Rachel asked.

"Go back in there." Elise whipped out her phone, dialed a number.

"Daniel," Ellie said. "How fast can you get here?"

Chapter Thirty

The manufacturers of Daniel's 4WD LandCruiser underestimated its top speed. Daniel pushed the vehicle to its limits, then skidded to a stop in Elise's driveway in a spray of rocks and dirt. Sam and Sean pulled up next to him, pouring out of their car and drawing their weapons.

Blade had sent them to assist with Madden's death earlier this morning. When the gun had gone off, Daniel had expected to be the one who'd been shot. Instead, Madden's lifeless body had slumped on top of him.

There'd been paperwork to do, a mountain of it, and red tape to get around. After the pressing details had been handled, the men had started to discuss Wilson's takedown scheduled for Wednesday night and had been in the thick of that conversation when Elise's frantic call had come through.

Max was barking frantically, and unable to silence him, Daniel left him in the car. Through the half-open window, Max gave him a sad, confused look, but it was safer this way. "Stay!" Daniel repeated firmly.

Daniel drew his weapon and held it in front of him, a glance at Sam and Sean confirming they too were armed and ready. Silently, Sean and Sam moved around the sides of the house.

Both hands on his weapon, Daniel walked a direct line to the front door, where he saw Elise huddled on the front porch beneath a blanket, Liam in her arms, Sally clinging to her other side crying. He had no idea what to expect when he entered the house. After Elise's call, he'd tried Rachel but got only static.

"Is there an intruder?" Daniel asked swiftly.

Elise shook her head.

"Is Rachel okay?"

Elise nodded, her eyes wide and unblinking.

Was Rachel the threat? Daniel thought of what had happened with Madden just a few hours ago. It was hard enough dealing with the demon as it was. How would he save her if it had gotten inside her? Pia had said Rachel would be safe from that while Madden was still alive.

Madden was now dead...

"Stay here."

Sam came back around the corner and took up position at the front door, back against the wall, weapon raised in front of him with both hands.

Daniel nodded at Sam. They were going in.

They entered the house, Daniel pushing the front door open with his boot. He didn't need to turn around to know Sam had his back.

"Rachel!" Daniel's chest clenched so tight he could hardly breathe. Where was she?

But then he saw her walking toward him, and his heart lurched, lodging in his throat. He assessed her critically, hating himself—and this situation—for his need to do so. Her eyes appeared normal. She wasn't carrying a weapon or an object that could be used as one. Her eyes were still gray, and other than being wide and bloodshot as though she'd been crying, they appeared to be responding correctly. They weren't glassy, or staring unusually, and her expression was familiar.

He moved to her. Leaving one hand on his weapon, he wrapped his other arm around her, brought her close to his chest.

"What's going on?" Daniel demanded, his eyes flicking around, taking in everything around them.

Sam followed close behind him. Rachel looked over his shoulder, eyes growing wide.

"It's okay," Daniel said quickly. "That's Sam."

"Oh, yes, I remember Sam. Hi. You won't need the gun."

Daniel eyed her carefully. She wasn't a sobbing mess like her sister out in front. She was calm. Almost too calm. Her eyes were narrowed, and her jaw was clenched. She was furious.

"You either," Rachel said, as though noticing Daniel's gun for the first time.

Sam and Daniel lowered their weapons but didn't put them away.

"Tell me what happened and make it fast." Sally was still sobbing on the front porch, her cries distraught, and here was Rachel, walking around the house like she wanted to take someone's head off.

Instead of answering, Rachel took his hand and led him down the hallway. Every step was like walking through thick, unpleasant mud. The very air he breathed into his lungs tasted stale. Daniel felt eyes on him, someone unseen watching his every move.

The hair on the back of his neck was standing on end, and a disturbing energy rolled through him. As though something walked down the hallway and right through him. The sensation was akin to a cold electrical shock, without the pain.

Daniel eyed the small child's bed that had been dragged out and across the hallway and instinctively raised his gun again as he entered the little boy's room.

He stood just inside the entrance. Daniel had been at the house all of sixty seconds, but each second had ticked by excruciatingly slowly, and he still hadn't determined the threat.

The room looked empty, but felt as crowded as a packed bar on a humid night. The air was thick, and sweat prickled across his skin, even though the room temperature was damn near arctic. His heart pounded erratically and he almost struggled to breathe.

His instincts were telling him he was about to be attacked, but he could see no visible imminent threat.

Rolling his shoulders, Daniel fought to find that ingrained state of alert calmness he usually slipped into so naturally during dangerous situations.

He flicked on the light, and that's when he noticed the wall, his blood turning to ice in his veins.

On the far side of the room were faces peering out from the wall. Shadowy and grainy, but clearly faces of men. Not on the surface like pictures or drawings, but somehow embedded into the wall. Peering out through it.

"What the ever-loving fuck is that?" Sam said at his side.

A foul smell permeated the room, its rank residue lining Daniel's nasal passages. It smelled of sulfur, of decaying flesh.

Icy fingers raked down his spine as the eyes of the faces seemed to focus on him.

"It's like looking at those old black-and-white photos where the old people stare at you without smiles," Sam said, stepping closer, but not too close. "Except these aren't photos. It's like the people are somehow actually coming in through the walls."

"Not helpful, mate," Daniel said, tossing a speaking glance at his partner.

Rachel stood back against the doorframe, shivering.

"I heard Liam laughing. I heard him talking to something." Rachel choked on the words. "Oh God, he was talking to the faces."

Daniel tucked his weapon into the waistband of his jeans, shrugged out of his jacket, and tossed it around her shoulders.

"Anything else I need to know about?" he asked softly.

"Is this not enough?"

Daniel glared at the faces, his fury needing an outlet. When he was after criminals, there was something satisfying about bringing about the resolution, taking them down. What the hell was he going to do here? Shoot the fuck out of the walls? And what about the strange goddamn feeling in the room, the sensation that someone—*something*—was standing in the corner watching their every move?

Feeding off their every reaction.

Drinking fear as though it were a lifeline.

Beneath his jacket, Rachel hugged her arms across her chest. Her face was deathly white, but her expression was hard, and she didn't meet his eyes. She was holding something back. What the hell had gone on here this morning?

Sean's bulky frame filled the door. "What the fuck?"

Sam grinned. "From this moment on, this is officially to be known as the 'what the fuck' case."

"Jesus H. Christ," Sean said, walking closer to the wall. Daniel took note that he stopped a full step back. Sean, who'd walk into a viper's nest without fear. "What the hell is this?" Sean rubbed his arms. "And why the fuck is it so cold in here?" He rolled his shoulders, and his eyes darted around the room. "Feels like I'm in a goddamn morgue. Smells like it too."

Yes, that's exactly what it felt like. The room was cold, the air heavy with the cloying stench of death.

"It's kind of like you've walked in on a crime scene," Sam said. "Except the bodies aren't bleeding all over the floor; they're coming out of the walls."

Rachel made a strangled noise, and Daniel tightened his arm around her shoulders.

"No need for you guys to stay," Daniel said to Sean and Sam before they really warmed up to their theory. Rachel was listening to their every word. The guys weren't deliberately being obtuse; it was just that not much could shock them anymore. This case clearly appealed to their curiosity.

"Thanks for coming. I can take it from here," Daniel said, crossing the room.

As creepy as fuck as this was, on a TSI level, there was no immediate threat, and Sean and Sam needed to get back to the Wilson case. Time was running out; they needed find Lilly Randall, and Daniel didn't want to tie up resources here when there wasn't a need.

The resources needed for this would come from Mark Collins and his team.

Sam shook his head in disbelief. "Glad I did. Wouldn't have believed it had you told me. This is something you have to see for yourself." He slapped Daniel on the back. "Glad it's you and not me. Give me Wild Wilson's gang of pussy peddlers over this any day. This is some fucked-up shit you've got here."

Daniel growled and flicked a glance to Rachel.

"Sorry, Rach." Sean apologized for Sam, as though just becoming aware she was standing there. "Sam was hiding behind the door when manners were being handed out."

"Hey! I've got fucking manners!"

Staring at the wall with narrowed eyes, Rachel didn't appear to be taking any notice of the guys' banter. She seemed to be vacillating between being angry, frightened, and downright murderous.

Daniel needed to get her out of there.

He took her hand, and she withdrew it with a wince. He grabbed her wrist and turned her palm over. It was red and raw, the skin blistered. "You burned yourself?"

Rachel blinked down at her hand, then tugged it back, wrapping her arms around her stomach. His chest tightened with concern.

Embracing her, Daniel leaned down, kissed Rachel firmly on the mouth, and held her against his side as he angled her out of the room.

Sean and Sam followed behind, and he knew they hadn't missed the way he was with Rachel. If they were surprised, they didn't say anything. That would happen another time. For now, he wanted them to know what Rachel was to him.

This wasn't just a case.

And although the guys tackled all cases to the best of their ability, when it came to the unit, when it came to family, their dedication rose to a whole other level. Rachel was family, and Daniel wanted that known.

"I let Max out of the car," Sam said, walking back in from outside. "He was going nuts in there."

A moment later, Max was growling at the wall from his position in the bedroom doorway. Every now and again he let out a bark, as though unable to stop himself.

On the front porch, Daniel left Rachel with her sister and kids. She put her arms around Ellie and lowered her head.

Daniel walked Sam and Sean to their cars.

"Let us know if there's anything else you need," Sam said.

"Thanks, mate, I will." Daniel walked directly back to Rachel.

"Oh God, oh God. I left him," Elise was saying. "When I got home, I went to the toilet first. I was bursting. I heard Liam awake in his bed, and I left him there! Oh my God. Oh my God. I left him in there with that... with..." Elise's voice was high, the words rushing out. She looked ready to hyperventilate.

Rachel rubbed her sister's arm. "Shh, it's all okay. It didn't hurt him. You didn't do anything wrong. This is all my fault, and I promise you I'll fix this."

Rachel's eyes connected with Daniel's, and although she was outwardly calm, the fierceness, the heavy guilt he saw in her eyes twisted him up. She was blaming herself, and damn it, he wasn't going to allow her to do that.

He'd make that clear to her, but he had some calls to make first.

The first one was to Mark Collins. The *Debunking Reality* team would know how to deal with the fucked-up wall.

The second call was to Ethan. Elise and the kids were going to stay in one of the TSI safe houses tonight. He'd increase the number of security guards. No one was getting near them.

Rachel was going to stay with him. That was not negotiable. He'd let her have her way last night, but now he was drawing the line. The situation had gotten out of hand, and it needed to be brought back under control. Stat. There were too many variables, too many unknowns.

Daniel hadn't forgotten the way Max had barked at Rachel's car. At her bag.

The same reaction he was having to Liam's wall. Until he worked out the connection and, more importantly, what to do about it, Rachel needed to be with him.

And away from her sister and the kids. He hadn't forgotten Pia's statement that Rachel might be safe from the demon while Madden was alive.

But now Madden was dead.

What did that mean for Rachel?

Chapter Thirty-One

Rachel wasn't able to take a full breath until the large black *Debunking Reality* van pulled into Elise's driveway next to Daniel's 4WD, and the team poured out. A black 4WD with tinted windows pulled up just behind the van, and a tall, muscular man dressed completely in black, his eyes hidden behind dark sunglasses, climbed out.

Daniel walked over to the man and shook his hand. He was the armed security guard assigned to take Ellie and the kids to where they'd be spending the next few nights.

While they'd waited for everyone to arrive, Daniel had made some calls and arranged backstage tickets to Sally's favorite show, The Wiggles, the following day. Elise pasted a smile on her face and told the kids they were going on holiday and that while they were away, their rooms were going to be redecorated.

Just hours ago, Ellie had opened up to Rachel about the cancer, how concerned she was that this not upset the kids' routine.

And instead of being a source of support and comfort, Rachel had caused them to flee from their very home.

She couldn't possibly have hated herself any more in that moment. But as appealing as it was, wallowing in self-pity wasn't going to help her sister.

Rachel had plans to get even.

No one, alive or dead, did this to her sister and kids and got away with it.

So, she gritted her teeth, helped Ellie and the kids pack up, then watched the paranormal team move into her sister's house while her sister moved out.

Hanging back, Rachel saw how Elise hugged Daniel, and how Daniel hugged her back. He then picked up Sally, who wrapped her little arms around his neck. He pinched Liam on the cheek and ruffled his hair, then lowered Sally to the ground. He was a natural with the kids. For all his tough exterior, Daniel had a big heart.

Elise appeared to be thanking him, something Rachel needed to do as well. Daniel had responded immediately when Elise had called. He'd arrived within minutes, taken charge, taken care of the kids, arranged a safe place for them to be. He'd handled the situation financially, emotionally, and in a way that minimized the trauma to the kids.

While he helped the kids into their car seats, Elise's glance connected with Rachel's.

"I'm so sorry," Rachel mouthed, tears rolling silently down her cheeks.

She expected Ellie to be furious, wouldn't have blamed her if she was. But Ellie ran up to her, threw her arms around Rachel's neck, and squeezed her tight. Then she pulled back and said sternly, "Now listen here, stop blaming yourself. This is *not* your fault. I wish I could stay and help you fight this—whatever it is—but the kids need me. As much as I hate it, it is best we leave."

Rachel's eyes burned. "I *will* fix this."

"Let Daniel and Mark's team fix it," Elise said. Rachel clenched her jaw. They could deal with the wall, but she would find out exactly what this demon was and what it wanted with her.

Elise gave Rachel another squeeze. "You keep out of the way and stay safe. I'll meet you back here after this is all over. Okay?"

Rachel hugged her tight. She didn't deserve Elise's forgiveness, her love. But Rachel would do her best to earn it.

Tears blurred her vision as the car carrying Ellie, Sally, and Liam pulled out of the driveway. Wiping her eyes, Rachel turned to face the house. It was time to deal with the mess she'd made of her sister's life.

Daniel came over to her. "Thank you," Rachel said, when he reached her side. Daniel caught her hands in his, ran his thumbs across her skin.

"We'll work this out," he said.

Rachel blinked and pulled away, unable to reply.

On the roof of the house, a black crow sat, head cocked, as if it were studying them, listening to them. Rachel felt the weight of its stare as they made their way into the house.

———◆———

Ellie's house was a flurry of action when Rachel and Daniel stepped inside. Mark signaled Ryan, who raised his handheld camera and pressed the button to record. Standing in the doorway to Liam's room, Mark whistled. His eyes glittered with excitement. "It's exactly as you said, Daniel. This is awesome. You getting this, Ryan?" Mark walked to the window and opened the curtains. "Joe, what's the temperature reading? It's freezing in here."

"Four degrees. That's Celsius, for all our overseas viewers," Joe added. "Damn cold. Especially when it should be up around eighteen."

"As you can see," Mark spoke directly into the camera, "these faces aren't shadows. The sunlight is streaming directly into the room, and the overhead light is on. If anything, the light is making the images clearer, not less so."

Ryan panned the camera, then zeroed in to do close-ups of each image.

"Six faces," Mark commented. "No, seven. There are seven faces."

The images were black and white, and grainy. But you could clearly make out from each of the shadowy images the shape of a face: hair, eyes, nose, and mouth. None of the faces were smiling, and the eyes held death's vacant stare…

Even under Daniel's leather jacket, Rachel shivered against a chill. She tugged it around her as tightly as it would go.

"My camera is playing up," Ryan said. "Keeps going in and out of focus. Cutting out when I zoom too close on the faces."

"The batteries in the EMF detector just died," Joe said. Mark pulled out his mobile phone. "Dead." He tapped it against his palm. As though that could magically recharge the batteries.

Rachel's stomach clenched, but she was not surprised. Her phone's battery had mysteriously drained on several occasions when she thought it had been fully charged.

"I've seen something similar before," Mark mused, examining the faces closely. "In a previous investigation at a house in the Northern Territory. The family had unwittingly built on an old Aboriginal burial ground, and the faces of those buried there were appearing in the concrete floor."

"If Pia was here," Mark said, "she'd be able to give us some insight as to who these people are. She's working another case right now, but we'll send her the footage later to see if she can get a remote reading."

Rachel knew exactly who the faces belonged to. She'd seen them in the scry sitting around the Ouija board with the captain.

"I know who they are." Rachel's voice was thick, and she barely recognized it as her own. She pressed her hand to her chest and tried to control her breathing. It was time to come clean.

"You do?" Mark looked at her in surprise. "Who?"

"That is Captain Edwards and his six crewmen."

Mark peered closer at one of the faces, tracing his fingers along the features. Then he checked his fingertips to see whether there was any residue. "You know, you might just be right. This looks like the captain's face."

"How did you know that?" Daniel asked in a quiet voice at her side.

Rachel swallowed. "I saw them."

Daniel narrowed his gaze. "How'd you see them?"

Rachel signaled for Ryan to stop filming. She didn't want her confession to be something the whole world witnessed. It was bad enough Daniel had to hear.

Mark didn't look happy, but he nodded for Ryan to switch the camera off. Joe grumbled his displeasure, and Daniel glared at him. The tension between them was thick anyway, but here in this room, the energy raked across everyone's nerves, putting them all on edge.

"Tell us how you know that, Rach," Mark said.

With all eyes on her, especially Daniel's penetrating stare, she hesitated. She thought of the scry buried at the beach. It had made no difference at all that it wasn't in the house. The ghosts appeared regardless. The scry wasn't responsible. The scry wasn't the link.

I am.

A wave of dizziness washed over Rachel, and her skin tingled. She rubbed her hands across her arms. Her skin seemed to sizzle, like she was charged with some type of static electricity.

I saw their faces in the captain's scry, she tried to say. But the words clung to her tongue. She couldn't speak them.

If she told them about the scry, they'd take it away. Which shouldn't matter. But strangely, it did. She'd gotten rid of it, but now she wanted it back. She *needed* it. She pictured the scry, buried in the sand, and wanted to go to it.

Even though she shouldn't.

She opened her mouth to tell them, but nothing would come out. She tried again, her mouth opening and closing like a fish out of water. She couldn't form a word. She rubbed her jaw and clamped her lips together.

"Rachel, are you okay?" Mark asked. Her eyes went from Mark's frowning face to Daniel's, heavily creased in concern.

She couldn't tell them. Not yet.

Maybe one day, but not today.

She had unfinished business with the scry.

For some reason, the scry had come to her. The captain had reached out to *her*. Whatever that reason was, it was tied in to the solution to all of this. If she gave away the scry, she gave away her power.

And her only way to reach the captain. Her only chance to stop this.

The scry had been delivered to her. Not Mark, not Pia, not Daniel.

To *her.*

Anger raced hot and fast through her veins.

She was the one who had the power to end this.

She was not going to give away her only connection, her only chance at finishing this once and for all.

"I saw them in a dream," Rachel said, ignoring the painful twist in her stomach.

How many lies did God forgive before even He'd had enough?

CHAPTER THIRTY-TWO

Daniel threw his scrub brush in the bucket and stood, rolling his shoulders. They'd been scrubbing at the faces in Liam's wall for over two hours, and instead of their efforts making the faces disappear, they were becoming more and more clear. The face that was the captain's was as sharply in focus as a modern day black-and-white photograph now, and as eerie as fuck.

They'd started out with a gentle approach, expecting the apparitions to wipe clean with a cloth and mild detergent. They'd then progressed to a kitchen cleanser, then to an industrial-strength bathroom cleanser, and finally they'd tried bleach. The more they'd scrubbed, the more the faces had risen up through the walls, their eyes becoming more focused, more alive with every moment. Eyes that seemed to follow a person's every movement no matter where they stood in the room.

Joe had set up numerous paranormal-investigation devices. He was monitoring the temperature fluctuations and had a laptop connected to a camera that mapped changes in the electromagnetic field. Various still cameras were positioned around the room, in addition to Ryan capturing everything on his handheld unit. They weren't going to miss a thing. Daniel felt like a bug under a microscope.

Max was waiting on the front porch, unable to stop himself from barking if Daniel allowed him inside. The room with the faces freaked Max out. Daniel couldn't blame him. It freaked the fuck out of him too.

Rubbing at his gooseflesh arms, Daniel surveyed the mess they'd made of Liam's once-sweet room. His bed was no longer out in the hallway, but pushed against the opposite wall with the furniture, and piled high with teddy bears and toys. The carpet was pulled up and back, and the team had managed to make a small flood with the cleaning supplies.

Rachel walked back into the room. She'd left a while ago, and he assumed she'd just needed a moment to herself. He crossed to her, wrapped an arm around her shoulders, and kissed the top of her head.

"Daniel, remember when I asked you to find Anna-Marie Edwards? Did you?" she asked.

He stilled, his heart a regular thud in his ears, memories of Madden's death outside the captain's wife's house that morning rising up.

He should tell Rachel that Madden was dead, but was now the time? He took in her pale complexion, the way she was wringing her hands, the fixed look of anger and frustration narrowing her eyes. She was going to be devastated when she found out. He'd tell her later, when he could comfort her in private.

"Did you find out where she is?" Rachel asked.

"Yes. About an hour's drive north of here."

She exhaled. "Do you have the address?"

Her question gave him pause. "Why would you need her address? Don't you want to hear what Zach found out?"

"Of course," Rachel said quickly. "That's what I meant."

"Fill us in, detective," Mark said, snapping a couple more pictures of the captain's emerging face. "Tell us everything you know about Captain Edwards and his sordid life," he continued in a theatrical voice.

Ryan laughed. Daniel ignored them; there was nothing funny about any of this, especially what it was doing to Rachel.

Daniel condensed Zach's lengthy report into a few sentences. "After Anna-Marie's husband had been lost at sea for over a year, she gave up hope of him ever returning, and she left Western Australia and went back to her family in England. She stayed there until her parents passed away. About eighteen months ago, she returned to the house she'd shared with her husband, Captain Edwards."

"The same time the ship washed up on shore," Mark said, pausing in his scrubbing.

"Which wasn't just a coincidence," Rachel said.

"I don't believe in coincidences," Mark said. "Do you have Anna-Marie's contact information? I'd like to interview her for the show if she's willing."

Daniel relayed her number and address from memory, and Joe wrote it down.

They continued to scrub, and the faces continued to grow more vivid.

"Jesus, if those things get any clearer, they'll turn into real people and step out of the fucking wall," Daniel grumbled. "How long are you guys going to keep this up?"

"As long as it takes," Mark said cheerfully. "What's this?" Mark asked, scrubbing away at the captain's image. There was something very disconcerting about Mark's enthusiasm for shit like this.

"It looks like… there's a crystal ball or something next to him. Ryan, get over here. Is this what Pia was telling us about?"

"Looks like it," Ryan said.

"Pia told you about the scry?" Rachel's voice shook, and all color drained from her face.

"Yes," Mark said absently, "that day in the coffee shop."

Rachel shook her head.

"Oh, that's right," Mark said. "She must have told us before you arrived. You were late that day, remember? How did you know to call it a scry? Most people would refer to it as a crystal ball."

Rachel sucked in a breath and tensed, and when Daniel reached for her, she pulled away. She knew she hadn't been late. She'd been right on time.

"You didn't tell me?" Rachel asked Daniel, the hurt in her eyes slicing though him.

The air quality in the room changed again, turning thicker somehow, if that were even possible. Everyone was taking deeper breaths, as though the oxygen in the room were being depleted.

"What else haven't you told me?" Rachel began to shake, and he moved to her. "Does your *girlfriend* know you fucked me last night?"

That was a very un-Rachel thing to say. Daniel frowned, Mark and the team stilled, staring.

"Rach," Daniel said, concern filling every inch of him. "What the hell are you talking about? I don't have a damn girlfriend." *Except you, if you'll stop pushing me away.*

What made her think he did? Daniel stepped closer, but she pushed him away.

"Liar! Stay away from me!" Rachel turned her back and ran out of the room.

Daniel went to go after her, but Ryan stopped him. "Let her go, mate. She's dealing with a lot right now. She probably just needs a little space. A time-out to calm down."

Daniel shuffled restlessly. He clenched his fists, then relaxed them and rubbed them along his jeans. He had no idea who she was referring to when she'd mentioned his girlfriend. What the hell had given her that idea?

It was all he could do to not run after her. But he didn't want to fuck this up, and he had no idea what to say. Ryan was right; she needed too cool off so she could think clearly. And then surely, she'd realize there was no other woman for him. Ever.

Daniel picked up a scourer and took his frustrations out on the wall.

"You know this is a losing battle, right?" he grumbled after a while. "Bulldozing the place is the only way to get rid of these things." He flexed his hand, stiff from scrubbing so hard.

Mark looked as though Daniel had lost his mind. "This is groundbreaking evidence of the paranormal. The last time faces were discovered leaching through a surface, it was purported to be a hoax. The paranormal investigators couldn't prove their validity, and skeptics had a field day driving holes through the evidence. We're treating this like you'd treat a murder investigation," Mark said. "When we match up the evidence, the images rising out of the walls, the electronic voice phenomena we've captured, the unexplained temperature changes, the fluctuations in the electromagnetic field, the batteries draining…"

Mark waved an arm around the room. "All this scientific evidence will be impossible to refute. We've disconnected the power to the house, turned off all mobile phones. Every event on every device is time-synced to the second. This investigation is going to be airtight."

Rachel still hadn't returned. Daniel tossed his brush in the bucket. He hoped she'd had enough space; he couldn't be without her another second. "I'm going to find Rachel."

"We'll be here," Mark said happily.

"Yeah, well I think you're all nuts. But be careful," Daniel said. "All of you. You know my number if you need me, and Sam and Sean will be in the area for the next few hours too."

Mark nodded, already focused back on the wall.

Daniel had given Rachel enough time alone. He needed her by his side. He couldn't shake the heavy feeling of dread that was hanging over him.

As though this was not the end, but only the beginning of what was to come.

━━━━━━ ◆ ━━━━━━

Unable to listen to one more word, or look at Daniel for one more second, Rachel walked through the house and out the front door. She crossed the front lawn and headed toward the beach.

Daniel had kept details about the captain, his scry, and what had happened on the ship away from her.

Why would he do that? Why would he keep things from her? She couldn't trust any of them. Especially Daniel. And that hurt the most.

She paused at the top of the sand dunes. The only thing that had told her the truth had been the scry. Strangely, she felt closer to that chunk of crystal than to any person she knew.

She was grateful Mark had asked Daniel for the address of Anna-Marie's house. Daniel had been starting to get suspicious of her questions. But now she knew where Anna-Marie lived.

All she needed was the scry. Getting rid of it hadn't made one scrap of difference as far as making this all go away. And when she'd seen the captain's image with the scry on the wall, she knew why the faces had appeared.

It was a message.

For her.

The scry held the answers she was looking for.

She was physically unable to tell Daniel or Mark because she wasn't meant to.

They had been keeping things from her. That was why the words hadn't come out.

They had known all about the captain and his cheating wife, and they hadn't told her.

But the scry had.

Head down, she crossed the dunes and made her way to the scry. The demon scared the hell out of her, but the captain didn't. In a strange way, she wanted to help him. Perhaps he wanted to help her too. Especially if she paid a little visit to his wife…

Rachel approached the place where the scry was buried. So what if she helped the captain take revenge on his wife? The stupid bitch should have kept her panties on. The captain loved her. How could she screw around on him?

And how could her father screw around on her mother?

And Daniel…? He had a *girlfriend!*

Trust no one.

Rachel counted six fence posts from the gateway. But she didn't need to count in two meters—she knew exactly which bush she was looking for. And it wasn't because it was the largest, greenest bush covered in the most flowers.

It was because it was dead.

CHAPTER THIRTY-THREE

Daniel let Max out of the car, and together they searched up and down the beach for Rachel. When they came back, he realized her car was gone. He checked his watch. It was approaching an hour since he'd last seen her.

His phone rang, and for a moment he thought it was Rachel, but it was Pia's name on his screen. He swallowed his disappointment.

"Daniel," Pia's voice came through before he even spoke. "I'm worried about Rachel."

"You and me both," he said, unable to shake the heavy sense of dread. Rachel had taken off in that car that Max didn't like, without telling him where she was going.

Why would she do that?

Why hadn't he heard her car leaving?

His fingers tightened on the phone. "Rachel has taken off somewhere. She was upset and said we were hiding things from her. About the captain and the scry. And yet, she seemed to know this stuff anyway. Have you spoken to her recently?"

"No," Pia said. "Not since the morning we took the Ouija board away. I tried calling her several times, but each time the call wouldn't connect."

"Any idea how she got her information?"

"No." Pia sounded surprised. "Didn't you just get confirmation about Anna-Marie yourself? Nate showed me the report from Zach that came through last night." The report validated what Pia had told them about the captain and his wife that morning at the coffee shop.

Despite her gift, Pia always seemed relieved to have her information confirmed.

It told him there were times when she was wrong. TSI relied on her a lot, maybe too much. She wasn't infallible.

"Madden is dead," Pia said.

"Yes."

"That's not a good thing."

Daniel's stomach clenched. He should have told Rachel when he'd had the chance.

He'd discharged the security patrolling the house when Elise and the kids had left earlier. There'd been no need for additional security while he was inside with Mark's team and Rachel. Especially with Madden no longer a threat.

But that also meant there had been no one to alert him that Rachel had left. Something he hadn't considered.

Where had she gone?

"I have a theory on that," Pia said, and Daniel realized he hadn't voiced the question.

"What's your theory?"

He put Pia on speaker, and shot off a quick message to Sam and Sean to let him know if they spotted Rachel's car.

"Remember when I was telling you the story of the captain back at the coffee shop? I said he had been messing with the Ouija board, but also looking into a scry."

"Yes." He had a sinking feeling he knew where she was going with this.

"Well, the Ouija board turned up in Rachel's bedroom, but I'm wondering if the scry didn't turn up at the same time."

"You think she kept it from us?" Daniel didn't want to believe it, but he had to consider the possibility. It would explain Max's behavior, why he'd growled at her backpack. "Why would she do that?" He'd seen how frightened she'd been of the Ouija board. Why wouldn't she be as frightened of the scry?

And more importantly, why would she *lie* about it?

Rachel had tensed when Mark had pointed out the scry with the captain on the wall, and she'd turned almost deathly white as she'd asked about it. And now he knew why.

"Because she didn't hear us discuss the scry at the coffee shop," Pia said. "She didn't know about my suspicions that it was possessed. Perhaps if she'd known, she wouldn't have kept it in the first place."

"But why didn't she tell us about it?" *Why didn't she tell me?*

"Possessed objects contain power, power that can meld with the energy of the person who touches them. If she was curious, played with the scry a little, its attraction might have been virtually impossible for her to resist."

Daniel thrust a hand through his hair. Jesus, he wished he could take back his decision to have her arrive later. He'd really fucked up.

"But... as I said before, I think it was always meant to be hers," Pia said thoughtfully. "Which means the connection would be even more powerful."

"Do you know where she is?" Daniel wanted to press Pia for more details about her cryptic comment that the scry was always meant to be Rachel's, but the most critical thing right now was making sure Rachel was back with him. Safe in his arms.

"She thinks you betrayed her," Pia said. "For some reason, Rachel has lost trust in you. She thinks you have—or will—hurt her."

"I haven't betrayed her."

"But she *believes* you have. And that's what matters here. Last night, I had another vision. The captain's wife *wasn't* screwing around on him. The scry lies." Pia's tone was grim. "If Rachel has been messing with the scry, I have no idea what she might have seen. What she might believe." She paused. "I think Rachel is in real trouble."

Daniel was already walking to his vehicle, checking his weapon, his comms, even as Pia spoke. He opened the passenger door, and Max jumped in.

"You remember me telling you I saw an old woman, a high priestess? I think the scry was originally hers, and I think she is the connection to Rachel."

Daniel's stomach churned. "How so?"

"From what I can tell, Rachel is related by blood to the old woman. It wasn't an accident the scry ended up in Rachel's hands. But it's not the same as it was when the priestess used it. It's been tainted."

"With the demon," Daniel said, his heart pounding in his chest.

"Yes. He scratched her again, Daniel. On the neck. With Madden dead, the demon is free to start oppressing Rachel. He's already messing with her mind. She is not herself."

"What can I do?"

"Just find her. Keep her safe from everyone *and* herself until tomorrow night. I'll know what to do when I see her," Pia said. "Oh God."

Knives twisted in Daniel's stomach. "What?"

"Oh, Daniel." Her voice rose. "I just saw Rachel in a vision. You have to stop her."

"What is she doing?" Daniel asked, even as he received a text message from Sam saying a patrol car had spotted Rachel's car speeding north along the highway.

"She's almost at the captain's wife's house, and the demon is with her. And Daniel, I can't see how, but it doesn't end well. I have a terrible feeling something really bad is going to happen."

He disconnected from Pia, no longer able to contain himself. Fury burned through him. Fury at himself.

"Fuuuck!" he bellowed.

By inadvertently giving Rachel the address, he'd sent her right into the demon's line of fire.

CHAPTER THIRTY-FOUR

With a dull roar reminiscent of swarming bees in her ears, Rachel keyed the address of Anna-Marie Edwards's house into her GPS. *Stick with me and we'll be there before the first snag's off the barbie*, the GPS informed her.

Rachel hit the open road and headed north. Gum trees soon gave way to a windswept landscape. Red dust collected on her car, and the low-lying scrub of Australian native bushland blurred as she sped along the highway.

With the pedal to the floor, the motor strained, the steering wheel shuddering, and she backed off the accelerator a touch. Wouldn't do to break down out here so far away from help. Wouldn't do to get a speeding fine either, now that she was unemployed.

She had a job to do. And she didn't need any interference.

Rachel synced her phone playlist to the car, and her favorite music blared out through the speakers. She turned the volume up as loud as the unit would allow, seeking to drown out the screaming inside her head.

To silence the voice screaming at her to turn around. To go back.

To silence the voice that was screaming even louder to kill the bitch. To kill Anna-Marie Edwards over what she'd done to her loving and loyal husband.

Wait. What?

Rachel wasn't killing anyone. She never would! Jeez! Her heart pounded as she tried to clear her mind, order her thoughts. What the hell was happening to her?

The images the scry had shown her, the images of the time she didn't remember, flashed into her mind.

But you did kill someone. Trey.

No! I couldn't. I just couldn't!

She passed a rocky outcrop of jagged limestone, her stomach churning. Her glance fell to the backpack on the passenger seat. The scry was inside it. Had it lied to her?

She fought a thick fog trying to cloud her mind.

I should have told Daniel where I was going.

No doubt about it, that would have been the sensible, rational, most *logical* thing to do. With Daniel and the TSI team, Rachel had access to the best security this country had to offer. The prime minister himself didn't have better resources.

And yet, there she was, a small-time singer—ex-singer—from Perth, traveling unarmed through the countryside on the advice of an inanimate object.

Nothing about what she was doing was smart, let alone sane.

And yet, here she was just the same, staying on course, barreling down the highway toward the dead captain's wife. But even if she'd been in Daniel's LandCruiser, she wouldn't have been able to drive fast enough to escape the crushing pain in her chest. The agonizing sensation of knowing that the man she loved was seeing another woman, just like Anna-Marie had been seeing another man. Plus, Daniel had been keeping important things from her. Things she deserved to know. Things she had a *right* to know.

And not just Daniel—they all had. Mark, Pia, everywhere she looked, those around her had been doing things behind her back. An image of them all sitting around in a circle, mouths open, heads thrown back, laughing at how they'd fooled stupid, naïve, *pathetic* little Rachel appeared in her mind. Rachel blinked it away in surprise.

It wasn't like that.

Was it?

But the images took root in the strange fog growing in her mind, and she imagined Daniel at the head of a table of a meeting she wasn't invited to. "We've caught Rob, but don't tell her that either," he said. "Rob saw everything that happened that night. It was Rachel. She's the real murderer. Let's lock her up!"

Rachel shook her head to clear the vision. It was bad enough knowing the things she knew were true without imagining anything else. But the more she drove, the foggier her thoughts became, until she struggled to sort fact from fiction.

Her whole life had become a mess of fantastical proportions. Perhaps she wasn't even alive anymore, and this was all a dream? Had she died that night on the ship with Trey and Rob, and was now trapped in a nightmare of her own creation, the way the captain was trapped in his nightmare on his ship? Spending an eternity trying to get back to the one he loved more than life itself.

Rachel concentrated hard on driving, on trying to clear her thoughts, her breathing becoming more and more labored. The car was swerving off the road, periodically sending sprays of red dirt and rocks up behind her. She blinked rapidly. She focused on something real. What was important? Her main goal. Her sister, her niece and nephew, and making this go away.

Rachel felt a rush of clarity.

That's what I'm doing!

She held fast to that thought with everything she had. Her sister had cancer, and Rachel had pulled a fuse out of a hand grenade and thrown it into Ellie's life. Rachel was sorting out the mess she'd made.

This had to end.

And… she could trust no one to help her.

Something cold was seeping through her veins. Her head started to throb, a headache beginning to claw into her brain.

Daniel.

Only thoughts of Daniel slowed the ice-cold numbness. She wanted him. Desperately. She needed him. She reached for her phone.

Wait. If she called Daniel, she'd have to tell him about the scry. She'd have to admit she'd lied. She'd have to admit she'd done nothing but lie to and deceive the people she loved since she'd arrived.

She'd have to tell him she'd killed Trey. She'd have to see the look of disgust on his face the next time he looked at her.

Rachel choked on a sob.

She didn't know this new self.

She hated who she'd become.

And she certainly knew Daniel would hate her when he found out what she'd done. All this time and effort trying to find Rob, and he was sleeping with the real killer.

What could she hope to achieve by visiting Anna-Marie Edwards? And what would she say when she got there? *Hi, Anna-Marie. Were you screwing around on your husband?* And then what? *Okay then, just wanted to know. Have a good day.*

What could she possibly hope to achieve?

Kill the bitch.

What? *No!*

That was *not* her thought. Something like that would never enter her mind. Jesus! What the hell?

She started to shake. What was *wrong* with her?

But anger toward Anna-Marie continued to build inside her. For what Anna-Marie had done to the captain. The captain loved her with every fiber of his being. He lived and breathed for her. She was his childhood sweetheart, and there'd never been another woman for him.

And the bitch screwed around on him.

Like her father had screwed around on her mother.

Rachel narrowed her eyes. And Anna-Marie, the lying whore, had gotten away with it. She'd probably kept screwing the other man; they'd probably laughed over it. "Poor Adam, poor foolish Adam," she'd say. How stupid he was to think he could satisfy a wantonly lustful woman like Anna-Marie.

Rage pumped through Rachel's veins. *How dare she!* The captain was a good man. All he'd done was love her. He'd named his ship after her, the passion of his life after the love of his life. The cheating bitch didn't deserve him.

That's what happened when you loved someone.

Love was fickle.

Hate was the only steady, reliable thing you could depend on. The only thing that would never let you down.

Rachel pressed her foot down on the accelerator, and the speedometer climbed higher.

She knew what had to be done. She knew what she was going to do when she got there. Anna-Marie had to pay for her sins. And Rachel was going to be the one who made sure Anna-Marie paid in full.

It was all clear to her now.

CHAPTER THIRTY-FIVE

Your destination is on the left, the voice in the GPS informed her. *Windows up, grab your sunnies, and don't let the seagulls steal your chips.*

Rachel stopped the car outside the neat little cottage with its white picket fence and immaculate rose garden. A large crucifix hung above the security door, and statues of the Virgin Mary were scattered around the garden.

Opening the car door, Rachel had to grasp the handle for balance. The waves of energy coming off the religious symbols were causing a strong reaction inside her. Her fists clenched, and she imagined herself smashing them to pieces with a hammer.

Why? Why was she reacting this way? Even though she wasn't overly religious herself, she had no problem with anyone who was. Quite the opposite. Rachel often envied people who could find peace in their faith, whatever the denomination.

She tossed the bag that contained the scry into the boot. "You stay here," she told the scry.

A shiver skittered across her skin, and an ache started at her temples. She had the sudden sense it was not happy.

Of course, that was ridiculous. A scry didn't have feelings.

She stood by the side of the car for a moment, forcing herself to focus on the large crucifix on Anna-Marie's front door. She took one deep breath after another. Gradually the sickness receded, and her mind began to clear.

Rachel walked up the neat little path, her steps heavy as though she were walking through thick sand. Her heart was pounding for reasons she couldn't explain, and her hand was shaking as she knocked on the front door.

A few moments later, she heard someone approaching the door from inside.

"Anna-Marie?" Rachel called out. "Anna-Marie Edwards?"

The door opened. "Yes?"

Even at sixty-six years old, Anna-Marie was still beautiful. She must have been a stunner in her youth. She still retained her elegance, her grace. She was slender, and although time had added lines to her mouth and eyes, her voice was clear and strong. She wore her hair pulled back in a bun, and stockinged feet poked out from beneath an ankle-length dress with long sleeves.

"Can I come in?" Rachel asked.

"What's this about?" Anna-Marie narrowed her eyes. "You're not a reporter, are you? The police told me not to talk to any reporters."

"The police?" Rachel couldn't hide her surprise.

"Yes. Someone was shot near the road behind my backyard." Anna-Marie made a sign of the cross over her chest.

"Do you know who it was or what happened?" Dread pooled in Rachel's stomach for a reason she couldn't explain.

"I can't see that part of the yard clearly from my kitchen window, too many trees in the way. And the police told me to stay inside. They'll be back to talk some more after they've informed the victim's family and whatever else it is that they do in situations like this. So, if you came looking for information, I don't have it."

"I'm not a reporter, I promise."

"Then why *are* you here?"

"I just want to—"

A brown and white fluffy little dog ran out of the house, down the pathway, and began barking savagely at the rear of Rachel's car. *At the boot.*

"Molly, come back!" Anna admonished her. The dog continued to bark and growl, and Anna-Marie chased after her. She scooped Molly up, and holding her firmly in her arms, brought her back to the house.

"Sorry about that," Anna-Marie said. "I don't know what that was about. The way she carried on over your car would make one think I never have visitors."

Rachel followed her inside, taking advantage of her distraction over the dog's behavior.

"She's normally such a good little puppy," Anna-Marie said, lowering Molly to the ground and giving her a treat she pulled out of a side pocket in her dress.

"What kind of dog is she?" Rachel asked while Anna-Marie filled up her water bowl with fresh water.

The scent of lemon furniture polish mixed with the smell of the freshly picked roses in the hallway vase. The floors were all plush carpet, and although it had likely been laid years ago, it was in immaculate condition.

"She's a King Charles Cavalier spaniel."

"Cute," Rachel murmured, moving to a side table filled with family pictures. The large picture in the center was of a younger Anna-Marie, smiling into the camera happily, with an older man on her arm who Rachel recognized as the captain. There were no recent photos showing her with another man. Or Anna-Marie with any other man.

With Molly seemingly happy again, Anna-Marie turned toward Rachel, slightly narrowing her eyes as she looked her over, head to toe.

"Do you want some tea?" Anna-Marie asked, showing Rachel into a sunroom and indicating the wicker table and chairs.

"That would be lovely. Thank you."

Anna-Marie disappeared into the kitchen, and after a few moments, returned with a pot of tea and a tray of what appeared to be homemade biscuits.

She sat down, back straight, but smiled pleasantly. *Regal* was the word that immediately came to Rachel's mind.

Anna-Marie poured the tea. "You're that girl, aren't you? That singer from that band. Trinity Flowers or something. The one in the paper. You and two friends went onto my husband's ship and one of them died."

Rachel released a breath. "Trinity Beat. And yeah, that's me." She managed a weak smile.

"And now you're worried his death has something to do with the ship, and you've come here to see if I can help you."

Rachel winced. So much for trying to get information anonymously. "Yes."

A large reproduction of da Vinci's *The Last Supper* hung on the wall to her left.

"Can you tell me about your husband?" Rachel asked gently.

"He was the love of my life," Anna-Marie said, her eyes misting.

"What happened?"

"He'd been at sea too long," she said. "It was time for him to retire. He said he was too young to retire, that retiring was something you did when you were old." Her hand shook as she raised the cup to her pursed lips. She set the cup back in its saucer, the chink of china the only sound in the otherwise silent house.

"He always worried about the age gap between us. Nine years was a lot when I was eighteen, and he twenty-seven. Over time, the years smoothed the difference, but Adam never forgot. He always worried I would think of him as old. He never was. He was as fit and tough as a man could be."

Rachel felt the same way about Daniel. There were seven years between them, but with Daniel strong, fit, and in the prime of his life, Rachel couldn't imagine him ever being an old man. He'd age well. Men like that always did.

"Do you know what happened to your husband?" Rachel asked. "To the crew?" Could Anna-Marie confirm what Rachel had seen in the scry?

A look of deep sadness settled on Anna-Marie's face, an expression Rachel suspected she'd worn many times over the years.

"They say he killed his crew, that the sea stole his mind. Something in the ocean air makes sailors see mirages, images of ships on the horizon that don't exist, mermaids. I don't know what happened to my husband, but whatever happened, he was a good man. I will never believe any different."

A good man, who lost his mind and killed his whole crew.

"After what happened," Anna-Marie continued, "I couldn't stay here anymore. I went back to England to spend time with my parents before they passed."

"And you've come back here now for good?"

Anna-Marie shrugged. "Enough time had passed that I found the strength to come back. I loved it here once. I loved my life. I loved my husband. I was happy here. I was finally strong enough to live with the twenty-eight years of good memories and forget the flash of bad at the end. I had to, you know?" Anna-Marie wrung her hands. "Otherwise my whole life was a waste. If I let that one event ruin a lifetime of wonderful memories, what do I have? So I came back to live out my twilight years remembering the life I'd loved."

Tears welled in Rachel's eyes. How Anna-Marie had suffered.

"Anna-Marie, I need to ask you something sensitive. I don't want to upset you, but it may be important."

Anna-Marie stiffened. People had likely been asking her questions for years, trying to understand how the captain could kill his whole crew before taking his own life. Questions poor Anna-Marie couldn't possibly have the answers to.

Rachel hesitated, not wanting to cause her any more distress. Life had given the poor woman too much already. But the question needed to be asked.

"I don't know if there is a sensitive way to ask this, so I'm just going to come out and say it." Rachel took a breath. "Were you seeing someone else at the time the captain died?"

Anna-Marie's eyes turned cold, her face flushed a deep red, and she stood from her chair. "How dare you insult me in my own house!"

Rachel stood as well. "I'm sorry to ask, really I am. But I just had to ask why your husband thought you were."

Anna-Marie went still as death. "How do you know what my husband thought?"

"I... uh, it's complicated."

Anna-Marie's face turned a ghastly white, and for a moment, Rachel thought the woman was going to have a heart attack. Rachel went to her side and assisted her back into the chair.

"I'm sorry," Rachel said. "I really am."

"I'd never do that to him. I loved him."

"He thought a man was coming around in the evenings—"

Anna-Marie frowned. "There was. But what I'm wondering, dear, is how you know?"

Rachel's heart sank. So it was true. Anna-Marie had been having an affair. Rachel had wanted to believe in a love that lasted forever. But that kind of love only happened in romance novels. Real life was far crueler.

"So he was right," Rachel said.

"What? No!" Anna-Marie seemed to come back to life. "The man who was coming around was an artist."

"You were seeing an artist?"

"I was getting a portrait painted for Adam's birthday. I had a local artist come around some evenings." She flushed. "The painting was a little… risqué. I was getting two. One for the wall, and a smaller one just for him for when he went away on his fishing charters."

"You couldn't have just gotten a picture?"

Anna-Marie's eyes flashed. "I'm not one of *those* girls. We didn't have those fancy digital thingies like you have these days. Back then, you had to get them developed at a shop." She placed her hands over her reddened cheeks. "I wanted something classy. Something tasteful. I wanted to surprise him."

Anna-Marie's lower lip began to tremble. "He spent the last weeks of his life thinking I was having an affair? How cruel."

Rachel's heart broke for her.

"Thank you for your help," Rachel said, not wanting to distress Anna-Marie any further. What could the old woman tell her anyway?

What am I doing here?

"Wait." Anna-Marie looked at her, her eyes sad. "I've thought about you many times these last few weeks. You looked like such a nice girl. That picture in the paper of you on your knees sobbing at the beach broke my heart. I often wondered what you three really did that night. I had my suspicions…"

Rachel had deliberately stayed away from reading the papers. She hadn't seen the picture, but her eyes started to well again, just remembering how she'd felt that day.

"You found the scry, didn't you?"

Rachel's mouth dropped open. "How did you know that?"

Anna-Marie had turned a worrisome color, like uncooked pastry, and she made the sign of the cross across her chest.

"Get rid of that evil abomination of Satan." Anna-Marie lunged forward and grabbed Rachel's arm, her fingernails digging painfully into Rachel's flesh. Anna-Marie's eyes were wide and slightly crazed. "Get rid of it now!"

A lump formed in Rachel's throat. "I don't think it's going to be as easy as that." Whatever it was, whatever it wanted, it was determined to be with her.

Anna-Marie stared at her long and hard.

"You," she said. "It was meant for you all along, wasn't it?"

"Uh… maybe?" Rachel said cautiously. This conversation had taken a disconcerting turn, and Rachel was on edge.

Anna-Marie stared at Rachel for a moment longer, then she deflated, her shoulders hunching forward like she had the weight of the world on her shoulders.

"You poor girl. Sit down. Wait here." Anna-Marie disappeared for a while, then came back several minutes later carrying an old book.

"After the police finished their investigation of the shipwreck, they returned Adam's personal items that they'd taken into evidence. One of the things was his personal diary. Different from his captain's log. The police believed the ramblings in the diary confirmed he'd lost his mind."

Anna-Marie ran her fingers across the cover, the skin of her hands as frail and thin as crinkled tissue paper.

"I must have read every word a thousand times. Everything is here. The police wouldn't believe a word of it, of course. No," she added bitterly. "*That* doesn't fit with their carefully crafted view of the world."

"What doesn't?" Rachel asked, even as she knew. What she had seen in the scry must be written in the diary.

"Adam described the cave where he'd found the Ouija board and the strange markings perfectly. I looked them up, searched and researched until I found the symbols. And what they meant."

Rachel was leaning forward, holding her breath, hanging on the woman's every word. "What did they mean?"

"They were symbols of protection. Powerful. The object they protected against contained an evil of the worst kind." Anna-Marie rubbed her eyes. "I'll never know what influenced Adam to stop the ship precisely there that day, why he felt compelled to walk off the ship alone, how he knew where the cave was, or what was inside it. Whatever it was, it had chosen him for a reason I never worked out. But now you're here. You turn up out of the blue, knowing things only he knew. And now I can't help but believe that reason was you."

Rachel's head swam. If that were true, Rachel was not just responsible for Trey's death, but also that of Captain Edwards and his entire crew.

"I'm still trying to piece this together myself," Rachel said, her voice thick. She rubbed at a tightness in her chest with a shaking hand. Her grandmother had tried to rid the family of the scry, and somehow Captain Edwards had been influenced to retrieve it.

It would have been unbelievable, had it not been happening to her.

Anna-Marie handed Rachel the diary.

Rachel opened the hard cover, breathing in the faint scent of the ocean, and a fragile slip of parchment fell out of the book into her hands.

"I didn't know what to do with that," Anna-Marie said. "Of course, I showed it to the police, said it looked important, but they just looked at me as though I was mad." She crossed her arms.

Rachel lowered herself into an armchair and ran her fingers over the old parchment filled with symbols and strange notations.

"It's dated 1817," Rachel said with reverence. "Two hundred years ago." The parchment appeared to contain two rituals: a summoning ritual on one side, and a banishing ritual on the back.

Both for a powerful archdemon called Sohn-Zae.

According to the notations, Sohn-Zae was one of the most powerful demons of Hell. A demon of jealousy and revenge.

From what Rachel could tell, the notations on the parchment had been made by a high priestess named Maia. Rachel's fingers froze on the page. Could this be the woman she had seen in the scry? The one who'd been trying to warn her? A strange recognition tingled inside her.

Had she been trying to warn Rachel about the demon? The one she herself had summoned. The demon that had turned on her and killed her. The demon that was still around, a hundred and fifty years later.

And now, in Rachel's hands, was the way to banish Sohn-Zae forever.

Was this the reason the scry had turned up in Rachel's bedroom? It seemed too much of a coincidence that Rachel had seen a woman in the scry, apparently Maia herself, and now she was holding a parchment filled with Maia's handwriting.

Rachel scanned the summoning ritual.

Tonight, I command the forces of darkness to stand as one with me, as we seek retribution… I send a curse to the woman who seeks my husband's bed. May she die slowly, a painful death until she turns into dust, dust, dust.

Rachel turned the page over, to the ritual on the back.

It outlined how to cast the perfect circle and listed precisely, step by step, what to do.

By the power of love and light, thrust back to Hell the demon Sohn-Zae and protect us from his evil intent—

"My God, Anna-Marie. Do you know what this is?"

Anna-Marie nodded. "Yes, dear. I suspect this is what is going to save your life."

Chapter Thirty-Six

Rachel slipped behind the wheel of her Lexus, filled with strength and determination after her discussion with Anna-Marie. She no longer felt powerless. In the captain's diary on the passenger seat was the solution to protecting them all.

Rachel tried Daniel's number, then Pia's, then Mark's. She couldn't wait to check in with them, to let them know what she had, but all the calls failed to go through. She tapped on the screen, as though that would somehow get a few bars of reception, but it was no use. She simply could not get service.

She had no other choice; she was going to have to drive back and then tell them what she'd found.

She left Anna-Marie's property and soon reached the highway. Rachel concentrated on the road ahead, wattle trees and scrubland blurring as she raced past them.

She understood now why the captain wanted her to see his wife. He didn't want Rachel to kill her. He wanted Rachel to get the ritual from Anna-Marie. All along, his wife had had the way to banish the demon. The captain was trying to help Rachel.

Just as the demon was using the captain's image to try to manipulate her into committing heinous acts on his behalf.

It pained her to remember her dark thoughts about Anna-Marie on the way there. But they were the demon's desires. Not hers. She would never willingly hurt anyone.

Rachel thought about what had happened to Jake, about what had happened to Mark.

How they'd been possessed.

Was that happening to her as well? She'd heard the demon's thoughts in her mind, right alongside her own.

She had to talk to Pia about what to do. How to keep the demon out of her head, how to perform the banishing ritual. Another twenty-four hours or so, and this nightmare would all be over.

A group of kangaroos was to her left, and she hovered her foot over the brake in case one tried to jump in front of her.

She reached over and patted the book.

The miles went by, and something caught the corner of her eye.

A gold and diamond rabbit pendant was dangling out of the corner of the glovebox.

Tears stung her eyes, blurred her vision. She blinked them back. Was it? Could it be?

My necklace! Rachel reached out, cradling the bunny in the palm of her hand. Sunlight glistened off its diamond eyes.

It was the necklace Rob had given her on her twenty-first birthday. It was their symbol. He always called her a scaredy-girl. Not a scaredy-cat. A reference to her gender, and the fact that her two best friends were boys. She was like a scared little rabbit, he'd teased her one day, pointing at a live one that had scampered between some bushes. He'd been trying to get her to swim with sharks without a cage. Although she'd made it a point to keep up with Rob's and Trey's challenges, she wasn't an idiot....

Rachel blinked. How had the pendant ended up in her car? She had lost it on the ship that night. How could it have gotten stuck in the glovebox? She would have noticed it there before, surely. But it *must* have been in here the whole time. Unless...?

Unless Rob put it in her car to let her know he was okay!

Rob was alive and close. And he still loved her. He didn't want to kill her. He wanted her to know that. Her heart squeezed. *I miss you so much. I love you, my friend.*

Rob must be fighting the demon too. Just like Rachel was. If only they could fight it together. He must be staying away from her to try to keep her safe.

Rob, please come back!

Daniel would love Rob too, once he had the opportunity to know him. To think of him as something other than a killer. Rob was a good man, with a big heart, just like Daniel.

She opened the windows to let some fresh air in. Taking a deep breath, Rachel found it in her to smile. She had the solution! Visiting Anna, finding the pendant, remembering her love for Rob and how much she loved Daniel had cleared her mind.

Time to try Daniel again. She picked up the phone. Still no signal.

She was driving through a windy stretch of road with double lines. She imagined telling Daniel what had happened, coming clean about everything, telling him about the scry. The relief she felt was immense. It was the right thing to do. The only thing to do.

Her heart squeezed. *I love you, Daniel.*

Yes, she'd tell him that too.

The decision felt *right*, and for the first time since she'd seen the faces on the wall, her head was in the right place. She smiled at Rob's bunny swaying back and forth. When she stopped, she'd find the key to unlock the glovebox and put it back around her neck where it belonged.

Happy at her new resolve, she smiled at a wolf at the side of the road.

Wait. A wolf?

There weren't any wolves in Australia. Perhaps it was a dingo. Or a wild dog. Must have been a wild dog.

But something didn't feel right. Rachel's stomach clenched and she sat up straight, gripping the steering wheel as she scanned both sides of the road. Her music turned to static. She fiddled with the knobs, and unable to work out what was wrong, turned the stereo off. Silence filled the car. She flicked her eyes to the GPS and blinked. It was flashing "no signal."

She passed an old man walking on the side of the road, his hair gray, his shoulders slumped. He stopped, looking up as her car neared. What was he doing out here? Did he need help? Rachel slowed, and he looked directly into her eyes as she drove past. Something about his gaze, so cold, so vacant, gave her a chill to the bone.

But she should stop. She wasn't one to turn her back on anyone who needed help. How much of a threat could an old man be?

She slowed and started to pull off the road. When she looked in her rearview mirror, the old man was gone. There was nowhere for him to hide; the bush was low-lying, and she would have seen him if he'd walked into it. But he had just… vanished.

Had she really seen him at all?

The hair on the back of Rachel's neck was standing on end, and her unease increased. There was no one traveling behind her, and she'd seen only three oncoming vehicles over the last five minutes. She was alone out here.

And yet, she felt as though she were being watched.

Rachel swallowed past the constriction in her throat.

She reached for her phone. She was calling Daniel. He could be as upset as he wanted, but she really needed to hear his voice.

Using one hand, she pulled up his number and called it. The phone began to ring, and she laughed in relief. She finally had a signal!

Things would be better once she'd talked to him. After she'd heard his voice. He'd talk to her and ease her nerves. Maybe she'd even keep him on the line while she made her way home. He'd probably prefer that. She knew how much he worried over her.

The phone rang twice, then stopped.

She glanced at the display. The phone was dead.

A shiver trickled down her spine.

There was another group of kangaroos on the side of the road. They all stopped, turned, and looked directly at her as she drove past, their black eyes trained on her. Again, she felt a bone-deep chill.

A little further up, a flock of crows swooped at her car. She hit one, sent it tumbling off to the side of the road. The rest swarmed around her like a black cloud, their loud cawing and the scraping of their claws over the top of the car raking across her nerves. Crows? Had she driven into an Alfred Hitchcock film? She tried to laugh, but it came out as a choked sob. She loved Alfred Hitchcock movies, but there was nothing funny about her life turning into one.

Her pulse racing, she pressed down on the accelerator, hands clamped on the steering wheel, and concentrated on keeping her shuddering car on the road. The swirling cloud of birds cleared away, and she again saw the bitumen stretch out before her.

Damn it. She was going too fast for the winding stretch coming up. She put her foot on the brake… and the car sped up! Had she put her foot on the accelerator by accident? She glanced down. Her foot was definitely on the brake. She pressed hard, then harder still, but the car didn't respond. Her heart lodging in her throat, Rachel watched the speedometer continue to climb. The landscape blurred and the car shuddered, the motor whining. She lifted her foot, then slammed the brake with everything she had.

She heard a sharp hiss and looked down.

A large brown snake had wrapped itself around the brake pedal. Its brown scaly head was raised near her ankle, and its beady eyes looked at her as she stared at it. Its mouth was open, baring sharp, deadly teeth. She could see all the way inside its hollow throat, could see the toxic venom dripping from its fangs.

She screamed, lifting both feet up to the seat. Her knees knocked the steering wheel, sending the Lexus careening over the road. The screech of the tires sent an icy rush of adrenaline coursing through her veins. Self-preservation kicked in, and she forced her shaking foot down on the brake, ignoring the feel of the snake's cold body brushing against her leg. Keeping her gaze firmly on the road, she held the steering wheel straight, somehow remembering not to overcorrect. And although the vehicle didn't slow, it stabilized.

The snake brushed against her ankle again and she shivered, trying not to scream as its body wound around her leg.

Driving on the white line in the middle of the road, she glanced down, knowing by how it felt what she'd find. The brown snake had wrapped itself around her shin and was slithering up her leg to her knee.

She whimpered, hot tears stinging her eyes. These snakes were deadly. One drop of venom could kill six adult men. Her only chance at survival was to stay calm. But it was so damn hard.

Think. She needed to get out of the car, but she couldn't pull over. The brakes weren't slowing the car. There was no way she could stop the vehicle without crashing.

The snake continued to climb, its flickering tongue touching her inner thigh.

The handbrake! Of course! Taking her hand off the steering wheel, Rachel raised the lever. The car responded, slowing down. The speedometer started to drop and hope filled her. She laughed, relief making her near hysterical.

Until the handbrake jammed.

The engine howled, fighting to speed up as the handbrake tried to slow it down. Rachel yanked the lever with everything she had. With a sharp crack, it broke off in her hand.

Oh Jesus, no!

Unrestrained now, the vehicle surged forward, the speedometer climbing toward capacity. She dropped the lever onto the seat and gripped the shuddering steering wheel with everything she had.

Stay still. Stay calm. Breathe… breathe in. breathe out. Think. Don't look at the snake. Don't look at the snake.

Unable to stop herself, she glanced down. The snake was now wrapping itself around the steering column, all the time watching her with calculating, lethally intelligent eyes.

The demon was *in* the snake. Controlling it. She knew it with every breath she took.

Her whole body trembled, and she panted wildly, struggling not to hyperventilate. At any moment the snake could strike. If she took a hit, she'd die for sure, so far away from medical help. She clutched the steering wheel; keeping the vehicle on the road was essential to her survival. She didn't know how this would end, how she'd get out of this. Time slowed to an agonizing crawl as second by terrifying second ticked by.

The snake popped its head through the steering wheel. It hissed, and when she saw its needle-like fangs so close to her hand, she whipped it away. She was whimpering continually now, unable to stop. Tears fell from her eyes as she looked around for a weapon.

On the passenger seat was the handbrake lever, and she grabbed it. Lining up her aim with the snake's head, she kept one eye on the road.

Disembodied laughter poured into her ear like an icy claw of pure evil. She couldn't tell if it was from the snake or if it was coming from somewhere else in the car. Either way, it was *wrong*. She stayed focused.

She lined up her target. Brought the lever down. Hard and fast.

And missed!

The lever skittered off the steering wheel and slammed into her leg. White-hot pain speared up her thigh. The snake reared its head, fangs bared, ready to strike.

No, it was *laughing*.

A hand grabbed her shoulder from the back seat and she screeched. The grip was chilling, three claws digging into her skin, as though she were being touched by the hand of death itself. She glanced in the rearview mirror and saw the demon's dark, twisted face, its glinting red eyes.

Sohn-Zae!

He meant to kill her. She had the key to his death, and he was going to make sure she never got to use it.

The demon's thin black lips curled into a snarl as the snake slithered over and around her wrist.

No!

She let go of the steering wheel and screamed.

The car careened off the road.

The demon laughed.

Rachel pressed hard on the brake, squeezed her eyes closed, flung her arms up to shield her face.

And braced for impact.

CHAPTER THIRTY-SEVEN

Daniel pushed his LandCruiser 4WD to its limits as it sped along the highway. He took no pleasure from the power of the engine and the racing wheels beneath him, his sole attention on reaching Rachel.

In the distance, a plume of smoke was spiraling into the sky, and somehow he knew it was Rachel. Fear tightened in his gut like a vise. He couldn't get to her fast enough; the pedal was mashed to the floor, the engine at full speed, but to Daniel, he was moving at a crawl.

He crested another small hill, and a blackened vehicle came into view. There was no way anyone could have survived that. Bile roared up his throat; he was going to be sick.

Tires screeching, he pulled up beside the overturned vehicle. The fire had burned itself out, but the intensity of the heat still radiating off the wreck stopped him from getting too close to the burnt-out shell.

He couldn't see anyone inside. Damn it. He had to *know*.

He whipped off his T-shirt and wrapped it around his hand. He lifted charred metal. He couldn't see her. His heart pounded out of his chest. Maybe it wasn't her car?

He walked to the back of the vehicle, his eyes finding the scorched license plate. He could still make out the numbers and letters.

It was Rachel's Lexus.

He sank to his knees in the dirt.

I never once told you I love you.

She'd died without knowing what she meant to him, that she was the very breath in his lungs. How could he have let that happen?

He'd thought he had time. She was young. Too young to die. Why had he thought they had their whole lives?

If anyone should have known better, it was him. In a single moment, life could change. Everything you knew, everything you loved, could be taken away.

And now it was too late.

How was he meant to carry on? Tears rolled down his cheeks as his world crashed in around him.

His Rachel. Gone.

CHAPTER THIRTY-EIGHT

When Rachel opened her eyes, the world was upside down. She blinked hard, then wiped grit and dirt from her eyes with a bloodied hand. Through the broken window, she saw an inverted tree. No, it was she who'd gone ass up.

She felt around for the seat belt and released it, falling against broken glass and a mangled dash and deflated airbags. She landed hard, white-hot fire spearing up her body, but she was free. Ignoring the pain, she gingerly pulled herself through the wreckage and grabbed the handle of the passenger side door.

It was jammed.

She shoved herself forward, using everything she had to push the door open. It wouldn't budge. Pain shot through her body with every attempt. There wasn't an inch of her that didn't hurt. Her body was covered in blood, but she couldn't tell from how many wounds. She touched her throbbing forehead and saw fresh blood covering her fingertips. She rubbed her fingers together almost disbelievingly. It was warm, sticky.

I've hit my head.

She grasped the thought as it tried to float past. That's why her head hurt; she'd hit it. For some reason, that was funny. She started to laugh.

Then abruptly stopped.

I can't worry about that now.

She was tired, and she needed to sleep. She hadn't been sleeping well lately, and everyone knew how important sleep was. She would have preferred her bed, but this would have to do.

Rachel lowered her head, wincing as it settled against something hard. She had to remember to buy some new pillows. These ones were no good. Her lids were heavy, and she closed her eyes. *Everything will be better after a good night's sleep.*

Something touched her shoulder. "Rachel, wake up."

"Go away," she said. Her mouth was dry and her tongue was thick.

"Rachel, you have to wake up. You have to get out of the car." The voice was urgent, insistent, and damn irritating.

"I need thleep," Rachel said, smothering a yawn. "Thee you in da mornin'."

"Rachel!"

Rachel blinked open her eyes to see Rob standing on the other side of the broken window. She began to cry, the tears washing the grit away. She closed her eyes, then opened them again, but Rob was still there.

"Oh, Rob! I killed Trey! I'm so sorry!"

She expected his anger, but he was smiling at her with his familiar grin. "No, you didn't."

Rachel blinked. "I didn't?"

He shook his head sadly. "You didn't kill him."

Rachel's vision wavered as she tried to focus. "I missed you." She sobbed. "I miss both of you so much." Emptiness was a great cavern inside her, threatening to swallow her whole. "Where have you been?"

Rachel reached out, her hand trembling. He smiled gently, but he didn't take it.

"I… I need you," Rachel sobbed, the pain inside unbearable. "Don't leave me again. Promise me, Rob. Don't you leave this time." *Don't you freaking dare. I need you. I can't get through the loss of Trey alone.*

"Come on, scaredy-girl," Rob said, his eyes flicking nervously over the vehicle. "You can't stay there. You need to get out of the car. Now. It's going to blow."

Rachel strained to focus on his words. *Scaredy-girl.* It wasn't her imagination— it really was Rob. He reached through the shattered window and touched the latch. The door came swinging open.

"Cool," Rachel said. "How'd you do that?"

"Hurry."

Rob held out his hand, and this time he let her take it. His skin felt cold in her fingers, and her heart clenched. He must be tired and hungry, having had to hide out here. Because of her.

"Did you cover Trey's murder up for me? Is that why you disappeared?"

Rob's expression was creased with effort as he pulled her from the car. She landed in a heap on the ground. Something was crackling. Was the car on fire? She smelled smoke and coughed.

"Don't stop now," he ordered. "Keep moving." Rob was standing just ahead of her, and she dragged herself across the ground toward him.

"More. Keep coming," Rob said. "Come on, scaredy-girl. You can do better than that."

Rachel tossed him a glare, and damn if it didn't feel like the best thing she'd done all year. She grinned stupidly up at him.

"Where have you been?" She choked on the words, and the tears began to flow again. "We can go back together; you can tell everyone what happened. I'll tell everyone what I did. It's not fair for you to be blamed for something you didn't do."

Rob took another two steps back. "Stop talking. You have to hurry. Don't stop now." He kicked his feet playfully, but his eyes kept flicking to the car. "Catch me, scaredy-girl. Come on. Hurry."

There was a loud pop and an intense heat flared over her skin.

The car *was* on fire.

A look of distress crossed Rob's face. "Hurry, Rach. Get up. You have to run! Hurry!"

Rachel crawled into a crouch, then pulled herself up onto her legs and half stumbled, half ran after Rob. He stayed just in front of her, teasing her, tormenting her, dancing just out of reach.

An explosion rent the air, and a blast of hot wind knocked her over. She pulled herself up and looked back at her car. It was a ball of flames.

"Wow." It seemed such an inane thing to say, and she began to laugh hysterically. "I almost died." Rob was watching the car too, a look of sadness on his face.

"That's my cue." He smiled at her gently and backed away. "I have to go now, scaredy-girl."

"No!" Her voice was raspy and raw, full of desperation.

"I love you, Rachel," he said, his eyes filling with tears. "I always have. You and Trey both. I'm sorry for everything."

"Wait!" Rachel cried out. "Don't go!" She scrambled forward, but he held up his hand.

"Do *not* follow me. Stay with the car. He's on his way."

"Who?" Rachel said. "Who's on his way?"

"He's a good guy, Rachel. It's meant to be, you know. It's time for me to go now." He looked over his shoulder, as though seeing something wonderful. He had such a look of peace on his face, of love. Of resignation.

"You sound like you're saying goodbye for good." Rachel choked on a sob.

"I am." Rob smiled tenderly. "Look after yourself, scaredy-girl. I love you. I always have. I always will."

The car made a strange rending sound, and Rachel turned to see what was happening. When she looked back, Rob was gone.

She frantically scanned the bush for him, but he was nowhere to be seen.

"Rob!" Rachel screamed, despite the razor blades slicing her throat. "Rob! Come back!"

She scrambled across the ground, thorns from a bush tearing into her skin.

"Don't go," Rachel sobbed. "Don't you *dare* go."

But it was hopeless. He was gone.

And this time, he wouldn't be coming back.

In the distance, Rachel heard a vehicle approaching. She was too smothered by pain to be relieved. She lay back on the ground and closed her eyes.

All she wanted to do was cry. Rob was gone.

Tires screeched as the vehicle came to a stop.

And then she was aware of every muscle she had, and each one ached, then turned to water. She wanted to rest, to stay on the ground and sleep.

You can't.

She'd die out here if she didn't get help now. Forcing her eyes open, she called out and struggled to her feet. She took a step, and her knee buckled. She swore at its inconvenient weakness, then took another step, only to stumble and fall on the ground.

She was just a scaredy-girl after all. Tears filled her eyes and rolled down her cheeks. *Rob, come back!*

But Rob wouldn't ever be coming back. He'd said someone else was coming for her...

"Daniel!" she croaked, her voice shredded.

"Rachel!" She heard his voice before she saw him. *Daniel.*

Then he was at her side, all six feet of take-charge male. He gently pulled her against his chest, his whole body shaking. She could hear his heart pounding as he kissed her head, his hands twining in her hair. His arms wrapped around her, he held her tight, like he'd never let her go. After long moment, he loosened his grip and pulled back so he could search her face. "Babe, are you okay?" His eyes were red, and she could see he'd been crying.

She nodded, unable to speak.

Seemingly unconvinced, he supported her while he assessed her, his free hand feeling along her arms and legs. "Nothing appears to be broken. Can you tell me who I am?"

For some reason, she found that question funny and choked on a laugh.

Daniel only looked more concerned. He pulled a white cloth from somewhere and dabbed at her forehead. She winced. When he pulled it away, it was bright with blood.

"It's all right, babe. It's not so bad." But his face was hard, his eyes filled with concern.

He continued to speak to her, his voice soft, tender, reassuring. Telling her everything was fine, that she was okay. He seemed to be convincing himself as much as her.

He placed one hand on either side of her face, leaned in, and kissed her. She wrapped her arms around his neck, and he lifted her into his arms as he stood.

"I think I can walk." She looked around her. Things seemed clear now, back in focus.

"No."

"Put me down," Rachel insisted.

"I can't," Daniel said, his voice deep and broken. "Letting you go is not an option." He held her eyes, his own brimming with emotion. "I love you, Rachel."

Her world shuddered to a halt. She blinked up at him, more stunned than when she'd woken upside down in the car. "You do?"

"I thought I'd missed the chance to tell you." His voice cracked, and he squeezed his eyes shut. "I love you, Rachel Sommers. I have loved you since you were eighteen."

Tears filled her eyes, and her whole body trembled in his arms. Her head pounded, and every muscle in her body ached. And her heart soared, a big ray of sun in her chest. "I love you too."

Daniel kissed her cheek as he walked to his car.

He helped her into her seat, strapping the seat belt carefully across her. "Does this hurt?" he asked, gently pressing her belly. Rachel knew he was worried about internal injuries, but all she could see was her burnt-out car.

Max nuzzled against her from the back seat, and she ran a hand through his thick pelt.

"Oh God, oh God!" she cried out.

"What is it?" Daniel immediately removed his hand. Eyes wide, he looked at her in concern. Max growled.

"The banishing rite!"

Daniel frowned. "What?"

Oh, dear God! The only way to defeat the demon was gone.

And she would have died had it not been for Rob.

When Sohn-Zae knew he had failed, that Rachel had not been influenced to kill Anna-Marie, but had in fact been given the way to destroy him, he'd driven her car off the road. That's why the snake had not bitten her. The demon wanted to ensure the destruction of the precious parchment. It had survived two hundred years, and had lasted less than an hour in her hands.

She pounded her forehead with her palms.

"Hey," Daniel growled, gripping her wrists.

How could she have let that happen!

The solution had literally gone up in flames.

What am I going to do now?

Chapter Thirty-Nine

At Daniel's large dining room table, Rachel's shoulders were slumped forward, heavy with the weight of the world. On her lap was his black leather jacket. She hugged it to her stomach as she slowly sipped from the cup of tea he had just made for her.

Max sat at her feet, his muzzle pressed to her leg, no doubt able to sense her distress. He'd barely left her side since they'd found her car wreck.

Daniel's heart squeezed, but he held onto the cold marble counter behind him instead of going to her. She was safe, and the fear that had gripped him when she'd disappeared, then seen her overturned car loosened—somewhat. Reality—life—began seeping back into him, bringing painful truths that hurt to acknowledge.

He loved Rachel, and he would never let her go. But they had things to discuss.

She had lied to him.

And it hurt like hell.

And those lies had almost gotten her killed.

He was still assessing her every movement, her every response to stimuli. Like all members of Taipan, Daniel had medical training for field emergencies, but he'd wanted her properly examined at a hospital. She'd needed a few stitches and had a mild concussion, but she had somehow escaped relatively unscathed from her ordeal. She was still distressed, but alert and aware.

Daniel had already called in Rachel's accident to his sergeant mate at the local police station, then reported in with Blade, who would handle the official obligations related to the accident. Rachel would be called in to make a statement, but that could wait.

Officially, it was just a traffic accident, and no one else was involved.

Unofficially, it was a hell of a lot more.

Without speaking, Daniel walked into the bathroom, turned the shower on, adjusted the temperature, and steam filled the space.

He'd almost lost her today.

That pain, that absolute devastation, was not something he ever wanted to experience again. He wouldn't survive losing her. Until this was over, she wasn't leaving his sight. But although he loved her and couldn't live without her, there were things between them that needed to be sorted out so they could move forward.

It was time for things to change between them.

Starting with honesty.

On both sides.

Rachel stood in Daniel's shower, the masculine scent of his soap all around her. The warm water soothed her skin, but it couldn't remove the chill embedded in her bones.

Daniel had helped undress her, assessing every scratch, every graze and bruise. And now he stood with one broad shoulder resting against the wall outside the shower, arms crossed over his chest, watching her.

His scrutiny made her feel exposed, naked—and not in a good way. There was nothing sexual in his dark gaze. He seemed to be assuring himself she was okay. And she was.

Because of Rob.

Now that she'd stopped shaking, her mind was able to go over the moments leading up to her accident. It was time for her to come clean with Daniel. About everything. So many things between them remained unspoken. On his side, as well as hers. It was time to lay herself bare.

But would he?

She shut the taps off, and Daniel was waiting for her with an oversized fluffy white towel. He helped her get dressed in one of his T-shirts. Draping a black robe around her shoulders, he pulled her roughly to him and squeezed her hard against his chest. She wrapped her arms around his waist, and for a long, delicious moment, she forgot everything. He smelled of leather and something dark and spicy. Forbidden. And he felt so good, so terribly strong. She clung to him, as though if she held him long enough, he'd make this mess go away.

He released his grip and said four little words that made her heart flutter—again, not in a good way. "We need to talk."

In the kitchen, Daniel placed a glass of wine in front of her and took a seat at the table. He was wearing a tight V-neck T-shirt and navy cargo shorts that hugged his incredible ass in just the right places. His wallet and keys were with his gun and belt just off to the side. His shoes were in the kitchen, where he'd kicked them off soon after they'd gotten in.

But it wasn't his incredible body that had her attention at the moment; it was the cool determination fixed in his expression. This was a man who intended to get answers.

"You lied to me," Daniel said. The pain in his eyes, the disappointment and hurt she saw there, shredded her. A defense instantly rose to her tongue. She wasn't the only one who hadn't been completely honest.

But she was fessing up, whether he did or not. "Yes, I did."

Daniel closed his eyes briefly in acknowledgment. When he opened them, his gaze penetrated right to her very soul.

"Why?" His voice broke on that one word, and she rubbed at the pain in her chest. "Why couldn't you trust me?"

"I'm sorry." Her pulse pounded in her ears. "I do trust you." Could he hear the truth in her words? She trusted him more than anyone on this earth. Why couldn't she see that earlier today?

Because of the scry.

The truth hit her like a sack of concrete. Something about that thing altered her perception, her ability to think clearly. It was a good thing it had been trapped in her burning car. No doubt it was a puddle of melted glass now.

Though why didn't that *feel* like a good thing?

"But you didn't trust me enough to tell me the truth," Daniel pressed. "The whole truth."

Rachel met his eyes, forced herself to hold his gaze. "What's even worse," she said, her voice little above a whisper, "is that even now, I can't be sure exactly which lie you're talking about."

Daniel took a long drink of his whiskey, placing the tumbler on the table with a little too much force. He didn't look up as he twirled the glass between his thumb and forefinger.

"How many are there?"

"Lies?" Rachel reached across the table, placed her hand on his. He stopped twirling his glass and stared at their joined hands.

"Too many," she murmured.

Daniel pulled away, and she felt the loss of their connection, the huge cavern between them.

"Goddamn it, Rachel. All I ever wanted to do is protect you. Do you have any idea how it felt to know that with everything I can offer you, all the resources available to me, you took off on your own without a single word?" His intense blue eyes locked onto hers. "Do you have any idea what it was like for me to find your car overturned and burned out on the side of the road? To know no one would have survived had they been in there? What it was like for me during those moments I'd thought I'd lost you?"

Daniel's voice was deep and roughened. "A piece of me died right there on the road with you. When you've looked into the eyes of death so many times and survived like I have, there's not much left in this world that can scare you. But you…" Daniel said, unshed tears glistening in his eyes. "Knowing I could have lost you? *That* fucking scared me."

Rachel placed her hand on his wrist, but he pulled it away and sat back in his chair, folding his arms across his chest.

She tucked her hands back in her lap. He wanted total honesty, and she was giving him nothing less.

"I went to see Anna-Marie."

"No shit," Daniel said, the softness gone from his eyes. "Tell me something I haven't already worked out for myself."

Rachel swallowed and raised her chin. "I didn't see the captain and his crew in a dream. I saw them in the captain's scry. I have it. *Had* it," she corrected. "And I'd been using it. You ask it questions and it shows you the answers. I saw the captain in it. He asked me to… uh, find his wife, and I asked you to locate her." Rachel thought of the brief periods of time she'd thought she would harm Anna-Marie, but pushed them aside. That was ridiculous. She would never hurt anyone.

"Why didn't you tell me you had the scry?"

"I couldn't," Rachel said, and it was the simple truth. She'd tried telling him, wanted to tell them all back at the house. "I wasn't able to."

His expression was pained, his chiseled jaw tensely working. He released a long breath. "I'm sorry. I told you to come half an hour late to the meeting with *Debunking Reality*. At the time, I didn't know what Pia would tell me. Didn't know what we were dealing with. I thought I was protecting you. But I was wrong. You deserved to know everything."

Would things have been different had she known how potentially evil the scry could be before she'd found it? Would she have feared it like she did the Ouija board? Perhaps. But she also knew the strangely compelling influence it had wielded over her from the first moment she'd seen it. It hadn't repulsed her like the board. It had *called* to her.

"I'm not angry anymore," Rachel said, clearing fond memories of the scry from her mind. "I know there is something off about the scry." She forced herself to remember barreling toward Anna-Marie's house with thoughts of murder on her mind. Thoughts that were *not* hers.

"Pia said the scry is tainted."

"I can see that." Rachel sighed. "But as much as it scared me, I also felt a very real connection with it. As though it was always supposed to be mine. But when I saw that… the demon in it, I panicked and buried it at the beach when I saw you this morning." Had it been only this morning?

"But this afternoon, when the demon appeared in Sally's room and the faces appeared on Liam's wall, I knew that getting rid of the scry didn't matter."

Rachel finished her wine, and Daniel immediately reached for the bottle in the chiller and refilled her glass.

She shivered, remembering how she'd held Sally in her arms, knowing her physical body was inadequate to keep Sally safe, but not knowing what else to do. "It's the worst feeling in the world not knowing how to protect someone from something you can't see or fight."

"No shit." She looked up into Daniel's stormy gaze, and her chest squeezed. To a man like Daniel, so used to being in control, to handling everything that crossed his path, a case like this must be torture.

"So, you've been communicating with the captain through the scry?" Daniel asked.

"Yes." Rachel lowered her head and rested her chin in her hands on the table. She took him through what had happened, how she'd felt an affinity with the captain when she'd seen his anguish in trying to get back to his cheating wife. How he'd gone mad at sea, killing his crew. She told him about her visit to Anna-Marie, about Anna-Marie giving her the parchment with the banishing rite on it.

She didn't tell him what she'd thought of doing to Anna-Marie on the way there. She couldn't. Daniel had told her he loved her. How could he love a woman who could think thoughts like that? Besides, nothing had happened.

And now that the scry was gone, something like that would never happen again anyway.

She told him about the old man on the side of the road, the wolf that shouldn't have been there, the western brown snake in the car with its strangely intelligent eyes, and the odd behavior of the animals she'd passed and the way they'd looked at her, the disembodied laugh, and then the demon she'd seen in her back seat through the rearview mirror.

"Jesus." Daniel leaned back in his chair, ran his palms across his shorts. He drained his whiskey and refilled his glass.

"I woke up and I was upside down in the car," Rachel said. "And Rob was there—"

Daniel knocked over the tumbler of whiskey and swore. Snatching a cloth from the kitchen, he dabbed at the spill. "You didn't really see Rob," Daniel said. "You mean you *thought* you saw him. You'd taken a knock to the head, you were imagining it."

Rachel shook her head, grabbing another towel, and helped him wipe up the floor. "No, I know he was there. I spoke to him." He'd called her scaredy-girl, and she'd felt his hand as he'd helped her out of the car. It was Rob; she knew it for sure.

"If it wasn't for Rob, I wouldn't have got out of the car," Rachel said firmly, taking the cloths to the laundry room.

"I had no idea the car was going to explode," she said, sitting back down at the table. "All I knew was that the door was jammed shut, and I was too tired to keep my eyes open, much less care. Rob woke me up. Kept talking to me. Forced me to stay alert enough to get out of the car. I followed him for a short distance, and then after the car exploded, he said he had to go, he couldn't stay. He said goodbye." Rachel's throat closed over, and tears pooled in her eyes. *I have to go now, scaredy-girl.*

"At least I know he's alive, and he's okay." Rachel sniffed. "You don't have to worry about him hurting me. He saved my life, Daniel."

Daniel kept his gaze on his drink. Then he took a long sip. Finally he met her eyes.

"Rach," he said softly. "I'm sorry, but Rob could not have been there with you at the car. He's dead. He died at eight-fifteen this morning."

Rachel's lungs locked up. "What?" She shook her head. "I saw him only a few hours ago."

Daniel rose, then dropped to his knees in front of her. He took her hand in both of his and looked up at her. "After I left you this morning," he said softly, "I found Rob tied to a tree out behind Anna-Marie Edwards's home. He wanted me to kill him."

"*You* killed him?" Daniel's words were a dagger to her heart. Rachel's breath seized, her vision blurring red around the edges.

That was the death Anna-Marie was talking about?

Anger welled up inside her, rolled in big fat tears down her cheeks. "How *could* you?! You promised me you wouldn't!"

She struck out at him, and he stood, catching her fists in his hands. He held them close to his chest and kissed her knuckles.

"I tried to bring him in," Daniel said, his brow furrowed. "I promised you I would. But—"

"But *what?*" Rachel demanded, wanting to lash out at him, wanting to make him hurt as much as she was hurting. "Rob was no match for you! With all your abilities, with all your experience, how hard would it have been to take him in? Admit it. You wanted him dead."

Daniel released a slow breath. "He was not himself. He knew it. I saw the real Rob briefly. He believed that dying was the only way to end it. To keep you safe," he added.

"But it hasn't kept me safe, has it?" Rachel choked out. "You should have helped him. Like you promised! You know how much he meant to me."

She was sobbing uncontrollably now. Her world was quicksand and she was sinking. She realized then just how much hope she'd placed on Rob being found alive. To have *both* Rob and Trey dead?

"Wait." Rachel pulled away, confused. How could what Daniel told her be right? It didn't make sense. She'd seen Rob just a few hours ago. Daniel had said he died early this morning.

"I thought there were to be no more lies between us! You can't have killed Rob this morning. I *saw* him." Rachel pushed up from the table, hugging her arms around her roiling stomach. She glared at Daniel to make it clear he shouldn't even consider following her. She didn't want his comfort, didn't want him anywhere near her. She was being honest with him. How dare he not give her the same in return!

She walked through the double doors, out onto the balcony, and looked over the darkened ocean. Numbness seeped through her, and she dug her fingernails into the cool metal railing. She *knew* she'd seen Rob mere hours ago. The stars above her spun in the sky, making her feel dizzy and disoriented.

She took a deep breath, the truth settling inside her. Daniel wouldn't lie about Rob being dead. So if he'd already been dead at the time of her crash, that must mean that Rob had somehow saved her life before he took his final leave of this world.

The notion was unbelievable, but if she wasn't crazy, it was the only thing that made sense.

She felt Daniel coming up behind her before she heard his footsteps. She tensed as he wrapped an arm around her shoulders.

"I'm really sorry about Rob," Daniel said, his voice thick with emotion. "There was nothing I could do. Rob was no longer himself, not the Rob you remember. I didn't break my promise to you. I tried to bring him in. But he knew." Daniel put his finger beneath her chin, turned her so that she was looking at him. "He knew what was happening to him, Rach. He felt the demon, and it was tearing him apart from the inside out. He wanted it over. He told me to tell you he loved you. If you want to know what I really think, I think what he did, he did for you."

Hot tears filled her eyes and rolled down her cheeks.

"I would have brought him in, if I could have. You believe that, don't you?"

Daniel pulled her into his strong embrace, and he held her tight as she sobbed for long moments for the loss of her best friend. For the loss of both of them.

There was no longer hope she would find them alive, that things would return to normal. Rob and Trey were both gone, and she'd have to find a way to live without them. Something she'd have to work out in time, because right now, she had no idea how that would be possible.

Daniel continued to hold her, murmuring he was sorry and gently kissing the top of her head as he ran a hand soothingly down her back. Eventually, her tears dried, and she calmed, listening to the rise and fall of his chest and the regular beat of his heart against her cheek.

"Where's the scry now?" Daniel asked softly, into her hair.

"You don't have to worry about it anymore." Rachel pulled back, surprised at the sudden bitterness in her tone. "It was destroyed with the car. It was in my bag in the boot." At that moment, it simply felt like yet another loss on top of so many.

But the scry wasn't good for her. Right?

She was cold, chilled from the inside out. Daniel tugged her back into his arms, and she clung to him, the sound of waves crashing below them.

"You can't trust what the scry shows you. It's evil. Pia said it lies."

"It tells the truth as well," Rachel said. "It's shown me things I couldn't have known on my own." Whatever else it was, its ability was genuine.

"Like what?"

"It told me you were at the restaurant on my eighteenth birthday," Rachel pointed out. "You confirmed it."

"*That's* why you asked about that?" Daniel thrust his hands through his hair. "Jesus Christ!"

Rachel looked down. "It told me the truth, Daniel. It showed me things." She had asked about Rob and been shown his location. She didn't know why he'd been outside her window, but when she'd looked, he'd been there.

"It *lies*, Rachel." Daniel's eyes were narrow. Intense. "Is it also responsible for your ridiculous comment earlier? The remark about my supposed girlfriend?"

Rachel squeezed her eyes closed, shutting out the image that had haunted her ever since she'd seen it in the scry. Daniel with that woman, her bare ass on the table, her legs wrapped around her man. *Her* man… Was he really hers?

"Long, blonde hair, legs that go on for miles. Her bare ass on a rustic wooden table, her Louboutin heels wrapped around your waist." Rachel almost choked on the words.

"Louboutin heels?"

"The ones with the red soles…" Rachel said weakly. At the flash of recognition in his eyes, bile rose in her throat.

"Cynthia."

Cynthia. I hate her.

"She's not my girlfriend. She's just a girl I… uh…" He shrugged. "Someone I used to fuck on occasion."

Rachel squeezed her eyes shut. Her whole body shook, not because she thought he didn't see other women. Of course, he did. It's just that she wasn't prepared for just how much it… *hurt* to hear him talk about it so casually. Let alone the pain of *seeing* the two of them together.

"She's not my girlfriend," Daniel repeated firmly. "She never was. You," he said, his voice softening, "you are the only one I've ever considered for that role."

Her heart banged around in her chest, and the world spun. He was saying things she'd always wanted him to say, things she'd never allowed herself, even in her dreams, to believe he ever would.

And still… it was another thing the scry had told her that had been the truth. She had seen Cynthia. More than once. Had been able to describe her enough that Daniel knew who she was talking about. Rachel crossed her arms and glared up at him.

"Something happens to you whenever you talk about that thing," Daniel growled, a muscle in his jaw clenching.

Her blood ran cold as she remembered something else the scry had shown her.

I murdered Trey.

She should tell Daniel. Hadn't that been her intention for this conversation, total disclosure? But she couldn't bring herself to tell him right now. Didn't want to see the look of… disgust on his face. Would he hate her? Arrest her?

"There's something you're holding back. What else did that scry tell you?" Daniel asked, and she glanced up.

She *couldn't* tell him.

Couldn't push past the sickening image of Daniel and Cynthia in her mind, as painfully vivid as if she'd walked in on them in real life. Like she had with her father.

Daniel wasn't the one, and she needed to stop wasting time thinking he could be.

She didn't want to look back on her life at some point and not know what it felt like to give her heart to someone.

Unconditionally.

To experience the same in return.

Her heart squeezed painfully, and she rubbed at her chest. Jesus, she wanted that. Wanted to feel that type of all-consuming love she'd read about in romance novels.

Daniel wasn't the man to give that to her.

And she wouldn't accept less. Not anymore.

"I want to go back to Elise's. I need to see what's going on with the wall. See if they're any closer to getting Elise's house back to normal."

"You're not going back there," Daniel said.

"You don't get to tell me what I can and can't do, Daniel." She said the words automatically and without heat. She was tired of arguing.

She looked around for her bag then stopped. It had burned up in the car.

No car. No money. No phone.

Awesome.

"Can you call me a taxi? Please?"

She felt the heat of his body at her back. He ran his fingers through her hair, lifting it off her shoulders and twisting it into a ponytail. His breath fanned over her neck, his lips touching her skin. She squeezed her eyes shut, and a tear escaped, rolling down her cheek.

"Please don't." *I can't bear your tenderness.* Her voice was a mere rasp. Raw, broken, and shattered, the way she felt inside.

"Stay." His voice was a soft whisper in her ear. "I know I'm not going to make good husband material. If I was a better man, I'd let you push me away. Give you a chance to find a man much more worthy of you. But on top of my sins, I'm selfish. I won't let you go." His voice cracked. "Don't make me."

His words shattered her. There was a time she would have settled for that.

But things had changed. The situation with Elise, the kids. She wanted more than to warm Daniel's bed when he was in town.

She no longer wanted to be someone's good time.

She wanted to be someone's *reason.*

"I want a lot more than you're prepared to give. I know I was convenient. But it's not enough for me. Not anymore."

He moved closer, eyes narrowed, his face inches from hers. "You think you were ever *convenient?*" The intensity in his gaze scorched her. "You couldn't be any further from the truth." Waves of heat rolled off his body. "Babe, the way I think about you is anything but *convenient.*"

He pressed himself against her, and she felt the evidence of his inconvenience in his pants. Well, he'd have to get over that. She turned her head away, and he used a finger beneath her chin to angle her gaze back to his. Her breath caught in her throat at the storm clouds of emotion in his darkened eyes.

"The way I can't get you out of my head after I leave is not *convenient*," Daniel continued. "The way I deliberately don't shower the day after so that I can smell you on my skin is not *convenient*."

He traced his finger down her neck and made circles on her shoulder. "The way I dream about you, the way you feature in each and every one of my fantasies, the way for the last year I chose women who looked like you to fuck in an unsuccessful attempt to get you out of my mind was also not very damn *convenient*."

Her skin was on fire, his finger a blowtorch.

"The way that merely hearing you were in trouble damn near ripped me apart. The team were close to breaking a major case, and all I could think about was getting to you. For the first time in my life, I found something more important to me than what I thought defined me: my work. I'd say that was pretty damn *inconvenient*, wouldn't you?"

He cupped her face in his hands, looked deep into her eyes. "Don't you understand? I *love* you. I've never said that to anyone before. Never felt like this before."

Her pulse skittered at the dark promise reflected in his eyes, his vehement tone stealing her breath.

"I don't know what I can promise you. That is something we have to work out. But Rachel, we *will* work it out. When this is all over, we will sit down—together—and decide how we can make this work. Because it *has* to work. Us. Because you are meant to be in my life. You always have been. All these years, it's always been you." His tone was low, gravelly, and she fell into his gravitational force.

He wrapped a strong arm around her waist, pulled her flush against his body. She felt his desire for her pressed hard against her stomach. "I want you to feel me, Rachel," Daniel said. "Feel every inch of me as I bury myself deep inside you. Not just into your flesh, but into your heart."

Rachel swallowed hard, totally overcome.

He loved her; he loved her the way she loved him. With every molecule, every cell.

"I'm going to kiss every inch of your skin, starting from your ankles, then work my way up." His lips feathered across her neck, his breath soft puffs on her heated skin.

Then before she could say a word, he scooped her up and carried her inside, where he laid her gently on the bed.

"I don't want to hurt you," he said, his eyes raking along her exposed skin, lingering on the scrapes and bruises from the accident. But she knew he meant emotionally, as much as physically. She shimmied her way up to the pillows, to the bed linens that smelled like Daniel.

His words of promise had sliced her, as surely as if he'd cut open her chest and laid her heart bare. She wanted everything, just as much as he said he did. Daniel was the color in a black-and-white painting of her life. Always had been.

Her body was hot, her skin on fire, as he tenderly removed her robe and T-shirt, kissing the scrapes and bandages he exposed along the way. Her hands fisting the covers, she lay back, baring her broken self to him, aware the gesture reflected their conversation, going much deeper than baring mere flesh.

Rising, Daniel stood next to the bed, his expression fierce as his gaze traveled across her heated skin. She felt it as powerfully as though he'd touched her with his fingers.

Her breath was coming in short gasps as he fisted his shirt at the base and pulled the material up and off, exposing the muscular torso with the defined V that she loved so much. He unbuttoned his shorts, pulled them down along with his sexy black boxer briefs, and kicked them across the floor. Perfectly naked, he stood there for a moment, as Rachel's eyes drank him in, as she felt the weight of his gaze on her. Although they weren't touching, the act of laying themselves bare for each other was deeply intimate.

Heat pooled hot and urgently between her thighs, and she opened her arms. "Come to me."

With a predator's grace, he moved to her, grabbed her ankle, brought it to his mouth. The action spread her legs, but he kept his eyes on hers, as his lips pressed along the tender flesh on the inside of her leg, sending white-hot bolts of pleasure racing through her bloodstream. Kneeling over her, he kissed and licked a path all the way to the place between her legs that was clenching with anticipation and need.

Daniel made a low guttural sound as his tongue flicked across her tender flesh. "You are so beautiful."

Rachel arched her back, pressing herself against his mouth, and he grabbed her thighs, bringing her legs over his shoulders. As his tongue flicked over her clit, his fingers inside her, she was nearly mindless with the need to orgasm.

He kept his eyes on hers, seemingly aware of every breathless whimper he elicited from her, keeping her on the precipice, but careful not to send her over.

She writhed beneath him, her head thrashing from side to side, calling out his name. The tension built to a painful crescendo inside her, then he stilled.

"Daniel!" Rachel arched her back, but he didn't move, his fingers still buried deep inside her.

"Please, Daniel," Rachel begged.

His eyes darkened, narrowed with intensity. "Tell me you love me." His voice was hoarse, and he held his breath as though her answer was the most important thing in the world to him.

Tears instantly stung her eyes. The raw vulnerability in his expression burned her.

He was studying her reaction to his demand, and she kept her expression open, allowed him to see the truth of her reply. "I love you madly, Daniel Jackson Smith." Her answer was breathless, but the truth was clear for him to hear. "There's never been anyone that could compare to you."

He swallowed hard, and his eyes, still intense, softened at the edges. "Ever since I saw you sing your first song, it's always been you."

He moved his fingers again, and her core tightened around him. His gaze was hot and possessive as it remained locked on hers.

"I love watching you come," he said hoarsely. "Come for me, babe. Now."

Rachel cried out his name as a searing orgasm ripped through her, ecstasy filling her. Her heart pounded, blood racing past her ears as wave after wave of pleasure careened through her. Once she was satiated and boneless, he lowered her legs to the bed and kissed his way up her body to her mouth.

His lips pressed to hers, and she wrapped her arms around his neck, her fingers tangling in his hair. He kissed her hard, and she rolled him over so that she was straddling him.

"Babe," he said, his voice husky, his lids heavy and oh so sexy. "Are you sure you're up for this?"

Yeah, she'd feel her injuries far more tomorrow, when the painkillers they'd given her at the hospital wore off. But for now, all she wanted to feel was Daniel. Every long, hard, sexy inch of him.

"Oh, Daniel… How can I not want this?"

———◆———

Daniel held Rachel's hips and thrust deep into her. She arched her back and cried out, her beautiful full breasts bouncing as she rode him.

He was hyperaware of her every move, her every breath, the clenching of her pussy around him. He fucked her fiercely, letting out the maelstrom of emotion that had warred inside him all day. Leaning forward, he hungrily sucked a nipple deep into his mouth, then nipped it, and she let out a breathy scream and squeezed his cock tight. He groaned. He desperately needed to come, but he kept a tight rein on it. She wasn't ready yet, and he'd be damned if he was coming before he got her off again.

Tossing her hair back, she brought one hand up to cup her breast and squeezed it firmly. She drew her bottom lip between her teeth, closed her eyes, and ground her hips deeper over him. She was so wet, so tight. She fucked him like there was nothing in the world she loved to do more.

He thrust up again, and she adjusted her angle so that she took him all in. He wasn't a small man, and she had a tight little pussy, but she took every inch he had to give.

It was all he could do to hold his orgasm back. His balls squeezed painfully. Rachel was going to be the death of him, but he didn't care.

God, he loved her!

She panted softly, a flush running up her chest to her cheeks. She was close. He brought his hand between them, fingered her clit rhythmically. He thrust upward, *hard*, and she screamed his name. "Daniel!"

His climax hit him with force, a wave of pleasure ripping through his veins, ripping through his heart.

Rachel leaned down, her nipples pressed against his chest, and suckled on the pulse point at the side of his neck. Then she bit him, with that perfect balance of pleasure and pain.

He hissed through his teeth, his cock pulsing inside her.

When she brought her mouth to his, he kissed her roughly, both of them short of breath, then he rolled her over, reversing their positions so that he was on top. Lids heavy with desire, he looked deep into her eyes.

He cupped her cheek in his palm, and she leaned her face into him.

"I love you." She smiled up at him. He'd never get tired of hearing that.

"I'm going to hate leaving you tomorrow night when we rescue the girls from Wilson. Promise you'll stay where I know you're safe. Wait for me. And after we end all this with the demon, it will be just you and me, and we'll work this out."

He'd finally found the love he'd thought would always elude him.

Then why couldn't he shake the feeling it was all about to slip through his fingers?

CHAPTER FORTY

Daniel strapped his shoulder holster on over his black fitted T-shirt, then tightened his ankle holster. Rachel held out his leather jacket, and he slipped his arms through the sleeves. She smoothed her hands along his broad shoulders, and untucked the hair that fell just inside the collar. He turned, circling her with his arms, and she breathed in clean, powerful male. He kissed the top of her head, then continued to get ready.

Earlier, he'd wordlessly slipped out of bed and walked to the shower. There was no fun "wanna join me" invitation. He was remote, disconnected. She'd witnessed his transition from lover to fighter, a one-man island of war.

When he was dressed, he popped the clip out of his pistol into his palm, looked it over, then reloaded the gun before securing it in the holster. His shoulders appeared even broader now, his presence even more formidable. The energy of a powerful male preparing himself mentally for battle rolled off him. It scared and excited her at the same time.

Rachel stood back, captivated, her eyes glued to his every move.

Finally, he looked at her. His eyes dark, his gaze focused. "It's time. I have to go."

"Did you find Lilly Randall?"

Daniel's eyes turned arctic, his jaw set. "We'll find her tonight." Rachel knew he'd consider it a personal failure if all six girls weren't rescued. It must tear him up not knowing where Lilly was.

Did he wonder whether his distraction with Rachel's case had contributed to their inability to locate Lilly?

Rachel certainly did, and she prayed her case didn't lead to Lilly's death.

Daniel cupped Rachel's face, kissed her on the lips. Then without a word, he turned and walked to his vehicle. Max jumped into the passenger side, and he closed the door after him. She stood at the window, her fingers digging into the sill, and watched them drive away.

Silence fell around her.

She walked to the balcony, through the open sliding doors, and stared out into the darkness across the ocean. A gentle breeze ruffled her hair, and she took a deep breath of the salty air. The low, rhythmic sound of the waves crashing to shore should have been comforting.

But wasn't.

It felt in every way *wrong* that she was here, in this exquisite house, with two armed men out front protecting her as though she were Lady Muck.

Rachel clenched her hands into fists. She felt helpless and powerless. Useless. Ridiculously unentitled to be in this luxurious place while everyone else, including Pia—and even Max—went to work saving young girls from a lifetime of addiction to drugs and working in a brothel. But what could she do about it?

There was a knock at the door.

Rachel's heart stilled.

Slowly she made her way to the door and peered out the peephole.

On the porch was a gray-haired man in a flannel shirt, his shoulders hunched with age. Rachel's heart skipped a beat. It was the old man she'd seen walking on the side of the road just before her accident.

Accident? Before she'd been *forced* off the road.

Two men dressed in black appeared at either side of the old man and began escorting him off the doorstep.

"Get your hands off me!" the old man growled. "I'm just trying to return her bag." He shrugged off the grip of the security guards, and they raised their brows as though surprised at his strength.

One guard grabbed a backpack from the old man and peered inside. He emptied the contents on the pavement and checked the lining. The other pulled out a handheld scanner and waved it over the bag. Was it for detecting bugs, or explosives? Either way, the guards seemed to be taking no chances.

Seemingly satisfied, one of the men repacked Rachel's belongings in the bag.

"Where did you find this?"

"On the side of the road," the old man said. "It had this address on a card, so I thought I'd return it."

The security guards looked at each other, shrugged, then escorted the old man off the property. He didn't appear to have a car, just walked off down the road. The guards stood at the end of the driveway, hands on hips, shaking their heads, clearly wondering the same thing as Rachel. What was an old man doing walking in the dark, miles away from anything?

One of the guards came to the door and rapped on it, using the knock that meant it was safe. *Overkill.* She could always look out the peephole, but Daniel had insisted.

The guard held out her backpack. "Is this yours?"

"Yes," Rachel said, taking the bag. "Thank you."

She closed the door and put her backpack on the table. How hadn't her bag been destroyed when the car had gone up in flames? Had she dragged it out of the car with her? She struggled to remember. Was it possible…? No. It had been in the boot.

And how had the old man gotten this address?

It was Daniel's address, not hers. This address was absolutely *not* on a card in her bag. Then how had the old man known where to return it?

The hair on the back of her nape rose, and a thin sheen of sweat broke out over her forehead. She knew what was in that bag.

The scry hadn't burned up with the car after all. It was now safely back in her possession.

But she wouldn't touch it.

Rachel made a cup of tea and sat down at the table, looking at the bag. Her leg jerked up and down, and she spat out a nail before nibbling on another.

The parchment with the banishing ritual hadn't been in her bag. That had been next to her on the front seat.

It hadn't escaped her notice that the only thing that mysteriously turned up in her possession again was the scry. As though it was meant to be hers…

Should she take it out? Just take a quick peek at it?

No. Absolutely not.

But it had come to her again. There must be a reason…

She took a sip of her tea, walked to the sink, and poured it down the drain. This situation called for something stronger than tea. She grabbed a wine glass, filled it with the Margaret River chardonnay she liked. Took a sip. Tipped it down the sink, and poured herself a glass of Daniel's whiskey.

She walked to the balcony, keeping her back to the bag on the table. Was it just her imagination, or did the house feel different with that thing in here?

She thought about the promises she'd made Daniel, about total honesty moving forward, and her chest tightened.

What she should do is take that scry out of her bag and smash it into a gazillion pieces.

No. It could be useful, somehow. She'd keep it safe for tonight, and she'd give it to Pia and Mark tomorrow. One night wouldn't make any difference.

Rachel's fingers tapped against the railing. Everyone was doing something. Something useful, and important. Mark and the *Debunking Reality* team were working back at Elise's house, and Pia and Daniel's team were rescuing young girls from a notorious drug lord's corruption.

And what was Rachel doing?

Sipping whiskey on a balcony overlooking the ocean.

It wasn't right.

No, it wasn't right at all.

She needed to be doing something to put this right. She was the one responsible for this mess in the first place.

Something fell in the kitchen, and she whipped her head around, her pulse racing, her breathing fast and heavy. Fighting off a wave of dizziness, she set her glass down.

When she walked back inside, her gaze was drawn to the bag on the table. To what was inside. But if she were honest, like she promised to be, she'd admit her attention hadn't left it for one second since it had been mysteriously returned.

Her feet crossed the room to the bag, all thoughts over the fallen object drifting away. Her fingers gripped the edge of the table. She was not going to get out the scry.

Pia had said it was evil. Possessed.

She'd be an idiot to even think about touching it again. A shiver rolled down her spine, and she rubbed at an ache behind her eyes. Her legs felt strange, her body hot and cold with fever.

She clung to the table's edge, and closed her eyes.

When she opened her eyes, she was sitting at the table, the scry in her hands.

She blinked in surprise. She didn't remember sitting down. She definitely didn't remember getting the scry out of her bag.

But… it felt right in her hands. She ran her fingers over its cool, polished surface. What was so wrong with it? Something niggled at her, some reason she shouldn't be holding it. What was it?

Oh yes, someone had told her it was dangerous. But why would that be? The scry had shown her the truth.

What if… what if…?

What if she used it just one last time? What if it could be used for good?

What if she could use it to find the sixth girl?

Perhaps the problem all along was that she wasn't using it correctly. After all, she'd had no idea what she'd been doing, especially at first. The scry answered questions; it was a divination tool. She was stronger now. She was in control. She would make sure her question was clear, that her mind was focused. Then the demon wouldn't be able to enter.

What if some good could happen out of all this evil?

What if she could make amends for what she'd done?

She held the answers in her hand.

All she had to do was ask.

Smoke began to swirl in the scry.

CHAPTER FORTY-ONE

Rachel took off her helmet and shook out her hair. She glanced up and down the street, ignoring the sharp stab of guilt she felt over taking Daniel's motorbike without his permission. But what choice did she have? Her car was barbecued, and it wasn't like the security guards were going to offer her a lift.

So she'd turned on an action movie with the surround-sound speakers cranked way up, sneaked out the back of the house, and waited until she'd pushed the bike a safe distance away before starting it. It wasn't stealing if you intended to return it, right?

All those years riding bikes with Rob and Trey had come in handy. Although the bikes she used to ride were a long way from Daniel's turbocharged Suzuki Hayabusa, which had a top speed of over two hundred and seventy miles per hour. A speed she went nowhere near. Although being on the back with Daniel at high speed… A delicious thrill rolled through her body, and she forcefully pushed the wayward thought aside.

Daniel would likely never speak to her again when he found out what she'd done. She took a breath and straightened her shoulders. She would not back out now. A girl's life—Lilly's life—was on the line.

Rachel walked along the side of the road toward the brothel, glancing behind her. Without stopping, she scanned the darkness, watching for moving shadows. She couldn't shake the feeling she was being watched. But she saw nothing.

Up ahead was the stone building that housed The Wild Dungeon, just as Rachel had seen it in the scry.

Fifty years ago, the location had been a slaughterhouse. She had seen and heard the anguished cries of the animals' final moments in the polished glass of the scry. She'd had to push through her instinctual response to withdraw, to shut out such horrifying images, before she'd been shown that Lilly Randall was here.

The music and voices were louder now that she'd nearly reached the edge of the parking lot.

She would slip in, grab Lilly, slip out.

The plan was as vague as it was simple. She had no idea what she was going to do when she got in there. All she knew was that she had to get in and find Lilly. She'd work out how to get them both out alive if and when she made it that far. Rachel stopped in the darkness across the street, took a moment to catch her breath, calm her racing heart.

Pulling out her phone, which had still been in her bag along with the scry, she turned her back to hide the screen's glow. She'd try one last time before putting her plan into action.

She phoned Daniel again, for the umpteenth time. Why wasn't the call going through? She tried Mark again too. His phone was off, and she went straight to voice mail. Then she tried Pia, hoping she could pass a message to Daniel through Nate. Again, the call went to voice mail.

For at least an hour, Rachel had been trying to give Daniel the information she'd received. Yeah, he'd be upset about the scry, but he'd see that the information had been useful. She could endure the lecture he'd give her.

But there wouldn't be a lecture, because no one was answering. And that meant she had no choice.

She took a deep breath and shakily let it out. She wasn't an undercover investigator. She was a singer.

And she could be Lilly's last hope. She tugged down the tiny black skirt, then laughed at herself. Hookers weren't known for their modesty, and she'd never pass for one if she didn't remember that. She tugged the skirt back up to show the tops of the garters she'd worn to cover the cuts and bruises she'd received in the crash.

She fluffed up her hair, pulled the V of her tight top down and puffed up her cleavage. Balancing on stupidly high heels, Rachel waited for an opportunity.

A car parked down the street, and a single man got out. This could be her what she was looking for. She waited for him to get closer and moved out of the shadows.

She approached him, deliberately swaying slightly on her heels as though she'd had a little too much to drink. His eyes lit up, traveling the length of her body, from her heels up her long legs to her breasts, where they lingered. She forced a come-hither smile on her face.

When he was close enough, she stumbled, falling into him. He caught her, and she rubbed her breasts against him.

"Sorry." She pushed off him and tugged at her top, yanking it too far down, exposing her full cleavage, then feigning surprise, she giggled, pulling it back up, exposing her stomach. She frowned, as though this confused her.

"What are you doing out here, honey?" the man asked. His voice was thick, his eyes almost bulging out of his head. If she played her cards right, he'd be the one to get her inside. He was a large muscular man, heavyset, in his fifties, with some excess weight around the middle.

"Oh." She touched her palm to her head. "I needed some fresh air. And I—"

Rachel turned her head, sniffed, and pretended to cry.

As she'd hoped, the man immediately put his arm around her shoulders, and she allowed herself to be pulled into his chest. He was an Aussie bloke, protecting a sheila.

"I recognized my next… friend." She blinked up at him innocently, as though he didn't know she was a hooker. "He was rough last time, and after the night I've already had, I just couldn't face him. I'm sorry." Rachel affected a frightened expression. "Don't tell anyone, or I'll get in big trouble." She pushed off him. "I'd better go back inside."

"Wait," he said.

Rachel stopped, blinking up at him.

"What if you already had a… friend?"

Rachel pretended to look uncertain. She shook her head. "No. I don't think that would work. He asked specifically for me. He always does."

"But what if you're busy?"

Rachel looked up at him through her mascara-clad lashes. "Then he'd have to wait."

"And maybe get impatient, and see someone else."

"That might work." Rachel gave him a grateful smile and moved into his arms. "Thank you, Mr.…?"

"Big," he said. "Call me Mr. Big."

"Like in *Sex and the City*?" Rachel giggled. "Thanks, Mr. Big," Rachel said in her best sultry voice. "I'm Carrie, and I'll make it worth your trouble."

"Actually, I prefer Samantha." He licked his lips, and her stomach turned, but she smiled through it.

"Samantha it is," Rachel said. "We'll have to sneak past the front desk." She giggled like a naughty schoolgirl, as though this were an adventure, and not the most dangerous and stupid thing she'd ever done in her life. Her heart was pounding so loud, she was sure he could hear it.

"You leave that to me."

Rachel's heart raced, and it was no small relief to find the front office bustling with activity. Music pounded from beyond the red door, and Big wrapped his arm around Rachel. With a nod at the bouncer, he led her straight inside. Clearly Big was a regular here.

Inside was a large bar, the tables packed, the waitresses wearing hot pants and colored pasties with long tassels, and nothing else. Money was exchanged for lap dances, and men were led into side rooms by girls in private-school uniforms, leather BDSM gear, and even some dressed as Wonder Woman. Looking around her, Rachel took note of where everything was.

She could see the renovations that had been made to transform the old slaughterhouse into a brothel. Among the changes, the concrete floors had been polished, and no doubt the patrons were unaware that the unusual swirling patterns beneath the polish were bloodstains.

It felt as though eyes were watching her from in between the human forms in the room. Her chest ached as she walked on shaky legs. She struggled to breathe, somehow forcing herself to remain calm. To not give herself away.

Playing up her seductive act, she disguised her shaking hands by wrapping them around Big as he led her down a long corridor. Her heart pounded. How was she going to give Big the slip so she could find Lilly?

Big licked his lips and raised a brow, silently asking which room was hers.

She swallowed. "The end one. But I'd really like a drink first."

"A drink?"

"Like a date," she added, rubbing her breasts against his arm. "Wouldn't you like to date Samantha?"

Big shrugged, then smirked. "Why not? I'm up for anything tonight."

"Go get us something at the bar while Samantha gets the room ready. I'll be just a minute," Rachel said.

Big frowned. Clearly that was not how things worked around here. Rachel put on a seductive voice, tiptoed her fingers down his stomach, then traced her fingers across the bulge in his pants. "Don't you think Sam's worth waiting for?" she asked in her best little-girl hurt voice, licking her finger and trailing it across her cleavage.

Big's eyes bulged again, and he nodded in lieu of words.

She gave him a little shove, blew him a seductive kiss, and walked in the opposite direction. Additional rooms, where guests could mingle and talk, had been built onto the original structure. From what Rachel could work out from the signs in the front lobby, you could buy a membership, come in for a drink at the topless bar, and hire some additional entertainment for an extra charge.

Of course, this late at night, entertainment was the main course.

Rachel kept her head down and ignored the strange looks she received from some of the girls. She might have fooled Big, but she wouldn't fool the ladies working here.

She moved in a way that was nonchalant, swaying her hips, as she watched the other girls do. She kept her head back, eyes half closed, as though she were waiting for someone, while checking every face, looking for Lilly.

She couldn't see her.

And she was running out of time.

Had the scry lied to her? Was this a setup by the demon? Luring her here to kill her?

At the bar, a beer in his hand, Rachel saw Big searching for her. He pushed off the wall and walked into the crowd of people. Rachel swallowed and peered into one of the private rooms. A glazed pair of eyes, devoid of emotion, stared back at her. Not her girl.

Moving quickly, Rachel moved onto the next room, and then the next. A man hurled abuse at her, and she jumped back, closing the door. Her stomach roiled. Each to their own and all that, but damn, she wished she could un-see that!

Rachel began to shiver. The hairs on the back of her neck were standing on end as though she were being pursued by something. Something a lot more terrifying than Big.

She glanced over her shoulder to see Big looking directly at her, a suspicious expression on his face.

Busted!

How the hell was she going to get out of this?

———— ♦ ————

Behind Wilson's "nightclub" in the center of town, the side door to a large black van slid open and TSI silently poured out. The rhythmic pounding of a bass line escaped through the walls of the club and drifted out into the warm, still night as the team members, weapons in hand, took their positions.

The boys moved as one finely honed unit, entering through the solid metal doors as though they weren't secured with dead bolts and security locks.

Blade, Ryder, Wynter, and Wells all went to the right. Daniel, with Max at his side, made his way left, to the door second on the right, where Pia had told him he would find Scotty Fryer.

The man who had murdered Daniel's father.

Daniel's boots glided across the polished concrete floor, not making so much as a squeak, not that such stealth was required with all the noise from the club.

He touched the door handle and dragged in a breath. All these years of waiting. And this was it.

Daniel threw open the door, his eyes landing on a woman on her knees wearing only a G-string, her face buried in the crotch of a man sitting on the bed. She whirled around when the door bounced off the wall.

"The fuck?" Fryer growled.

Daniel trained his weapon on Fryer and crossed the room. The woman immediately scuttled out of the way, her wide eyes flicking between Daniel and the large German shepherd at his side baring its teeth.

"Will he attack?" she asked.

"Only if I tell him to."

Daniel picked up a silky piece of clothing from the end of the bed and threw it at her. She clutched it in front of her, but didn't put it on.

"Get out."

Giving Max a wide berth, she scrambled out of the room, her bare ass jiggling as she ran. Time was limited; she'd go straight for help. Keeping the gun trained on Fryer, Daniel kicked the door shut with his boot.

"Who are you?" Fryer said, cupping a hand over his naked crotch and standing.

"1993," Daniel said. "Driving a stolen Holden Commodore, you killed a man in the driveway of his own home."

Fryer frowned as though trying to place the incident and simultaneously work out what was happening right now. He took his time thinking. How many men had he killed the same way?

"Twenty-four years ago, a little boy was waiting at the window for his dad to come home, only to see him gunned down and die in his own driveway."

Recognition finally lit Fryer's eyes. His gaze connected with Daniel's, and there was no doubt. The killer's eyes had been burned into Daniel's memory all these years, had haunted his nightmares.

"Let me guess, you're the boy," Fryer said with a sick grin. "I remember now. That was the cop."

"He was my father."

"So?" Fryer shrugged. "What's the death of one cop?"

"Why?" Daniel was conscious of the seconds ticking away, but he needed to know.

Daniel closed the distance between them, while Max stayed where he was. He wouldn't move unless Daniel gave the order. Fryer knew he was going to die; Daniel read the recognition on his face. You didn't live this lifestyle and not know when your time was up.

"Tell me why you did it," Daniel said.

"Five grand." Fryer rubbed his chin. "Would have done it for less. Needed the cash bad back then."

Daniel's fingers twitched on the trigger. He wished he had time with this son of a bitch, had the chance to make him suffer. But someone rapped on the door, the pattern marking it as coming from the team.

It was time to go.

"Who ordered the hit?"

Fryer smirked. "I've always worked for Wilson. I don't ask why. I just get the job done."

Another rap on the door.

"This is for you, Dad," Daniel said softly. His eyes stung as he briefly glanced skyward. He blinked and his eyes were clear. His gaze cold, hard, and focused, he squeezed off one shot, dead center mass. Fryer's naked body slumped to the ground.

Daniel had expected to feel something more profound. A strong sense of relief, or closure perhaps. Instead, there was nothing. Just an emptiness. A cool acceptance that something that needed to be done had now been finished.

Another rap at the door.

He took one last look at Fryer, made sure he wasn't breathing, then turned to go.

The team piled into the van, Daniel and Max barely making it inside before they sped off. Daniel slid the door closed and held the handle for balance as the van took a corner hard.

Daniel stared out the tinted back window. Wilson's men were giving chase in a black sedan. The guy in the passenger seat leaned out the window, peeled off a round of shots, the bullets hitting the back of the van with heavy thunks. The windows were bulletproof, but Daniel instinctively angled his body to shelter Max at his feet.

Just before their pursuers' vehicle slammed head on into a traffic light.

Daniel grinned. Fortune was smiling upon them.

With any luck, Wilson's men wouldn't survive the crash.

In the front seat of the van, a girl huddled against the door. She looked small and frightened. Pia was holding one of her hands in both of hers.

Daniel's heart rate normalized. Partially numb, with blood rushing past his ears, Daniel wiped his palms on his jeans. Killing a man, no matter how justified the reason, never felt the way you'd think it would. Perhaps he'd feel something later, in the silence of night, at a time when he was alone with his whiskey.

But there was no room for emotion on the job.

"Oh God," Pia said, twisting her body and speaking to him through the metal bars from the front seat. "I just saw where Lilly Randall is!"

"Where?" There was still time. They had five of the girls; if Lilly wasn't far away, they could still pull this off. Wilson would know for sure by now what TSI had done.

"Where is she?"

"She's with Rachel."

Daniel's heart slammed in his chest, and Pia turned wide eyes on him. "Rachel is with Lilly at The Wild Dungeon."

Chapter Forty-Two

Rachel pasted what she hoped was a seductive smile on her face and gave Big a coy little wave with her fingers. She licked her index finger with her tongue and held it up in front of her, as though to say, one more minute.

Then she placed her finger in her mouth and sucked, her blood red lips pouting suggestively. Big tracked her movement with eyes glued to her finger.

Someone touched Big's shoulder, and he turned and greeted the other man. He looked back at Rachel and mouthed "One minute."

Rachel swallowed. Big wouldn't wait much longer.

Lilly had to be here. Or was this a huge mistake? Where was her evidence? The goddamned scry? She felt ridiculously foolish and unreasonably frightened. There was a subtle shift in the air, as if some unseen menace had entered the brothel. An argument broke out near the bar, and a woman yelped in pain as her partner grabbed her too hard. A shout came from the front reception, and it sounded like a bouncer had shoved someone into a wall.

What was going on?

Behind it all, the music still pounded its low dark sultry beat.

Rachel swallowed past the lump in her throat. She'd checked all the rooms and hadn't spotted her girl. She should forget this whole idea and get out before she ended up with concrete slippers at the bottom of the Swan River.

She hurried through the sprawling building, looking for an exit. An open back door or window would be perfect. After searching for longer than her promised one-minute return to Big, Rachel finally located a back door. People were milling around, so she waited, her back against the wall, while she applied lipstick with a handheld mirror.

A door opened to her right and Rachel glanced up. Long blonde hair, young, tiny frame. Lilly! She had opened the door, and a man exited the room. Lilly gripped the frame as though it were the only thing holding her upright. Rachel's stomach clenched, her fear dissolving in a rush of anger. Lilly's eyes were glassy and vacant. Track marks bruised the inside of her left arm, and her right cheek was swollen and streaked with concealer.

Rachel moved to her, took her hand. It felt cold, delicate as a bird's wing. Lilly blinked vacant, but sad, eyes up at her.

"Come with me."

The girl was so out of it, she didn't even put up a fight when Rachel put an arm around her and led her away. She was so resigned, so removed from her body, Rachel could have done almost anything to her. Rachel's heart squeezed. That was the exact reason why the girl was this way. People had been doing anything they wanted to her. And she'd had no choice but to let them.

Not anymore.

Adrenaline lit a fire in her veins. "Lilly Randall, I'm Rachel, and I'm not going to hurt you. You're coming with me. Play along."

Rachel half-steered, half-carried the girl toward the back door. She talked the whole time, trying to make it appear that they were having a conversation. The group that had been cloistered in the back room had moved on, and it was now empty. She moved more quickly now, heading for the door and freedom.

"Where are we going?" Lilly asked. "We're not allowed to go out there."

"Shh!" Rachel hissed.

The girl planted her feet and shook her head. "No, no. I can't. I *can't* go out that door. He'll kill you. Kill me." Lilly's eyes were wide with fear.

"I'm here to help you. I'm getting you out of here."

"I can't leave!" Lilly shrieked, and two nearby people turned to look.

Rachel's heart pounded, and she saw Big walking in their direction. Ah hell, she was screwed.

They had to run!

Rachel dragged the girl to the back door. Lilly screamed, and Rachel yanked the handle.

Locked!

Oh God. Shifting restlessly on her feet, Rachel looked at the knob. The handle turned freely. Then why wasn't it opening? People began to shout behind her. Her eyes raced up the length of the door, stopping when she saw a deadbolt. With fumbling fingers, she slid the bolt back and threw open the door.

Cold night air slapped her face, and she raced out the door, tugging on Lilly's arm. Now that they were outside, the girl finally stopped fighting her, and they ran across a courtyard. Rachel scanned the area. Empty tables and chairs littered the space; it was obviously a daytime alfresco area. The walls were high, the wrought iron gate locked with a giant padlock.

They were trapped. What had she expected? An open carpark?

Heart hammering in her chest, Rachel let go of Lilly, dragged a table up against the wall, and told her to climb up onto it. She did as told, but couldn't reach the top of the wall. Rachel grabbed a chair and placed it on the table. "Hurry!" she said. "Climb up and over." Big and two other men dressed in black and carrying handheld radios rushed toward them. Lilly stood on the top of the rickety chair and struggled to get a leg over the wall.

Rachel stood on the table, trying to find purchase on the vertical surface of the wall. The rough limestone abraded her knees, and then a hand closed around her ankle.

She screamed.

A large bald man, with a full beard and piercing eyes, yanked at her leg. She held onto the top of the wall with everything she had.

More people poured out the door, filling the small area with shouts and confusion.

And then there was an almighty roar.

A shot was fired into the air, and people ran screaming from the courtyard back inside.

The goon holding her ankle let go, reached into his pocket, and pulled a gun. "You bitches stop where you are, or I'll shoot!"

Several dark figures climbed over the wall and jumped down into the courtyard. Out of the corner of her eye, Rachel saw the goon drop to the ground and be dragged away.

Rachel climbed on top of the teetering chair, saw hands reaching for Lilly. "Jump!" someone called.

Rachel recognized that voice. Daniel! "It's okay," Rachel said. "You can trust him."

The girl disappeared over the wall, and Rachel extended her hand over the edge, hoping Daniel would grab it.

Instead, someone grabbed her leg and yanked her off the table.

Rachel landed hard on the ground, and for a moment she was stunned. She was expecting to see another of Wilson's goons looming over her, but when she opened her eyes, she saw only objects circling around in the air.

Who had grabbed her ankle?

A chair flew past, crashing into the opposite wall. There was a scream and shouting, and then the courtyard cleared. Three men she recognized as part of the TSI team trained their weapons on Wilson's thugs.

"Get inside." Ethan's command was a harsh I'm-going-to-kill-someone, who's-going-to-be-first bark. Sam rushed to Rachel's side. "Stay here," Sam ordered. "Wait for Dan." Sam darted a frown at the wall, as though unsure as to what was keeping him.

Sam moved off with Ethan and Sean inside the building as more of Wilson's men rushed to the scene. Rachel heard the muffled sound of three shots being fired, following by screaming and shouting.

Now alone in the courtyard, Rachel felt cold and vulnerable. Something evil was watching her. Her heart was racing out of her chest, and suddenly being inside with Wilson's men was more appealing than being here alone. Rachel rushed to follow TSI into the building, but an icy wind blasted her backward, and she hit her head against the brick wall. Stars in black smudges blurred her vision.

From the other side of the wall, she heard Daniel shouting her name frantically.

A menacing presence lurked nearby. Blood thrashed past her ears. She struggled for breath and trembled uncontrollably.

Something was on the far side of the courtyard, a shadow darker than the shadows.

The pained cry of a thousand wounded lost souls screamed in her ears, and she breathed in the cloying odor of death. The spirits of animals rose up from the concrete floor of the old slaughterhouse and seeped out from the walls: pigs, cows, and sheep howling in pain as blunt knives sent them far too slowly to their deaths. Their souls pressed down on her, forcing the breath out of her lungs. She wanted to run, but her limbs refused to obey her commands. She was frozen to the spot.

Rachel turned her gaze and faced her enemy. Sohn-Zae. The demonic face from the scry.

He moved closer, and she hissed in pain as the scratches on both her back and her neck burned viciously. Her hiss turned into a scream as the pain intensified, and a chilling laugh came from right above her.

The demon whipped his hand through the air, and her legs were swept away from beneath her.

Rachel dropped to the ground like a lead weight.

Behind the demon, the dead animals watched with cold, lifeless eyes.

———— ◆ ————

Daniel's gut twisted painfully. Something was stopping him from climbing over the wall. It was an eight-foot limestone wall. Shouldn't be a problem. He jumped, but every time he gripped the top of the wall, his hands were somehow shoved off.

Max had started barking the moment they'd pulled up and refused to quit, so Daniel had no other choice than to leave him in the vehicle. Daniel didn't need Max's animal instinct to know there was something seriously fucked up with the atmosphere around this place.

The frustration churning in his gut was brutal. Rachel screamed out his name, and a powerful surge of adrenaline ripped through his body. An animalistic growl roared out of his mouth as he jumped, scaling the wall in a way he wouldn't have thought possible. Sheer *need* to get to Rachel gave him strength he hadn't known he possessed.

Or had whatever it was that had been forcing him back finally decided it was ready for him?

From the top of the wall, he saw Rachel lying on the ground, her hair fanned around her.

He hadn't believed it when Pia told him what she'd seen. That Rachel was at The Wild Dungeon. Not until he'd seen her helping Lilly Randall over the wall.

He was too angry, too terrified to admire Rachel's courage, too amped up to wonder how the fuck she'd known where Lilly was when his team and the best psychic in Australia hadn't known.

His questions would have to wait, because Pia was standing near Rachel's prone body and was angrily chanting words he couldn't quite make out. Floating above Rachel was a dark shadow, as solid as a storm cloud, as dark as a bottomless pit dropping into the deepest earth.

The entity did not need a physical form for Daniel to recognize how dire the threat was to Rachel.

Fury raced through his veins, distorting his vision. He ignored the table and jumped off the wall to the ground. Landing in a crouch, he pulled his weapon out of habit, aimed it at the shadow, a presence as menacing as any human he'd ever encountered. The screams, the pained squeals of animals being tortured, rolled through him.

"Leave her alone!" Daniel roared, wild with rage, his frustration and fear more intense than any he'd ever experienced. Rachel lay unmoving. If the demon had hurt her…

Daniel raced toward her, only to slam into an ice-cold wall of energy.

"It won't let you get near her," Pia shouted. Daniel threw himself at the virtual wall, but it held him back. Relentlessly, he pushed forward, his body taking hit after pounding hit from unseen fists. The courtyard swirled with a bitterly cold wind, which formed a vortex at its center. Daniel focused through the red spots rage had formed in his vision, cursing the entity right back to Hell.

"Get away from her!"

Pia sprinkled something from a bottle she was holding, and the virtual wall separating him from Rachel suddenly parted. Daniel threw himself on her, covering her body with his. Something sharp ripped down his back, and he sheltered Rachel's limp body with everything he had. If he lost her, he had nothing. Let the demon tear him to shreds; Daniel would be dead anyway without her.

Pia screamed, and Daniel glanced up to see her standing on the table, Nate in front of her, sheltering her from stones that began pelting in their direction. More stones thudded into Daniel's back, and he wrapped his arms around Rachel's head, protecting her.

Nate sheltered Pia as the storm raged on, until eventually, after seemingly never-ending minutes, Daniel could hear Pia chanting what sounded to his untrained hears like Bible verses, her voice eventually drowning out the misery and suffering of the animals. One by one, the rocks stopped mid-air and fell to the ground.

An image of a horned, demonic face, with black soulless eyes, curled horns, and a pointed chin, flashed in his mind, and then the air split, and the face disappeared.

The storm was over, all silent, except for a painful ringing in Daniel's ears. Debris littered the courtyard. Daniel sat back on his knees, gently picked up Rachel's limp body, and cradled her in his arms, pressing her cheek to his chest.

Her arms hung at her sides, and he willed her to raise a hand, run it through his hair. He listened for her breathing, couldn't be sure. Her pulse beat faintly beneath his fingers. He made a strangled noise in the back of his throat.

"You're going to be fine, baby," Daniel vowed fiercely.

He brushed the hair off her face and leaned down and kissed her cheek. A moan wrenched itself out of his chest.

Pia rushed over, and kneeling next to him, took a pendant from around her neck and placed it on Rachel. "You need to get her out of here. Hurry."

The back door to the brothel slammed open, and Nate, Sam, Sean, and Ethan poured out, their expressions grim as they eyed Rachel's prone body on the ground. Daniel rose, with the most precious thing he had in the world firm in his arms.

"If she doesn't pull through this, I'm going to follow you into the pits of Hell and kill you for the rest of eternity!" Daniel shouted to the courtyard, hoping the demonic son of a bitch could hear him.

"I'll follow you down," Sam said grimly.

"Not without me," Sean added.

"Fucked if I'm going to be left behind," Ethan growled and Nate nodded his agreement.

Daniel meant it with every fiber of his being. Nothing was more important to him than the woman in his arms.

And as his mates grouped around him, he knew they'd kill for her too. Rachel was a part of the brotherhood, as much as Pia, as much as Sage.

Daniel's heart squeezed painfully in his chest.

Rachel was going to be okay.

She had to be.

He'd never survive it otherwise.

CHAPTER FORTY-THREE

A warmth spread through Rachel's body, the radiant heat from the flickering flames of a fire on a winter's night. It seeped through her veins, warmed her heart.

She knew she was in Daniel's arms.

It was the way he held her, the gentle strength in his muscles as he clasped her body to his. The rhythmic pounding of his heart, his scent, his whiskey-deep voice as he spoke quietly to someone above her.

She stretched her body as sounds and movement told her she was in a vehicle. A cool nose nuzzled into her, sniffing and licking. *Max.* Rachel smiled, making her head pound. She groaned.

"Rach?"

She opened her eyes and looked directly into Daniel's. His were dark, his lids heavy, his lips pressed tight with concern.

"Daniel."

"Hi, sleepyhead." He lowered his mouth to hers, cupping the back of her skull and kissing her tenderly. His lips trembled against hers, and she wrapped her arms around his neck. He rested his forehead against hers, his ragged breathing matching her own.

He pulled back, his gaze searching her face. "Are you all right?"

Rachel struggled to sit up, and he adjusted his hold so she was sitting in his lap. "I can't let go of you just yet," he said into her hair in a voice only she'd be able to hear.

"Hi!" Pia said, twisting around from her position in the front seat.

Rachel gave her a wobbly smile. "Hi."

Ethan was in the drivers' seat, not Nate.

"Nate is driving Sam and Sean back to Perth," Pia said, answering Rachel's unvoiced question. "Ethan is catching the red-eye back to Adelaide." Back to Sage and baby Celeste.

Ethan glared at her in the rearview mirror. "Well, if that wasn't the most goddamned stupid thing I've ever seen anyone do in my life. What the hell were you thinking going into a Wild Wilson establishment like that? You could have been killed."

"Hey!" Pia slapped his arm.

Daniel made a sound in the back of his throat.

"Those are my lines, mate," Daniel said. "However, I was going to wait to be sure she was all right before I said them."

"I'm right here," Rachel grumbled.

"Well, you almost weren't," Ethan said.

"That's enough," Daniel snapped. "Although, my tactless mate does have a point." He softened his voice. "What were you thinking, babe? Do you have any idea the danger you put yourself in tonight? There's a reason TSI go in as a full team."

"Lilly is safe, isn't she?" Rachel had seen Daniel reach up and pluck her from the wall. Had she somehow landed back in the hands of Wild Wilson's crew? Had tonight been all for nothing?

Or worse. She put a hand over her mouth as her stomach roiled. Had she jeopardized the lives of the other five girls? A tear rolled out of the side of her eye and down her cheek.

Max, sensing her distress, placed his paws on her lap. She ran her fingers over the top of his head.

"Lilly is safe," Daniel said.

"And the other girls?" She held her breath.

"All safe. We got all six back tonight."

A warmth filled Rachel's chest. Then she started to shiver as the enormity of what she'd done started to sink in.

"Six girls will be going home to their families tonight. We all played a part in that," Pia said, glaring at Ethan. "And it would have been only five, if not for Rachel."

Despite Daniel's current mood, Rachel consoled herself with the fact she'd helped save Lilly's life tonight. And it felt good.

Except... Rachel peered up at Daniel's expression and winced.

"How did you know where Lilly was?" Ethan's question was characteristically terse. Ethan was never one to mince words; he was a formidable presence on the best of days. There'd also be no skirting around with her answers. Sage must be a hell of a woman to handle a man like that.

Rachel risked another glance at Daniel. She had her own pissed-off alpha male to deal with.

A heavy, sinking feeling filled her.

"You took a huge gamble trusting that thing," Pia said, and Rachel no longer had the need to answer.

Daniel's jaw clenched, waves of anger rolling off him and filling the car. She shifted out of his arms and into the seat next to him, and he let her go without resistance.

"I'm sorry," she whispered to Daniel.

He didn't look at her, and she saw his throat work as he swallowed. "You had the scry. You lied to me." His voice broke, but his expression was set in steel. "Again."

In his eyes, she'd broken the first real promises they'd ever made to each other. Within twenty-four hours. Surely that didn't bode well for them. Their relationship was so new and so very fragile.

"Lilly is alive because of the scry," Rachel reminded him weakly.

"The demon wasn't trying to save Lilly," Pia said. "The demon didn't give a toss about her. This was about *you*. He was making another attempt to possess you now that you no longer have the way to banish him. He got you onto his turf. It was no accident you ended up on Wild Wilson's premises tonight."

Rachel sucked in a breath. She wasn't sure how many more of these events that weren't coincidences she could take. It was a creepy feeling not being as in control of your destiny as you thought you were.

Twisting around in her seat, Pia held Rachel's eyes. "The demon showed you where Lilly was to get you there. To have you vulnerable."

"Then why didn't it succeed?" Rachel couldn't help asking, even as a shiver raked down her spine.

To her surprise, it was Ethan who answered. "Love."

Pia smiled. "Yes. Only love in its purest form can defeat evil at its most primal level. Hate is the polar opposite of love, and hatred from a demon is most pure."

Pia and Ethan shared a private glance, and she briefly squeezed Ethan's hand on the steering wheel with her fingertips in what Rachel suspected was a shared memory of what had happened to Ethan and Sage last September.

"Where is the scry now?" Pia asked Rachel.

"At Daniel's house." To him she said, "Sorry about borrowing your bike without asking."

Daniel whipped out his phone and fired off a message.

"What are you doing?" Was he arranging to get rid of the scry?

Fear gripped Rachel and simultaneously sickened her. Her forehead broke out in a feverish sweat. The panic that gripped her was akin to someone taking her own child.

It's mine! a part of her roared. *You have no right to take it from me!*

"Getting my bike back," Daniel said.

Oh. Of course, the bike. "I thought you were arranging to take the scry away."

"How do we get rid of that fucker?" Ethan demanded. Rachel's heart raced.

"We don't," Pia said from the front seat. "The scry needs to be with her. It belongs to her, and because of her ancestral connection to it and the demon, she's the one who needs it to end this."

"I know it sounds crazy, but I'm drawn to it. I feel like I'm supposed to have it. For some reason, I feel that it's mine."

"It *is* yours," Pia said. "That woman you saw in the scry? The high priestess, Maia? She's a blood relative of yours. The scry has been handed down through the bloodline for generations. You have it now."

Rachel felt the truth in Pia's words, felt the sense of knowing, as though she'd merely confirmed something Rachel had known all her life.

"But why me?" Rachel asked. "Why not Elise? Or Mum?"

"Abilities skip generations and siblings at will. No one knows why one person is born with an ability, and another is not. Why can some children instinctively play a piano or guitar? Some people are born painters or singers. We've all watched in awe as a ten-year old belts out a Whitney Houston song and wonder how the hell a voice like that could come out of such a small girl. You might have experienced some paranormal events when you were young, but Sally was born with a true gift."

"That's why Sally can see the demon and the captain without the scry," Rachel breathed.

"Yes. I feel the demon is biding his time until Sally is old enough to control through the scry."

"I won't let that happen," Rachel said, determination molten steel in her veins.

"Sohn-Zae is an archdemon of jealousy and revenge," Pia said, her voice grim. "I saw what he was tonight when he hovered above you. He uses jealousy to control. Love is the most powerful emotion in the universe; it trumps hate, anger, everything lower. But the demon knows that the more powerful the love, the more powerful the emotion if that love is betrayed. A decent, law-abiding man finding his lover in bed with another man is capable of committing murder, where nothing else in life would otherwise cause that to be possible."

Rachel remembered the rage she'd felt on the captain's behalf when she'd believed Anna-Marie had been unfaithful to him. The rage she'd felt on her mother's behalf. On her own.

"That was when I felt the demon's influence the strongest," Rachel said, recognition weighing heavily. "He used my feelings about what my father did to my mother to manipulate me."

"Yes," Pia said. "That's how he works."

Rachel's eyes stung, and she blinked back her tears. "I had the solution," she said, her voice thick. "Anna-Marie gave me the banishing ritual. But it burned up in the car."

Pia closed her eyes, her face twisted in regret. "I know. Daniel, you won't like this, but I don't know any other way around it."

"I'm almost afraid to ask," he growled.

"Rachel, I want you to cast a circle tomorrow night and contact Maia directly to ask for the banishing rite. I'll take you through what to do. I'll do my best to hold the demon back while you get whatever information you can that might help. We need the ritual, and she is the one who knows it."

Daniel glared out the window, a muscle twitching along his jaw. Rachel ran her fingers across his clenched fist, and her heart squeezed. She knew what keeping quiet was costing him.

She didn't know the first thing about casting circles, or how she'd contact Maia, but she was prepared to do whatever it took.

"Without the rite, there is no other way. You are the connection, Rachel. You are the one who has the power to end this."

Rachel nodded, her jaw firming. "I'll do it. I just need you to tell me how."

Ethan slid a glance at Pia. "Nate know what you're planning?"

"He will when I tell him," Pia said.

Ethan shook his head in exasperation.

"Why did the faces of the captain and his crew appear on Liam's wall?" Rachel asked.

"The demon wanted you out of the house," Pia said. "It wanted you out on the road alone. There was too much love in the house with your sister and the kids. Divide and conquer. Your sister's love for her children was a powerful protection against his influence. That's why the faces appeared when she was out of the house."

Pia paused. "And you were at a low point."

Rachel looked up and met her eyes.

"Your sister had told you about her illness, and you were in a state of fear. Fear for her, for her children. It was the crack through which he gained access. When the faces appeared, you felt a strong sense of guilt and responsibility, especially in light of your sister's illness, and you reacted with extreme anger. You reconnected with the scry. The demon then influenced you, using the jealousy and anger that were already inside you, and you drove off to Anna-Marie's house. Alone."

Rachel slumped down horrified over what could have happened. She remembered seeing the demon in the back seat.

"You had the parchment, the way to send him back to Hell. He tried to kill you. Would have succeeded..."

Except Rob's love had saved her.

Rachel opened the window, took a deep breath of cool air. "This ends tomorrow night."

She wouldn't allow the demon to get anywhere near Sally. Or her cancer-stricken sister.

Rachel would do whatever it took. Pay whatever price.

Like Ethan had done for Sage, like Nate had done for Pia.

She glanced at the man she loved sitting stonily beside her. The man she loved more than life itself. She would do this for Sally, she would do it for Daniel.

"The verses I was chanting might have helped shift the negative energy tonight," Pia said. "But it was Daniel's love for you that saved your life. Gave you the greatest protection from the demon. Love trumps everything," Pia said, referring to her words from earlier.

Rachel's heart skipped, and Daniel met her eyes. She saw the truth in Pia's words reflected in his gaze. She knew Daniel loved her, as she loved him with every fiber of her being. But love was not simple. It was complicated. Messy. It was time to bare the final part of her soul to him.

Ethan pulled up in front of Daniel's house.

She needed to tell Daniel the truth. All of it. Even if it meant losing him forever. It was time he knew he was in love with a murderer.

It was time he knew she'd killed Trey.

Chapter Forty-Four

The warm, sweet fragrance of peach and vanilla wafted out of the open bathroom door and wrapped around Daniel. He inhaled the scent of Rachel's body wash and closed his eyes, as though drawing it inside himself would chase away the chilling knowledge that he'd almost lost her again tonight.

Daniel closed his eyes as updates from WAPOL rolled across his screen, willing the lingering fear and nausea to pass.

He could still feel her fragile, unmoving body in his arms, the mind-numbing chill of the devastation that had threatened to take him over. He shook his head to clear the image.

Did she have no comprehension of the risk she'd taken tonight? A human life meant nothing to Wilson. He was a psychopath who killed without warning, without reason, and without conscience.

But whether or not Rachel fully understood the danger, she had risked her life for a stranger. Something that hadn't escaped his team's attention. Rachel had earned the respect and loyalty of his team—his mates—tonight.

As though on cue, Nate's name flashed on his phone.

"You made good time," Daniel said, flicking a quick glance at his watch. Nate had dropped Sam and Sean off in the city and was already on his way back. A childhood spent at the track with Formula One drivers had cemented Ryder's lifelong love of nice cars and driving at high speed.

Nate chuckled. "Heard from Blade that all six girls are in the hospital being checked over, and their parents have all been notified. Got intel from Zach that the cops are raiding The Wild Dungeon as we speak. Not a good night for ol' Wilson."

Daniel smiled. The feeling of a successfully completed case never got old. Tonight's arrests would be minor in the grand scheme of Wilson's criminal empire, but the inconvenience—not to mention the loss of Fryer—would piss him off, and for that Daniel took some satisfaction.

"You've got one helluva ballsy chick there, mate." Daniel could hear the grin in Nate's voice.

Daniel's neck cracked loudly as he stretched it from one side to the other.

Nate laughed. "Ah, come on. You love it."

"Not so much right now," Daniel grumbled.

"Yeah, well. Join the club."

Rachel fit in well with Sage and Pia, two of the most fearless women he knew. But despite the promises made to each other only last night, she had still lied to him about having the scry. Why?

"As per your instructions," Nate said, "the team have been reassigned, but I'm coming with you tomorrow night. Tonight," he corrected. "I'm forcing Pia to rest for a few hours, but you know her." Nate let out a resigned sigh. "She'll no doubt stay up, doing as much research as humanly possible. To be honest, I think she's more worried about tonight than she's letting on. I haven't seen her like this since September last year when she was helping Sage. She's trying to be all cool around Rachel, but I've seen the pained expression on her face when she thinks I'm not paying attention. It's got me nervous. Don't let your guard down tonight."

"Thanks for the heads-up," Daniel said, his chest expanding on a deep inhale. Although he didn't need the warning. His instincts were screaming at him, something sharp in his gut twisting like a knife. But what the fuck could he do? It was torture of the worst fucking kind to have to leave most of tonight's strategy to someone else. Especially when it involved *his* Rachel.

"I'm not letting Pia out of my sight," Nate said. "I suggest you keep similar tabs on Rachel. I well know that Pia can't be trusted to keep herself out of harm's way. I've seen the types of risks she takes."

"Yeah, the same risks Taipan takes," Daniel said. The same risks Rachel took tonight. But he was still too cut at her to feel proud.

"What time are we meeting you at the ship tomorrow?" Nate asked, and Daniel heard Nate's Porsche run through the gears.

"Sunset." The shower shut off in the bathroom.

"Don't be too hard on Rach, mate," Nate said. "She did good tonight."

"I know." They said their goodbyes. Daniel clicked off and slowly closed the laptop.

Yes, Rachel had done well. But at what cost?

As pissed as he was about she'd put herself in danger, he grudgingly had to admire her selflessness in acting on the intel when there was no other option. Regardless of how she'd gained the information.

Why hadn't she told him about the scry? She must have hidden it from him, lied about it to his face last night when she'd told him it had burned up in the car. That was the part that sliced him to the bone. He needed to be able to trust her. Trust her to tell him the truth. No matter what.

Why his security guards hadn't told him she was no longer in the house was another matter entirely. Two of the best men money could buy—other than Taipan—had been shocked to see her arrive back with him. He'd seen their "How the fuck did she get out?" glances at each other. They hadn't even known she was gone!

Daniel leaned his forearm against the window and stared unseeingly across the dark, tumultuous ocean. He was going to do some serious ass-kicking when this was over. TSI's list of approved security providers was going to go through a major overhaul. Blade would be just as pissed when he found out. And no one wanted to be on the receiving end of a Blade shitstorm.

Daniel sensed Rachel's presence without having to turn around.

Lifting his head off his arm, he eyed her reflection in the floor-to-ceiling window. Her dark hair hung in damp curls around her shoulders, sexily tousled from being towel-dried. Her long, tanned legs were showcased by her short silky sleep shorts, and her generous breasts pushed at the soft ribbed cotton of a white tank top.

When he caught her soft gray eyes in the reflection, Daniel's breath lodged in his throat. She chewed on her bottom lip, her gaze sliding the length of his body. She was captivatingly beautiful, and she looked at him as though she thought the same of him.

He'd had enough of danger; it was time he added a dash of peace to his chaotic existence. He wanted a base, a home. A proper one where dinners were had with a family at a table, and not out of a take-away container.

And he wanted that with Rachel.

"Mine," he whispered.

He had her for now.

But it was not enough. He wanted her forever. He just had to work out how to make that happen.

Chapter Forty-Five

Rachel's breath hitched as she took in the long, lean profile of the man she loved standing at the full-length window, the stormy ocean as a backdrop. He looked so strong, so powerful, and so… *broken.*

Through the reflection, she watched him struggle, as though enough attention to detail would put this situation in a place where it all made sense. Rachel glanced at her bag on the kitchen table, the scry dropped off by Sam a short time ago, and her heart squeezed. There was no neat, logical little box to put any of this in.

She was entirely responsible for the distance that was once again between them, and it gutted her. While she'd been in the shower, Daniel had changed into black sweats and an old gray V-neck T-shirt. She knew how soft that worn fabric was, the way it smelled like him, that scent uniquely his. Leather and something spicy, dark and erotic. She fought the urge to go to him, held back by his stillness, and the tension that radiated outward from him.

I'm sorry. I wish things hadn't happened tonight the way they did… but they turned out all right in the end, didn't they?

"I love you," she said instead. Nothing else mattered, did it?

Daniel turned then, crossed the room with long strides, and wrapped her in his arms. He thrust a hand through her damp hair and held her head against his chest.

"I love you too," he said, his voice a deep rumble against her cheek. "But we need to talk."

On the plush outdoor lounge, Rachel sat with a hot coffee. The sky was slowly becoming lighter, pastels transforming the black night sky. A crisp ocean breeze snapped at her face, whipping across the surface of the coffee she sipped.

Daniel took a seat close by, not at her side, but facing her, his back straight, his jaw clenched.

"Don't be upset with your security guards," Rachel said, remembering how he'd fired the other guards. "It wasn't their fault."

His eyes narrowed, a storm raging in them. "That is not your concern."

Rachel bristled, but he had a right to be pissed at the guards. She imagined they were being paid a considerable sum to keep her safe. They hadn't expected her to slip away.

"I tried to call you when the man returned my bag," Rachel said, jumping right into her defense. "But the calls wouldn't connect." Maybe she could have tried harder. Maybe she could have called out to the security guards to get a message through.

But she had tried to call Daniel and the others, multiple times. That *was* the truth. And she was determined to be honest, no matter what. Through the window, she glanced at the bag holding the scry. *No matter what.*

"What man?" Daniel narrowed his eyes.

"They didn't tell you?" She thought the security guards were supposed to report everything.

"No."

"Oh." Rachel cleared her throat and through the soft morning light watched a seagull land on the sand. "I didn't lie to you, Daniel. When I told you the scry was burned up with the car, I honestly believed that. But when the old man turned up at the door, saying he'd found my bag on the side of the road, I realized that I must have taken it out of the car with me before it blew up." It had sounded logical when she reasoned it that way. Except...

"How did he know to find you here?" Daniel asked.

Yeah, except for that.

He looked through the window at her bag. It was almost impossible to believe it was still with her after everything that had happened.

Daniel walked inside and picked up the bag with one hand, his face scrunched up as though he were holding something disgusting, repulsive, like a dead animal carcass.

"What are you doing?" Rachel fought the urge to run to it. Adrenaline flooded her body, sending blood racing past her ears.

He hurled the bag against the far wall. Rachel let out a small cry of distress. She wanted to run to it, protect it. *Fight Daniel for it.*

Crossing to the bag, he picked it up and peered inside. "It should be smashed to pieces, but there's not a fucking scratch on it." He tossed the bag back onto the table, and it slid to a stop next to a large vase.

"Even if the demon himself was standing right there and I threw that rock at him, it wouldn't touch him." His voice was angry, but broken. Fire blazed in his eyes. "I can shoot at him, and the bullets won't do a goddamned thing. A sword can't cut him, dynamite won't blow the fucker up. I can't physically hurt him. Yet…" Daniel squeezed his eyes shut and when he opened them, she saw his vulnerability. "And yet he still has the ability to physically hurt you."

Rachel started to speak, and he held up a hand. She closed her mouth and gave him a moment. He thrust both hands through his hair, his face creased into tortured lines. His hands shook, the anguish he was suffering at her expense ripping her in half.

"I do everything I know how to keep you safe. And then, as if it's a matter of no consequence, you give the armed security the slip and go out alone, unprotected, and enter a fucking brothel owned by Australia's most notorious drug lord no less, dressed as one of his girls."

Daniel angled his head and she couldn't see his eyes. "I died a thousand deaths tonight worrying about you. I know you saved Lilly's life. But your half-cocked rescue mission could just as easily have ended up costing you yours. It very nearly did." His voice broke and he clenched his jaw.

"What hurts," he said tightly, turning back to her. "What hurts the most is that you had no comprehension of what that would do to me. I love you, damn it! And you're *killing* me."

Rachel choked up, hot stinging tears filling her eyes.

Her heart was pounding, her throat strangled. She crossed the room, placed her hands on his chest. "I feel just as frustrated as you. You are powerless to stop this, to protect me, and I feel powerless to stop this from hurting everyone I love, from hurting my sister and Sally if I can't end this."

Tears rolled down her cheeks. "Tonight… you were all out doing something, and I was left home by myself. When the scry came back to me and I asked it where Lilly was, I just wanted to do something *right*."

"I understand that. Hell, if anyone does, it's me. But you went about it the wrong way. Look." Daniel grabbed her shoulders. "You have to get over your guilt. It's making you reckless. You are not responsible for this situation you're in."

"You keep saying that, but I am!" Rachel shouted. She stepped back, waved a hand in front of her. "*All* of this is my fault." Her voice was thick. "Everything! What happened to my sister, what happened to Sally, to Liam. Including the fact that you were called away from your investigation and weren't there to find Lilly yourself. On top of that, I put you all at risk tonight when my own rescue attempt went to shit." Rachel began to shake.

"Even though I didn't ask for it, this is all happening because of *me*. And it's not even over yet. Tonight, once again, I'll be putting my friends in danger. Pia will risk her life, so will all of you. Trey is dead. Rob is dead. Everything that happened and will happen is because of me. And Daniel?"

She hesitated so long, her lips trembling, that he broke the silence. "What?"

"You might want to read me my rights."

"What the hell are you talking about?"

Rachel's legs wobbled, but she found the strength to speak. "I'm a murderer, Daniel."

She sobbed, her knees giving way. "I killed Trey."

CHAPTER FORTY-SIX

What the hell are you talking about?" Daniel gripped Rachel's shaking shoulders. "What do you mean you killed Trey?"

Rachel swayed on her feet, and he caught her before she hit the floor. She looked so fragile, so devastated. She shoved his hands away, but he grabbed her and pulled her up and into his arms. She struggled a moment, then gave in, sobbing into his chest. He had no idea what she was talking about, but he gave her a full minute before he pressed her.

"Talk to me."

"I pushed Trey down the stairs," Rachel said, lifting her head off his chest. "He died because I pushed him."

"No, you didn't," he said slowly. That cause of death didn't match up with the evidence. "What makes you say that? Has your memory come back?"

She looked up at him, and what he saw in her eyes damn near broke him.

"I saw it in the scry."

Tension turned his body to stone. That goddamned fucking thing! He wanted nothing more than to smash that demon-possessed rock into a gazillion pieces. If that were possible. When they were finished with it tonight, Daniel reserved the right to be the one to obliterate it.

"Babe, you didn't kill Trey."

"But I *did!*" Rachel sobbed, her agony shredding him. How long had she been suffering with this?

"Rachel," he said calmly, firmly. "You didn't. Trey didn't fall down the stairs. He was stabbed. Rob's fingerprints were on the handle of the knife. Trey had defensive wounds, and it was Rob's skin beneath his nails, not yours. We ruled you out in the first few days. Sorry," he added when she blinked up at him. "You had to have known you were the prime suspect originally."

Rachel nodded slowly. "Yeah, I think I must have known that." Daniel watched her internal struggle. "He *didn't* fall from the stairs? Are you sure? Maybe Rob stabbed him after he died to protect me?"

"Then Trey wouldn't have had Rob's skin under his nails. All his wounds are consistent with a struggle; they're the type of defensive wounds incurred during a knife attack. He had no bruises or other injuries consistent with a fall."

"Are you sure?"

"Yes. Why are you struggling with this?"

"It *lied* to me?" Rachel seemed just as distressed about that as when she'd believed she'd killed Trey. "I can't believe it lied to me—" Her voice was a broken whisper.

There were no pretty words to make this all okay. The situation was out of the ordinary, six hundred and sixty-six shades of fucked up.

She tugged away from him, and he let her go.

"Daniel?" She turned, blinking at him uncertainly. "Can you do something for me?"

"Name it." *I'd find a way to pluck the stars right out of the night sky if you asked me to.*

"Can you make me forget about all this? Just for a while," she whispered. "I'm so tired. I can't keep thinking about what might happen tonight. There are no guarantees about how it will end. For just a short time, I want to forget I'm frightened." She softened her voice, ran her hands across his chest. "If something happens to us, I don't want to regret wasting this time together."

"Nothing is going to happen." Razor blades churned in his stomach. He understood how she felt all too well.

"Right here, right now, it's just you and me," she said softly.

"It's always been about you and me, babe."

He swept her off her feet and into his arms.

Chapter Forty-Seven

A gentle sunrise lightened the sky, pale pastels erasing the restless darkness of the stormy night. The wind turned still, the clouds clearing, allowing the golden sunlight to wash across the balcony, giving Rachel's silky smooth, tanned skin an almost ethereal glow.

Daniel pressed Rachel against the glass balustrade, hooked his thumbs in the waistband of her shorts and tugged them down. He reached beneath her white tank top, ran his palm up the gentle curves of her stomach, and whipped the material off, tossing it aside.

He kissed the tender pulse point at her wrist, then kissed a trail down the inside of her arm, across the curve of her breast. Drawing her nipple into his mouth, he sucking deeply, enjoying the sweet sounds of pleasure he elicited from her. He gently nipped it as he pulled back, enjoying the way the cool morning air pebbled it into a hard, sexy peak. After he did the same to the other nipple, he stepped back to admire the results.

Naked in the morning sunlight, with her dark hair cascading in silky waves behind her, Rachel was nothing short of stunning. She had her arms out to the sides, hooked over the balustrade, with one long leg slightly bent. She had killer curves and a body that sent men to their knees.

And she is mine.

She lifted her head, caught his eye, and gave him a slow, seductive smile that made his cock strain painfully.

"You are so fucking beautiful," he said gruffly, totally enamored of her. She smiled peacefully, tilted her face to the sun, and took a slow, deep breath as though savoring the morning. Her chest swelled on the intake, pushing out her full breasts.

She straightened, and Daniel affected a frown, which caused her to widen her eyes slightly.

"What's wrong?"

He pretended to consider. "Something isn't quite right…" He moved to her, loving that she held her ground, didn't go all self-conscious on him. Her message was clear: this is me, all of me, exposed, bare and vulnerable.

Daniel took the worn silver chain from his neck for the first time in twenty-three years.

"I don't have any diamonds for you yet." He ran the flat, silver links through his fingers. "My dad gave me this on our last camping trip together." He took off the black tourmaline Pia gave her, and secured his chain around her neck. "I've worn it every day since."

Rachel was silent, staring down at the chain, the thick scuffed links masculine against her soft skin, and for a moment he wondered if he'd made a mistake. He hadn't considered that she might not like it.

"You don't have to wear it—" He reached for it, and she placed a hand protectively on the links. When she glanced up at him, tears were glistening in her eyes.

"I love it," she said, her voice thick with emotion. "And I love you." She threw herself into his arms, and he had to step back to steady them, or she'd send them both tumbling to the ground. Although, that wouldn't be such a bad thing.

She wrapped her legs around his waist and her arms around his neck, her hair cascading down around them. He held her close, for as long as was humanly possible. He was, after all, merely a man with a stunningly naked woman wrapped around him.

He set her down in front of the glass balustrade. She leaned her naked body back against the glass, wearing nothing but his silver chain.

He scratched his chin, pretending to consider. "Perfect," he said drawing out the moment, so the image of her against the sunrise would be permanently seared into his memory. Her smile made his heart skip a beat.

"You'd better remember to put Pia's tourmaline on when we go back out on the ship," Daniel said. "But don't take mine off when you do."

"I won't," Rachel promised. "This means everything to me." She touched the chain, her hand pressing against her heart.

"*You* mean everything to me," he replied, and another tear slipped from her eye and rolled down her cheek.

"Why did we wait so long, Daniel?"

He shook his head. "Nothing worth having ever comes easily." Though he regretted not telling her how he felt earlier, this specific culmination of events at this time in their lives was perfect. Looking back over their years together before this, he couldn't imagine them having such a powerful realization of what they meant to each other at any other time. Certainly not in just the short weekends when he was in town. "It was destined to be this way."

"Yeah, well destiny thinks you are wearing far too many clothes, and I agree." She stepped up to him. Her fingers brushing against his skin as she lifted his shirt sent delicious shivers through him. When she trailed her fingertips along his biceps and across his chest, he bit back a moan.

"I love how hard your muscles are," she breathed. "I love your chest. Your body."

"Not as much as I love yours," he said, walking her backward so that she was pressed against the glass again.

She laughed, and the sweet trill washed through him, sending his heart souring. He dropped to his knees, lifted one of her legs over his shoulder.

He flicked his tongue across her sensitive, soft folds, breathing in the delicate fragrance of her desire, enjoying the sweet taste of her. He drew her clit into his mouth, sucking and flicking it with his tongue until she was a quivering mess above him. Her fingers tangled in his hair, and he drove her relentlessly to a fierce climax.

"Oh God!" she screamed, her leg curling around his neck, her nails digging into his scalp. He continued until the last tremor subsided, then, when she was boneless, he carried her to the white outdoor lounge, laying her on the cushions. He stripped out of his remaining clothes.

Her skin was flushed a delectable pink, her eyes glistening through lids still heavy with desire.

She spread her legs provocatively, and he lowered himself in between them.

On top of her warm body, he was cocooned by the fragrance of her skin. "Tell me we'll work out how to be together when this is all over," he said gruffly.

Her expression softened into the most beautiful smile he'd ever seen. "We'll work it out."

"Because we have to," he said, keeping his eyes fixed on hers. "I can't stop loving you, so we need to happen. Tell me you know how to do that."

Rachel cupped her hands on his face, leaned up and kissed him on the lips. "I'll be wherever you need me to be."

"Tell me *what* you need me to be, because I don't know how to do this."

Unshed tears pooled at the edges of her lids. "I only want you to ever be you. You are perfect, just the way you are."

There was nothing unfinished between them now, no lies, no secrets. Just the two of them, bare, open, vulnerable. A tremor rippled through him as he fell helplessly into uncharted territory. He had to trust she'd catch him, show him the way.

"I'll make mistakes," he said, desperation bleeding into his tone. "I know I will. I don't know how to do what comes after this. How do you take two lives and make them one? Especially one like mine."

"Shh." She pressed her fingers to his lips. "We'll work it out. Together." He let her quiet confidence fill him with hope.

"I love you," he said, sliding his cock deep into her slick heat, relishing the way her eyes closed in pleasure, the way her breath hitched, the soft cry she let out when he filled her completely.

He would never get enough of her. He craved the feeling of being inside her, never fully complete until they were at one like this. She was his only peace in this crazy fucked-up world. He increased the intensity of his thrusts, enjoying the bliss on her face.

Cupping his hands beneath her ass, he lifted it up to penetrate her deeper. Her hips bucked as he thrust harder… faster. She lifted her head, moistened her lips with a pink tongue, and looked deep into his eyes.

Unable to contain a ferocious surge of emotion, he leaned down, kissing her savagely. She wrapped her arms around his neck and kissed him back, matching his intensity.

Her orgasm surprised them both, rippling over his cock, her pussy clenching him so tight he came undone. He drove into her until he climaxed with a force that left him trembling in her arms.

Naked and sweaty on the outdoor lounge, they held each other tight as their breathing slowed, the frantic beating of their hearts finally returning to a regular pace.

He kissed the top of her head and felt her body relax beneath his.

And in her arms, Daniel found a peace he never thought he'd have.

CHAPTER FORTY-EIGHT

Lying flat on his back, Daniel woke to the cold steel of his six-inch blade pressed against his neck, and the weight of a body on top of him. Max was barking furiously inside the house, jumping onto the glass of the French doors.

A rush of adrenaline cleared the fog of sleep from his mind, but Daniel lay predator-still. His mind was sharp and focused, the pounding of his heart loud, but regular.

He kept his arms deceptively relaxed at his sides as he assessed his opponent's intentions, calculating and reassessing his course of action based on the smallest movement. He concentrated on his attacker's gaze, for the eyes always gave away the opponent's hand—an advantage that often meant the difference between life and death.

He'd have only a split-second warning between threat and intention.

He loved Rachel, but he wouldn't let her kill him.

"Who is she?" Rachel's eyes were wild, the gray irises dark, almost black.

"Put the knife down, babe," Daniel said softly. Firmly.

She blinked rapidly, as though his voice momentarily confused her. Tears swam in her eyes, but anger kept them from falling. "I. Said. Who. Is. She?"

He glanced over her shoulder to the table, to find the scry out of her bag. He slowly released a breath.

"The knife," Daniel said, his voice steady, authoritative. "Put it on the white glass-top table." Giving more specific instructions was often more effective than a generic "Put the weapon down." Telling them *where* to put the weapon often shifted their focus.

"I *saw* her put her arms around you," Rachel said, her voice thick with emotion, her eyes glassy and wild. "It was at the Ocean Bar, which means it happened during this trip. You saw her! While you were telling me things had changed, that you love me... you were with Cynthia. Did you tell *her* the same thing?" Tears poured in heavy rivulets down her cheeks.

"Tell me what you think you saw."

"I saw her put her arms around you. Long blonde hair, ironed straight. She was wearing a tight red dress, black heels, and she rubbed her big fake tits on your arm."

"You saw that?" Daniel asked slowly. "Did that evil piece of shit scry show me grabbing her wrist and pushing her away?"

The quiet conviction in his tone seemed to give Rachel pause. She frowned, her hand wavered, and he felt the sharp burn as the knife sliced into his skin.

Daniel grabbed her wrist, then used his other hand to gently prize the knife from her shaking fingers. He pushed her off, and she fell, dazed, back onto the chair. She pulled her legs to her chest as he put the knife on the table. She could still reach it, if she wanted to. But he knew she wouldn't. Already her eyes were beginning to clear, to become the clear satin gray he knew and loved.

"It didn't show you that part, did it?" Daniel asked softly.

She shook her head, her whole body trembling.

"The scry lies. Remember? It's tainted. You can't believe what you see."

He watched her blink in confusion, bring her hands to her head and squeeze as though trying to order her thoughts. "Everything is foggy." Her voice shook.

"Rach, babe. Look at me."

She looked at him, but her gaze traveled through him.

"I'm scared," she said. "My head is spinning and pounding and I—" She glanced around the balcony. "I keep wondering where I am. *Who* I am. Yet I know saying that makes me sound crazy. Have I lost my mind?" She shivered, her whole body shaking as if she had a fever.

"Babe, no," he said, running his palms up and down her arms. "Take a deep breath, and shake it off. I'm here. I'm not going anywhere. Everything is going to be all right."

He glanced at his phone. He needed to call Pia.

"Oh, God! Please make it stop!" Rachel let out a pained cry, then covered her mouth with her hand as though she were going to be sick.

He assisted her to her feet. He opened the glass sliding door, and Max, seeing Rachel in his embrace, calmed down. Max was right at Daniel's side as he half-carried Rachel to the bathroom and held her hair back while she splashed cold water on her face. Huge shudders wracked her body, and for a moment, the three scratches on her back glowed a vivid red.

He barely held back the urge to punch something. The demon was hurting her, right in front of him! And there was not a fucking thing he could do to stop it.

Eventually, her breathing returned to normal, and he grabbed his Taipan T-shirt out of her bag and helped her put it on.

She straightened, looked at her reddened face in the mirror, and threw the wet washcloth at her reflection. The mirror shuddered, and water splattered back onto them. Rachel spun around, wrapped her arms around his neck, and buried her face in his chest. She nudged him backward out of the bathroom as though she couldn't bear to look at herself anymore.

She bent down, ran a hand over Max's back. "I'm sorry I worried you." Her voice was raspy. Broken. "I don't deserve you," Rachel said, and his heart twisted painfully. "Either of you."

"Yes, you do."

She shook her head, the devastation in her eyes complete.

He took her back out to the balcony, to the fresh air, helped her sit down on the couch. He took the knife from the table, put it back in the kitchen, and returned with a tall glass of ice water.

Then he walked to the table, grabbed the scry, and threw it as far as he could into the ocean.

Fuck you, scry!

And fuck its influence over the woman he loved.

Rachel stood at his side, her hands gripping the balustrade as she looked out across the water. "Pia's going to be mad at you."

Daniel slanted her a glance. "But not you?"

She shook her head. "I don't like what it does to me." She shook as though a shiver rolled down her spine. "What it turns me into." Her breath caught. "Daniel! You're hurt!" she said on a broken sob, apparently just now noticing his neck. "What happened?" She rushed inside and came out with a clean, white washcloth. Tenderly, she mopped at the blood. "Did *I* do this?"

"You don't remember?"

"I remember how I was feeling. Not what I did. But I can put two and two together." She looked at the blood, stark red on the white washcloth, and tears streamed down her cheeks. "Oh God, I'm so sorry!" *Damn that fucking scry and what it's doing to her.*

He wasn't worried about tossing the scry into the ocean; no doubt it would be back.

"I don't know what made me get up, walk to the scry," she said in a small voice. "I don't know why I asked it if I could trust you. But I did, and it showed me you and Cynthia—"

Jealousy was a bitch, the one thing that could drive an otherwise sane person to the brink of insanity, give them the ability to kill. Love was the most powerful emotion in the universe. Betray that love, and the pain was intolerable. The greater the love, the greater the pain, the greater the need for revenge.

With all his training, control, and experience with handling extreme situations, Daniel couldn't predict what he would do if he caught Rachel in the arms of another man.

But he wasn't with another woman, and Rachel wasn't with another man.

Because when you truly loved someone, that absolute love that Daniel felt for Rachel, you couldn't be with anyone else. You simply didn't want to. The mere thought of it repulsed you.

"You are the only woman for me," Daniel said. "And I will spend the rest of my life proving that to you."

"But… how do I know?" her voice shook, and his heart ached.

"You don't know," he said. "You trust."

"Mum trusted Dad."

"*Babe.*"

"It would kill me, Daniel. If you cheated on me like that. I wouldn't survive you."

"Nor I you."

Her brow creased. "But you're so strong."

"Not when it comes to you." He traced his fingers across her silky skin. "A year ago, the last time we were together, the sun was just beginning to rise. We were lying in bed, and you said something to me."

He rarely slept well, often resorting to simply lying in bed with his eyes closed as he focused on his breathing. That was what he'd been doing that last morning with her. He'd sensed her quiet contemplation, felt her eyes on his face.

"You kissed my temple and told me you loved me," Daniel said. "You whispered it so softly, I almost believed I had imagined it, had it not been for the way your words made my heart squeeze in my chest."

"I remember that. I didn't know you'd heard me."

"I didn't let you know I'd heard you because—" He briefly closed his eyes. "I didn't know what to say to you. Telling you I loved you scared me where few things in life can."

"Oh, Daniel."

"Hearing you tell me that rocked my world. I never stopped thinking about you, but after I left that morning, you became my every waking thought. I began trying to piece together how to make it work between us. I even paid attention to Blade's relationship with Sage for clues. But the truth is, I needed you to tell me again, when you knew I'd heard you. I wanted to follow your lead. But you cut me off. You told me you loved me, then you stopped taking my calls. I respected your right to do that, told myself I was giving you space, but time kept slipping by, and soon it was a year, and I had no idea how to bridge the gap that had opened up between us."

Rachel fell back into his arms, and he held her tight.

"Family to me has only meant pain. The pain of losing my father. The pain of my mother's bitterness. The pain of finally getting revenge for my father's death and discovering it didn't give me the peace I expected it to."

"You killed the man who murdered your father?"

Daniel nodded. "Last night. I looked him dead in the eyes and shot him. Coldly. Without remorse. The way he shot my father."

"Oh, Daniel." She cupped her soft hand over his rough cheek.

"It had to be done. It always felt like unfinished business." He traced a finger along her skin thoughtfully.

"That's why you chose a career in the police force."

"Walking in his footsteps was the next best thing to having him walking next to me."

"You're a good man, Daniel."

His heart squeezed. "When I'm with you is the only time I feel that's true."

She leaned in, and he caught a hint of peach and vanilla before her soft lips pressed against his.

"I'm sorry I hurt you," she said, her gaze falling again to his neck. "I hate that I did."

He placed his finger beneath her chin, raised her eyes so she was looking at him.

"Together, we will beat this. I won't let the demon come between us, no matter what. That's what he wants."

Rachel shook her head in disbelief. "I can't believe you still want me, knowing what you do about me. I know people come with baggage..." Her lips twisted wryly. "But with this demon, I come with my own storage container full."

He kissed her forehead, tucked a lock of hair behind one ear. "I love that you're imperfect," he murmured, "because it allows me to be imperfect for you."

"You are a rare man, Daniel Jackson Smith."

Their lips pressed together.

The hair on the nape of his neck stood on end. Her eyes flicked to the glass sliding door. They were not alone. Rachel sensed it too. The demon might no longer be influencing her the way it had been, but it certainly wasn't gone.

Evil stood by the door.

Watching their every move.

Waiting for another opportunity to strike...

Chapter Forty-Nine

As the sun slipped fully into the horizon, the warmth of the day disappeared with it, leaving a brisk chill in the air. The moon was high and full, its silhouette having appeared in the sky long before the sun went down.

The early evening was crisp, calm, and unnaturally still. The waves made barely a sound as they lapped against the hull of the shipwrecked fishing trawler.

On the rusting deck of the *Anna-Marie*, a shiver of trepidation rolled through Rachel. She hung back from the others, the scry a dead weight in the bag on her shoulder. She'd been both relieved and terrified to see it glistening in the sun on the beach when she'd peered over Daniel's balcony earlier this afternoon.

She fingered Daniel's chain, next to Pia's black tourmaline around her neck, and thought of Daniel. Of how far *they* had come in such a short time.

She'd spent years unable to resolve the seemingly insurmountable conflict between them, and yet the last two weeks had wrought changes that she'd never thought possible. It was far too easy to procrastinate, to coast along, never giving yourself the opportunity to fight for something. It was too easy to give up.

A crisis forced you to dig deep. Discover things about yourself you'd only hoped were there. Daniel faced challenges all the time in his work, situations that tested his limits, his strengths. But Rachel would never have known what she was capable of had the demon not drawn her into his web. She'd kept her life simple, coasting from one singing gig to the next, her two best friends making it easy to stay busy, to keep Daniel at a distance.

On the surface, it seemed as though a haphazard series of random events had led her to this point. But when she looked back, it was clear that all of it had been carefully crafted to have her standing right here where she was.

There were no coincidences.

Rachel felt the weight of the possessed object in the backpack hanging over her shoulder, and sensed its influence, as though someone were trying to inject venom in her veins. Her fingers traveled across the silver necklace Daniel had given her.

Love triumphed over all.

This ends tonight.

The *Debunking Reality* team worked like a well-oiled unit, wordlessly setting up recording equipment, while Pia paced out a perfect nine-foot circle, casting its form with sea salt, stones, crystals, and various herbs from a bag she was carrying.

Daniel and Nate were searching the ship to ensure they were alone and that there would be no surprises later on.

"We have done this before," Pia reminded everyone when they were all back together on the top deck again. "Back in South Australia for Sage. I'll be using the same protection ritual, the one from the grimoire, as it's the most powerful one I have. But there is a significant difference this time. Back then, we were dealing with a demon associated with a prophecy; this time, we are dealing with a summoned demon and a cursed object. There will be differences in what happens, in how the demon can influence us, and in how we need to respond. Most of what we are attempting is untried; as such, it is impossible to predict how the night will unfold.

"We have a circle of seven," she continued. "Mark, Ryan, Joe, Daniel, Nate, Rachel, and myself. Stay on the edge of the circle, but just inside its protection at all times. Its high energy is the only defense we have. I shouldn't need to remind either of you, Nate and Daniel, that your weapons are useless here, so both of you can leave your guns in your pants." Joe snickered, and Pia sent him a hard look. "Nothing about this is funny."

She paused a moment, then adjusted her tone for emphasis.

"The scry is *not* to be touched under any circumstances once we begin. It's the open doorway that allows the demon into our dimension. There are boundaries a demon cannot ordinarily cross; something needs to happen to give it permission. Maia gave Sohn-Zae, a very powerful archdemon of Hell, permission to cross that night one hundred and fifty years ago when she summoned him, causing the scry to become cursed. The demon can now inflict harm through the scry and use it to possess people, wreaking death and destruction along the way.

"As we now know," Pia continued, "he's appeared in this century in our generation because of Rachel's blood connection to Maia. The events of the past few weeks have been carefully orchestrated to connect Rachel with the scry and to lead her to this point in time. This is the last chance we have to stop Sohn-Zae before he kills anyone else."

The silence was weighted as everyone in the circle absorbed the enormity, the *responsibility* of that. And the understanding that there were no guarantees any of them would make it off the ship alive.

"Maia was a Wiccan witch. Wiccans typically don't believe in the Devil and Satan. Such things are a Christian construct. But in Maia's anger and despair over her husband's betrayal, she was tempted by the promise of retribution, and when she came across an ancient spell book, she turned her back against generations of pagan beliefs to summon a demon of revenge."

"When the time comes to use the banishing ritual, which is akin to an exorcism of a person, I will need to summon Sohn-Zae by name. He's a demon of Satan, which means he will react strongly against any Christian religious items or terminology. When the time comes, I will be using words and symbols to call him out that will provoke intense aggression. All of you will need to be careful. Do not take any unnecessary risks. Stay on the boundary, but within the circle."

"Rachel, you will be especially vulnerable the moment Sohn-Zae realizes his power over you is slipping. The instant he knows he can't control you—oppress or possess you—he will try to kill you. The only reason you are still alive is because he believes you will be of use to him, as Maia was." *For a short while, before he killed her...* "I believe it's his plan to make you his new High Priestess of Darkness and use you to lure many followers as you form his Satanic cult. You will be useful to him until Sally is old enough to take over. Your power is but a fraction of hers. The moment your usefulness to him is gone, you will be expendable."

Rachel's chest tightened, and a heavy feeling settled in the pit of her stomach.

"Once we have made contact with Maia and know the specific banishing rite to use, it will be touch and go for a while as we summon the demon. That's when it can go either way for Rachel. If we don't banish him in time, he'll kill her."

Daniel growled his displeasure.

"I'm sorry to be so blunt, but I don't have time to mince words. Everyone needs to be informed of the risks, both for the big picture and themselves."

Pia paused, her eyes darting around nervously. "Can you feel that?" She shivered, as though a chill rolled down her spine. "The cold lifeless eyes of death are already watching us."

Rachel felt the tension in the group increase.

Pia cleared her throat and seemed to regather herself. "Sorry." She rubbed her hands together. "Are there any questions before we start?"

"Isn't there something we can do with less risk for Rachel?" Daniel was beside Nate. Both men stood with wide stances, shoulders back, and expressions set in stone.

"For all of us," Joe grumbled. "We're all fucked if this doesn't work."

Pia shook her head. "I'm a psychic, not a high priestess or a Wiccan witch. The truth is, all this is an educated guess. This is just as dangerous for me as it is for Rachel, as I am susceptible to spiritual energies more than most."

Nate grimaced and crossed his arms.

"Maybe we should get a priest?" Ryan suggested. "Or an experienced exorcist?"

"You want to pack this all up and wait until we find one who's willing to come out here?" Pia asked. "I doubt we'd ever find one that reckless."

"Everyone, please," Rachel said immediately. "Sally is in danger. I—" She cleared her throat, glancing at Daniel. "I don't want to stop now. I am a danger to those I love. Who knows what I'm capable of doing? Whoever wants to leave, can. I completely understand. But I'm staying. I have to give this a shot."

"Well?" Pia demanded of the group, clearly meaning to stay herself. Ryan and Joe grumbled their assent, and Mark, Nate, and Daniel firmly said they were staying.

"Well then, that's decided," Pia said. "Now if anyone has any better ideas, I'm happy to hear them. If we had the parchment, it would have been less risky as we could have skipped straight to the banishing ritual, but as it stands, this is our best chance."

"How do we protect Rachel at the time she's most vulnerable?" Daniel asked.

"Trust your instincts," Pia said. "Be guided by your heart, not your mind. That's the best advice I can give you. All of you."

Daniel shook his head, his jaw working like he was grinding his teeth. "Was hoping for something a bit more helpful than that," he growled. "What kind of bloody plan is that?"

"The only one we've got," Pia snapped. She continued to prepare for the ceremony, explaining what she was doing along the way. She gave everyone a large piece of black obsidian to place by their feet to help absorb negative emotions, like anger and fear.

She lit four candles, putting one in each cardinal direction, north, south, east, and west, speaking a prayer or ritual of protection and asking her angels and guides to join with them to keep them safe. She then added some herbs in a large metallic incense burner that swung on a heavy chain, and smoke began to plume and spiral out of the top.

"To cleanse and purify the air," Pia said, then spoke a few verses in another language Rachel thought could be Latin. Pia handed the incense burner to Mark while she lit five more candles and placed them around the circle to represent the five elements: earth, fire, metal, water, and wood. When she spoke the ritual to surround them in white light in a mixture of languages, Rachel could have sworn she felt a shift in the tension of the air within the circle.

A soothing calm washed over Rachel, bathing her in a gentle warmth that seemed to spread through her body from the inside out. Her heartbeat slowed, and her breathing evened out. It felt like she'd woken from a long, languid afternoon nap. Rachel hid her surprise at how well Pia's ceremony was working.

But outside the circle, the shadows came to life. Rachel kept seeing movement out of the corner of her eye, but when she turned her head, nothing was there. A gust of wind swirled around, sending something clattering along the rusty metal deck.

Off to one side were black candles, like the ones the captain had used, the ones Rob had used. They would be lit when it was time to summon the demon to the circle.

Waves began to crash high against the rusting frame of the ship, and a stiff ocean breeze kicked up. Rachel used both hands to scoop the hair off her face and tighten her ponytail.

Breathe. In… out… Stay in the circle… I've got this.

Rachel thought of Sally's bright sunny smile and sweet face framed with pretty blonde curls and mentally blew her a kiss. *I love you, kiddo. I'm doing this for you.*

Whatever happened tonight, Rachel would at least know she'd done everything she possibly could to protect Sally. So that she might live her life like a normal little girl and not have the weight of this on her shoulders.

Rachel's grandmother had done the best she'd known how when she'd hidden the scry in the cave. But it hadn't worked. The spell she'd used had either not been strong enough, or it had been the wrong one.

Rachel was armed with more knowledge than her grandmother had had. It was imperative she succeed this time. If only she'd had the opportunity to get to know her grandmother more during her childhood, she would have been better prepared. If only she'd known her grandmother hadn't been crazy, but had been trying to protect the family…

Keeping herself fully inside the circle, Pia crossed to Rachel and placed a pendant around her neck. It was large, a group of colorful crystals bound with gold wire. It sparkled, and Rachel almost believed she saw a purplish haze glowing around it. It chinked against the tourmaline pendant Pia had given her previously. The second pendant felt warm and comforting against her skin.

"Additional protection for when you go through the doorway," Pia said.

Dark clouds swirled above, smothering the light of the moon and covering them in gloomy darkness. The light from several battery-operated lanterns placed around them flickered, and one went out entirely. Pia cast a nervous glance around them. "We'd better hurry."

Daniel squeezed Rachel's hand briefly. Rain began to pelt down horizontally as the wind grew stronger. It put the candles out, and Pia frowned. Relighting them would be pointless.

"Stay in place," Pia shouted above the wind. "The circle might get washed away, but the energy of protection I created while casting the circle should hold."

Then, as suddenly as the downpour began, it stopped. Her wet clothing clung to Rachel's body as she shivered from the chill. Her hair was plastered to her face, and she raised a shaky hand to brush the sodden strands away from her eyes.

As Rachel stood at her place in the circle and Pia's voice grew stronger, Rachel's mind began to clear. She had the sense she was stepping out of a dream, or out of a dark movie theater into the sunlight.

Her memory started to return.

Images she'd rather not have remembered began to flash before her. They were out of sequence, but they were starting to make sense. Like a jigsaw puzzle coming together, Rachel began to remember portions of that night on the ship. The night Trey had died.

The air thickened, making it hard to breathe. Just as it had that night.

A wave of dizziness came over Rachel, and flashes of that evening appeared in her mind. Her body swayed, yet the flashes kept coming. She felt as though she were falling... falling into the room below deck, where they'd sat around the Ouija board. The place it had all started. She saw herself, Trey, and Rob.

She was laughing. They all were. Her initial fear over Rob finding the captain's board eased quickly when nothing happened. They began to make jokes about it, Trey cracking them up with a hilarious ghost story.

Feeling emboldened by the lack of activity, Rachel asked the board a question. "Yo, captain psycho," she had called out, the residual alcohol in her body making her bold. "If you're here, why don't you come out and talk to us. Tell us why you flipped out and killed your crew."

Back in the circle, Pia continued her protection ritual, recasting the circle that had washed away, while Rachel relived that night, feeling sick at her irreverence to an energy, another entire dimension, she'd not understood. They'd taunted a powerful demon. Dear God! Had she really been so stupid?

She pounded her head with her palm as she remembered what had happened next. Her knees felt weak, and she placed her feet shoulder width apart for balance.

Rachel began moving the Ouija board's pointer herself, her answers hilarious. At least Trey had thought so. Rob was getting annoyed with them, and Trey was telling him to lighten up. That there was no such thing as ghosts.

Her stomach tightened, a tendril of unease worming its way through her gut. She felt something at her back, a menacing presence breathing down her neck.

Trey raised his arms, waving them around like a ghost. "Woo ooo."

"Sit down, you idiot," Rob said. "Something is here with us, can't you feel that?"

Yes. Rachel could feel it, and it didn't feel good. The smile fell from Trey's face, and his gaze connected with hers. She didn't like Rob's words, or the tone he'd spoken them in. And neither, it appeared, did Trey.

Then Rob asked a question of the captain, and this time Rachel wasn't moving the pointer, even though it was traveling across the board. She immediately looked over at Trey, but the way his eyes went wide told her it wasn't him either.

It clearly wasn't Rob, who, taking this whole thing seriously, had his fingertips barely touching the top of the pointer. Shocked and surprised, she watched the planchette closely as it started to spell out words, trying to spot who was moving it. Rob was applying no pressure;

there was no way he could move it from how he was holding it, and Trey had turned an odd shade of green.

None of them were moving the planchette.

Something else was.

"I feel you here with us. Use my body," Rob said. "Use my energy to speak to us…"

Rob closed his eyes, then opened him, his gaze flat and cold. "You've been fucking Trey," Rob said furiously. His voice had changed, the words he spoke not in his usual cadence.

"No," Rachel said. "He's like a brother to me. Like you are. We'd never cross that line." She forced away the memory of Trey's earlier admission that he loved her. Rob didn't need to know that.

But Rob's eyes narrowed, as though he did in fact know that. "I saw you. Both of you in the captain's crystal ball." Rob's lips twisted. "It's fascinating what secrets that little thing can tell you…" He let the words trail off before he continued. "I saw Trey kissing you on the deck, while I was down below. You telling me that didn't happen?"

Rob was watching her face intently. "It didn't; the ball lied to you. The only thing that happened was Trey told me he—"

Rob shoved her, and she fell backward, landing hard on her back.

"The only liars are both of you!" Rob's eyes were black. Crazed. "Screwing each other behind my back. How long has it been going on? Years?"

Rachel picked herself up off the floor, ignoring a sharp shooting pain in her spine. "What the hell, Rob!" she yelled. "There is nothing going on between Trey and me, but so what if there was? We're all adults!"

She wiped her mouth and tasted blood. She must have bit her lip when she'd fallen. "There are no rules between us. You are like brothers, but you are not my brothers. I could have screwed you both. At the same time if we'd all wanted to, but we didn't. Why? Because I don't look at you like that."

Rob's eyes flared with a flash of violence. "I saw you screwing," he spat, seething. "I was forced to watch."

"No." She wanted to back away from the crazed look on his face but held her ground. "I don't know what you saw, or how. But it's wrong. This ship is wrong. We have to get off. Now. Snap out of whatever has got a hold of you, and let's get off this boat. I want to go home. Now."

Rob looked at her with cold black eyes she didn't recognize. He nodded, as though in answer to a question she couldn't hear. "Yes, I agree," Rob said. "He must die."

"That's not what I said!" Rachel screamed, jumping on Rob's back, but he shrugged her off with unnatural strength and she slammed into the wall.

Rob's face twisted into an expression Rachel didn't recognize, and he began laying into Trey.

Trey, briefly stunned, raised his arms in defense. But when Rob's fist connected with Trey's jaw, the two began to fight in earnest.

Rachel screamed at them to stop, trying to put herself between them. Rob was crazed, striking Trey in a frenzy. Blood ran from the corner of Trey's mouth, the side of his head.

Rachel tried to desperately tune out the sound of fists pounding into flesh. She screamed for them to stop. Just stop...

Blow by blow, Rachel watched Rob beat Trey until he was a bloodied mass on the floor. Then Rob grabbed a knife she'd never seen before from a nearby table, went back to Trey's barely conscious body, raised his arm, and plunged the knife deep into Trey's chest.

She cried out, tears blinding her vision.

The ship was spinning, and Pia's voice seemed so far away. Clouds were still swirling strangely overhead, but the air was again calm. Still.

"Babe?" Daniel said, at her side. "You're starting to sway."

Rachel shook her head, metaphorically shaking the sickening memories away. It was true—she *hadn't* pushed Trey down the stairs. It was exactly as Daniel had said. Rob had killed Trey, but he had clearly been influenced by the demon when he'd done so. The demon had oppressed Rob, using jealousy to turn him into a beast capable of murder.

Jealousy, the most insidious of all the deadly sins.

"You bastard!" Rachel shouted into the night, her anger meant for Sohn-Zae.

She took a deep breath. She couldn't fall apart now. She rolled her shoulders, tried to stay in the moment, stay grounded.

Daniel's arms wrapped around her.

"I'm okay," Rachel said. "I just remembered what happened that night on the ship."

"Babe—" Daniel pulled her close, and she rested her cheek against his chest. The rhythmic beat of his heart was soothing.

"Daniel," Pia said sternly. "Keep your place in the circle."

Daniel glared at her, clearly not used to being told what to do, but he took a step away, keeping the space between the seven equal. From his place in the circle, he kept his gaze on Rachel, watching her intently, hands clenched into fists at his sides.

The scratches on Rachel's back started to burn, and her heart pounded erratically. The warm balm of Pia's protection was wearing off, and fighting a rush of panic, Rachel looked around at the faces of her friends. The people who were risking their own lives to help her. She would be indebted to them forever.

She now knew what she wanted to do with her life if she made it out of this alive. She wanted to work with Daniel and TSI, to help people in whatever way they'd allow her to. Singing was fun, but she wanted to do something more rewarding, something that helped others.

Rachel studied Daniel, who stood shoulders back, his legs wide apart. His face was a study in chiseled anger, his eyes narrow and hard. His confidence and force of will radiated outward in powerful waves, his strong presence filling the circle.

The forces of darkness crowded around them. The shadows were alive and moving. The hair on the back of Rachel's neck prickled; her pulse raced, and sweat beaded in a fine layer across her skin. She wouldn't even pretend she had this.

Her terror was real.

"Rachel," Pia said. "Put the scry in the center of the circle. We need to protect the doorway from Sohn-Zae while we reach out to Maia."

Swallowing hard, Rachel took a deep breath. What if she lost herself and touched the scry? Just hours ago, she'd abruptly come to, holding a knife to Daniel's throat. Never, *ever*, did she want to experience the horror of something like that again.

Her heart in her throat, she took her bag to the center of the circle, opened the zipper, and let it roll out. Swiftly, Rachel stepped back, taking her place in the circle before she did something crazy like pick the scry up.

Her fingers itched at her side.

Pick it up.

You need to!

She let out a cry of anguish. It felt like she was throwing her own baby to the lions. All she wanted to do was hold it…

Pia spoke. "You're doing well, Rachel. Leave the scry there."

That's when Rachel realized she'd taken a step forward. She stepped back and ground her teeth. "When the scry is cleansed, I can have it again, right?"

Pia looked at her with concern. "I can't give any guarantees right now," she said carefully. "Let's just focus on making it out of this safely. If we're successful in banishing the demon tonight, I'm going to attempt to seal the doorway."

Rachel's stomach knotted. "By destroying the scry?"

"I'll do what needs to be done," Pia said firmly. "Now I need you to focus on me, on my words. Okay? I'm going to continue with the protection ritual." Pia held Rachel's eyes. "You with me?"

Rachel glared at Pia; she shouldn't, but she couldn't seem to control her face. Her head throbbed like it was going to explode, and the stench of rotten flesh swirled in an arctic wind that whipped at her face. What was happening?

"Pia, I'm scared," Rachel said, her body starting to tremble uncontrollably. A fever burned inside her; she shivered and broke into a sweat.

She didn't deserve these people. Trey was dead, Rob was dead. She'd lost her two dearest friends, and it was all her fault. She'd even tried to kill the man she loved more than life itself earlier today.

Kill them. Kill them all.

Fear clawed its way up her body and constricted her throat. "I feel him!" Her voice was high with the onset of panic. "He's on me… *in* me. Pia! Oh God, please help me! I don't know what I'm capable of doing."

The temperature plummeted as though Rachel was suspended in pure ice. She was cold, so cold, shivering hard enough to rattle her bones. She hugged her arms around her waist and tucked her hands in her armpits. Her teeth began chattering and she bit her tongue, the metallic taste of blood filling her mouth.

Her lids were heavy. She struggled to keep them open, but she knew the moment she was in Daniel's arms. Felt his warmth, his strength. Her whole body shook, and he tightened his arms around her. She clung to him as though she were drowning, and he was her only lifeline.

"Daniel!" Pia's voice penetrated the fog of Rachel's mind. "Get back to your place."

"Manage without me," he growled. "Look at her. She's deathly pale. She's about to collapse any second."

"She'll be fine," Pia shouted, her tone angry and frustrated, and totally not like her. She was more concerned about what they were about to do than she was letting on. "If this goes wrong..." Pia squeezed her eyes shut, then when she spoke next she was calmer. "I know you are worried, but the way you can help is to stay in your place, hold this circle open and protect her from the demon."

Rachel felt Daniel's whole body tremble, as though letting her go was one of the hardest things he'd ever had to do. He kissed the top of her head. "I love you," he whispered, before gently releasing her. "Always."

"You need to concentrate now," Pia said firmly. "I'm holding a circle of light. Rachel, I want you to keep your eyes closed, but blank your mind. Breathe in... Breathe out... Concentrate on the rise and fall of your chest, the sound of my voice..."

Pick up the scry. You need to!

No! Rachel screwed her eyes shut and concentrated on her breathing, in... out... in... out...

After an interminable amount of time, a calmness washed through her, followed by a profound awareness, as though she'd become somehow bigger than her body. More alert, her mind sharper.

"Good," Pia said, relief clear in her tone. "You've got this. Now, I want you to reach out with your mind. Call your angels and guides for protection and reach out to your distant relative, the high priestess, Maia. Call for her. Picture her in your mind, and float upward and outward. Let go. Trust that I have you and that I can bring you back when the time is right."

On a long exhale, Rachel felt herself rise up, out of her body. She followed the rise and fall in the cadence of Pia's voice as she reached out.

A woman filled Rachel's vision. She wore a hooded cloak, but the eyes that stared out at her were the same ones Rachel saw when she stared into the mirror. When she looked at Sally.

Maia smiled, but Rachel saw the fear in her eyes.

"I see her," Rachel said out loud to Pia.

"Ask her for the banishing ritual. Tell me the impressions you get. The words she speaks."

Rachel focused, but Maia's image slipped away.

No!!!

"I can't hold onto her," Rachel said.

"You're trying too hard," Pia said. "Let go and trust. Don't see her, feel her. Your physical eyes aren't the ones you need to use."

Rachel took another deep breath. In… out… in… out… And after a while, the outside world faded away, the ship, the ocean crashing against the rusting frame… Once again, Maia came into focus. Sharper this time, as though Rachel were really floating above her, witnessing firsthand, one hundred and fifty years in the past. She felt the breeze blow back her hair, heard a bird call from a tree next to her.

The high priestess stood with her coven in her inner circle of seven. Maia rang a bell, six times, then six times, then six times more.

Rachel began describing out loud what she could see. She started to feel Maia's anguish washing over her. Maia had been betrayed, humiliated, abandoned by the man she loved more than life itself… He deserved to feel her pain, he deserved to die.

She loved him. She loved him so much!

But it was the opposite of love that Maia summoned now. The parchment she read from trembled in her hands, the words she chanted gathering a terrible power.

Oh God! Rachel was witnessing the *summoning* ritual.

Rachel kept her feet firmly in place as Maia spoke.

"In the name of darkness, I summon forth the archdemon Sohn-Zae."

The coven repeated her words, albeit without their usual gusto. They'd never summoned a demon before.

Maia peered into the depths of the scry, trying to see her husband and his lover.

The scry had once been used for good. It had been a wonderful divination tool. Once.

Maia formed the shape of a cross over her chest, but she did it with her left hand, the order of the movements reversed.

The seven members of Maia's coven shifted uneasily, casting fearful glances at each other. But none dared challenge her. She was the most powerful seer of their time.

Maia checked the spell, then added the final ingredients to her cauldron: chili peppers, for the burning damnation of their souls; blood from a wild fighting dog, for an eternity of aggression and anger; a sprinkle of grave soil, for their deaths.

"I curse thee, the woman who seeks my husband's bed. May she die a slow and painful death. May she suffer long past this life and into the next. May she never find peace, her soul tortured in Satan's playground for eternity."

Meeting the surprised looks of her coven, Maia acknowledged each member as their gazes hardened, then lowered, in a display of their support.

Maia stirred the cauldron with a bone into which she'd carved specific demonic symbols and continued the rite until a beast's image formed in the flames, a horse-like face with a giant mouth lined with sharp, needle-like teeth. Two horns curled from its head, and arms like tentacles speared from a defined, almost human torso. Six-fingered claws formed hands that cradled skulls and human bones.

The beast looked up, locked eyes with Rachel. One hundred and fifty years in time and distance melted away to nothing. She was there, then, as the demon was here with her, now. This moment in time was predestined; this connection had been forged well over a century ago.

Shockwaves ripped through her body.

Rachel screamed and jumped back. Her heart was pounding, racing uncontrollably, her breathing coming in huge, wracking inhales.

Pia's voice cut through the air. "Saint Michael, the Archangel, defend us in battle, be our protection against the malice and snares of the devil…"

"Rachel!" Pia said urgently. "Go back in and get the banishing ritual. You've only witnessed the summoning."

Everyone in the circle continued to hold hands as Pia chanted more verses, some Rachel recognized from the Bible and some in another language she didn't know.

Something fell behind her, and she glanced over her shoulder. The air on the outside of the circle was foul and sour, and Rachel gagged as she sucked in a deep breath.

"Rachel!" Pia's voice whipped through her. "Hurry. Before you lose the connection."

Right. The banishing ritual… Rachel's head swam, and she struggled to focus. She squeezed her eyes closed, shut out fear and doubt, and Maia came back into focus. Rachel asked to be shown the banishing ritual. The high priestess started to speak, and Rachel repeated her words verbatim to Pia, knowing the cameras that were filming the whole ceremony would record every detail.

"Well done," Pia said when Rachel couldn't hold the link anymore and her words trailed off.

"Let's do this," Pia said. "Ready, everyone?"

Feeling more like herself again, Rachel swallowed a tremor of trepidation. Her voice was strong and clear as she said, "Yes."

"In the name of light, I summon the archdemon Sohn-Zae."

Rachel repeated Pia's words, adding her own energy. Wind whipped around them, and a low growl vibrated through the metal ship beneath their feet. A foul stench permeated the air, the putrid smell of rotting flesh.

I will not *leave!* Rachel heard Sohn-Zae's words, as though he shouted them directly into her ear. They sliced her like razor blades.

She screamed. "Hurry, Pia! He's here. Start the banishing ritual!" Sohn-Zae's icy breath skittered over the back of her neck, and his claws gripped her shoulders. Rachel shivered, as malice and hatred of the purest kind penetrated her very soul.

You're mine. You always will be. I am part of you.

Rachel screamed. She couldn't help it. Sohn-Zae was on top of her. Inside her. Smothering her with his evil.

She planted her feet, fought an overwhelming urge to run away, jump from the ship, and swim to shore.

Daniel was at her side again, and she gave him a little shove on his rock-hard chest, whispering urgently that she was fine, to do as Pia said. To keep his place in the circle.

"Step into the middle of the circle," Pia said.

"He won't go," Rachel said, panic making it hard to breathe. A chilling disembodied laugh echoed in her ears.

You are weak, pathetic. This childish routine is a joke.

"*You* step into the circle, Rachel," Pia said.

Rachel tried to lift her foot, but it wouldn't budge. She was rooted in place, held fast by a force she couldn't see. "I—I can't." Her head was pounding, her stomach churning.

"We revoke your permission to be here. You have no permission to be on Earth!" Pia shouted. "You do not have permission to be inside Rachel. Tell him, Rachel!"

"I… uh… you have no permission…" Her words trailed off. The people around her spun, and she felt she was going to fall. Where was she? What was happening?

Visions pressed into her mind. Rachel saw the beasts rising up from the floor of Wild Wilson's slaughterhouse, the animals crying out as their throats were slit. She slapped a hand over her mouth and doubled over. She was going to be sick.

A large coil of rope rose up into the air, like a giant snake come to life. The rope was heavy gauge, its weight too much for a man to pick up on his own. The coil came down like the sweep of a giant's hand, whipping through the group and knocking them off their feet, scattering the stones and the outline of the circle.

"Nooo!" Pia screamed.

Rachel trembled. Crimson rivers of blood flooded from the sides of the boat, sliding in thick, sticky waves and covering the deck she stood on. The sharp metallic tang of blood filled her mouth, and she gagged.

Sally appeared in the center of the circle. Her blonde curls bounced around her head, and a smile lit up her face. She bent down to pick up the sparkling crystal ball at her feet.

"No!" Rachel screamed. "Sally! No!" Rachel ran into what was left of the circle, snatching the scry from Sally's hands. Rachel's legs trembled and she slumped to the deck, her knees slamming into the metal.

It was only then she realized that Sally wasn't there, that Sally had never been there. There was no blood pooling on the deck.

But the scry was now in Rachel's hands.

Chapter Fifty

Daniel could never have imagined how much the image of Rachel sitting in the middle of the scattered salt and crystals with that scry clutched in her palms would affect him. His whole body was as tense as steel, and fear for her safety was acid in his stomach.

It took every ounce of strength he possessed not to grab her and get her the hell off the ship. He could hardly believe how fast she'd become the most important thing in his life. His life up until now had been about seeking retribution for his father's death, about ridding the world of Scotty Fryer and men like him. He'd believed that Taipan, his brothers, and what they stood for would be enough for him in life. He hadn't been looking for romance, he certainly hadn't been looking for love.

Until Rachel.

Rachel had changed everything. Turned his life upside down. And now he risked losing it all. If he hadn't already. Rachel had that same glazed look on her face that Madden had had. The same unfocused, slightly wild look in her eyes.

Daniel's heart stopped dead in his chest.

He kept the circle in his attention, what Pia was doing with the ritual, but his focus remained unwaveringly on Rachel, sitting in the middle of the scattered salt and crystals with the scry clutched in her palms.

He hoped Pia knew what the fuck she was doing.

The cost of her making a mistake could not be higher.

"In the name of light, I banish the archdemon Sohn-Zae back to the fiery pits of Hell!" Pia shouted, continuing as though the circle had not been destroyed, as though Rachel were not sitting in the middle with a foreign expression and glazed eyes.

Miniature tornados swirled around them, sending objects spiraling into the air and careening across the deck. It didn't take a psychic to know something was wrong. That this was not going according to plan.

Should he stay in place? Trust Pia? Or did he say fuck it all and rush to the side of the woman he loved?

Nate placed a hand on his arm, warning him to stay in place, as though aware of his inner torment. Daniel shrugged it off. He was seconds from acting.

A vile stench of… decaying shellfish made Daniel's stomach roil violently. Clouds swirled unnaturally fast in the sky above, and the temperature hovered at a bone-chilling degree somewhere near freezing.

The ship rocked violently. A ferocious roar rent the air, and a whirlwind filled the circle.

The demon had arrived.

The face of a beast appeared in the crystal in Rachel's hands. Horns speared out from a horse-like face, its eyes an evil red. Hands with six sharp claws reached out from the scry, and tentacles wrapped around Rachel's arms, burrowing into her flesh, tangling around her neck.

"No!" Daniel threw himself onto Rachel, grabbed the scry and endeavored to wrench it away. She held on to it with abnormal strength. The demon inside the glass smiled, drool dripping off its needle-like fangs.

"Leave her alone, you son of a bitch!" Daniel roared.

Rachel swatted him away with the swipe of one arm, and Daniel was thrown backward. He jumped to his feet, his boots slipping on spilled salt and herbs from the circle.

Pia was shouting for everyone to not panic, for Daniel to get back in the circle. But Daniel couldn't take his eyes off Rachel. Slowly, she got to her feet. She looked around with wide glassy eyes and a smile he didn't recognize.

Daniel took a step toward her, tentatively reached for her. Then stopped. Rachel's lips curled into a snarl and she hissed at him, spittle landing on his cheek.

Clutching the scry to her chest, she held up a hand as though it were a claw and lunged at Daniel. Nate grabbed Rachel's arm to restrain her, but Rachel wrenched herself away from Nate, dislocating her shoulder with a sickening pop as she did so.

"Careful!" Daniel shouted to Nate. "Don't hurt her!"

"Both of you, get back to your places." Pia's voice was panicked, but Daniel couldn't leave Rachel there, vulnerable, with tentacles of evil wrapping around her tender flesh.

Rachel's wild gaze held his own as she gripped her shoulder and wrenched it back into place with a disturbing crunch. Daniel's fists clenched and unclenched at his sides, but he had no outlet for his anger.

If someone had hurt Rachel like that in front of him, the fucker would be dead right now. But what could he do when the thing hurting Rachel was inside her?

Daniel's heart hammered in his chest. A hellish chill pulsated over him in thick repugnant waves. Disembodied cries and whispers echoed all around, and a heavy sadness filled the air. Desperation and sorrow were draining his energy, and as he looked around, the team were similarly affected.

Pia started to cry. "This is all going wrong." She tried to rebuild the circle, but the swirling wind kept scattering the crystals and candles, sending them careening across the deck.

Fuck this! Daniel rushed to Rachel's side, reached out to take her in his arms, but she grabbed his fingers, and with a jerk of her wrist, she bent them backward and snapped them.

Pain shot through his hand and up his arm, and he instinctively raised a fist in the air, but he couldn't bring it down. This was Rachel. *His Rachel.*

How the fuck was he going to help her?

Nate grabbed one of Rachel's arms, and Mark rushed to assist, taking her other arm, restraining her. The scry dropped, landing at her feet.

"Careful of her shoulder," Daniel ordered, wincing as he sucked in a breath and realigned his fingers. They were broken and needed to be strapped, but that would have to wait.

"This happened to me, remember," Mark said, his face twisted. His eyes glistened with unshed tears, even as he held onto Rachel with all his strength. "Don't forget the Rachel we know and love is still in there," Mark said desperately. "If she makes it out of this alive, it's going to kill her to realize what she's done, who she became."

"She'll make it out of this alive," Daniel snapped. She had to.

Mark met Daniel's gaze. "She might survive the night, but she still has to survive herself after."

"Don't say shit like that," Nate said, casting a worried glance at Daniel. Daniel didn't know what was on his face, but it was taking every ounce of his control not to grab Rachel and get her the fuck away from here. From all of this. The son of a bitch demon was ripping her apart from the inside out.

And there was not a fucking thing he could do about it.

"Let's retry the banishing ritual," Pia said.

Rachel's eyes turned from glazed and out of focus to black and wild. She was swearing, using language Daniel didn't recognize. Cursing in words Daniel knew she didn't know. She thrashed wildly, screaming, and fearing Mark's ability to restrain her, Daniel pushed him aside to take over. Nate glanced down at Daniel's swollen fingers and cursed, but Daniel shook his head. "Remember, this is not who she is."

Nate clenched his jaw, a look of pure thunder on his face. Daniel understood; the bond in the brotherhood was fierce. If one of them was hurt, the whole unit felt the pain and sought retribution.

"This is the same woman who risked her life for a complete stranger last night," Daniel said fiercely. "Don't forget that."

Rachel spat in Nate's face, thrashing with her whole body to get free. Daniel held firmly to her injured arm, enough to keep her restrained, hopefully not enough to do permanent damage. Rachel hissed and screamed, bucking and kicking at his shins like a wild brumby.

"LET. ME. GO!" Her voice was deep, guttural. It sounded nothing like Rachel, and everything like the demon.

Rachel shouldn't have been a match for Nate and Daniel—either of the men— under any circumstances. The strength she was exuding was unnatural. Daniel could see the physical damage on the outside—her face contorted, her skin lined with bulging veins, her shoulder a dark purple bruise.

What was the beast doing to her on the inside? What damage had already been done? Daniel remembered Madden's last moments, how weighed down by hopelessness and despair he'd been. He'd tied himself to a tree out of desperation, to protect others from atrocities he had no control over committing. How urgently he'd pleaded for Daniel to kill him. What hell had he endured to view death as a relief?

Daniel held Rachel tighter, burying his nose in hair that smelled of peach and vanilla. A sob rose up and wedged itself in his throat.

He was powerless to help her.

And it was the worst fucking torture of his life.

"Pia!" Daniel shouted. "Do something. He's going to kill her!"

Pia sprang to life at the words, grabbed a bottle that Daniel suspected was holy water, and began sprinkling it around them. When that was empty, she grabbed another bottle and handed it to Mark. A drop landed on Rachel's foot through her sandal, and she howled with pain, nearly bucking both Daniel and Nate off.

"Sohn-Zae!" Pia called out, her voice loud and clear. "Your permission to be here is revoked. You no longer have any permission to be in this dimension. You do not have permission to be with Rachel, the scry, or any person on Earth." Ryan, Mark and Joe stood behind Pia wide-eyed and shaking, but firmly showing their support, adding their energy.

Pia began speaking verses in Latin. Rachel threw her head back and keened like a wounded animal.

"May the heavenly universe rebuke Sohn-Zae, the dark demon of jealousy and revenge," Pia shouted as a series of shudders rocked the ship, sending Ryan and Mark stumbling across the deck.

Rachel jackknifed, her body contorting as she struggled to free herself from Nate's and Daniel's grips. She hissed and cursed; her eyes bulged, and she spat in Pia's face. The howls of a hundred wolves sounded in the distance.

Daniel had no way of knowing whether what Pia was doing was helping, but his fear that Rachel would slip away like Madden had increased with every second that ticked on.

The ship shuddered again, and everyone adjusted their footing so as to not lose their balance. A sound reverberated through the metal, an unhealthy grind and whir.

"What the fuck?" Ryan's eyes were wide.

"Is that the motor starting up?" Nate asked incredulously. "That thing should have seized up years ago."

Rachel growled, low and deep, the threat unmistakable.

"The demon is trying to take the ship back out to the ocean," Pia yelled. "We mustn't stop now. He wants to take Rachel with him!"

"Shut up, bitch!" Rachel shouted at Pia, frothy yellow bile rolling out of her mouth.

Daniel tightened his grip. Like fuck the demon was taking Rachel anywhere!

The ship jerked, and Daniel stumbled. Mark's holy water splashed over Rachel. Her scream ripped through Daniel, and her skin bubbled and blistered as though she'd been hit with boiling water. Her eyes rolled back in her head, exposing the whites.

"What can I do?" Daniel demanded, his voice breaking. "Tell me what I can do to help her."

"Give this a chance," Pia said. She continued to chant, as the ship trembled and shook, wind whipping around and through them.

"Leave her alone!" Daniel roared at the beast. "Take me!"

Rachel's mouth twisted. "You think you can order me about?" A deep laugh came out of her mouth. Her head began to turn from side to side.

Pia came closer, her words louder and clearer over the roaring engine as the *Anna-Marie* strained to dislodge itself from the sandbar.

"Will the ship be able to get free?" Daniel asked. In normal circumstances the answer to that would have been highly bloody unlikely.

But these were anything but normal circumstances.

Pia's glanced around her uneasily. "Perhaps."

The ship's motor continued to strain, and all around them the ship seemed to come to life. A captain barked orders at his crew, heavy, booted footsteps sounded up and down the stairs, and Daniel could have sworn something raced right past him.

He looked at Rachel's arms, at her small hands, her fragile wrists engulfed by his and Nate's much larger grips.

Rachel blinked, licked her lips, and started to shake.

Daniel stilled.

Rachel's eyes blinked into focus as she searched the ship, stopping when they connected with his. His heart shuddered to a halt, and he held his breath.

"Daniel?" Her voice was a broken, breathless whisper, her eyes red and glistening with moisture.

A lump lodged firmly in his throat. "Rachel?" His voice was a choked rasp. "Babe, is that you? Are you okay?" He twisted her around to face him. "Let her go," Daniel ordered Nate.

"Not a chance," Nate said, and although Daniel didn't like it one fucking bit, he understood. It seemed a cruel irony that Rachel had risked her life to save a complete stranger just last night, but tonight Rachel was the one to be feared.

Daniel traced his left hand carefully down her face. "I need to know you're okay."

Rachel squeezed her eyes shut and shook her head. Tears streamed down her cheeks, and her lower lip trembled.

Daniel turned to Pia. "Rachel's back. Is she free from it now?"

Pia was looking around her, her eyes following the sounds of movement as though she could visibly see what the rest of them could only hear.

Pia shook her head. "I don't think he's going to go that easily."

The ship's engine strained, and the *Anna-Marie* shuddered, metal screeching. "The engine's going to blow if it keeps revving like that," Nate said grimly. Daniel had to agree.

"What do we do now?" Daniel asked Pia. "Can we leave?" A sense of urgency flooded his body. Instinct told him this was merely the calm before the storm. That the demon hadn't just disappeared. It was a window, like the one he'd had when talking to Madden, before the demon had returned.

They should never have attempted this. He should never have exposed Rachel to this danger.

What the hell had he been thinking, allowing her to come back on this ship?

Suddenly there was a loud bang, and an explosion shook the ship.

Joe ran below deck. A few minutes later, he came tearing back up the stairs.

"Everyone get off!" he shouted. "The ship's about to blow! There's a fire; it's only a matter of minutes before the flames reach the fuel tanks."

"Throw the fuel tanks overboard!" Nate shouted.

"Tried that," Joe shouted back. "Can't shift them."

"Jesus," Nate growled. Mark and Ryan accompanied Joe and bolted downstairs to see what they could do.

Pia reached into her pocket, withdrew a crucifix, and with a powerful wrench, Rachel threw herself onto the ground and away from Nate and Daniel. She scrambled to her feet and rushed at Pia, sending her flying backward.

Pia landed against the side of the boat, her head hitting heavily on the metal deck. Rachel jumped on top of her. She got one good swing into the side of Pia's face before Nate and Daniel pulled her off. Nate shoved Rachel away hard and knelt beside Pia, pulling her into his embrace.

Thick smoke rose up from below, and Mark returned with Joe and Ryan close behind. "It's no use. We've got to get off now!"

Mark rushed to Pia. "What the hell?" he demanded, looking at her lying in Nate's arms.

"Is Pia okay?" Mark glared at Rachel, and Daniel's heart squeezed.

"Make sure the tinny is ready," Nate said, rising with Pia in his arms. He tenderly kissed her forehead. "It's going to be all right," he said softly. "You're going to be just fine—"

Mark, Ryan, and Joe rushed to the side of the ship where the tinny was. Nate held Pia while the boat was being prepared.

"*She's* not coming," Nate said, glaring at Rachel.

"The fuck she's not!" Daniel exploded. "I'm not leaving her here."

"There's not enough room on the boat to keep her restrained," Nate said. "She'll kill us all before we reach the shore."

Rachel struggled furiously in Daniel's arms, and he strengthened his hold.

"This is not her fault." Frustration churned like shards of glass in his gut. "We can't just leave her here to die."

Heat from the fire below deck penetrated the soles of his boots. They were out of time.

What was he going to do?

Nate was right. Rachel couldn't go onto the boat with them.

"Go," Daniel ordered. "Get Pia to safety. She needs medical attention."

Nate met his eyes. "How do you want this to work?" he asked quickly. "I've got my cuffs. Let's secure her to the ship."

Daniel's jaw clenched. If anyone other than Nate had said that... "The fuck I'm leaving her!"

"You have no choice!" Nate shouted, his face reddening. "It's her or us."

"Go!" Daniel growled through clenched teeth.

Another explosion rocked the trawler, and Daniel and Nate stumbled and almost fell. Daniel readjusted his grip on Rachel. Flames rose into the sky at the bow.

"I'm not leaving you, so you'd better work out how you're going to handle Rachel, stat." Nate looked around, heat from the flames washing over them. "We could lock her in the captain's quarters if we're quick."

"Don't fucking talk about Rachel like that!" Daniel bellowed. "I'm not leaving her here to die!"

"She's *already* dead, mate!"

A choked noise rose up and out Daniel's throat, and pain unlike anything he'd ever felt shredded him. He shook his head vehemently.

"Don't fucking say that! Don't you fucking dare! This. Is. Not. Her. Fault. She's a victim here, not a fucking criminal. Would you give up on Pia?"

Nate looked down at Pia, her body limp, her long red hair flowing over his arm. Then he met Daniel's gaze, awareness flickering across his eyes; there would be no changing Daniel's mind.

Daniel had seen Rachel—the real Rachel—only moments ago. His sweet Rachel was still in there. He wouldn't give up on her.

All he needed to do was get Rachel off the ship and let it blow into smithereens, taking the scry and everything with it. Seal the doorway forever.

He refused to concede defeat to the demon. Not while there was breath in his lungs. He'd die before he let that fucker win.

Rachel is mine!

"Maaate!" Nate growled, making one last-ditch attempt. "Think about this, will you?"

"Already have."

Daniel had said he'd die for Rachel, and he would. Without question. Failing that, Daniel was dying with her. The fuck she was dying out here alone.

"I'm not leaving her," Daniel said.

Nate glared at him, and Daniel glared back. The ship shuddered, sending them both off balance. It was moving, somehow refloating itself and motoring off the sandbank.

"Come on!" Mark called from the tinny, its motor revving. "There was a lot of fuel down there. We'll all die if you don't hurry up!"

Nate looked torn. Daniel set his jaw and nodded in the direction of the boat.

Ryder closed his eyes. As much as it would kill Nate to leave Daniel here to face certain death, he wouldn't risk Pia's life. It was the only card Daniel had left to play. "Go. Save Pia."

Nate's eyes snapped open. "Blade is going to fucking kill you when he finds out." Daniel grinned at the irony; he doubted there'd be anything left of him to kill when this was over.

Glancing at Rachel, Nate shook his head sadly. "Best of luck, mate. I hope whatever you've got planned works."

Daniel choked up. He had nothing planned. All he knew was that he wasn't leaving Rachel to die on this fucking ship alone.

Tears glistened in Nate's eyes. "Love you, brother." Nate rebalanced Pia in his arms and placed a fist to his chest. Then he turned and jogged off with Pia in his arms.

Nate had said his final goodbye.

A few moments later, the little motorboat roared off.

Daniel released his hold on Rachel and spun her around to face him. They stood on the deck, and Daniel faced the beast—through the eyes of the woman he loved.

Chapter Fifty-One

Rachel felt herself slipping in and out of consciousness. She had no real memory of what had happened, just fragments, but from the seconds of time that she had been aware, she could put enough pieces together.

She'd killed Pia.

She'd seen the devastation on Nate's face as he'd cradled her in his arms.

Rachel scrubbed a palm over her eyes, but it didn't wipe away the image of Pia's bloodied body beneath her just before Nate and Daniel had dragged her off or the feel of Nate's death grip on her wrist as he'd stopped her before she could lay in another punch. Rachel doubled over. Tears burned her eyes, and a lump filled her throat. How could she have done such a horrible thing?

To her last day on this earth, she would never forgive herself for what she'd done to Pia.

Her eyes still closed, Rachel sucked in a deep breath, tried to focus. The decking beneath her feet was hot, the ship shuddering. Her shoulder was on fire. The slightest movement sent pain shooting down her arm. What had happened?

Opening her eyes, she found herself facing Daniel. Something flared inside her. Hope. Love. She rushed forward, but stopped dead when she caught his expression.

His eyes were stony, his features set in a mask of murderous violence. Rachel instinctively shrank back, and Daniel's face softened.

Then she realized why.

The demon would never have recoiled.

A heavy weight fell over her. Daniel might never look at her the same way again. Not that she could blame him. She wouldn't be able to look at herself the same way again. Not after what she'd done.

And what else *had* she done?

Where had everyone gone?

"Rach?" Daniel's voice was tentative, his expression wary.

"I'm here." Her voice was not much more than a rasp. His gaze pierced right through her, but something he saw in her face must have reassured him because he grabbed her fast, hugging her to his chest in a viselike grip. His heart pounded beneath her ear, and his hand ran soothingly down her hair.

Hot tears stung her eyes and soaked into his shirt. She was wracked with tremors, shaking like an addict in the grip of withdrawal. She didn't deserve his love, but she greedily took what she craved more than anything else.

"We've got to get off the ship," Daniel said urgently.

Only then did Rachel become aware of the flames that engulfed the bow. Daniel supported her with one arm and half-carried her, half-dragged her to the edge. "I know you have questions, but they'll have to wait. First thing is getting you off this ship safely. I'll go in first," he said. "Then you jump. You'll hold onto me until we make it to shore."

"We're swimming?"

Her eyes watered with the sting of smoke, but it wasn't only that. They were the only two left on the *Anna-Marie*. The fact they were swimming meant everyone else had left with the tinny.

Daniel had opted to stay behind.

For her? She was desperately unworthy of such kindness.

Of such selfless love.

"You can swim, can't you?" he asked.

"Of course." Given the injury to her shoulder, maybe not well, but with Daniel's help… She eyed the waves, calm only moments ago but now rising into frothy whitecaps. After what she'd just been through, she felt no fear over what would have terrified her yesterday.

"Don't worry, babe. All you need to do is jump and keep your head above the water. I'll do the rest from there."

"I'm not worried." She looked into his eyes, at his calm confidence. What would it take to rattle him? With the flames spitting and rising high into the night sky, the roar of the fire loud in their ears, the fact there could be an explosion at any time… Daniel was the bit of calm in the center of a cyclone.

Rachel followed him to the edge, the heat becoming unbearable. He put a hand on the railing. Two of his fingers were swollen and purple.

"What happened to your fingers?" she gasped.

Something flitted through his eyes, then he glanced down at his hand and shrugged. "Got hit during the explosion."

She took his hand tenderly in hers and brushed her lips over the injury. "You need to get these looked at."

He looked deep into her eyes, cupped her face between his palms. Kissed her. Hard. "I love you. We're going to be okay. Trust me."

Another small explosion rocked the belly of the ship.

"Count to five, then follow me in." Daniel jumped into the water. He surfaced, and with a flick of his head, cleared the hair out of his eyes.

"Now!" he ordered. Another explosion went off, a little louder than the last one, the trawler shuddering. Something crashed to the deck near her.

"Rachel! Jump!" he yelled.

She climbed up onto the edge, and something tingled inside her. A tug on her awareness. Anger churned in the pit of her stomach; the demon was still nearby. The banishing ritual hadn't worked.

A sob rose up and choked her throat. She fought to remain present, to stay focused. Something was different this time. She could sense Sohn-Zae's presence, but he wasn't inside her like he'd been earlier. He seemed to be watching her from a distance.

But that didn't mean he wouldn't force his way inside her again. She was still marked; the scratches on her back and neck burned. She couldn't go through that again. What she'd done to Pia. She thought of Daniel's fingers. Had she done that too? Probably—she'd tried to slit his throat not that long ago.

What more could she be capable of and not even be aware of doing?

Daniel bobbed in the waves below, staring up at her. She loved him with every fiber of her being. This man, this wonderful man, who'd stayed when everyone else had left. This man who'd risked his life to save her, even after she no longer deserved to be saved.

"I love you!" Rachel called out. Tears rolled down her cheeks.

"Rachel, jump!" His desperate plea ripped at her insides, but she'd made her decision.

"I can't risk it." *I can't risk you.* She loved him so much, too much to hurt him any more than she had already.

She'd held a knife at Daniel's throat; she'd killed Pia.

What if she inadvertently hurt or killed her sister, or dear God, Sally or Liam? *Sally.*

Rachel's grandmother had tried and failed to rid their family of the scry and Sohn-Zae. Rachel was not ready to concede defeat. She owed it to Sally to fight to her dying breath.

How could she live with herself otherwise? It sickened her to know she carried this nefarious legacy in her bloodline.

"I'm sorry, Daniel," Rachel called down. "I have to give it one more shot."

She closed her eyes and dragged a shaky breath of salty air deep into her lungs.

It seemed such a waste now, to look back on all the years she and Daniel had fought their attraction to each other. The excuses they'd made so they didn't have to risk their hearts.

It had all been bullshit. Because their hearts had already been at risk.

But the past couldn't be changed. She had his love today and that had to be enough to sustain her. Forever.

She held his chain close to her heart, fingered the strong, smooth links, and stepped down off the edge.

The ship rocked, and the scry rolled over to her, bumping against her foot. She picked it up; oddly, she felt no connection to it now. It was a dead weight, nothing but a cold rock in her fingers.

Rachel went to Ryan's camera, unclipped it from its tripod. She rewound it to the section where Maia gave her the instructions on how to banish the demon. She would repeat the ritual until she got it right. Until it worked.

Pia had been incredible in getting them this far; Rachel would be grateful to her forever. But it was Rachel's destiny to end this.

It always had been.

Rachel was the blood relative of the woman who had summoned this evil into the world.

It was only right that Rachel would be the one to banish it.

Adrenaline pumped through her veins, giving her mind sharpness and clarity of purpose. She knew what needed to be done and she was prepared to do it.

She would face Sohn-Zae one last time in a battle to the death. And she'd be the one to send that fucker back to Hell.

"Rachel!" Daniel screamed her name again and again, and she closed her eyes, tears welling up.

She was ready to battle Sohn-Zae.

But first, she needed to say goodbye to the only man she'd ever loved.

CHAPTER FIFTY-TWO

Daniel rode the waves in the cold water as he looked up at the ship, at the angry reds and oranges of flames rising against the inky black sky. The only part of the ship not on fire was the small section at the stern where Rachel stood. The ship was one explosion away from becoming fully engulfed.

"Jump!" he demanded furiously. For the first time since they'd boarded the ship that evening, Daniel felt as though he had some semblance of control. He had a plan. All he had to do was get Rachel off the ship. And she refused to go!

Getting back on the ship and forcibly removing her wasn't an option. There wasn't time. She had to get off now. He should have taken her with him when he'd jumped, but he hadn't wanted to risk losing sight of her, even for a second as they went under when they first hit the water. Better he watch where she landed so he could instantly grab her. Now he doubted the wisdom of that decision as Rachel climbed down off the edge of the ship.

She disappeared from his view for a few moments. "Rachel!" he shouted, his voice desperate, hoarse.

He shouted her name several more times, then she came back and looked over the railing.

She shook her head firmly. "I'm doing this, Daniel."

"Rachel, no!"

But she just shook her head.

"Rachel… please?"

She was breaking his fucking heart.

Tears coursed down his cheeks. Rachel's eyes squeezed tight, as though unable to witness his pain.

"This is bigger than us," she said, her voice breaking. "I can't be selfish. How could I ever look Sally in the eyes if I don't try again?"

"No!"

"Promise me," she begged, sobbing openly. "You'll remember me how I was. Before this—"

She hugged her arms around her stomach. "Don't remember me like I am now." She was visibly trembling.

"I don't want to *remember* you! I want to hold you. I want to wake up and feel your warmth in my bed. I want you wrapped in my arms every night as we go to sleep. *Together.*"

"Oh, Daniel—"

"Rachel! Damn it, get off the fucking ship!" His voice was raw and shaky.

She glanced over her shoulder. "I feel him. I don't have much time before the fire reaches here."

Panic rose like acid to his throat. "Rachel Sommers! Don't you dare!"

"I love you, Daniel Jackson Smith." She put a fist to her mouth and choked on a sob. "*Really* love you. I've never loved anyone but you. And I never will. It's always been you. In this life and the next."

"Rachel, for fuck's sake, just jump!"

"This lifetime wasn't for us," she said. She glanced around her. "My destiny was for something else."

"No!" he howled.

"I'll see you on the other side." She touched her lips to the palm of her hand, and through her tears, tossed a kiss into the ocean. She turned and walked away, back to the circle to continue the ritual—to fight the demon—on her own.

How could he make her listen? How could he convince her to get off the goddamn ship?

"Take me!" Daniel roared into the night as he began to swim furiously to her.

"Let her live, and take me." He fought the waves toward to the ship, the smell of smoke curling around him like a python.

The ladder was on the other side. His broken fingers hindered his ability to move swiftly through the water, but he pushed through the pain.

Waves drove him back, swallowing every inch of progress he made. Another explosion rocked the ship, and he felt the vibration through the water.

"Goddamn it!" he screamed, punching through a wave with his fist. It was like one of those dreams where you were being chased, and your legs were pushing through concrete. He couldn't get closer to the ship no matter how hard he tried.

He kept fighting with everything he had until his muscles fatigued, and he could barely keep his head above water.

Then came a god-awful noise. A deafening roar as a mighty explosion ripped through the ship. He looked up to see Rachel's body fly through the air and fall into the ocean. A rush of fiery heat washed over him, and he slipped beneath the water to let it pass.

When Daniel resurfaced, the ship was well alight.

"Rachel!" he cried out her name, swam to the spot where he remembered seeing her land. The water was ice cold, but adrenaline filled his veins, keeping the chill at bay. He rode the waves, straining his eyes for any sign of her. Twice he thought he'd glimpsed her hair, her smile. But both times, it had been an illusion.

Daniel continued to search, diving and swimming, until he could barely keep afloat in the water himself.

Mark returned with the tinny and eventually dragged him into the motorboat and took him to shore.

Without her.

Chapter Fifty-Three

Daniel sank onto the cold, damp sand, his gaze on the burning ship glowing red against an inky sky. People rushed around him, lights strobing behind him from various emergency vehicles. Professionals mixed with the curious or the morbid. Local police were asking questions and taking notes. Occasionally someone would stop, ask him if he was okay. Always something in his eyes kept them moving and not prying further.

Daniel was not okay.

His flesh was still warm, but he was stone cold dead on the inside. There was no warmth in his heart.

Rachel was gone. Max was gone too. The only things he loved in life had disappeared. Darkness, a great vast emptiness, threatened to swallow him whole. And he'd willingly go if only it would wipe out the pain eating away at his insides like acid.

"I'm sorry, mate. There's still no sign of Max," Mark said, placing a heavy hand on his shoulder. Daniel squeezed his eyes shut.

The first thing Daniel had done when he'd been back on shore was seek out his little buddy. If there was ever a time Daniel had needed him, it was now. But Max was gone; he wasn't with Daniel's 4WD where he'd left him with the window down and the command to stay. It wasn't like Max to jump out of the vehicle and run off. Something must have happened.

Daniel had lost the woman he loved and his best friend, his constant companion for a good portion of his adult life, on the same night. Life could be a mean son of a bitch sometimes.

The sky eventually lightened to blue, nothing left of the ship but a charred outline against the sunrise. The scry was destroyed, as was the ship. But it was all too late.

Too late to save Rachel.

Occasionally Daniel inhaled the scent of smoke when the wind blew the right way. The last of the emergency services had left, only a few uniforms lingered, with the odd onlooker coming and going. Faces changed, only Daniel was the constant.

He was in no hurry. He had nowhere to go.

What he'd had with Rachel had been a gift. And he had squandered that gift. Taken it for granted, and wasted the chance they'd both been given. If only he had his time over again…

Daniel sucked in a breath. But you didn't get your time over again. You had today, that was it.

Now that the anger had subsided, he was closer to understanding her decision. Selfishly, he wished she had chosen to jump, had chosen him. But she'd tried to fix things, to keep the demon from using her, from using Sally and future generations of their family.

Daniel couldn't fault Rachel's actions, as much as he regretted her choice.

It was just that it hurt so damn bad…

It took incredible strength to make the decision she had. On some level, he knew that.

But he was still furious with her.

Rachel had taken action to protect those she loved. Had Daniel been faced with the same unwinnable choices, undoubtedly, he would have done the same thing.

He had, actually. By staying on the ship, Daniel had been prepared to give his life to save hers.

Something caught his eye, and he turned his head. A lone purple flower poked up over the prickly sand dune plants. Daniel's throat closed over.

His vision blurred as he made his way over to the flower, reached down, snapped it off.

A beach morning glory. One single plant, with one purple flower.

He held the flower to his nose, imagined it smelled of peach and vanilla.

Imagined it smelled like her.

He scanned the sand dunes. There was not another single plant, not another purple flower. It was like a message from her. That she was still here. She was still with him somehow.

Overwhelming sadness engulfed him, and his throat closed over, tears running unchecked down his face. He didn't care if anyone saw, thought him a pussy. There was nothing left inside him that cared.

Daniel carried the flower back to the shore, then walked into the ocean. He walked past the breaking waves, to the calm water beyond. Tears stung his eyes as he looked out into the vastness of the sea.

"Oh, Rachel." His voice was broken, like his heart, his shredded soul. *Losing you hurts so much.*

He ran his fingers over the delicate petals of the morning glory, remembered how it had looked tucked behind her ear. Remembered the shine in her eyes as she'd looked up at him through long lashes.

He pressed his lips to the flower.

"Take this to her," he said. "So that wherever she is, she'll remember how much I love her. Just how much she came to mean to me in this lifetime."

He set the flower on the water, watched until it floated out of sight.

He closed his eyes, fighting to find a way to stop this mind-numbing, bone-deep pain.

He cried out, slamming his fist down on the water, the salty waves splashing him in the face.

How did he find the strength to carry on in this life without her?

But in the silence, he found it.

Just not in the way he thought.

CHAPTER FIFTY-FOUR

In the silence between waves crashing against the shore, Daniel heard a dog barking. He held his breath, every sense on alert. After all the commotion of last night, the beach was mostly deserted.

There it was again.

The bark.

Max.

It wasn't his imagination.

Daniel angled his head to hear better against the sea breeze. He waited. And, faintly, he heard it again. Carried on the wind. An answer to his prayer.

Daniel walked through the water, pushing through the resistance of the waves, in the direction he believed the sound to be coming from. Back on the beach, he moved toward the sound, one foot after another sinking into the thick white sand.

He walked for a long time like that, along the beach, heartened each time he heard Max's call. His dog was tired, his barks rasping. As though he'd been barking all night. And likely he had. Max had been calling for him, and by the grace of a higher power, Daniel had finally heard him. He thanked heaven he'd chosen to stay and hadn't left with everyone else as he'd been pressured to do.

Daniel walked out into the ocean to round a rocky outcropping, slipping several times on the seaweed-covered rocks, some jagged, some smooth. All of them hazardous beneath the white frothy waves as they crashed against the shore.

A morning sea breeze kicked in as he stepped back onto the sand. Max's bark was louder. Daniel stood, listening. His tiredness, his exhaustion, vanishing in an instant when he saw Max off in the distance. He was lying down on the sand.

Was he hurt? What had happened to his little buddy? Daniel moved as fast as his legs would carry him to reach Max. As he drew closer, Daniel's heart stopped dead in his chest. Max was lying on top of a body.

Daniel continued forward, his heart sinking with every step. As he pounded down the beach, he steeled his nerves, prepared himself for what he would find.

When Max saw him, his tail started wagging. Thank God Max appeared to be okay. But he didn't run to Daniel as he normally would. Instead, he stayed on the body.

It was Rachel.

Daniel could see her hair fanned out beneath her.

Max was protecting Rachel.

Hot tears burned Daniel's eyes, and he blinked them back. He couldn't break down now. It was some consolation to find her body; at least she hadn't been eaten by sharks. Nobody wanted to go out like that.

Daniel dropped to his knees as he reached them, and Max finally moved off her. He licked Daniel's face briefly before nudging Rachel with his nose. He whimpered.

Acting on sheer need and desperation, Daniel scooped Rachel up into his arms, his medical training flying out the window. He knew not to touch a victim before assessing them for injuries, but his need to hold her was far too great.

Her skin was cold, and her head lolled back over his forearm, her hair dangling in the sand. He shifted her weight in his arms so that her head fell against his chest. He watched for the rise and fall of her chest... and saw one. He held his breath, watched for another, just to be sure.

"She's alive?"

Max barked, his tail wagging.

Daniel checked for a pulse, his own heart stopping as he waited for the result. It was weak, but he found one. She was alive! Barely, and he didn't know how much longer she would be. He felt the warmth of his dog on her body and realized that was what had saved her life. Max's warmth had stopped Rachel from dying of exposure. He'd kept her warm.

Daniel's throat closed over. "You saved her life, didn't you, little buddy?" Max nosed Daniel's arm, and he ran his palm over Max's head. "You are the best thing that ever happened to me. And now you've given me back Rachel."

Max wagged his tail, then barked again as if to say, *Hurry!*

"You're right. We have to get her to help. Fast." Daniel kissed Rachel's cold, salty lips and quickly checked her for obvious injuries. She'd likely suffered broken bones, concussion, shock. There'd been some blood loss. How much, he couldn't be sure. She was so very pale. If Max hadn't stayed with her, keeping her warm...

He stopped that thought in its tracks.

Tenderly, as though she were made of fragile tissue paper, he laid her down, stripped off his shirt, and wrapped it around a significant wound on her leg.

Satisfied he'd done all he could for her visible injuries, he lifted her up into his arms and stood.

He looked around the deserted beach. There was no one around for miles. The cliffs on this part of the beach were limestone rock, too perilous to climb in his condition, and not with Rachel in his arms. The only option was to walk back the way he'd come. With energy borrowed from somewhere higher than himself, Daniel quickly moved through the thick sand, step by step.

If Rachel made it through this, *when* she made it through this, he would not squander his second chance. His priorities in his life had become clear in these last few hours.

It had taken almost losing her to realize how... *essential* she was to his life. He'd already known he loved her, but he hadn't known just how deep that love ran. He'd never known how all-consuming love could be.

He'd give everything for her; he'd give his life for her. He'd proved it to himself by staying on the ship. Without hesitation, he would have given himself to the demon in exchange for her life.

There was no greater power in life than that.

His love for Rachel made him a better man.

Chapter Fifty-Five

Six Months Later

C ome and watch me swing, Auntie Rachel!"

Rachel smiled at Sally, whose golden hair fanned out behind her and glistened in the afternoon sun as she kicked her legs to go higher.

The delicious scent of steak and sausages cooking on the barbecue made Rachel's stomach rumble.

Elise's backyard was filled with laughter, great conversation, and the warmth of coming together as a family. Sage and Ethan were there laughing at something Pia said, little Celeste, as always, in Ethan's arms. It was astounding the way such a hard man looked at his wife and daughter so tenderly, like they were his sun and his moon. Which, of course they were.

Sam and Sean were holding beers and tongs, working the barbeque. Ryan, Joe, and Nate were sitting at the large outdoor table, where Mark appeared to be entertaining them with a funny story. After the airing of the "Ghost Ship" episode, *Debunking Reality*'s ratings had skyrocketed even higher.

The only people missing at the barbecue were Rob and Trey. Not a day went by that Rachel didn't think of them, but whenever the pain of their loss became too much to bear, she tried remembering the happy memories they'd shared growing up together. They'd been such a big part of her life, and so much of what made her the person she was today.

Not wanting grief to cast shadow on the celebration today, Rachel forced her attention back to the present. She could barely believe how her family had grown from just her and her sister and kids to this large group, seemingly in an instant. And she was grateful for them all. She'd always wanted a large family, and it finally seemed as though all her dreams had come true.

Rachel and Ellie were still estranged from their father. Perhaps that would change with time, but for now, it was how it needed to be.

Sally jumped off the swing and rushed to Rachel. "Auntie Rachel, can I go to the beach and collect shells?"

Rachel glanced over at Ellie, who was now deep in conversation with Pia and Nate, and made the call. "Sure. Just stay where I can see you, okay?"

Elise's tests had come back clear. For now. There was never any guarantee once you developed that insidious disease, but they were determined to remain positive. If Rachel had learned one thing from her ordeal, it was to treat each new day as a gift.

When Elise had gone to the city for tests and treatment, Daniel and Rachel had stayed to look after the kids. Daniel was patient and fun with Sally and Liam, and Rachel couldn't have loved him more. Was there anything sexier than a man who was great with kids? Her stomach fluttered.

She sensed him behind her, without needing to turn and look. Daniel's arm wrapped around her shoulders, and she leaned into him, looking up at him then. He smiled down at her, the love shining through his eyes making it difficult for her to breathe.

"Max barely leaves your side." Daniel's deep voice in her ear sent a wave of warmth throughout her body.

Rachel smiled down at the shepherd pressed so close to her leg, he was lying across her foot. "That's because I'm always with you."

But that wasn't entirely true. Although Daniel and Rachel had rarely been apart since the accident, Max had become very protective of her, leaving her side only if he went somewhere with Daniel.

After Rachel had been released from the hospital, Daniel had taken her home. To their new home. Daniel had bought a house only an hour's drive from Elise and the kids, and Rachel couldn't have loved it more. Together, they'd chosen furniture, moved their possessions in, made it their own. Max had his own brand-new bed but mostly opted for sleeping on the end of Rachel and Daniel's bed. There were few rules for Max where Rachel was concerned, and Daniel was always pretending to get her into trouble for spoiling the dog.

Daniel's hand slid down her side and across her stomach. She placed her hand on top of his, the diamond on her left hand sparkling in the sunlight. Her heart filled with warmth as she traced his strong fingers with her fingertips.

"Are you ready, Mrs. Smith?" Daniel asked, his breath a caress on her neck. There was a softness in him now that hadn't been there before.

Rachel smiled up at him, her eyes meeting his. Her heart skipped, the way it always did. The way she knew it always would. There were no longer any doubts or trust issues between them. Their love was solid. They had that innate confidence survivors had, the knowledge that they could handle anything life threw at them.

"I'm ready."

"Can I have your attention," Daniel said. There was no need to tap on a glass or bottle with a spoon; Daniel's voice held the tone of command people instinctively listened to. "Rachel and I have something we'd like to share."

Ellie met her gaze and smiled, tears dancing in her eyes. Her sister knew, even without having been told. It was rare for everyone to be in one place at the same time, and even though it wasn't three months yet, Rachel didn't want to waste the opportunity to tell everyone at once. She no longer let chances slip through her fingers.

Daniel pulled her in front of him and placed his arms around her. He let one hand fall to her stomach, and everyone's eyes widened with excitement as they realized what he was about to say.

He didn't even get the words out before their friends—their family—raced forward, each wanting to congratulate them. Sage reached them first, followed soon after by Pia, then Nate, Ethan, Sam, Sean, Ryan, Mark, and Joe.

It was too early to tell, but if it was a boy, they were going to name him Robbie. Robert Trey Smith.

Rachel looked around their group of friends, basking in their love. Through her new family, she'd finally found the peace she'd spent her whole life searching for.

"Auntie Rachel! Auntie Rachel!" Sally came running up to them, holding something wrapped in her pink T-shirt.

"What is it?" Rachel asked, smiling down at the pretty little girl with sparkling eyes.

"Look what I found!" Sally thrust out her arms, flattened her palms. Nestled in her little niece's hands was the scry.

Rachel's world shuddered to a halt. She couldn't breathe, her heart pounding erratically in her chest.

Rachel instinctively reached for it, but Sally pulled it away, skipping a few steps back. Memories of the night on the shipwreck came rushing back to her with the force of a hurricane. Chilling fear gripped Rachel's throat, and she had to swallow twice before she could speak. "Give that to me."

As much as touching that thing sickened her, it was far more disturbing seeing such evil in the sweet and innocent girl's hands.

"Mine!" Her tone made it clear she wouldn't give it up without a fight.

Oh no! Oh no! Oh no!

"You've got to be kidding," Daniel growled next to Rachel, tension rolling off him in almost tangible waves.

The crowd around them fell silent, the only sound the distant crackle of the barbeque. For a tense moment, time stood still.

Bile rising in her throat, Rachel prepared herself to lunge forward, physically wrestle the scry from Sally's arms if necessary. Whatever it took to keep her niece safe.

"Rachel, wait." Pia slowly knelt down to the Sally's level and smiled gently. "Can you show me what you found?"

Sally hesitated for nearly a full minute, but after Pia's persistent and gentle encouragement, Sally eventually handed over the crystal ball. But only after she'd secured Pia's solemn promise to give it straight back.

Pia held the scry in her hands and closed her eyes. After a nail-biting moment, she opened them and smiled. There was an audible sigh of relief from everyone.

Pia gave the scry back to Sally, then stood, placing a calming hand on Rachel's arm. "You don't have to worry anymore. You managed to successfully exorcise Sohn-Zae from the scry. There's nothing evil attached to it now."

"Yes. But what if the demon comes back?" Rachel whispered urgently, wringing her hands.

"The demon didn't attach itself to the scry," Pia said. "It was summoned. Through a specific and complex spell. The scry itself is magical, but not harmful. Things are back to how they were supposed to be."

"The scry should have blown to smithereens with the explosion," Daniel said, his tone indicating he was far from pleased by its return. "It seems an almost unbelievable coincidence that it washed to shore right at the specific time Sally was there to find it."

"It wasn't a coincidence," Pia said. "Some things are destined. You and Rachel should know that better than anyone by now."

Rachel couldn't argue with that. If she'd learned one thing from nearly losing it all, it was that life would have its way with you, regardless. You might as well stop fighting the tide and ride the waves.

And if that was true for Rachel and Daniel, it was true for Sally as well.

"Can I keep it?" Sally asked, blinking up at her mother. "Please, Mummy? I'll take good care of it."

Elise looked to Pia before answering. "It's safe," Pia said. "I'm certain."

The horror of that final night on the ship was bitter acid in Rachel's stomach, but she knew Pia was right when she'd assured them the scry was cleansed. Rachel clearly remembered the moment the banishing ritual had finally worked. She'd followed the ritual outlined on the parchment to the letter, without fear, as she'd already resigned herself to fight to the end. Rob and Trey's deaths would not be for nothing. Rachel was determined to do whatever it took to keep Sally safe, so that no more lives were lost to the beast.

When she was about halfway through the ritual, Rachel felt her grandmother on one side, and then Maia on the other. She felt a tingling warmth and imagined them surrounding her with a golden light and linking with her in some surreal and indefinable way. Then, as the ritual's power proved to be working, weakening the demon's influence, Rachel's strength and confidence grew.

The sickening screams of the wounded beast, the moment his eyes had connected with hers, would stay with Rachel forever. Its ear, then anger, the pure unadulterated hatred as the demon's form transformed into a black, terrifying shadow that then disappeared as though being sucked away through a ventilation system. For a too-brief moment, Rachel had rejoiced in her victory before the final explosion had catapulted her into the ocean, and the ship had been engulfed in flames.

She must have been knocked out, because she had the strangest dream she was being cradled in her grandmother's arms and carried above the waves, lovingly to shore.

There had been a gentle kiss on her forehead, and the next thing she remembered was Max, standing guard over her. Covering her body with his, keeping her warm. She'd had the sense her grandmother had called Max to her. When her strength had started to give out, and she'd felt herself succumbing to the peace of darkness, Max had licked her face, barking at her when necessary to stop her from slipping into unconsciousness.

But of course, Rachel kept her thoughts over what she believed happened with her grandmother and Maia to herself. To others, those memories would be considered nothing but a product of the trauma she'd survived.

Rachel leaned down and ran her fingers through Max's soft fur, smiling as he licked her hand in response.

"I see swirling smoke," Sally said, excitedly staring into the scry. Rachel smiled to hide the tremble that rolled through her body. Maybe one day, she'd be able to look at the scry without fear.

Rachel bent down, hugged Sally tight, and gradually the knots twisting her insides loosened. She would not ruin this moment with worry and concern over what the future might or might not bring. The only thing Rachel had any real control over was the here and now.

The moment she stood, Daniel pulled her into his arms. Looking around, she absorbed the happiness of the family around her, the vibrant energy that flowed through the gathering.

For too many years, fear had stolen love from her, stopped her from experiencing the beauty available to those brave enough to surrender.

Brave enough to be vulnerable.

She was the luckiest woman in the world to have lost it all and traveled through the darkness to find Daniel waiting for her in the light at the end.

And to realize that he'd been there all long.

Rachel was no longer a hostage to fear. No longer paralyzed by the dread of being hurt.

No longer living with her heart half closed off, expecting a betrayal that would never come.

There was no room for demons now; they no longer held any power over her. She had stripped herself bare.

For Daniel, she was willing to risk it all.

Her life, her soul, her fragile, broken heart.

She'd taken a chance on love.

And she would never look back.

THE END

AUTHOR'S NOTE

Thank you for reading *When Darkness Follows*. If you enjoyed *When Darkness Follows*, please consider writing a review to help others learn about the book. Every recommendation truly helps, and I appreciate anyone who takes the time to share their love of books and reading with others.

To hear about my new releases, you can sign up for my mailing list at:

http://www.athenadaniels.com/home/subscribe/

Thank you for your support!

Athena

ABOUT THE AUTHOR

Athena Daniels is the #1 International bestselling author of the award-winning Beyond the Grave paranormal romance series and romantic thrillers *The Scream Behind Her Smile* and *Desperate*. In 2016, Athena was nominated for Author of the Year and Best New Author in *AusRom Today*'s Reader's Choice Awards. Her latest novel, *The Scream Behind Her Smile*, won the Silver Medal in the 2019 Readers Favorite® International Book Awards.

Girl Unseen won the Silver Medal in the 2017 Readers' Favorite® International Book Awards and was awarded a Silver Medal in the 2017 Literary Titan Book Awards, and finalist in the TopShelf Book Awards 2018. *Girl Unseen* is a semi-finalist in The Kindle Book Review Awards, "Official Selection" in the New Apple Annual book Awards and nominated for 2017 Book of the Year in *AusRom Today*'s Reader's Choice Awards.

When Darkness Follows won the Bronze Medal in the 2018 Readers' Favorite® International Book Awards, Silver Medal in the 2018 Literary Titan Book Awards, and was nominated for the TopShelf Book Awards 2019 and nominated in the Australian Romance Readers Association (ARRA) 2018 awards for Favourite Paranormal Romance.

The Seer's Daughter was the solo Medalist Winner in the Suspense/Thriller category of the 2016 New Apple Annual Book Awards for Excellence in Independent Publishing.

The Seer's Daughter was also a finalist in the 11th Annual National Indie Excellence Awards in Suspense and in the 2016 Readers' Favorite® International Book Awards. Additionally, *The Seer's Daughter* was nominated for 2016 Book of the Year and 2016 Cover of the Year in *AusRom Today*'s Reader's Choice Awards.

Girl Unseen and *The Seer's Daughter* are both 5-star Top Picks at The Romance Reviews.

Athena holds several qualifications in metaphysics and natural therapies. She is a neuro-linguistic programming (NLP) practitioner, life coach, and feng shui specialist.

Athena lives on the northern beaches of sunny Western Australia. Follow her on Twitter @AthenaDaniels11 and on Facebook at /AthenaDaniels11.

athenadaniels.com

www.ingramcontent.com/pod-product-compliance
Lightning Source LLC
Chambersburg PA
CBHW032001130726
47903CB00012B/435